MIDNIGHT'S MASTER

DONNA GRANT

St. Martin's Paperbacks

This is a work of fiction. All of the characters, organizations, and events portrayed in this novel are either products of the author's imagination or are used fictitiously.

MIDNIGHT'S MASTER

Copyright © 2012 by Donna Grant.
Excerpt from *Midnight's Lover* copyright © 2012 by Donna Grant.

For information address St. Martin's Press, 175 Fifth Avenue, New York, NY 10010.

ISBN: 978-0-312-55248-0

Printed in the United States of America

St. Martin's Paperbacks edition / June 2012

St. Martin's Paperbacks are published by St. Martin's Press, 175 Fifth Avenue, New York, NY 10010.

10 9 8 7 6 5 4 3 2 1

To all of Donna's Dolls around the world!

My street team members are the most awesome readers around. Thank you so much for your continued support. It means so very much to me. This book is for y'all.
::smooches::

ACKNOWLEDGMENTS

Thank you to my brilliant, marvelous, beautiful editor, Monique Patterson. I know I say it all the time, but you are the bomb! Thanks for pushing me when I needed it, encouraging when I hesitated, and for teaching me how to hail a cab (even though I'm still trying to master it!).

To Holly Blanck—what can I say besides the truth—you rock! To everyone at St. Martin's who helped get this book ready, thank you.

To my amazing, marvelous agent, Amy Moore-Benson. Thank you. For everything!

A special note to Leagh Christensen, Melissa Bradley, and April Renn. Thanks for all the help, especially when I needed it the most.

To my kiddos, parents, and brother—thank you! A writer makes sacrifices when writing, but so does the writer's family. Thanks for picking up the slack, knowing when I'm on deadline that I won't remember any conversations we might have. And for not minding having to repeat anything. lol

And to my awesome husband. Steve, my real-life hero. You never mind spending dinners talking about upcoming battle scenes or helping me work through a spot I'm stuck in. Thank you for the love you've given me, for the laughter you brought into my life, and for . . . everything. I love you.

CHAPTER ONE

December 18th

Gwynn Austin clenched the arms of her aisle seat, her knuckles white and her breath locked in her lungs as the airplane finally touched down in Edinburgh.

God, she hated flying. She barely made it through short trips across the US without being sedated or drinking heavily.

But the message from her father had changed everything.

Gwynn let out her breath as the plane taxied down the runway to the terminal. She was starving and nauseated at the same time. It had taken all she had not to get sick on the plane, so eating was out of the question.

As the plane stopped at the terminal, however, she was ravenous and couldn't get off the plane fast enough. And wouldn't you know, there was a man two rows in front of her who wanted to look through his carry-on and hold up the rest of the plane?

Gwynn wanted to shove the guy, to knock him on the back of the head for being so rude. Her mouth dropped open as the guy suddenly gave a grunt and fell over in the aisle. He lifted his head, looking at everyone staring at him.

This wasn't the first time Gwynn had wished something and it happened, though she didn't look too deep into herself to find out why. Too bad she hadn't been able to wish herself to Scotland instead of having to fly.

Looking away as the guy scrambled to his feet, Gwynn ignored the tingle of awareness that lodged itself in the base of her spine. She had always had a fascination with Scotland and its supposed legends and myths of magic, Druids, and Highland warriors.

Gwynn stretched her shoulders as she finally stepped off the plane and followed the signs to baggage claim. Worry over her father's cryptic message pushed aside her nausea.

It had been three weeks since her father's message. Three long, worry-filled weeks with little sleep. He was known to get deeply involved in his research and forget to call for a day or so, but never for three weeks. It's what had spurred Gwynn to buy a plane ticket and spend eleven hours on the flights from Houston to New York, then on to Edinburgh, with her mind conjuring all sorts of accidents that could have befallen her father.

Gwynn collected her small suitcase and adjusted the strap of her purse over her shoulder as she looked around for the rental car sign. As soon as she saw it, she made a beeline for it while dodging other people and their luggage.

It took no time at all to rent a car, but as Gwynn stood beside her small red Fiat Punto she had to wonder if she could drive it. Not only would she be driving on the wrong side of the road, but she'd be sitting in the wrong side of the car. A manual car.

"I'm an idiot with my left hand," she mumbled as she

tossed her suitcase into the back and climbed behind the wheel.

But she had to know what had happened to her father. He was all she had left. Her mother had died three years before, leaving just Gwynn and her father to cope. Her mother had kept the family bound together.

It had been a loose bond, but it was still a bond.

Her father, Professor Gary Austin of Rice University, the most prestigious private university in Texas, was the professor everyone hated to get. He loved his field of anthropology, and he expected everyone else to love it as well.

It was that love that had taken him from his family. Gwynn's mother had merely smiled as she watched her husband succumb to some new finding that would keep him at the university far into the night doing research.

Gwynn had hated him for it. Weeks would go by before he would return home or check on his wife. Gwynn had learned to distance herself from him, to forget that she still had a father.

Until her mother died.

It was as if Gary had looked at her for the first time and realized he had a daughter.

From that moment on, he'd made an effort to call her at least every other day while he was off finding new research all over the globe. While he was at home, Gwynn made sure she cooked for him every Sunday night.

It had taken her mother's death, but Gwynn had gained a father. Somewhat.

Gwynn pulled out the map and bit her lip as she used her finger to find the road she would need to take to the west side of Scotland and the isles there.

She folded her map and turned on her phone. Gwynn blew out a harsh breath when she saw no messages waiting for her. She was expecting two calls: one from her father telling her he was fine and there was no need to worry, and one from Rice. Hopefully the university could tell her exactly what had sent her father off to Scotland within an hour of finding some ancient book.

Gwynn rubbed her tired eyes, wincing at the sandpaper feel behind her eyelids, and started the car. The first thing she had to do was find something to eat. All she wanted was to curl up and sleep, but it was ten in the morning in Scotland, and she had traveling to do. She could sleep for a week once she found her father.

No sooner had Gwynn found first gear and uneasily let out the clutch than her phone rang. She was in such a hurry to grab the phone she had tossed on the seat next to her that she stalled the engine.

She fumbled for the phone, uncaring what happened to the car.

"Hello?" she said breathlessly, hope spreading in her chest that it was her father.

"Is this Gwynn Austin?" a nasal male voice asked.

Gwynn closed her eyes and rested her head against the seat. "It is."

"This is Phil Manning from Rice University. I'm returning your calls about your father."

"About time." She didn't bother to keep the testiness out of her voice. She'd been calling Rice for about a week. No one would take her calls, nor would anyone return them. Maybe it was the threat to call the FBI that had gotten things moving along.

"Yes," the man said, and she could just imagine him rolling his eyes. "Your last message left us little choice."

"Why there was a choice to begin with, I wouldn't know."

"Your father's whereabouts are no longer our concern."

A sick feeling filled Gwynn's stomach as she clutched her cell phone tighter. "What do you mean?"

"He resigned his position here almost a month ago. He refused to listen to reason or even agree to take a sabbatical. He was one of our best professors, Miss Austin. He'd been with the university for decades. None of that meant anything when he quit."

Gwynn swallowed and let his words sink into her fuzzy brain. "So, you're telling me the university didn't send him to Scotland to investigate some artifact he wanted to research?"

"No."

That one word opened the floodgates. Tears began to fall unheeded down her cheeks. "Do you . . ." She paused and cleared her throat. "Do you know what he was looking for?"

"He took all his research, Miss Austin," the man said, his tone softer. "I am sorry we cannot be of more help."

She nodded, then realized he couldn't see her. "Thank you. If you happen to find anything of his he might have forgotten, or something that might help me find him, please let me know."

"Of course. Good luck, Miss Austin."

Gwynn hung up the phone and put her forehead on the steering wheel as she sniffed. "What the Hell is going on, Dad?"

Her father loved the university. Rice had been his life. He had sacrificed years in order to gain the position of professor. What would have made him leave so suddenly?

Gwynn lifted her head and wiped her eyes before she started the car again. She drove until she found a convenience store where she bought a soda, a bag of chips, and the one sandwich that didn't look questionable.

She didn't allow herself to think of the conversation

with Mr. Manning at Rice. She'd let her mind speculate enough on the plane ride from the States. It was time she had facts. Until then, she would keep her mind focused on getting to her destination.

And not leaving the transmission on the road while she learned to shift with her left hand.

CHAPTER
TWO

The blackness, the unending void, ate away at Logan as he was yanked out of the year 1603 and thrown forward in time. He felt himself falling and desperately reached for something to hang on to.

The wind rushed by him, hurting his ears with the high-pitched sound and drowning out any noise. The wind took his breath, making it difficult to breathe. He was tossed first one way, and then the other. Determining which way was up was soon forgotten.

Where were the others? Ramsey, Arran, and Camdyn? The Druids had told him they didn't know where any of them would end up. All Logan could pray for as he felt the years and decades pass by was that he landed in the right time.

Around him, the inky darkness began to shimmer—the same shimmer that had appeared when the Druids cast the spell to send Logan and the others traveling through time.

Almost instantly, he was dumped out of the abyss onto his hands and knees in the midst of a vicious rainstorm.

Logan swallowed and gave himself a moment to let his

head stop spinning. He pushed his fingers into the wet ground and smiled when he felt the dirt between his hands.

He sat back on his heels and looked around. It was day, but the storm had darkened the sky. An urgent need pulled at him, called to him to return to Eigg, but he pushed it aside. He had to find Ian. That was his duty.

Logan wiped off his hands and took stock of his whereabouts on a hillside, the tall grass swaying with the howling wind. But what grabbed his interest were the dots of light below him.

Logan blinked through the cold, torrential rain and climbed to his feet. Those weren't fires he saw flickering in the valley. What they were, he didn't know. Yet.

He rose to his feet and ran a hand through his hair to get it out of his face. It was time to discover just where the Druids had managed to toss him in the future.

On his way down to the valley, Logan crossed a road that had been covered with some hard, black substance with bright white lines painted on it.

He squatted down to touch the surface and felt the rumbling of the ground beneath his fingers. Logan rose and stepped back as something large and loud came rolling down the lane.

As the object passed, Logan spotted a person inside who looked like they controlled the loud contraption.

More confused than ever, Logan walked over the road and down to the town. He could hardly believe his eyes when he reached the village to find buildings lined down the street, one right next to the other. They were all painted the same bright white with many more of those noisy contraptions lining the road as well as traveling down it.

Logan kept to the side of the road where he saw other people walking. A few gave him odd glances, but most paid him no heed.

He passed store after store, trying to learn the language

written on the signs. The fact that he had a primeval god inside him, a god so ancient his name had been forgotten, was the only way he was able to pick up this new language so quickly.

"You're soaked through, lad," said an elderly woman as she opened a door to a store Logan was walking past.

He gave a slight nod and felt the knot in his belly loosen as he heard her brogue. He was still in Scotland. Now, to determine *when* he was.

"Ah, not much of a talker," she said and laughed.

Logan smiled. "What year is it?"

She blinked and cocked her gray head at him. "You've quite the brogue, lad. It's been many a year since I've heard one so thick." She smiled, a faraway look stealing across her face.

Logan took a step toward her. "The year, lady?"

"Oh." She chuckled and patted her chest. "Forgive me. It's 2012. What an odd question."

"I've been living by myself . . . away from everyone."

"And everything," she said as she eyed his kilt.

Logan looked around him and shrugged. "What village am I in?"

This time the old woman frowned as she watched him. "Salen, not far from the Isle of Skye."

He knew the village, but the last time he had seen it, there had barely been anything there. It had grown tremendously since then.

What else had changed in the four centuries since he had left his friends behind at MacLeod Castle?

"I thank you," he said to the woman and walked on before she could ask more questions.

Logan looked at the town of Salen with new eyes. If this almost nonexistent village could grow so much in just a few centuries, what had become of Edinburgh or Glasgow? And did he even want to know?

He paused as a young woman ran in front of him to one of the contraptions sitting on the side of the road. She jerked at the handle as she held a bag over her head in an effort to keep from getting wet. It wasn't working.

"Rory! You wanker! Unlock the bloody door so I can get in the car!" she yelled over her shoulder.

Logan turned his head to see a thin man come out of the shop, walk around the . . . car, insert something small into the door, and open it.

The woman yanked on her door again then banged on the window above it. "Rory. Unlock the bloody door now!"

After another moment, Rory leaned over the door and pulled on something. A moment later, the woman got in. She was still yelling as the car rolled away.

So, the contraptions were called cars, and apparently people rode them much as Logan rode horses. He sighed and continued forward. It wasn't just the landscape that had changed. The people had changed as well.

No lady Logan had known would ever have spoken as the woman with Rory had. Not even whores spoke so crudely.

Logan heard footsteps coming fast behind him. His muscles seized and fangs filled his mouth. Logan spun around, claws lengthening as he readied himself to behead whoever thought to attack him.

He pulled his hand back, stopping himself just in time as two young lads ran past him, laughing and soaking wet. Logan stepped into the doorway of an unused building and took a deep breath.

Was he so used to fighting that he would attack anyone? Even children? He shook his head and struggled to tamp down the god inside him.

Athleus. He was the god of betrayal inside Logan, an ancient god who wanted nothing but death and destruction. It had taken decades for Logan to gain control over his god.

But sometimes, that control slipped.

Logan carried enough burdens. He didn't need to add the death of two young lads to the weight.

Once his fangs and claws had retreated, and Logan was sure his skin wasn't the silver of his god, he stepped out of the shadows and lengthened his stride as he exited the town. The urge to return to Eigg was sharp and true in his chest.

If anyone found out that he had a monster inside him, that he could release the god and become a beast, Logan was sure they'd kill him.

But he didn't just have a god inside him. He was able to use Athleus's power, a power able to control water. And Logan was going to the Isle of Eigg, an isle surrounded by water.

He wasn't sure when he had made that decision, only that he had. Logan couldn't hold back the desperate need to return there as soon as possible.

The last time he had been to Eigg, which to him was just a matter of hours—not centuries—earlier, he had been looking for an artifact hidden there by the Druids.

Not only had he not found the artifact, but his friend and fellow Warrior, Duncan, had been killed by Deirdre. Deirdre was a *drough*, a Druid who had given herself to evil and black magic. She was on a mission to take over the world, and as great as her magic was, Logan feared she might just win.

It had been Deirdre who had unleashed the gods inside the Warriors. And it would be Warriors who would help end Deirdre once and for all.

But first, Logan had to find Ian, Duncan's twin.

He couldn't imagine what Ian was going through. Ian

and Duncan, as twins, had shared a god, and with Duncan's death, the full power and rage of their god would overtake Ian. If he couldn't control his god, his god would control him and he would be ripe for Deirdre to claim. Which is just what she had wanted when she killed Duncan.

Logan had no idea where Ian had gone, but he knew Deirdre. She had leaped forward in time to 2012 in order to thwart him and the others in their mission to find the artifacts before she did.

He frowned. Or had she?

If Deirdre could travel through time whenever she wanted, why hadn't she done so before now? She could have changed the outcome to anything that hadn't gone her way, including gaining the artifacts before the MacLeods.

If Deirdre hadn't traveled through time on her own, that meant someone had to have helped her.

But who? And, more importantly, why?

Logan wasn't sure he'd have those answers anytime soon. Regardless, in order to defeat Deirdre, the Warriors would still need the artifacts. The one he had been sent to get was on Eigg.

He paused and looked around him. None of the other three Warriors who had volunteered to look for Ian had landed with Logan. He wasn't even sure if they had been taken as he had.

Yet, he knew the Druids at MacLeod Castle. Each one was powerful in her own right, and together, they wielded magic and quite literally took his breath away.

He had no doubt they had succeeded in tossing the others forward in time along with him. He had no means of communicating with anyone, nor could he take the chance of traveling to MacLeod Castle yet. He had to find Ian before Deirdre did.

If she didna have him already.

Logan hated the voice in his head, especially in moments like these.

He wished he weren't alone. He wished one of the other Warriors had landed with him. They would help him remember the man he had become.

Logan had created a new version of himself after he had escaped Deirdre's mountain, Cairn Toul. It was a mountain full of evil, a mountain Deirdre called her own, where she imprisoned hundreds of men in case they carried a god inside them waiting to be released.

But she also hunted and captured Druids so she could kill them and steal their magic.

Logan's attempt to become someone he wasn't had been more than successful. No one knew the guilt he carried. No one except Duncan, who was now dead.

Deirdre had told Duncan Logan's secret right before she had ended Duncan's life. Logan could still see the surprise and regret in Duncan's eyes before the life faded from them.

If that was any indication of what awaited Logan if he told the others he had gone to Deirdre to have his god unbound, that he had willingly given himself to her—then he would never tell his friends the truth.

He regretted his decision to go to Deirdre every moment of every day. The only way he could make up for what he had done to his family was to put an end to anyone who dared to side with such an evil bitch.

It was his mission. That and finding the artifacts that could end Deirdre once and for all.

Logan stepped into the road and looked first one way, then the other. The storm was passing, but it would most likely rain the rest of the day and into the night. He knew Scottish winters well, and the nip in the air was just the prelude to the snow and ice to come.

He lifted his eyes to the sky and frowned as he considered Eigg and Ian. Maybe Ian had gone to the place where Duncan had been killed. Maybe that was why Logan was being pulled toward Eigg.

He could use his enhanced speed and reach Eigg in a matter of moments, but then he wouldn't be able to search the villages for Ian. He didn't know how he was going to find his friend, but he had to look.

If Logan knew Ian, the other Warrior would try to go off on his own while battling his god for control.

Unless Deirdre had Ian already.

Logan refused to think of that possibility. He would find Ian and help him. Somehow, someway he would.

It was too bad Broc hadn't come with them, Logan mused. The god inside Broc gave him the ability to find anyone, anywhere. They had discovered just how potent a power Broc had when he was able to determine that Deirdre and Ian had traveled four centuries into the future.

Logan chuckled to himself. He'd been the youngest of the Warriors at MacLeod Castle. He'd barely reached the century mark. Now, he was five centuries old.

"Five hundred years," he murmured. "And I doona remember any of it."

He had to chuckle. Jesting with himself—things weren't looking good.

A loud sound drew his attention. Logan looked to his left and saw a small red car come around the corner. He jumped back as it flew past, and in that moment he saw the profile of a woman.

A very beautiful woman with black hair.

It was too bad he didn't have time to dally. He'd have liked to get a better look at the woman and her beautiful black hair she wore tied behind her.

Logan squared his shoulders and moved back onto the

path as he started toward Eigg. He kept his eyes open for any wyrran. Only a few had been pulled into the future with Deirdre, and Logan didn't know how much time had passed since she'd arrived in the year 2012.

It could have been plenty of time to create many more wyrran. He hated the creatures. Deirdre created the small, hairless, pale yellow beasts with her black magic. They had long claws on their hands and feet, and mouths so full of teeth that their thin lips couldn't close over them. Their yellow eyes were large in their small, round heads.

Their shrieks could make a person's blood turn to ice. There was something inherently evil that mortals recognized in the wyrran. It wasn't just that they were ugly. The evil that created them oozed from their bodies like a plague.

Logan could never kill enough of the vile beasts. And with every one he killed, two replaced it. Deirdre considered the creatures her pets, and they obeyed only her.

He came upon a man who looked to be in his mid-thirties and stopped. "Have you seen anything unusual around here?"

The man chortled. "Here? Are ye daft? Nothing happens around this sleepy town. All me life I couldna wait to leave, and then when I did and saw what was really in the world, I couldna get back here fast enough. So, nay, mister, there's been nothing odd."

"Are you sure? Any sounds? Anyone looking out of place?"

The man raised his pale brow. "Besides yourself, you mean?"

Logan glanced down at the man's pants, thick tunic, and what appeared to be a cloak with sleeves. "Does no one wear kilts anymore?"

"Och, most certainly. Just no' quite like you do."

Logan didn't know what to make of his statement. He wasn't certain he could wear the man's attire, nor did he think he wanted to.

"If there was anything out of the ordinary, Mrs. Gibbs would let us know. There's been nothing."

"I see."

"Do ye expect something to happen?" the man asked, his brown gaze sharp. "Are ye working with Scotland Yard?"

Logan didn't know what Scotland yard was, but he wasn't working with anyone. "Nay."

"I understand. You can no' tell me." The man gave a nod and grinned. "Is there a number where I can reach you in case something does happen?"

"Number?"

"Aye. Your mobile number."

"Mobile?"

The man frowned. "You act as though ye have no idea what I'm speaking of."

Logan hadn't a clue.

"How can I tell ye anything if there's no way to contact ye?" the man asked, becoming agitated. "They always want us to help, but they never want to help us."

Logan was sure he didn't want to know who "they" were, but whoever they were, the man certainly didn't like them.

"Do ye have a mobile?" the man asked.

Logan shook his head.

The man turned on his heel and entered his store without another word. Logan bit back a grin and kept walking. The people in this time were certainly odd. If he was looking for anything unusual, it was all around him.

Ian roared his fury as he opened his eyes to find himself lying atop a boulder. His leg was healing from a broken thighbone, and his back ached as the bones and muscles knitted back together after being severed in half.

But that wasn't what caused the turmoil in Ian.

It was his god. Farmire, the father of battle, demanded blood and death. He demanded Ian do his bidding.

Ian ignored the pain of his healing body and launched to his feet. The anguish, the soul-shredding agony of losing the link to his twin ripped through his body.

He fell to his knees, his arms out wide and his face lifted to the sky, as he bellowed his misery and grief. And his rage.

The full extent of his god's power ran rampant through his veins. The frenzy was building, the power awesome. Farmire called to him, begging him to give in to the seductive pulse of energy coursing through him.

It would be so easy to give in. Just a mere thought. Ian tried to hang on to his memories, tried to recall those who had meant something to him.

Their faces blurred as their names left him like sand in the wind. But one name remained—*Duncan*.

Nothing could make him forget his twin. Or how Duncan had been killed.

"Deirdre," Ian growled.

He didn't try to hide his Warrior form. He gloried in the pale blue that covered his body. He smiled at the blue claws that extended from his fingers and the fangs that filled his mouth.

Ian would hold off Farmire for as long as it took him to find Deirdre.

Inside, Ian could hear his god laughing at him. Each moment Farmire batted down his defenses, each breath more evil filled him.

Blackness encroached on Ian's vision. He knew his god was taking over.

But there was nothing he could do.

CHAPTER
THREE

The rain was falling so fast Gwynn could barely see to drive, and the windshield wipers weren't helping at all, even at top speed.

It was all Gwynn could do to see the lines on the road so she didn't run anyone over. All the while reminding herself she had to drive on the left side of the road, which just felt . . . wrong.

She passed a few towns as she followed the road signs to the small fishing port of Mallaig. She was nearly finished with her two hundred mile drive from Edinburgh, and she couldn't wait to get out of the Fiat.

Gwynn had to slow the car and squint out the window to see the sign that proclaimed she had reached Mallaig.

"Just a thousand people," she murmured. Surely someone would recognize the photo she had brought of her father.

She rubbed her temples and leaned forward as she looked for the hotel she had found on the internet. It took her longer than she wanted, but finally she pulled up in front of The Marine Hotel.

Gwynn didn't even try to avoid getting wet as she

climbed out of her rental. She was exhausted, cold, and hungry, and she just wanted a moment to close her eyes and think straight.

She grabbed her suitcase and yanked up the handle to roll it behind her as she trotted to the door. After four hours in a car and eleven on an airplane, Gwynn was ready to get her bearings and find her father.

Fortunately, the hotel had a room, and after a short conversation about her Texas accent she had a key and made her way to the bed that awaited.

She didn't even look at the room. She let the door close behind her as she released her hold on her suitcase, dropped the key onto a table, and let her purse fall to the floor as she collapsed face-first on the bed.

She let out a breath and rolled onto her back, not caring that she was getting the bedspread wet from the rain on her jacket. She stared at the ceiling for several moments as she once again went over the last time she'd seen her father.

He'd been so excited, but he wouldn't tell her about what. It was some find, she knew. He kept telling her it would give everyone the answers they had been searching for.

Gwynn snorted and shook her head as she recalled how his light blue eyes would light up when he found something of interest.

"Everyone has questions about everything," Gwynn said into the empty room.

She sat up and removed her jacket before she reached down to unzip her favorite black boots. Once they were off, she rose and wiggled out of her damp jeans.

Though Gwynn wanted to start looking for her father immediately, she knew she couldn't string two words together in her present state. She needed to get cleaned up, get some food in her, and then she could begin.

Gwynn jumped in the shower and stood beneath the steaming water, letting it course down her body. She couldn't decide if she was angry at her father or worried. A little of both, at the moment.

"Dammit, Dad," she said and braced her hands on the shower wall.

He was all she had, all she had allowed herself to have since her mother had died. She had used the excuse that she needed to care for her father when men asked her on a date.

But the simple truth was, she didn't think she could ever get close to anyone again, knowing they would eventually die. Losing her mother had hurt too badly; the wound was still raw even years later.

Gwynn hurriedly washed her hair and body. After drying off, she wrapped the towel around her and rummaged in her luggage for her comb and mousse.

Once she'd blow-dried her hair, she looked in the mirror and grimaced at the dark circles under her eyes. She pulled out her makeup bag. She loathed putting on makeup, but she always carried it with her. It didn't take her long to dab on some concealer and base. A hint of blush, some eyeliner, and a quick stroke of mascara, and she was finished.

"At least I no longer look like death warmed over," she said to herself in the mirror.

Gwynn padded out of the bathroom to her suitcase. She pulled out thick cashmere socks to cover her icy toes. She had been born and raised in Houston, where it never got very cold. Though she had expected chillier weather in Scotland, she hadn't been prepared for it to be quite so wet and frigid. She had yet to warm up since arriving.

Next came dry jeans, a long-sleeved shirt she tucked into her jeans, and then her favorite plum angora sweater. It was pretty, but it did little to help keep her warm. With her boots back on, Gwynn found the scarf and beanie she'd brought, along with the matching gloves.

With her father's picture in her pocket, she headed to the lobby of the hotel. She asked everyone she ran across, but no one at the hotel had seen her father.

That didn't discourage her. There were many B&Bs in Mallaig as well as another hotel. If she had to, she'd stop at every one. Her father had to be in Mallaig. He just had to.

She'd looked up the GPS tracking on his phone from his last call to her, and the coordinates had led her to Mallaig. She didn't want to think about what it would mean if he wasn't still in the area.

"One problem at a time," she told herself.

Gwynn walked out of the hotel, thankful the rain had slowed to a drizzle, and looked up and down the shore. The clouds were still dark and heavy. The air had gotten even cooler than before, and the brisk wind from the sea made Gwynn shudder, the little warmth she'd had gone in a heartbeat.

After inhaling deeply, she turned and started for the first B&B on her left. When she was finished asking people at the B&Bs and the other hotel about her father, she'd start at the dock.

Someone, somewhere had to have seen her father.

Logan wished he knew what it was about the Isle of Eigg that bade him to answer its call. He'd tried to ignore it, but the isle was insistent. Resolute. Tenacious even.

So he walked toward the isle. Along the way he questioned what few others he saw. He didn't travel along the road, preferring to walk across the land instead.

He didn't like the poles sticking out of the ground with what looked like thick rope strung between them. They were everywhere, taking away from the wildness and beauty of the land.

Logan put aside his distaste of what had become of his Scotland and concentrated on Ian, looking for any places where Ian might have hidden if he had landed near the sea.

It would take Logan decades to check all the caves along the coast, but most of them were near people. If there was any part of Ian left at all, he knew the Warrior would try to distance himself from others as much as he could.

Yet as he walked closer to Mallaig, he knew something was coming. He didn't know what, but it was there.

Maybe it was because that is where he'd been when everything had changed. Deirdre had ambushed the Warriors and killed Duncan. And Logan had learned that Malcolm had been made into a Warrior and was working with Deirdre.

Then Deirdre and Ian had disappeared right in front of Logan's eyes. Everything he and the other Warriors had been fighting changed in the blink of an eye.

What worried Logan most was how much damage Deirdre could inflict in this time.

There were more people milling about than in 1603. More people in Scotland meant more people around the world, which meant more people bowing down to Deirdre.

Logan paused when he crested a hill and looked into the valley where Deirdre had killed Duncan. Malcolm and the other Warriors with Deirdre had been pulled into the future with her. Logan was lucky he had gotten away in time, or he might well be imprisoned by Deirdre again.

He clenched his teeth. "Never," he vowed.

He would kill anyone associated with Deirdre. And he would help to end her and whatever evil had pulled her into the future.

Logan scanned the valley as he recalled the words

spoken and the battle that had taken place there. His gaze fell on a small monument in the middle of the valley.

He made his way to the valley and paused beside a stone cross that rose as high as his waist. He squatted beside it and ran his hands over the beautiful knotwork chiseled into the stone. The cross was worn and chipped in places.

He had no doubt his fellow Warriors had placed the cross in the valley in remembrance of Duncan Kerr.

"A brave Warrior, a good friend," Logan said. "I willna let you down, Duncan. I will find Ian and help him battle his god for control. I may no' have been able to save you, my friend, but I will save your brother. I give you my vow."

The rain slowed until it became nothing more than a drizzle, and for just a moment, the thick clouds split and a ray of light fell upon Logan and the cross.

Logan smiled and touched the cross once more before he rose to his feet and continued on to Mallaig and then Eigg. Maybe he would find some answers there.

Maybe he would find the artifact he'd been sent to find.

He'd taken only three steps when he felt the tingle of magic. Eigg had once been home to a large group of powerful Druids. They had protected Eigg from any attacks Deirdre had sent them.

Could there still be Druids there?

Logan lengthened his strides and hurried toward the port town of Mallaig. Before he'd been tossed through time, he'd felt the power of the Druids on Eigg from Mallaig.

His steps slowed as he reached Mallaig. It had grown just as Salen had. Logan let his eyes roam over the town, disappointment heavy in his gut. To his frustration, he barely felt any magic at all. Either the Druids had left, or they no longer practiced their magic.

Neither possibility was good.

Neither would help him against Deirdre.

He walked to the docks and looked out over the sea to the isles beyond. Eigg was the smallest of the isles, but it had been a great defense against Deirdre and anyone else the Druids didn't want on their land.

"Lookin' for something, lad?"

Logan turned to the bent, white-haired man to his left. By the weathered look of his face and the deep lines grooved into his cheeks and around his eyes, Logan could tell the man had seen many years.

"Are there many who live on Eigg?"

The man cocked a white brow and lifted a shoulder in a shrug. "No' too many. It is said centuries before there was a large sum of people who called Eigg home. But things change."

So it would seem, Logan thought. "Have you lived in Mallaig your entire life?"

The old man chuckled and sat on a stool as he rubbed his knee. "Aye. Fishin' was me life. It's what me family has always done."

"Have you seen anything unusual lately?"

"Lad," the man said with another laugh, "we get a lot of tourists, so we see all kinds."

Logan wasn't sure what that meant, but he presumed it meant the old man hadn't seen anything out of the ordinary, which was good.

In a way.

Logan looked out over the water toward Eigg. It would be a good place for Ian to hide, or for Deirdre to look for the artifact. If there weren't Druids guarding the isle as they once had, it gave Deirdre a prime opportunity to get what she wanted.

"Ye have the look of a man with the weight of the world on his shoulders," the man commented.

Logan grunted. "Perhaps I do. My name is Logan Hamilton. What can you tell me about Mallaig?"

"Well, Logan, I can begin by tellin' ye me name is Hamish Fletcher. Sit down and I'll tell ye anythin' ye be wantin' to know, lad."

Logan was lowering himself to another stool beside Hamish, when he felt the tingle of magic again. It was stronger than what he had felt before, but still weaker than the power he was used to feeling from the Druids at MacLeod Castle.

He looked around, hoping he'd discover the source of magic. And that's when he saw the little red car that had nearly run him down earlier.

CHAPTER
FOUR

As Logan listened to Hamish speak of Mallaig and its trials, he found himself thinking of his childhood and his family.

He usually kept memories of his parents and younger brother pushed far in a corner of his mind, but as soon as he had reached the mainland port of Mallaig those memories had bombarded him.

He hadn't tried to rid himself of them. In fact, he allowed himself a few moments to remember a happier time, a time when life had been pleasant. A time when he had been a good son.

A time before he had betrayed his family.

Memories he had hidden away were returning with a force too strong for him to shove away easily.

He didn't know what was in store for him in the coming days, but whatever it was he knew it would alter the course of his future. He didn't care what happened as long as he could continue to fight against Deirdre.

The oath Logan had made to put an end to her rode him tirelessly. He hadn't felt as if he were doing enough, which was why he had stepped forward to find the next artifact, the Tablet of Orn. The tablet would lead the Warriors to the place where Deirdre's twin, Laria, slept.

Laria was the only one who could kill Deirdre.

Logan took a deep breath, Hamish's words barely registering. The sounds of conversations, haggling, and laughter assaulted him at every angle along the dock.

In the distance Logan spotted an outdoor market. A person could find any number of items at such a place, Fruits, vegetables, cloth, baskets, ribbons, and even weapons. It was a visual spectacle he hadn't realized he'd missed until that moment.

The sights, the sounds, the smells were all just as Logan recalled. The only thing missing was his mother examining a piece of cloth they couldn't afford while his younger brother begged for a coin to buy a sweetmeat.

An ache, bone deep and crushing, began in Logan's chest. He couldn't breathe or move. He could do nothing to hold back the tide of memories.

If he gave in, if he allowed the memories to overtake him, he would be lost. They were as demanding and insistent as his god, Athleus.

He curled his hand into fists, thankful when his claws plunged deep into his palms and blood dripped between his fingers.

It was that pain, though momentary, which allowed him to get the upper hand in his recollections and shove them back into a deep, dark corner of his mind.

When he opened his eyes he glanced down at his skin to confirm it hadn't turned the silver of his god. Only then did he raise his gaze.

"Mallaig has survived," Hamish said, his voice low and full of pain.

Logan could understand the old man. "We all survive. There is no other choice."

Hamish lifted his gaze and gave a single nod. "Aye,

lad. Ye've the right of it. What have ye survived, being one so young?"

"Naught you'd believe, old man," Logan said with a smile he knew didn't quite reach his eyes.

He turned his head to look around him and stiffened as his gaze collided with a woman's. But not just any woman. She was stunning.

Dazzling.

Mesmerizing.

For a moment, Logan couldn't form a coherent thought as he drank in her extraordinary beauty. She stood still as stone, her wide, expressive violet eyes trained on him.

Her black hair hung thick and straight just past her shoulders where the ends lifted and swirled around her in the breeze coming from the sea. Her skin was unblemished, the color of cream, and beckoned to be touched. He longed to stroke it, to see if it was as soft and smooth as he imagined it would be.

Logan's blood began to pound. His balls tightened, and he was eager to know the taste of her lips and the feel of her curves against his. He grew hard just thinking about holding her, of skimming his hands along her body.

Logan had always enjoyed women, but never in all his years had one affected him as this one did. She intrigued him in a way that made him wonder if he should approach her or run the other way.

She was bundled against the weather with a hat of some kind in various shades of pink stripes. She was of average height, but there was nothing common about her. She was a siren, an irresistible enchantress.

And he was smitten. Besotted. Infatuated.

He had to know her, but more than that, he had to taste her. Touch her.

Claim her.

Logan rose, intending to discover her name and every secret she had when he felt it glide over his body. Magic. It was soft, almost hesitant, but it was magic.

A delicious, succulent feel that he had never experienced before.

"Now, that is a woman," Hamish said, and whistled softly.

Logan nodded, uncaring if Hamish was looking at the same woman or not.

"She's got the look of a tourist."

"Tourist?" Logan said and frowned. He glanced at Hamish and confirmed they were speaking about the same woman.

"Aye, lad." Hamish's old eyes narrowed in suspicion. "People who visit places. Tourists."

Logan sighed. Many things had changed, and he needed to learn quickly in order to find his answers.

"How do you know she's no' from here?" Logan asked.

"Her clothes for one. Look around ye, lad. And though her coat is heavy enough, her scarf and gloves willna stand against our harsh weather."

Coat. So that's what she's wearing.

Logan assessed the woman as he let his gaze roam down her lean legs encased in form-hugging pants that disappeared into boots that reached almost to her knees and were decorated with four big silver ornaments on either side going up from her ankle.

To Logan's delight, the woman licked her lips and started toward them.

"Ye've caught her attention, lad," Hamish whispered and slowly rose to his feet.

Logan reached out a hand and helped steady the old man as the woman reached them.

"Hello."

Her voice was as warm as the sunshine, as bright as

the sun. Logan looked into her violet eyes and was again taken aback. He'd never seen eyes that color, made more dramatic by how large and expressive they were.

Her face was heart shaped, her lips full and succulent. Black brows sliced delicately over her amazing eyes. She had a stubborn lift to her chin, and a vulnerability that made him want to pull her against him and shield her from the world.

The magic seemed to grow and fill the space between them, beckoning him, inviting him ever closer to the lovely, bewitching woman before him.

"Ah, an American," Hamish said, smiling at her.

Logan grunted as Hamish jabbed an elbow into his ribs. "How can we help you?"

"I'm . . . uh. I'm looking for someone."

Logan had never heard her accent before. He found it altogether charming, and combined with her nervous smile, he imagined she didn't want for anything.

"Who, lass?" Hamish asked.

She reached into the pocket of her coat and pulled something out. "My father. Gary Austin."

Hamish took the thin, square object and looked at it before handing it to Logan. Logan could only stare at what was in his hands. It was a man looking back at him. He noted the similarities between the man and the woman before him, but they were few. Logan turned the object over and looked at the back, but it was blank.

"What is this?" he asked.

"It's a picture of my father," the woman said.

Picture? *What the hell was a picture?* Logan cleared his throat and handed it back to her.

"Have you seen him?" the woman asked. "He called me three weeks ago from Mallaig, and I've not heard from him since."

Logan hated that he couldn't help her. He wanted to be

the one who took away the worry that filled her beautiful violet eyes. "I've no' seen him."

Hamish scratched his grizzled cheek. "He looks a wee bit familiar. Three weeks, ye say?"

"Yes," the woman said, hope flaring in her eyes.

Logan felt another wave of magic, this one more potent than before. There was no mistaking that it was coming from the woman. A Druid. Did she know what she was? Did she know how close she was to a land where Druids had ruled?

Hamish had called her an American. Did that mean she knew nothing of the magic in her blood? Her magic was strong, but . . . unfocused. As though she didn't use it.

"I'm old, ye ken, and me memory isna what it used to be," Hamish said, "but I think I recall seeing him board the ferry for the isles."

The woman lifted her eyes and looked out over the water. "Do you know which one?"

"Nay," Hamish said with a click of his tongue. "Sorry, I can no' help ye more, lass."

"It's more than I had before," she said softly.

Logan wasn't ready for her to walk away—not until he found out if she knew she was a Druid. If she did know, she could help him, and right now, he needed her help more than he wanted to admit.

"Are you staying here?" Logan asked.

She narrowed her eyes at him. "Why?"

"So if I remember more I can tell ye," Hamish answered for him.

She looked from one to the other. "I'm at The Marine Hotel. My name is Gwynn Austin."

"Gwynn. I'm Logan Hamilton."

A chill raced over Gwynn when the tall, model-perfect man repeated her name. She'd first caught sight of him when she'd scanned the docks. He was, without a doubt, the most gorgeous man she'd ever laid eyes on.

She let her eyes linger on his tall form. He was wearing a kilt that had seen better days, as if it were his second skin. His pale brown locks, highlighted with gold, tangled about his face in the breeze. She drank in his strong jawline, committing it to memory.

He had a wide forehead, an aquiline nose, a square chin, and cheekbones that even made her jealous. The shadow of a beard darkened his cheeks, giving him a rugged, primal look that made her heart miss a beat.

He had a face that guaranteed passion and pure, wonderful, breathtaking sin.

Gwynn's gaze lifted to his, and she was ensnared in the hazel depths, caught in the pull of his direct and lethal gaze. In his greenish-gold eyes, she glimpsed sorrow and . . . guilt that were quickly hidden by his all too charming smile.

Gwynn was taken aback by Logan's vitality and masculinity. She could tell that he was a man used to command, a man used to action and battle.

A warrior in every sense of the word.

She wasn't used to seeing such men. Her heart raced and her palms grew clammy. She wanted to be near him, to know what made him who he was.

At the same time, she sensed a current of danger that swirled around him. If she got too close, he was likely to pull her down with him.

Gwynn was the one who did everything safely. The one who never took chances, the one who kept herself—and her heart—closely guarded. Yet she found she wanted to take a chance with this bad boy named Logan.

It was a chance, however, she knew she would never be able to take.

Gwynn licked her lips and drew the frigid sea air into her lungs. The air was heavy with salt and the smell of fish. The wind whistled around her, carrying with it the crash of the waves, the cries of the gulls, and the conversations among the fishermen still on the dock.

Despite everything around her, Gwynn couldn't tear her gaze from Logan and the lean sinew and hard body she glimpsed beneath the saffron shirt and kilt. She'd even forgotten what they'd been talking about.

"Gwynn, I'm Hamish," the old man said, reminding her that she and Logan weren't alone. "I sit on these docks every day. If I see yer father, I'll be sure to let ye know."

She forced a smile. "Thanks, Mr. Hamish."

He chuckled. "Nay, lass. Just Hamish. I hope ye find your father. No' many get lost around these parts."

"What was he doing here?" Logan asked.

Gwynn tried not to look into his hypnotizing eyes, but she couldn't help herself. "He was here on research."

"What kind of research?"

"I'm . . . I'm not sure. He found something, a book, that led him here."

Logan's brow furrowed. "Here? To Mallaig? In all the places in Scotland with standing stones and history, he came here?"

Gwynn had thought the same thing. "If I knew what he was looking for, I would have a better chance of finding him. All I have to go on is the coordinates I got from his cell when he called me."

"Cell?" Logan repeated.

"Mobile phone," Hamish said and scratched his chin.

Gwynn kept forgetting that the Brits had a different word for just about everything. It wasn't a cell phone here. It was a mobile phone.

Mo-bile, she thought with a grin.

Yet, Logan hadn't seemed to understand what a mobile phone was either which was beyond odd. Everyone knew what a cell phone was.

She pulled out her iPhone and held it up. "This," she said as she showed Logan. "People talk on it."

His gaze narrowed as he stared at her phone. "Of course."

She wasn't buying it. He didn't know what a cell phone was, and what person in the last fifteen years didn't know that?

Her curiosity about who Logan was only increased. "Of course," she repeated.

Hamish glanced over his shoulder toward the isles. "Most folk who come to Mallaig come to see the isles."

"That's my guess as well," Gwynn said. "Especially since I checked every bed and breakfast and hotel here."

"That didna take you long," Hamish said with a laugh.

Gwynn couldn't help but smile at the old man. "No, it really didn't."

Silence stretched between the three, and though Gwynn didn't want to leave, she had her father to find.

"Thank you, gentlemen. Y'all have been helpful."

She started to walk away when Logan reached out and touched her arm. Gwynn paused and looked at him. "Yes?"

"I could help you. Locate your father."

Gwynn had always loved the sound of a Scottish brogue, and Logan's certainly made her blood race. But if he was near, she wouldn't be able to concentrate on finding her father. There was something that potent and alluring about him.

It reminded her that she was a woman. And he was a man. It made her think of kissing, of naked bodies gliding together, of sinful pleasure and mind-melding bliss.

He was trouble, and the quicker she got away from him the better.

"I appreciate the offer, but I must decline."

"Is it safe for women to walk around by themselves in this time?"

She cocked her head to the side at his words. "In this time? What do you mean?"

Logan shrugged his thick shoulders, the saffron shirt molding to the hard muscle. "I'm merely concerned for your safety."

"I've got mace, and I know enough karate moves to take care of myself."

Confusion clouded Logan's face. It was as if he didn't understand anything she said.

"Where are you from?" she asked.

"Scotland, of course."

She rolled her eyes. "I know that, but you act as if you don't understand anything I'm saying."

"It's yer accent, lass," Hamish quipped. "It takes some gettin' used to."

Gwynn knew it was more than that. "Do you understand me?" she asked Logan.

"Some."

She was surprised he had answered her at all, but more surprising was the truth she heard in his words. "Goodbye, Logan. Hamish."

"Good luck, lass," Hamish called as she walked down the docks.

Gwynn was tempted to look back and see if Logan watched her. Instead, she kept walking, her gaze locked on the ferry that was loading.

CHAPTER
FIVE

Logan found himself looking for Gwynn for the rest of the afternoon. Everything he needed to know he learned from Hamish.

As the sun began to set and the fishermen returned with their boats, they all stopped and spoke with Hamish. It gave Logan the chance he needed to question others.

But once again, there was nothing.

Maybe he had arrived before Deirdre. It could be that Ian had not been pulled forward in time as well.

Logan couldn't know for sure.

Part of him wished he could use one of the mobile phones that others had and talk to those at MacLeod Castle. He wasn't sure how it worked or if those at the castle would have one.

He needed to talk to them, to hear their voices and laughter. They were his family now. Duncan's death was a huge weight on his shoulders, made heavier because he hadn't been there to see his friend buried.

All because Deirdre had been pulled into the future. There hadn't been time to see Duncan buried. Logan had made the decision to jump forward through time to find Ian. To save Ian.

Since Logan hadn't been able to save Duncan.

He owed Ian at least that much.

Logan's mind was full of all the new things around him, yet he saw some of what he had always loved about Scotland was still there. The loyalty of her people, the love of the land. He saw it in each Scot's eyes.

And that made him take an easier breath.

He had never thought what his land would be like in the future, because he'd been too busy trying to keep Deirdre from destroying it all.

"These old bones can no' take the cold as they used to," Hamish said as he rose to his feet. "Besides, me missus will have me head if I doona get home for dinner."

Logan smiled as he helped Hamish stand.

"Yer welcome to join us."

Nay, there where things about Scotland and her people that would never change. "I must decline for tonight."

"Ye doona ken what yer missin'. Me Mary makes the best haggis in all of Scotland. If ye change yer mind, follow the road up the hill and take a left. Me house is the third one. Ye can no' miss it."

Logan waited until Hamish was deep in conversation with another man as they made their way off the docks before Logan turned to the sea.

Soon, the activity on the docks died down until it was just Logan and a few others. The temperature continued to drop, and the clouds far in the distance heralded a horrendous snowstorm.

As soon as the sun dipped below the horizon and the night descended over Mallaig, Logan closed his eyes and opened himself up to feel magic.

The last time he had done this was when he and Galen

had searched around Loch Awe for a group of Druids who had hidden away in fear of Deirdre.

Worry began to spread through Logan the more he searched for magic and the more he found only a thread. That thread was so faint it was almost nonexistent.

But he knew the feel of that magic. It was Gwynn.

"Gwynn," he murmured, his blood heating just thinking of her.

He wanted to know what had happened to the incredibly powerful group of Druids who had made the Isle of Eigg their home. They'd had unbelievable magic, the sheer might of it enough to keep even Deirdre away.

Logan wished once more that MacLeod Castle wasn't on the other side of Scotland. He should probably have gone to the castle first thing. Sooner or later he would find himself standing in front of the gates of MacLeod Castle.

His thoughts, as they had often that day, returned to Gwynn Austin. There was something about the woman that wouldn't allow her to leave his thoughts.

It was more than her beauty, more than the steel beneath her fragility. More than her magic, even. Logan couldn't put his finger on exactly what it was that drew him to her, but it was powerful enough that he knew where she was at all times.

Almost as if his body was attuned to hers, which was impossible.

Or was it?

Scotland had always been steeped in magic and unexplainable occurrences. The Druids helped to draw the magic around them, but maybe there didn't need to be Druids for him to sense, to feel the essence of whatever magic was left.

Logan smiled and opened his eyes when he discerned Gwynn watching him from the window of the building she was staying in. What had she called it? Ah, aye, a hotel.

His smile grew when she left the hotel and walked toward him. Her steps were quick and sure as she neared him.

"It's after midnight," he said when she stopped behind him.

"The time change has messed me up. Where I'm from it's only five. I'd be thinking about dinner right now, wondering if I wanted to go out or cook."

He wanted to ask what she meant but decided to stay quiet and see what it was that brought her to him.

She lowered herself to sit beside him and let out a deep, heartfelt breath. "I've wanted to come to Scotland for as long as I can remember."

"Is this your first time here?"

"Yes," she said with a wry smile as she glanced at him. "And I'm not enjoying any of it."

"You can still see my land as you search for your father."

She looked at him, her violet eyes searching. "It wouldn't feel right. I can't explain it, Logan, but I feel it in my gut that something is wrong, that something has happened to him."

"I learned long ago never to question my feelings. Listen to your instinct, Gwynn."

Her shoulders drooped as she leaned her head back and looked at the sky. "So many stars. Back home, I never get to see the sky like this. It's like everything is different here. I wonder why?"

"Magic."

Her head snapped up and she looked at him. "What did you say?"

Logan didn't miss the wariness that stole over her stunning face, or the fear that flashed in her eyes. "I said magic. Have you never heard the legends of my land?"

"I have," she admitted softly. "When I was a little girl,

my grandmother would tell me the most wonderful stories about the Druids who once roamed this land."

A thrill rushed through Logan. Maybe she did know what she was, after all. "Did she, now? What else did she tell you?"

"As with all stories, there was a villain."

"Did this villain have a name, perhaps?"

Gwynn shrugged. "I don't remember. All I do recall is that she was very evil. Despite the villain, I remember Grams painting a picture of Scotland that made me yearn to be here. As silly as it sounds, it made me feel as if this was where I belonged."

Logan decided to see how much Gwynn knew. And how much he would have to tell her. "There are all kinds of stories about my land. So many good men have died in battle fighting for it. Do you know the story of Rome and Britain?"

"I do," Gwynn said with a smile. She shifted toward Logan. "That was one of the stories Grams told me. I don't recall much, other than that the Celts ran Rome off."

"Shall I tell it?" Logan offered.

"I would like that very much."

Logan wasn't sure how much of her grandmother's telling was the original story, but he was about to find out. The "story" he would tell her was the truth about how he, and others like him, became Warriors.

"The Celts fought long and hard against Rome for many years. Several decades before the Druids had divided into two groups."

"Two?" Gwynn asked.

"Aye. The *mies*, who used the pure magic that flowed within them to heal people. They used their wisdom to guide the leaders of the clans and to help crops grow, among other things."

"And the other group?"

Logan swallowed, hating to even talk about them. "The other Druids were called *droughs*. They craved power more than anything. They underwent a ceremony where they cut their wrists. Their blood, along with a spell, bound their souls to *diabhul*, the devil. That connection gave them the ability to use black magic. And with it they wore a small vial around their necks with their *drough* blood inside. It's called a Demon's Kiss and it, along with the cuts on their wrists, were how *droughs* were recognized."

"Good and evil," Gwynn murmured. "It always seems to come down to that."

"And it always will. You can no' have one without the other."

"How do the Druids figure into the story with Rome?"

"After years of fighting with Rome and keeping them from pushing too far north, the Celts realized they needed something more to get Rome to leave for good," he said. "They turned to the *droughs*."

"Why the *droughs*? Why not the *mies*?"

"Because the *mies* didna fight unless they had no other choice. They would defend those around them in a battle, but they didna seek out war. The *droughs*, however, were a different animal. They had an answer for the Celts, one that would change history."

"What was it?" She leaned closer, her gaze eager.

"The *droughs* called up gods that had been locked in Hell. These gods were so ancient their names had been lost over time. They were vicious and bloodthirsty and they were just what the Celts needed to defeat Rome.

"The best warriors from each tribe agreed to host the gods. Once the *droughs* released the gods from their prison, they took over these men, creating Warriors."

Gwynn's brows lifted as she blew out a breath. "None

of this was in any history book I read, but I do recall some of it from Gram's stories."

"This wouldna be in any book, Gwynn. These Warriors defeated Rome in quick order. Rome couldna leave our shores fast enough, but once they departed, the Celts were left with men who were more god than mortal. The Warriors turned on each other and anyone who crossed their path. Where our rivers and land had run red with the blood of the Romans, now it ran with the heart and soul of Britain."

Logan paused as he watched Gwynn. She knew the story, or at least part of it. That meant there had to be a Druid somewhere in her family. It was the Druid's role to pass the story to their descendants so the same mistakes wouldn't be made.

"The Celts begged the *droughs* to remove the gods, but despite the powerful black magic the *droughs* possessed, they couldna force the gods to abandon their hosts. With no other choice, the *droughs* turned to the *mies*. It was the first—and last—time the Druids worked as one. Since no spell they cast could remove the gods, they devised a way to bind the gods inside the men."

"Bind them?" Gwynn asked. "I don't understand."

"Aye. With the binding in place, the gods couldna control the men. The men woke with no memories of what they had done to the Romans or their own people. They never knew of the gods still inside them, gods that moved through bloodlines to the strongest Warrior of each family. The Druids, however, remembered. They stayed close to the Warrior families in case they were ever needed."

Gwynn tucked a black lock of hair behind her ear and stuffed her hands in her coat pockets. "I'd like to think this is just some tall tale, but . . . somehow I know it's not. The story doesn't end there, either, does it?"

"It does no'."

"I'm not sure I want to hear the rest."

Logan liked how at ease Gwynn was around him. Would that change when she discovered that he was a Warrior, that he had one of those primeval gods inside him?

"My imagination has always been vivid," Gwynn said as she looked anywhere but at him. "Yet, while you spoke, it was as if I was there, that I was one of those Druids. I saw everything, Logan." She finally looked at him. "How can that be?"

"I told you. It's the magic of my land." The real reason was that Gwynn was a Druid, but he wanted to wait before he told her everything. Wait and see just how much she knew.

"You believe there really were Druids?"

"I know it for a fact, lass. I know several women who are Druids."

She blinked in surprise, then shrugged. "There are many people who claim to be something they're not."

"You doona trust easily, do you?"

Slowly, she shook her head. "Not when there is no one worthy of giving my trust to."

CHAPTER
SIX

Gwynn wanted to discount everything Logan had told her. But she couldn't. Somehow, someway, deep in her soul, she had not only heard his words before, but she knew they were truth.

Fact.

Reality.

The question was, how did she know?

"Will you finish the story?"

Logan's hazel eyes flecked with gold met hers. She glanced at his wide, thin lips and wondered what it would feel like to have those lips on her. To have his large, callused hands hold her against all that hard muscle of his body. She mentally shook herself and huddled deeper into her coat.

"If you're sure you want to hear it."

"I don't think I do, but I think I have to."

Logan gave a single nod. "The gods stayed bound inside the men for many years. The *droughs* and *mies* divided once more and life continued as it was. More invaders came to Britain, but no one, least of all the Druids, wanted to unleash the gods, for fear of no' being able to bind them again. No one wanted to see Britain destroyed, but the loss of its people was feared even more."

"So Britain fell, first to the Saxons and then to others."

"Aye. Until one day a young *drough* found a scroll long thought to have been destroyed. That scroll had the spell to unbind the gods, and it gave the *drough* one clan name—MacLeod."

Gwynn blew out a breath. "I don't think I've ever heard this part of the story."

"This *drough* took the scroll and left her village. She hid in a mountain."

"Cairn Toul," Gwynn said, then covered her mouth with her hand as she stared at Logan. "How did I know that?"

His gaze was unwavering as he said, "You've heard the story."

"The *drough's* name? What was it?"

"Deirdre."

A shiver raced down Gwynn's spine. She had heard part of this story before. The villain in Grams's stories was always named Deirdre. "What did this Deirdre do with the scroll?"

"She looked to the great MacLeod clan to find a warrior who had the god inside him. She discovered three brothers equal in every way. She destroyed their clan, killing everyone but the brothers. She tricked them into her mountain where she unbound each brother's god. And created Warriors once again."

"Wouldn't they be as uncontrollable as the first Warriors?"

"Nay," Logan said softly as he turned his head to the sea. "This spell limited the gods' powers. However, the god could gain control if the man was no' strong enough to hold him back."

Gwynn stared at Logan's profile. There was something in his words, pain and regret and shame, that told her this story was more than just words to him.

"After that, Deirdre began to find other men who had a god inside them," Logan continued. "All the while, she hunted and captured Druids who she killed in order to steal their magic."

Gwynn didn't know what to say, didn't know if there was anything to say. The story was too wild to be true, yet how could her Grams have known the exact same one?

Logan cleared his throat, bringing her attention back to him. "The MacLeods escaped her, but others were no' so fortunate. Many Warriors fell to their god, which allowed Deirdre to use them to her advantage. But there were others who banded together with the MacLeods to fight her."

"What happened to her? Did the MacLeods win?"

Logan's face hardened as he swung his head to look at her. "I doona know, lass. The battle still rages."

For a second, Gwynn believed him. Then she laughed. "You had me there for a minute, Logan. You're an incredible storyteller. Is that what you do for a living?"

He frowned. "I doona know what you mean."

"That's the second time today you've said that. Why don't you know the meaning of my words?"

"If I told you, you wouldna believe me."

"Try me."

He shook his head. "If you doona believe the story I just told you, then there's no use."

But Gwynn wanted to know. Her curiosity was urging her to beg, to plead, anything to discover what made Logan so different from other men. What made her want to know every secret he had. To know the man she sensed he kept hidden.

"Look at the isles," Logan urged her.

Gwynn raised a brow, but when Logan just looked at her, she sighed and looked across the sea. "Okay. Now what?"

"Close your eyes."

Again, she hesitated.

Logan leaned close and whispered in her ear, "Trust me, Gwynn."

With her hand on the can of mace in her pocket, Gwynn let her lids slide shut.

"Good," Logan murmured. "Now, think of Scotland and the wild, untamed beauty of this land. Let the magic that has been part of Scotland and her people surround you and fill your soul. Hear the call of the past. Feel the ancestors who once called Eigg home. Sense the power, the might of the Druids."

With every word Logan whispered into her ear, Gwynn felt herself falling deeper inside herself. The sound of drums and soft, melodic chanting filled her ears.

Sparks of color flashed behind her eyelids as the chanting grew louder. She didn't understand the words, repeated over and over, but she recognized the power in them.

Something flared inside her, the same something she had pushed aside years ago. But it wouldn't be denied now. It pulsed within her, growing, rising just as the chanting did.

Magic.

Gwynn's eyes flew open, her gaze locked on Eigg. Suddenly, she could hear Grams's voice in her head telling her about her ancestors, about the Druids who had lived on a small isle called Eigg on the west coast of Scotland.

How had Gwynn forgotten that? She had been a small child when Grams had died, but until this moment with Logan, Gwynn hadn't recalled anything about Eigg.

Or Druids.

Gwynn turned her head to look at Logan. "What did you do?"

A slow, satisfied smile pulled at his lips. "Your magic is . . . strong. Either the Druids of Eigg are gone or they've squashed their magic, just as you nearly did."

Gwynn climbed to her feet and shook her head as she glared at Logan. "Stop it. I don't have magic."

"There's no use denying it. No' only can I feel it, but you can as well. Now. Why did you bury it?"

Memories of small, unexplained things that occurred when she was just a child filled Gwynn's mind. She used to make her mother's plants grow; used to watch as a seed sprouted and matured in a matter of moments with her help.

She had eventually refused to listen to the call of her magic after her mother took her to all sorts of doctors to find out what had made her daughter so "wrong."

"Oh, God," Gwynn said as she began to feel ill.

Logan was suddenly standing beside her, his hands on her arms to steady her. "You feel it, your magic?"

"Why?" she asked him. "Why did you make me remember? Why did you make me feel my magic again?"

"Because I need you, Gwynn. We all do."

She backed away from him, out of his hold, out of the warmth that had begun to surround her. "I have to find my father."

"What do you really think brought your father here?" he asked as she took a step away from him.

"I don't know."

"You do," Logan insisted as he tracked her step for step. "Why, Gwynn?"

"What's your interest in Eigg and the Druids?" she demanded.

He paused, as if considering what to say. "It's why I

was brought here. You have no idea how verra important you, as a Druid, are."

She glanced at her hotel and tightened her fingers on the mace. "You're insane."

"Nay. I'm telling you the truth. You may no' want to hear it, but I am. Now tell me what would bring your father here?"

Gwynn didn't know what made her even consider telling Logan, but after everything she had experienced that night and the memories that now flooded her mind, she couldn't *not* tell him.

"My mother hated that I was . . . different. Between the doctors and the medication they put me on, I made myself forget about what I could do. My father, on the other hand, thought it marvelous. They argued constantly, and when I stopped doing the things that upset my mother, my father lost interest in me. But never in his ancestry. He was obsessed with learning about his past. My great-great grandmother came to America from Scotland. It was said that she was a witch."

Logan raked a hand through his shoulder-length golden brown hair and smiled ruefully. "Could your father do any magic?"

"Not that I know of. He was always researching magic and its effect on cultures as an anthropologist."

"If he came to Mallaig in search of Druids, he might have stumbled across something he should no' have found," Logan said.

Gwynn shivered. "I know."

"Are you going to the isles in the morn?"

"I am."

Logan took a step closer to her. "Allow me to accompany you, Gwynn."

There had been a flash of something fierce and animalistic in his hazel eyes. "Why?"

"If someone harmed your father, the same fate could befall you when you go searching. I can no' allow that."

She hadn't thought of that, but Logan had a point. "And how do I know I can trust you?"

His eyes blazed with intensity. "I gave a vow to protect Druids with my life."

"Oh." She wanted to discount his words, to walk away and forget about him. But she couldn't.

Nor did she want to.

CHAPTER SEVEN

No matter how hard she tried, Gwynn couldn't sleep for more than a half hour after leaving Logan on the docks.

Everything he'd told her mixed in her mind with memories of her childhood until her head pounded from the strain. To make matters worse, while she drifted in her thoughts right before sleep claimed her, she recalled a fight her mother had had with Grams about Gwynn's "magic."

Gwynn finally gave up on resting and rose to pace her small hotel room until the night sky lightened with a new day. She combed out her hair, dressed, and quickly brushed her teeth before she walked out of her room. She was pulling on her heavy black peacoat as she descended to the lobby.

"Good morn, miss," called the cheerful redhead behind the desk.

Gwynn forced a smile. "Good morning."

It wasn't good. Nothing was good right now, and it wouldn't get any better until Gwynn found her father.

She wasn't surprised to see Hamish and Logan once more on the docks. Gwynn wasn't sure if Logan had somewhere to go or if he just preferred staying by the sea.

In order to get to the ferry, she had to walk past the two men. When she'd rather have bypassed them altogether. Logan's knowing grin told her he knew she didn't want to speak with him.

"Did ye rest well, lass?" Hamish asked.

Gwynn shook her head.

"Och. That's no' good. Have ye eaten?"

Gwynn sighed, searching for patience that seemed to have deserted her that morning. "No, I haven't."

Hamish *tsk*ed and frowned. "It's no' good to start a day without a decent meal."

"I've got a bar in my purse," Gwynn said and glanced down at the black bag on her shoulder. "I'll be fine."

"Shall we go?" Logan asked.

Gwynn had debated with herself all night about whether or not to have Logan accompany her. She didn't know him, so she was leery. Yet a part of her, a part she had felt again last night for the first time in years, recognized his words as truth.

That still didn't mean he could be trusted.

Gwynn sighed. Logan was a Scot, and that meant he would be able to take her places she might not otherwise know to look for.

As if sensing her reluctance, Logan said, "I give you my word as a Highlander that I willna allow any harm to come to you, Gwynn, whether by me or someone—or some*thing*—else."

"All right," she agreed. "But the minute I think you're trying—"

"That time willna come," Logan stated, his face set in hard lines. "I've given my word."

Hamish nodded solemnly. "A Highlander's word is ta be taken seriously, lass."

"We shall see." Gwynn gave a wave to Hamish and set off for the ferry.

The sound of Logan's boots behind her helped settle her nerves, which were suddenly on edge. She stepped onto the ferry and walked to the railing where she could see the isles.

"You didna sleep," Logan said.

"After everything you told me last night you expected me to sleep?" Gwynn asked, as she cut him a look to let him know just how irritated she was.

Logan shrugged. "You were past exhausted yesterday. If you doona take care of yourself, Gwynn Austin, you willna be in any condition to find your father."

She blinked her scratchy eyes, which were made worse when the ferry pushed off and the wind began. "Why do you want to come with me?"

"Because you're a Druid."

It was all she could do not to roll her eyes. "Tell me again how you knew," she said as she turned to look at him.

His hazel eyes, green and blue mixed with flecks of gold, watched her as if he had found the most interesting thing on earth. It made Gwynn fidget. Men didn't look at her that way.

"Well?" she prompted when he didn't speak.

Logan's lips lifted into a crooked smile that made her heart miss a beat. "Last eve you didna want to believe me. Now you do?"

"I feel it," she whispered and glanced around to see if anyone heard her. "Inside me."

"I knew what you were because I, too, felt your magic."

"How is that possible?"

"I'm no' sure you want to know the answer to that."

She wasn't sure she did, either, but she had to know. "Will you tell me?"

"Aye, if that is your wish."

"You don't want to, though, do you?"

His nostrils flared as he exhaled and glanced at the dark blue waters that surrounded them. "You've just learned what you are. You might have been told parts of the story I retold last night, but deep inside you doona want to believe me."

Gwynn turned so that her back was against the railing. "All you say is true, but how can I really know what is going on if I don't know the entire story?"

"I may have put you in grave danger by reminding you of your magic. If I doona tell you more, she might overlook you."

"Who?"

He raised his golden brows, his lips flattened.

"Deirdre," Gwynn murmured.

"Aye. She's verra real, Gwynn. If you believe nothing else, believe what I've told you about her."

Gwynn looked away from his mesmerizing eyes and his rugged features to find everyone on the ferry was looking at him.

She dug her Chapstick out of her purse and applied it to her lips as she scooted closer to Logan.

"What is that?" he asked as he watched her recap the lip balm.

It was just another thing that made her frown. Who didn't know what Chapstick was? Instead of answering him, she said, "Your kilt looks authentic. Almost as if you've worn it for years."

The interest in his hazel eyes faded as he became aware of the other ferry riders. "You say this because people are watching me."

It wasn't a question, nor did she treat it as one. "There

are Scots looking at you as if they've never seen someone like you before. Then there are the women, who are practically drooling over you. You didn't know what a cell phone or Chapstick was. Those are common items everyone recognizes."

His jaw clenched as he held her gaze. "Once you know, there's no turning back."

"I wouldn't have it any other way."

"You say that now."

"Just what do you think will happen to me if I know?"

Logan waited until the ferry docked before he took Gwynn's elbow and ignored the flash of desire that simple touch caused. He ushered her onto the isle and maneuvered her away from the crowds.

"Logan," she said in warning.

"You want to know what will happen to you?" he asked as he came to a halt.

Gwynn whirled to face him, her black locks flying in the wind. She wore the same pink cap, which fit snugly over her head and covered her ears. The mixture of pinks only brought out the vivid color of her eyes even more.

"Yes," she said. "I want to know what could happen to me."

"Deirdre will hunt you down. She will take you and drain you of whatever magic you have and then kill you. She likes to torture the Druids for any information that could help her. You can be brave now, Gwynn, but I've seen what Deirdre does to the Druids. You doona want any part of that."

Wariness stole over Gwynn. Every time she thought of Deirdre, a coldness swept through her. No matter what she wanted, she couldn't discount that feeling. "I'm not sure I should believe you."

"There's only one way to prove it, and that's with Deirdre. I'd rather no' bring her into this."

Gwynn looked at the ground. "You're scaring me."

"Good. I'd rather have you frightened than no' to heed my words."

"All right," she said and squared her shoulders. "What isle are we on again?"

"Eigg." Logan was saddened by the loss of the once powerful Druids who had called the isle home.

Gwynn's eyes became distant and she moved past him to walk along the shore. She would pause every now and then to look at something, as if her mind had taken her far away.

"What is it?" Logan finally asked.

Slowly, she turned to face him. "I don't know. It's almost . . . it's almost as if I know this place."

"If your ancestors came from Eigg, it would make sense that you would recognize it because of your magic. The magic of Druids is endless, Gwynn. The stronger the Druid, the stronger the magic."

"Maybe," she said with a shrug. "I've never been here before. I've never even seen pictures. How can I feel a connection to a place I didn't know about until recently?"

"Magic is a potent entity. The Druids may be gone from this place, but residual magic still lingers. You belong here."

"I think I do," she said as she closed her eyes. "Do you feel that?"

Logan was instantly on alert. "What?"

"I feel magic, but it's different from mine. This magic is old. Very old."

Logan squatted and placed his hand on the ground. "I came here once to find an ancient artifact that would help end Deirdre. The object, the Tablet of Orn, held great magic. That could be what you're feeling."

"Do you not feel its magic?"

"I do now," Logan said as he stood. "I hope that means the artifact is still here."

"Why didn't you get it before?"

Logan moved away as a group of tourists neared them. "Deirdre. I was with another Wa . . . friend. We'd been sent here to convince the Druids to allow us on the isle. After that we'd either talk them into giving us the artifact or we'd steal it. Before we could get to the isle, Deirdre attacked and killed Duncan."

When Gwynn didn't have another question, he turned his head to look at her. She was watching him thoughtfully, as though she were piecing a puzzle together. "You were trying to get to Eigg when the Druids were here?"

"Aye." And then he realized his mistake. He hadn't wanted to tell Gwynn who he was or when he'd come from yet. She was already skittish enough without adding more weight to her shoulders.

"When was that, Logan?"

He sighed and rubbed the back of his neck. "A long time ago."

"How long?" she persisted.

"Gwynn. You doona really want to know."

"Oh, but I do."

Logan knew there was no way of getting around telling her. He could lie, but if he wanted her to believe everything else he had told her, he had to be truthful now as well. "The year was 1603."

For several heartbeats Gwynn did nothing but stare at him. Then she began to laugh.

"How do I attract the crazy people?" she asked no one in particular.

Logan wasn't sure what "crazy" meant, but he had an idea. "I'm no' daft, Gwynn."

"Oh, but you are," she said as she glared at him, her

violet eyes shining brightly. "There is no way someone can live for more than four hundred years."

"Actually, there are a couple of ways. I arrived in this time yesterday, which is why I doona know what that tube is you put on your lips, or this mobile phone you spoke of."

She shook her head and rubbed her temples with her fingers. "This cannot be real."

"Most believe that of magic as well, but you feel it within you. You used it as a child. If magic is real, why is it no' believable that I traveled from my time to yours?"

"Because time travel isn't possible," she ground out, the laughter gone and replaced with anger and frustration. "How, exactly, did you time travel?"

"I was sent here by the Druids at MacLeod Castle. They pooled their magic together and sent me and three others here."

"There are more of you walking around?" she said, her eyes wide with horror.

Once she knew of the god inside him, he wondered if that horror would be directed at him. "Aye."

"Why were you sent here?"

"Because Deirdre was pulled from our time to this one. She took another of us with her. We're here looking for Ian, and to complete our mission."

"Finding the artifact?" Gwynn asked.

"Indeed."

She started walking and Logan fell into step beside her. They continued in silence for a time before she halted and turned to him.

"Say I believe everything you've told me. How would you find Ian and Deirdre?"

Logan shrugged. "I'm no' sure. I would be able to feel Deirdre's magic. Ian is a different story altogether."

"Why would she take Ian?"

"Duncan was his twin. I believe that when Deirdre

was pulled through time, there was a connection between her and Duncan that transferred to Ian."

"Which is what made him time travel," she finished. She shook her head of midnight hair. "This is all so surreal."

"It's the truth," Logan vowed. "I was looking for Ian when I was drawn once more to Eigg. For me, Duncan died just a few days ago. I thought his death was what urged me to the isle, but then I met you. I'm no' sure if it was Duncan, my mission, or you who called me here."

"If everything you've said is true, then you need to find Ian."

"My vow is to protect Druids. That means you. Once I know you're safe from Deirdre, then I will look for Ian."

"And the artifact?"

He smiled. "Are you saying you believe me?"

"I'm indulging you," she said with a haughty lift of her chin.

Logan's smile grew. For now, that was enough.

CHAPTER
EIGHT

Deirdre hadn't thought she could loathe anyone more than the MacLeods, but apparently she'd been wrong. Hatred burned brightly inside her for Declan Wallace—the man who thought he could rule her.

But no man ruled Deirdre.

"I thought the new clothes would at least grant me a measure of a smile," Declan said as he leaned against the doorway of her chamber.

Deirdre glanced down at the new clothes she now wore. The leather pants fit tightly against her legs and bottom. The top was of the same black leather and molded to her breasts and torso.

It felt odd not wearing a gown, but she enjoyed the freedom the pants gave her. Not to mention how they made her body look.

The black high-heeled boots had taken a bit of getting used to, but Deirdre found she quite liked the height they gave her.

Regardless, her pleasure over the clothes couldn't dispel her anger. Or the vengeance she plotted.

"What do you want, Declan?"

His grin grew bolder as he pushed away from the door and walked toward her. He looked as if he had been blessed by the sun with his golden hair and skin. Those golden locks fell about his face in what looked like disarray, but Deirdre had seen him preening before the mirror, getting every strand perfect.

She glanced at his clothes and struggled to remember what he had called them. Ah, yes. A suit. The material was black and had been tailored just for him. The crisp white shirt brought out his bronzed skin.

Declan, with his strong jaw, full lips, and intense blue eyes, was more than handsome. But Deirdre wasn't impressed with his looks or his magic.

"What I want," Declan said with a sly grin, "is you, Deirdre."

"And what makes you think you can have me?"

"Because I have the means to give you everything you've ever wanted."

She raised a brow. "I was well on my way to getting what I wanted without you."

Declan chuckled and moved with slow, measured steps toward her. "You failed. How do you think I was able to bring you to my time? Had you succeeded, you would have ruled everything. Yet, look around my world, Deirdre. No one even knows your name."

She fisted her hand, wishing with all her might she could send a blast of magic through him.

"Druids are all but vanished," Declan continued, unaware of her fury. "The MacLeods bested you. They ended whatever reign you thought you had. I intervened before the MacLeods could win."

Deirdre inhaled deeply and crossed her arms over her chest. "So you say. How do I know you don't lie? How do

I know you didn't yank me to your time so you could share in my glory?"

Declan stopped in front of her. "Every mention of you speaks of your unusual white hair and eyes. And of your beauty. They doona lie."

"Compliments? Why?"

"Because I want you. No' just by my side to rule this pathetic world, but in my bed. Let my seed fill you. Let us bring forth the child of the prophecy."

"The child I was to have had with Quinn MacLeod?"

"The very one."

Deirdre considered Declan. It would be easy enough to take him to her bed. She'd glimpsed his body beneath his fine clothes and seen the hard definition of his muscles. Declan was nearly as vain as she was.

"Where are my Warriors?"

His knowing gaze told her he realized that she was changing the subject. "They are . . . learning to adjust."

"I need to see them."

"No' just yet," Declan hedged.

Deirdre let her hands drop to her sides. "And my wyrran?"

"They are also adjusting, though more loudly than the Warriors. It appears you inspire loyalty."

Deirdre ignored the rich furnishings around her. For all the lavish furniture and luxurious material, there were no windows in her room.

"Where are we, Declan?"

"In Scotland, as I told you before. You're in my home."

"So you say. Let me see outside."

He shrugged. "Soon."

"Do you intend to keep me prisoner?"

Declan ran a finger down her leather-encased arm. "I've no intention of letting you go, Deirdre. You were meant to be mine, and I intend to have you."

Unease rippled through her at his words. She didn't know how much magic he had, but he had put spells in place that prevented her from using her own magic.

For the moment.

She didn't intend to stay in his home for long. Her mountain was calling to her.

"Make yourself comfortable," Declan said as he turned and headed for the door. "There are many interesting shows on the telly. I'm sure you recall how I showed you to work it."

Deirdre stared at him as he paused at the door and looked at her over his shoulder. With one last smile, he was gone. The door closed and locked behind him.

She whirled around, anger rippling through her. Her magic swam inside her, eager to be used.

And she would use it.

For three months she had been locked in Declan's home. The first month she had been so crazed with fury that he'd restrained her. She had never felt so . . . helpless.

And it only bred her anger, until it consumed her.

The second month, after she had made herself calm, he had brought her to this chamber, that she had come to hate. There was nothing to do, nothing to see. It was made worse because she couldn't use the magic inside her.

Nor could she answer her mountain's call.

Deirdre walked to the dark blue chair in the corner of the room. She sat and closed her eyes. She might not be able to use her magic, but nothing could keep her from her wyrran and Warriors.

A smile pulled at her lips as she heard the wyrran in her mind.

"Soon, my darlings," she whispered. "Tell me what you see."

* * *

Gwynn showed her father's picture to everyone she encountered on Eigg, and still she learned nothing.

"It's as if he just vanished," she said. Whatever hope she'd felt the day before was gone.

Despair had set in, and she wasn't sure she could push it away.

"We'll find him."

Logan's deep voice sounded next to her. She'd been so lost in her thoughts she'd forgotten he was there.

He wasn't like any man she knew. He didn't talk about himself or whatever he thought he happened to be good at. He was simply there for her. He listened as she spoke, and offered his opinion if she needed it.

Where had he been all her life?

In the seventeenth century.

Gwynn inwardly winced. How could she believe he had time traveled to her time?

But how could she ignore it when she felt the magic within her?

Magic!

It wasn't supposed to exist. Oh, sure, there were telekinetics, who could supposedly move objects with their minds, and psychics, who could see into the future.

But magic?

If she accepted the magic within her, and that she was descended from Druids, then she had to accept everything Logan had told her as truth.

"Did it hurt?" she asked him as she came to a stop. "When you were pulled to my time? Did it hurt?"

Logan shrugged casually as he crossed his arms over his chest. "Nay. It was the absence of any light or sound that bothered me the most. Why? Do you wish to travel through time?"

"Not at all," Gwynn said hastily. "I like my life in Texas."

"Tex-ez," he repeated slowly.

Gwynn chuckled. "Yes. Texas."

"And this place is where?" he asked as he touched her arm to guide her away from an approaching group of people.

As his hand dropped, his fingers skimmed hers. Heat seared her skin where Logan's fingers touched her. That simple contact caused her heart to race and her body to sway toward him.

Awareness of his masculinity, of his strength, and the power that radiated from him engulfed her.

She wanted to move closer to him, to feel his warmth. And his hands on her.

"Gwynn?"

She blinked and tried to bring her body under control. What was wrong with her? Never in her life had she reacted to a man as she did to Logan.

"Your face is flushed," Logan said as he put his hand on her lower back and maneuvered her to a bench.

Gwynn had the insane urge to lay her head on his shoulder. The feel of his hand, even through her clothes, only helped to build the need growing inside her. A need that both scared and intrigued her.

"Sit," Logan said as he gently pushed her down. "You need to eat."

Gwynn swallowed and reached into her purse for a PowerBar. They weren't the tastiest things, but they were quick and easy food.

"I'm fine. Really," she said as she unwrapped the bar.

His hooded gaze slid to her. "Is that why I felt an increase in your magic?"

The bite she'd been attempting to swallow got caught in her throat. Thankfully, she had a bottle of water in her purse that she quickly reached for. After several swallows, she recapped the bottle.

"My magic grew?"

He answered with a brisk nod.

"And you can feel that?"

He sighed dramatically. "Lass, I've already told you I can feel the magic of Druids. What caused you to pull your magic around you?"

Is that what she'd been doing? No, she was pretty sure she'd been in the middle of thinking about Logan touching her, kissing her. Would that have caused her magic to flare?

"I don't know," she finally answered, and bit into her bar.

The look Logan sent her told her he didn't believe a word she said. "If you doona trust me, Gwynn, I can leave. I'll still watch over you to make sure no one harms you, but I'll stay out of sight."

It was a way out for her, a way to get Logan and his all-too-tempting body away from her. But she was tired of searching for her father alone. Maybe Logan could protect her, and maybe he couldn't. Just having him with her, however, had helped to ease her tension.

"Trust is a delicate thing. I'm not sure I do trust you yet, but I'd rather have you with me."

He smiled, and her stomach felt as if a thousand butterflies had just taken flight.

"I'm glad to hear it. You can trust me, and I'll prove it."

Gwynn finished her PowerBar and water in quick order. She tossed her trash in the can and was turning to Logan when something slammed into her, through her.

Her knees gave out and she pitched forward. Strong arms caught her and held her against his chest.

She clutched at Logan's saffron shirt and kilt as she tried to make her legs work again. Gwynn closed her eyes as one of Logan's hands came up to cup her head.

He lowered her back to the bench, but he didn't release her. "Can you move?" he whispered.

"My arms and legs don't feel like my own."

Logan tucked Gwynn against his side and scanned the people around them. "It was magic that struck you."

"I know."

Gwynn's voice was soft and muffled against his chest. He quite liked having her against him. She held him, as if he was the only thing keeping her there.

His balls tightened when she moved closer to him. He could feel her shivering. Whether from the cold or the magic, he didn't know.

He'd like nothing more than to hold Gwynn in his arms, but he needed to protect her. That meant finding the Druid who had attacked her. Yet no matter how hard he looked, he couldn't find anyone.

"I can no' sense another Druid."

Gwynn shifted and raised her head, but Logan kept his arm around her. "I don't think it was meant to harm me," she said.

"Really?" he asked as he looked down at her. "You nearly fell on your face."

"I know," she said, their gazes locked.

Logan told himself not to look at her tempting lips, not to think of kissing her, but he couldn't help himself. Not when it came to Gwynn.

She made him . . . feel. Really feel.

Her tongue peeked out to wet her lips, and Logan bit back a groan. She had no idea how enticing she was. Or how close to losing control he was.

Before he knew it, his head was lowering to hers. All he wanted was a taste, a brief kiss, so he would know her essence and calm the need that was driving him to take her.

She briefly lowered her lashes and pulled away from him a fraction. She rubbed the center of her chest. "Ever since it happened, I feel . . . something. I can't explain what it is, other than to tell you it's magical."

Logan forgot about his desire and was instantly on alert. There were no other Druids on the isle, but that didn't mean there wasn't residual magic in its soul.

Could the Tablet of Orn still be on the isle? If so, why had it sent magic to Gwynn?

CHAPTER
NINE

Gwynn turned her head to the right. "We need to go this way."

"Why?" Logan asked.

"I don't know. I just need to."

They stood together. Gwynn hated when Logan's arm fell from around her. His comfort, his strength had been the only things to keep her from falling under the tidal wave of magic that had gone through her.

And the all-too-powerful, needy ache that even now pounded through her.

"That was a great amount of magic directed at you," Logan murmured as they walked along the shore.

"It didn't hurt me."

"Dinna look that way to me."

Gwynn grinned at his surly tone. His protectiveness proved that he would take care of her if she got in trouble. "I think it was trying to tell me something."

"We'll soon see."

They hadn't gone far when an old woman with white hair pulled away from her face in a loose bun stepped in front of them. She was bent over and used a cane, but her dark eyes were so piercing, they stabbed Gwynn.

"I know what ye are," the woman said and pointed at Gwynn. "Ye've that look about ye."

"What look?" Logan demanded as he moved to put himself between Gwynn and the woman.

But Gwynn wasn't afraid of her. She stepped to the side of Logan. "Yes. What look?"

"A Druid," the woman said and frowned. "'Tis been many a year since any magic has touched this isle."

Gwynn clutched Logan's arm. "You know of magic?"

The woman snorted and leaned both hands on her cane. "Any Druid would. Most have forgotten what they are, or they refuse to see it. The old ways are gone. The once mighty magic of the Druids of Eigg is fading."

"There are tales told of an artifact here. The Tablet of Orn."

The woman's dark eyes swung to Logan. She looked him up and down. "I know what you are, too."

He bowed his head toward her. "I protect Druids, old woman."

She considered him a moment before she asked, "What do you want with the Tablet?"

"Is it here?" Logan asked again.

Gwynn could tell the woman wasn't going to answer him. "Please," Gwynn said. "is it here?"

"What do ye think sent that magic to ye? Me? There is no more magic running through my bloodline. I may not have any magic, but I can sense it."

"You have magic," Logan said. "It's no' much, but it's still there."

The old woman's lined face brightened. "Ah, ye've made my day, lad. I'm one of the last Druids on Eigg. When I'm gone, there will be no one else to tell of the days of old."

Gwynn ached for the woman. She didn't know much

about the Druids, but she remembered the way Grams had spoken of them with such reverence and awe, as if there was nothing better to wish for than to be a Druid.

"A Druid is born, not made," the woman said. "Ye returned to us."

"No. I came looking for my father. He was here three weeks ago, and then disappeared," she said and pulled out the photo.

The woman shook her head. "I keep to myself unless I sense other Druids." Then she took a step closer to Gwynn. "Yer eyes, lass."

Gwynn looked at Logan before she turned back to the woman. "What about them?"

"Violet eyes are unusual."

Gwynn shrugged. "I guess."

"There was a Druid on Eigg long ago who had violet eyes. With her magic she could look through the eyes of animals. She was also the Keeper."

"Keeper?" Logan repeated.

"Of the Tablet of Orn."

Gwynn rubbed her chest as she felt the urgency increase to find the place that was calling to her. "What does the Keeper do?"

"She keeps the Tablet safe. She's the only one who knows its location, the only one who can take it from its hiding spot."

Gwynn cleared her throat. "That wouldn't be me. I've never heard of the Tablet before today."

"The Tablet always has a Keeper," the old woman says. "You have the blood of the ancients of Eigg. The Tablet recognized that and sent its magic to call to you. It has chosen you to be its Keeper."

"Ah," Gwynn said and took a step back, but Logan's arm came up to wrap around her waist. "I need to find my father."

The old woman shrugged and began to hobble away. "Ye cannot ignore the Tablet's call, lass."

Gwynn blinked and dragged in a shaky breath. "No one seems to care about my missing father. It's all about magic and Druids."

Logan turned her and held her by her upper arms. "I told you we'd find your father. And we will."

"I'm not stupid, Logan. I know you were searching for this Tablet of Orn."

"You think I had something to do with this?"

"You could," she said and tried to ignore the spark of anger she saw in his hazel eyes. "All this could be some big hoax."

He dropped his hands from her arms and took a step back. His face was devoid of expression when he said, "I had nothing to do with the magic you feel inside you. Nor did I have anything to do with the blast of magic toward you a moment ago."

Gwynn stared into his eyes and saw remorse and guilt as well as anger and resolve. "How do I know what to believe?"

"Look to your magic. Every Druid, if their magic is powerful enough, has a certain gift such as healing or talking to trees."

"Talking to trees?" she repeated in surprise.

"Reaghan is able to see truth or lies when she looks into people's eyes as they speak to her. Maybe you can do that as well."

Gwynn was once again forced to consider the magic inside her. Logan couldn't have had anything to do with that. She hated not knowing what to believe. If only there was a way to discern what was the truth.

A gust of wind swirled around her. Gwynn froze in her tracks as she swore she heard the wind whisper in her ear.

"What did it say?" Logan asked.

Gwynn looked at him, startled. His hazel eyes watched her with curiosity. She hadn't realized she'd said anything out loud. "I thought the wind said the word "magic" in my ear."

"What were you thinking before you heard the wind?"

"I was wishing there was a way I could learn the truth of everything, of whether to trust you or not."

Logan nodded. "I can no' help you in this search, but I can tell you some of the things I learned from the Druids I knew. Maybe something will help."

"You aren't angry that I don't trust you?"

One side of his mouth lifted in a heart-stopping grin. "I'd be more worried if you believed everything without wanting proof."

"And you can give me proof?"

"If Deirdre is here, then aye. If no', it'll be a might more difficult. It will mean a trip to MacLeod Castle."

"There is no MacLeod Castle."

Instead of being taken aback, Logan's grin grew. "Oh, aye, lass, there is. And that I can prove to you."

An unexplainable thrill rushed through her at the prospect. She had no idea why. She'd never even heard of a MacLeod Castle until Logan. Still, something, her magic maybe, urged her to find the castle.

"How can you prove it?" Gwynn asked as she began walking down the path. "I know there's no MacLeod Castle because I've had a fascination with castles all my life. I researched every castle in Britain through the years. There's still MacLeod land, though for some reason no one has built on it in centuries."

"Aye. Because the MacLeods are there."

Gwynn jerked her head to him. "The MacLeods from the story? The brothers?"

"The verra ones."

"Once we find my father, I would like to see this castle that doesn't exist."

Logan winked at her. "It's a promise then. I'll take you there myself."

Gwynn shook her head and kept walking. Logan was charismatic and entirely too charming, but beneath that exterior she caught glimpses of a different man, a darker man.

He'd told her about Deirdre's attack and Duncan's death, but Gwynn knew he was keeping something else from her, something he wasn't ready to share. And might never be ready to share.

She was deep in thought about Logan and her magic when she crested one of the many hills on the isle. The view literally took her breath away.

"Oh my God," she whispered.

The wind alternately howled around her and caressed her skin. She was rooted to the spot, transfixed. Awed. Gwynn found herself reaching for the wind as if she could touch it.

"Look inside yourself," Logan murmured in her ear as he came up behind her. His nearness, his warmth spread around her, easing her just as the wind did. "Look to your magic and see if you can discover the answers you seek."

"Here?" she asked, her gaze on the startling view of the windswept sea and land before her.

"Here. Sit, Gwynn. Trust your magic."

For the first time that day, Gwynn wasn't cold. She lowered herself to the icy ground and closed her eyes as the wind's gentle fingers caressed her cheek.

"*Gwynnnnnn* . . ."

"I'm here," she answered.

"*We've waited a very long time. You could never hear us.*"

"I hear you now."

"You need to build your magic. War is coming. Danger is coming. Beware of Deirdre."

"Deirdre?"

"Hear the music of the ancients. Listen to their words. Feel their magic."

Gwynn did as the wind asked. She searched for her magic, and surprisingly it answered her quickly. The magic, pure and sweet, surged within her, filling every cell and making goosebumps rise on her flesh.

The magic was the most beautiful thing Gwynn had ever felt. It burned bright and warm as white tendrils grew from the center of her chest and seemed to merge with her bone and muscle.

Gwynn wasn't frightened, though. It felt right, as if the magic had been waiting years for her to recognize it. As if the magic had been waiting to become part of her.

She opened herself to it, and as she did, she began to hear distant drums beating in a steady, hypnotic rhythm. With every beat of the drums she found herself floating toward them, yearning to see what secrets they held.

And then she heard the chanting.

Hundreds of voices rising together, speaking words she couldn't possibly understand.

The drums and chanting grew louder, until she was part of it all. Out of the chanting, Gwynn heard a voice. The female voice began to speak in . . . Gaelic.

Gwynn's heart leaped in her throat, because she understood the woman, understood a language she had never learned. And as the voice continued, Gwynn found herself hearing the same tale Logan had told her the night before.

When the tale ended, the voice faded into the drums. Gwynn reached for the speaker, but the voice was gone. Gwynn screamed, begging the woman to return, for anyone to return and give her the answers she needed.

"Gwynn? Gwynn!"

Her eyes flew open to find Logan looking down at her as he held her in his arms. His face was lined with worry.

"Gwynn? Are you with me?"

"I heard them," Gwynn said. "I heard the drums and the chanting, and then a voice came out of it and told me the story of the Celts and Romans."

Logan's hand paused as he rubbed her back. "Did the voice tell you anything else?"

"No. But the wind did."

"What?"

Gwynn took a deep breath and slowly released it. "The wind, Logan. The wind spoke to me. It told me war was coming."

CHAPTER
TEN

Logan rested his chin atop Gwynn's head and took in what she'd told him. He knew a war was coming. It was destined for this time the moment Deirdre arrived here.

"Did the wind say anything else?" he asked.

Gwynn once again pulled out of his arms and gained her feet. She swatted her butt to wipe away the dirt, which only drew Logan's gaze to her perfectly shaped behind. He cursed his quickening blood that pooled in his cock. He had to keep Gwynn safe, not seduce her.

Even though it was all he wanted to do.

He rose to stand next to her and handed her the cap he had inadvertently pushed off her head when he'd grabbed her. When she'd called out, he'd not thought twice. He'd just wrapped his arms around her and did everything he could to reach her.

"Gwynn?"

She blinked and looked at him as if seeing him for the first time. "I can hear the wind, Logan. It's like several voices talking at once."

He smiled at the excitement growing in her violet eyes.

Her face was still pale against the black locks of hair tangled about her face.

"The voices said they've been waiting for me for years. They said they had tried to talk to me before."

Logan tucked a strand of hair behind her ears. "You had pushed aside your magic. Of course you didn't hear them."

The smile she gave him made his heart skip a beat.

"Their voices are the most beautiful sound I've ever heard."

"Did they have other warnings?" He hated to ask her, but if she could talk to the wind as Sonya spoke to trees, then they could learn a lot about Deirdre.

"They warned me that danger was coming. They told me to beware of Deirdre."

Logan glanced around them. "We need to get somewhere safe."

"No," Gwynn said and jerked her arm from his grasp. "I have to find my father."

Logan silently prayed for patience as he faced Gwynn. "You can no' find your father if you're dead or captured."

"You'll be with me," she argued. "You can keep me safe."

Logan clenched his teeth. "You have the rest of the day. As soon as the sun begins to set, I want you in your . . ."

"Hotel," she supplied.

"Aye. Your hotel."

After a moment she nodded. "Fair enough, I suppose."

He waited for her to begin walking, but she kept looking over her shoulder. "What is it?"

"I don't know."

Logan followed her as she walked to the edge of a small cliff. Below them water swirled as the waves crashed and water was dragged back out to the sea.

"The tide is going out," Logan commented. "You can see the rocks beneath the water."

"I see it. Though I don't know what I'm looking at. Something told me to come here, but there's nothing."

"What is the wind saying?"

She looked up at the sky for several moments, then let out a loud sigh. "Nothing. Either I'm not doing it correctly, or it doesn't want to talk to me."

"Come. You have the rest of Eigg to talk to about your father."

For hours they walked along Eigg as Gwynn stopped everyone she saw and showed them the picture of her father. A few looked at the picture longer than others, but eventually said they didn't recognize him.

Gwynn and Logan were about to board the ferry to return to Mallaig when Logan spotted a man watching Gwynn with lust in his eyes. Logan growled before he realized what he was doing.

Fangs filled his mouth when he saw that Gwynn was heading toward the man.

"Hi," Gwynn said as she handed him the picture. "I'm looking for my father. He was here about three weeks ago. Did you happen to see him here?"

The man started shaking his head, then paused and took another look at the photo. "I think I do. Did he like to carry an old leather satchel with him?"

"Yes," Gwynn said excitedly. "Where did he go? Who did he speak with?"

The man shrugged and handed her back the picture. "That I cannot tell you, lass. He got off the ferry and someone bumped into him, spilling the contents of his satchel. That's the only reason I recognize him. I doona know where he went or when he left Eigg."

Logan gave a terse nod to the man and led Gwynn onto the ferry.

"He was here, Logan," Gwynn said as she walked to the front.

"It seems he was."

"Where do I go from here?"

"First, you need to rest. You can no' continue as you are."

She nodded and looked back at Eigg as the ferry departed, the setting sun casting everything in a deep golden hue. "Something tells me we'll be back to Eigg soon."

Logan agreed with her, but not because of her father. He knew they would return to Eigg because that's where Gwynn would learn more about her magic.

And if the wind had warned her of Deirdre, then something was definitely coming for her. The when and the what were the questions he couldn't answer.

He walked her to the door of her hotel. "I'll see you in the morn."

"Where are you staying?"

"I'll be around."

She rolled her eyes. "I'm tired, Logan, not an idiot. You don't have anywhere to stay, do you?"

"I doona require much sleep."

"It's still early. Why don't you come with me? I'll order us some room service and we can talk about our plans for tomorrow."

Logan knew he should walk away. Gwynn was too tantalizing, too intoxicating. Too lovely. But he couldn't make his feet move. Instead, he found himself saying, "All right."

Gwynn was dead on her feet, but seeing the way Logan looked at everything around him with a mixture of awe and wariness made her take a look at her world with new eyes. Everything she took for granted was something Logan had never seen or experienced before—if she could believe his claims about time traveling.

If his story about Deirdre, the Druids, and Warriors was true, why would he lie about time travel? She found herself believing him, as she warned herself to be cautious.

Yet how could she not believe him when it was obvious he had no idea about anything in her world?

When she unlocked the door to her room, he went inside before she could. A second later, he bade her enter.

Gwynn rolled her eyes at his protectiveness, but then she recalled the warning from the wind. A warning that even now made it feel as if ice were in her veins.

She closed the door behind her and locked it out of habit. After tossing her purse aside, Gwynn took off her gloves and shoved them into the pockets of her coat before removing her scarf.

Logan inspected her open laptop while she unzipped her coat and threw it over her purse. "It's a computer," she said.

"What does it do?" Logan asked without looking up.

"It surfs the internet."

His hazel eyes lifted to hers. "It does what?"

For the next hour, Gwynn explained the internet to Logan and showed him how to use the laptop. To her surprise, he learned rapidly and was soon using it himself.

She watched him for a long time, amazed at his curiosity. His intellect was remarkable. She'd asked how he was able to read modern English, since languages had changed so much during the past four hundred years. His response was a shrug.

No matter how many times she asked, he evaded her questions until Gwynn let it drop. For now. With Logan immersed in the computer, she ordered room service and made herself comfortable on the bed.

"Tell me what has happened in the last four centuries," Logan urged her.

Gwynn didn't know where to begin. She started back

as far as she could remember in the eighteenth century and hit upon anything she could drag from her memory.

When she got to the twentieth century, she went into more detail. Logan had plenty of questions, and she answered any she didn't know by looking it up on the computer and showing him pictures.

By the time she reached the current year, Logan's expression was perplexed. And worried.

"Would you know if anything odd happened?" he asked.

She shrugged. "Most likely. The news likes to report on anything out of the ordinary, but then again, they'll pass over good news for something that will shock the public or send us into an uproar."

"I doona know when Deirdre arrived in your time, but if she's already here, she would have made herself known."

Gwynn was shaking her head when she recalled a story that had caught her interest. "A few months ago there were these videos posted on the internet showing a creature no one had ever seen before. It made the news for a day, but when no one could find the creature again, everyone forgot about it."

"Can you show me this creature?"

Gwynn pulled the computer onto her lap and typed in the URL. When the picture popped up, she turned the laptop where Logan could see it from where he sat in the chair next to the bed.

"Shite," he muttered.

"Shite?" Gwynn asked with a laugh. "Don't you mean shit?"

A smile split his face. "There are some things that never change." The smile fell when he looked back at the computer. "That's a wyrran, Gwynn."

She'd been afraid he'd recognize the creature. "Which means Deirdre is here already."

"Aye."

"What are these wyrran?" she asked

"Creatures made by Deirdre using her black magic. They issue shrieks that pierce your ears. It's an unmistakable sound, a sound I doona hope to hear around you."

"As far as I know the wyrran hasn't been spotted since this was taped three months ago."

"Good. It means Deirdre is no' out and about. Yet."

"What does that mean for us?" she asked as someone knocked on the door.

Logan rose swiftly into what was obviously a battle stance.

"It's just our food," Gwynn said as she scooted off the bed and went to open the door.

She thanked the man and took the food. When she turned around Logan was directly behind her, his gaze fastened on the man walking away.

"Hungry?" she asked.

He looked down at her and nodded. "Aye. It's been awhile since I last ate."

"That's what I was afraid of. I wasn't sure what you liked, so I ordered a bit of everything."

He helped her uncover the dishes she'd set on the small table. Gwynn's stomach growled, proving that she was also famished.

It was the best meal Gwynn had had in . . . years. Not because of the food, but because of Logan. He tried everything, all the while asking her what each dish was and how it was made.

Some of his questions she could answer; others she couldn't. She nearly choked on her food when he tasted a bit of her Coke and quickly handed it back to her. He preferred the beer she had ordered.

Gwynn was so intent on watching Logan that she didn't realize she had eaten her entire sandwich and all of her chips until she reached for another one and found the bag empty.

She crumpled it up and wiped her hands and mouth. "What did you think?"

"Some of the food is delicious. I've never tasted so many spices."

"Good." She glanced at his bared knees where his kilt had fallen when he'd sat. "Not that I don't love a man in a kilt, but what do you think of getting some clothes to help you fit in?"

"You think I should change out of my kilt?" he asked with a frown.

"No. What I'm saying is that having some different clothes will help you fit in and become invisible when you want to." Though Gwynn didn't think a drop-dead gorgeous man like Logan would ever be invisible.

She'd seen the women looking at him, and salivating much as she had been. He was tall and striking, which only added to his appeal. Add in his sleekly muscled body without an ounce of fat, and women were ready to pounce. Literally.

Gwynn should know since she was one of them.

"This kilt is all I've ever worn."

"I know," she said as she looked at the worn, frayed edges and cuts that had been repaired. "We could find you a new kilt if you'd like. They make them for every clan. I'm sure we could find one just like what you have."

He considered her a moment. "I'll think on it."

The silence that followed made Gwynn fidget. She wasn't used to being alone with a man like Logan. Her last boyfriend had been over a year ago, and it hadn't ended well. She'd stayed away from men after that.

But there was no staying away from Logan. He was like a magnet, pulling her attention and her gaze no matter how hard she tried to resist.

How would it feel to have those sleek muscled arms around her? How would it feel to run her hands through his long, glossy hair? To have his wide, firm lips on hers?

She was once again taken aback by his vitality and masculinity. He was a man used to command, a man used to action and battle.

A warrior in every sense of the word.

CHAPTER
ELEVEN

Logan's body was on fire for Gwynn. He'd tried his best to ignore it all day, but every touch, however innocent, had only made him hunger for her more.

Being alone with her in her chamber while sharing a meal only reminded him of their close proximity. And how he shouldn't touch her. Couldn't touch her.

Wouldn't touch her.

Gwynn was special. She could well be the last of the dying Druids, and she didn't need to be sullied by Logan and what he was.

It would be easier if he hadn't seen the way her hand shook after they touched, or how her eyes fell to his mouth. There had been an attraction the first moment he'd seen her, and it was becoming more and more impossible to ignore.

Especially when all Logan wanted to do was pull her into his arms and kiss her lips that had been tempting him for two days.

Gwynn cleared her throat and looked away. Logan let out a sigh and silently thanked God for the reprieve.

"You've learned a lot about my time," Gwynn said. "And we know Deirdre is here. What's the next step?"

Logan rubbed his chin and felt the whiskers scrape his fingers. He needed a shave. And a wash. "We need more information on Deirdre. She's here, but why has she no' done anything? That's no' like her."

"Maybe she's waiting for something."

"Is there any way you can discover what it was that brought your father to Mallaig?"

She bit her lip and played with the condensation on her glass. "I've already tried. The university wouldn't tell me anything."

"Your magic—which side of the family did it come from?"

"My father's," she answered. "Why?"

"Has he always been interested in it?"

Gwynn nodded. "Oh, yes. He was obsessed with it."

"Do you no' find it unusual that he came to the verra place of your descendants?"

"Not really. He'd always wanted to come here."

"And then you came and no' only discovered you have magic, but that you're the Keeper of the Tablet of Orn."

Gwynn's eyes rounded. "You think he came for the Tablet?"

Logan shrugged and rose to get her laptop. "It's a thought."

He did a search on the Tablet of Orn as Gwynn had showed him. Logan didn't know what Bing was, but it always came up with the very things he searched for. So he wasn't surprised when information came up on the Tablet.

"Oh, my God," Gwynn said as she leaned next to him to read the screen. "Is there a picture of it?"

"Nay," Logan said as he clicked one of the links and began to read. "But it says here it was believed to have been on the Isle of Eigg and reputed to have helped the Druids strengthen their magic."

"This site could have been put up by anyone. Who knows if what they say is true."

"I do," Logan said. "Whoever this is knows more than they have alluded to on this . . . site. Is there any way to determine who wrote this?"

Gwynn took the laptop. "Maybe. Let me see."

Logan watched as her fingers flew over the keys. He didn't have to wait long to hear her groan.

"Whoever it is has their information blocked," Gwynn said.

"I can no' help but think your father coming here is somehow connected to your ancestry and the Druids."

Gwynn rubbed her eyes. "I feel like we're being blocked at every turn."

Logan felt the same way, but he wasn't about to give up. Gwynn needed his protection, especially now that he knew for sure Deirdre was there. It was just a matter of time before Deirdre found Gwynn.

Time.

Logan bit back a groan as he realized he could be protecting Gwynn for months or even years. Normally, spending that much time with the same woman would make him fidgety. But he let the knowledge settle inside him and found he wanted to spend that time with Gwynn, wanted to share the days, and most especially the nights, with her.

Which told him he was definitely in trouble.

Declan didn't hesitate to unleash a blast of his magic that sent one of his guards flying backward to slam into a wall. Declan held the man there, pushing with his magic until he could hear his bones pop over the guard's screams.

When the guard was silent and his body a mass of broken bones held together with sagging skin, Declan let him fall to the floor.

"Get him out of my sight," he bellowed to the other guards.

Declan then spun around to face the captain of his men. "What happened, Robbie? I thought you had control of your men."

Robbie's eyes narrowed. "I do have control of my men."

"Then tell me how the wyrran and Deirdre's Warriors have gotten loose from my dungeons!"

"You would know better than I."

Declan hated Robbie's insolence, but he couldn't afford to kill him. Even if he'd like to do nothing better. Robbie wasn't only good at controlling the mercenaries; he was also Declan's cousin.

"You used your magic on the cell doors," Robbie said. "They weren't supposed to be able to get out."

A headache began to throb at the back of Declan's neck. "I know that my spells have inhibited Deirdre from using her magic. I assumed it would do the same to the wyrran."

"And the Warriors?"

"Ah, but they're different," Declan said. "As powerful as those Warriors are with their gods, magic can impede them."

"If the magic is powerful enough."

"Deirdre is the cause of this. The wyrran would never leave her unless she told them."

Robbie crossed his arms over his massive chest, his muscles bulging—muscles he'd gotten by using steroids for too many years to count. "They'll come back to her then. As long as you have Deirdre, who cares about the wyrran and a few Warriors?"

"I care," Declan stated as he whirled to point a finger at his cousin. "They are linked to her. If I have them, I can use them. Now they're gone."

Robbie shrugged. "I can find them."

"No, I doona believe you will. But I know how I can." Declan stormed out of his office and down the hallway to the stairs that took him up to Deirdre's room.

With a wave of his hand he unlocked the magic holding the door and let it bang open. He gnashed his teeth when Deirdre didn't so much as look his way from her chair when he barged in.

"Something the matter, Declan?" she asked as she idly ran her finger along the table next to her.

"You know what's the matter. Where did you send the wyrran, Deirdre?"

She shrugged her slim shoulders and smiled contentedly. "I have no idea what you're talking about."

"Ah, but you do, you deceitful bitch."

She rose to her feet in one fluid motion, her long white hair falling around her like a cloak. Declan had thought her beautiful in her black gown, but in the black leather he'd chosen for her, she was simply stunning.

Deirdre was everything he had ever wanted in a woman. He'd waited too long, worked too hard to get the infamous *drough* to his time. She would be his. No matter how long it took.

"Watch your mouth," Deirdre stated, her white eyes burning with hatred.

Declan looked her up and down, letting his gaze linger on the swell of her perfectly shaped breasts. "Your pets might have escaped, but you never will."

"If there's one thing I've learned in my millennia of existence, Declan, it's that one shouldn't ever say never. No man holds me prisoner."

"I am," he said with a smirk.

"And that's why when I do get out of here I will make it my mission to capture you and drain you of your magic as I've done to countless other Druids."

Declan wasn't stupid enough to dismiss her threat. He knew how powerful she was. It was why he'd put so many spells on his mansion, and her room especially, to prevent her from leaving.

"Doona fight fate," he said.

Suddenly she smiled. "I command fate."

Behind him Declan heard a grunt. He turned in time to see a maroon Warrior behead two of his guards. That same Warrior was headed toward him.

Declan used his magic to halt the Warrior. He smiled as the Warrior growled. And then he heard the shrieks.

He turned his head to see three wyrran coming at him. Declan knew he couldn't hold them off with his magic, so he did the only thing he could do. He stayed alive.

Declan glanced at Deirdre to see her confident smile an instant before he touched a panel on the wall that opened a secret compartment. He slid into the doorway and sighed once it shut.

No one, not even a Warrior would be able to get into his hideaway. It was triggered with his magic, and his magic alone.

That didn't stop the wyrran from clawing at the expensive wood paneling or the Warrior from trying to punch through the door.

Declan's shoulders sagged with relief when the shrieks and growls subsided. He waited another half hour before he cracked open the door, which was directly across from Deirdre's room, to find her gone.

He shouldn't have been surprised. It had been her plan all along to distract him while her wyrran and Warriors attacked. In his haste to save himself he hadn't locked her into her room. Not that it would have done any good. The wyrran wouldn't have stopped until they found a way to free her.

Declan sighed as he looked into the empty room. Deirdre was gone. And with her his dreams of having her. He knew he'd never capture her again.

But maybe he could prove he was her equal.

"Declan."

He turned to find Robbie walking toward him with his black T-shirt in tatters and blood coating him. "How many did we lose?"

"All but six."

"I'm going to need more, Robbie. And while we're at it, I think it's time we find some Warriors of our own."

A gleam shone in Robbie's eye. "About time, cousin."

Declan looked at Deirdre's room once more before he turned on his heel, and with his hands clasped behind his back, strode to his office. It was time to begin the war that would end in his ruling all. Most especially Deirdre.

CHAPTER
TWELVE

December 20th

Logan had decided that spending the night in the small chamber with Gwynn was asking too much of himself. He'd climbed out of her window and sat atop the roof of the hotel when he wasn't patrolling the area looking for any wyrran or Warriors.

Or Deirdre.

His mind kept going over everything that had happened the day before on Eigg. It was too much of a coincidence for Gwynn's father not to have been on Eigg for the artifact.

By the time the sun rose, Logan had more questions than ever.

While Gwynn was still sleeping, he stole back into her chamber. She was in the same position on her side that she'd been in when he left. For long moments he simply watched her, his body demanding he crawl into the bed with her. That he take her into his arms and kiss her. Touch her. Make love to her.

Logan wanted it so badly he shook with the need. He'd

never turned away from the prospect of bedding a woman. But Gwynn wasn't just any woman. She was different in so many ways that had nothing to do with her being from a different time.

He couldn't put his finger on what set her apart. He only knew that she was. And because of that, he should stay away from her.

If he could.

Logan made himself turn away from Gwynn and walked into the small room Gwynn had called the bathroom. She'd shown him how to use the shower, toilet, and sink. This was one room he could certainly get accustomed to. Hot water with a mere twist of a knob.

Logan removed his boots and set them side by side next to the wall. He unpinned the brooch over his heart and laid it on the counter next to the sink as his kilt fell to the floor.

He didn't look in the large mirror over the sink as he removed his saffron shirt and stared at the bloodstains that hadn't completely come out, no matter how many times he'd cleaned the shirt.

His kilt looked little better. The thought of not wearing his kilt made his chest hurt, but maybe Gwynn was right. Maybe he did need to blend in. And she had said they could get him a new kilt.

That, he wouldn't mind having. He didn't deserve it though.

"Hell, I doona deserve to wear the Hamilton kilt as it is."

Not after willingly going to Deirdre. He'd acted selfishly and recklessly. And it'd cost him his family.

Logan could still hear his little brother, Ronald, calling after him. Begging him to return.

With a curse, Logan closed off his memories. They would do him no good other than to remind him what a daft fool he'd been. He leaned into the shower and turned the knob with the big H on it.

It took just a few moments before steam from the hot water began to fill the bathroom. Logan turned the other knob with the C on it until he found the temperature he liked.

He stepped into the shower and smiled as the water sloshed over him. It pounded on the tense muscles of his shoulders, easing him.

Logan wet his hair and used what Gwynn had told him was soap for his hair.

"Shampoo," he read aloud off the small bottle.

With a shrug, he dumped some of it into his hands, amazed that it smelled good. He lathered it into his hair, scrubbing his scalp before rinsing.

He scrubbed his body three times and still he wasn't ready to leave the shower, but he wanted to make sure there was plenty of hot water for Gwynn.

Logan shut off the shower and shook his head as he looked at how far mortals had come. He reached for the fluffy white towel and began to dry off.

He padded naked to the sink and ran his hand over the mirror to wipe away the steam that had fogged it. For several long moments he stared at the man before him.

In all his years Logan had never really seen his reflection. Oh, he'd seen it distorted in a loch, but it wasn't the same as seeing it now.

The man who stared back at him was a stranger. The hazel eyes so like his mother's held none of her warmth or kindness. His skin was bronzed from the sun, and though his body held none of the scars he'd gotten as a Warrior thanks to the healing power of his god, he saw them anyway.

They were branded into his soul.

Logan turned his head to the side and looked at his

face where a beard had begun to take shape. It had been several days since he'd shaved. He looked . . . unkempt. His appearance was certainly not something Gwynn would find appealing.

He allowed one of his claws to lengthen. Just as he prepared to use it to shave, he saw the small pink thing next to the sink. What had Gwynn called it? Oh, aye. A razor. She'd shown him how to use it on his face, but as he looked at it in his hand, he couldn't imagine a man using it.

Logan looked between the razor and his claw. With a shrug, he stared into the mirror and began to use the razor.

Gwynn stretched and rolled over to find sunlight shining through the open curtains. She sat up and rubbed her eyes.

She could hear water running in the bathroom sink. A smile pulled at her lips as she thought of Logan. She'd slept for the first time in days because she'd felt safe with him in the room with her.

Though it had taken her a while to actually fall asleep. The idea of him in her room, the tall, masculine outline of him as he sat on the couch while she lay in her bed had brought an ache between her legs.

She didn't take risks. Ever. Yet she had almost given into the desire that flooded her and invited him into her bed. Even now she wondered why she hadn't.

But she knew the answer. She was chicken. What if he said no? She couldn't take that, not now.

So she had kept silent, the need clawing at her, growing with every thought of his large hands touching her, of his lips sliding over her mouth, and his hard body pressed against hers.

She had only managed to sleep after that because of pure exhaustion. Tonight, however, would be a different scenario.

Gwynn threw back the covers and shivered at the chill in the room. Her body would never get used to the cold in Scotland. She rose and wrapped her arms around her middle as she walked to the bathroom door.

And stopped dead in her tracks when she found herself staring at Logan's naked backside.

Her mouth went dry as she looked at his long, muscular legs. The muscles in his back bunched and flexed as he leaned close to the mirror to shave.

Those broad shoulders tapered to a narrow waist and hips. And his perfect butt.

It took her a moment to realize Logan had stopped moving. She lifted her gaze to find him watching her in the mirror. Desire smoldered in his gaze before he blinked and looked away.

Gwynn ran her fingers through her hair, knowing she looked a fright. "I'm sorry. I . . . ah . . . I didn't realize you would be naked."

He wiped his face and bent to pick up his clothes and boots. Gwynn turned away so she wouldn't stare, when it was all she longed to do. She'd never seen anyone with a body like his, and she couldn't get her fill of him.

"I think you're right," he said as he paused next to her.

She stared at the wall in front of her and tried to calm her racing heart. "About what?"

"I need to blend in."

As if he ever could. Then she realized what he was saying. "Oh. Clothes," she said, turning her head to look at his face.

His hazel eyes were more green than usual as he captured her gaze. "Would you help me?"

"Yes," she replied nervously, all too aware of his nudity and her yearning to look. "Of course."

With a nod, he walked to the couch.

Gwynn had the insane urge to crawl back into bed and

see if he'd follow her. She stepped into the bathroom and closed the door behind her instead.

She got ready in record time. Maybe it was the thought of taking Logan and fitting him in jeans, but Gwynn couldn't wait to get him into a store.

As they approached the only one in Mallaig, she could practically feel Logan's hesitance, but he never backed out. The store didn't have a lot. Mostly it was gear the fishermen would need, but with a guy like Logan, anything looked good on his muscular frame.

She handed him several pairs of jeans and sweaters and directed him to the dressing room. She had no idea what his size was, so she'd guessed.

Gwynn waited impatiently outside the dressing room, which was nothing more than a closet with a curtain between them.

"How does everything fit? I can get you another size."

The curtain opened and Logan stepped out. "You tell me."

Gwynn didn't think she'd ever seen someone look so hot in a pair of jeans and a hunter-green sweater. "You look—"

"Bloody hot," said the female clerk who had come up behind Gwynn.

Logan winked at the clerk and looked at Gwynn, brows raised. "What do you think? Will I blend in?"

"I think you'd look good in a wool sack," Gwynn murmured.

He frowned. "A what?"

"Nothing," Gwynn hurried to say. "The clothes look great on you. Do you like them?"

"I doona know. I've never worn the like before, but if you say this is what I should wear, then I'll wear it."

Gwynn smiled. "Oh, yes. I wouldn't steer you wrong."

"Then I'll take these."

"Great. I'll go pick up a couple more jeans and sweaters. What about shoes?" she asked when she saw his bare toes.

"I have my boots."

"They'll be a little difficult to get on with the jeans."

A half hour later Logan had a new pair of boots and several pairs of socks. When Gwynn reached for her wallet to pay, Logan's hand lightly touched her arm.

"I'm no' without coin."

She looked down at his hand to see the coins. "Ah," she hedged. "I don't think those will work here. Let me pay."

"Then you take these."

She gaped at the handful of gold coins that fell into her hand. They were likely worth a fortune. She closed her fingers around them and was about to hand them back, but she took one look at Logan's face and knew better than to try to return the coins.

They left the store and were walking back to the hotel when Logan said, "Is there somewhere besides your computer were we can do more research on how much is known about the artifact?"

"There's a heritage center. We could start there."

"Would Eigg have something similar?"

Gwynn nodded. "I'm sure they will. If something was recorded about the Tablet, it would be likely to be around here."

Logan dropped off the bags in her room as Gwynn got directions to the heritage center from the clerk. In a matter of minutes, they were walking toward the Heritage Centre.

Gwynn was stunned at how much the center offered. There were exhibitions about fishing, the railways, the first roads, steamers, and ferries. In addition, they had an exhibition called "Find-a-face" featuring photographs from Mallaig schools dating back as far as 1906. There were other photos besides those from the schools, and Mallaig was trying to identify who everyone was.

Gwynn found herself staring at the photos, wondering if any of them were relatives of hers.

"See anyone you know?" Logan whispered in her ear from behind.

"No," she said with a smile.

"There is a section of books I've found."

Gwynn turned to face him. "Then we need to start looking."

They walked together to the shelves of books. "What do we look for?" Gwynn asked.

"Anything to do with the area dating from sixteen hundred and older."

Gwynn blew out a breath and tilted her head to the side as she read titles. She found several books and took them with her to the table where she began to leaf through them.

At noon Logan closed a book and blew out a harsh breath. "Nothing. There's no' a single word about the Tablet in any of these books."

"Maybe because it's Eigg's history. Maybe we need to go there."

"Why do I see doubt in your eyes then?"

Gwynn leaned back in her chair and softly closed the book she'd been looking through. "If my father found something, then it would be in some obscure text or book no one would have ever heard of."

"Do you have access to those books?"

"No." And then she sat up. "Oh, God. I didn't even think of it."

"What?"

"My father often used my computer when his laptop

battery would go out, so he had both machines set up on a network."

Logan's brow furrowed. "What does that mean?"

"It means, Logan, that I can access his computer and possibly discover what he was working on."

CHAPTER
THIRTEEN

Logan watched as Gwynn's fingers moved with lightning speed over the keyboard. They had returned straightaway to the hotel where she'd wasted no time in opening the computer.

"The connection is so damn slow," she murmured.

Logan didn't think she was talking to him. Her gaze—and her mind—were on the computer. Nothing else existed at the moment.

He made no move to distract her, but he was near if she needed him. As he always would be.

The realization should have surprised him, but, oddly, it didn't. It just seemed . . . right.

Patience had never been something that came easily to him. Sitting idly was even more difficult. Yet if he wanted to avoid distracting her, he couldn't get up and pace the small confines of the chamber as he longed to do.

He closed his eyes and thought of MacLeod Castle and how everyone had looked when he'd last seen them. Marcail's stomach had just begun to show with her and Quinn MacLeod's child.

Broc and Sonya had finally found the love they'd held

for each other. With Cara and Lucan, Fallon and Larena, Galen and Reaghan, and Hayden and Isla all finding love, the castle was becoming more than just a refuge from Deirdre. It was a home.

Every Warrior there would defend the castle until his last breath to protect the Druids, most of whom were their wives.

Logan smiled as he thought of Hayden. He may not be Logan's brother by blood, but their bond went much deeper. It was a bond he shared with the other Warriors as well.

Hayden had been so eager for battle, the quickest to jump into a fight. And finish it. The first time Logan had seen Hayden with Isla, he'd witnessed his friend's hard eyes soften. He'd seen Hayden, who had always been the executioner, become the protector.

Even when Hayden learned Isla was a *drough*, the very thing Hayden had sworn to kill, he still couldn't take Isla's life.

At least Hayden had found Isla, who had removed the hate from his heart. Logan didn't think there would ever be anyone who could do the same for him.

There was hate in his heart, hate for himself. But there was more remorse and shame than anything else. No matter how many times he killed wyrran or Deirdre's Warriors, it wouldn't remove the stain of his regret.

Only ending Deirdre once and for all would give Logan some solace.

"Yes!" Gwynn shouted.

Logan's eyes flew open to find Gwynn smiling at him.

"I did it," she said. "The university hasn't deleted the codes for me to get in. I'm surprised. Usually they do that as soon as someone leaves. It's a security measure."

Her voice trailed off as she frowned at the screen.

"What is it?" Logan was keeping up as best he could in this new time, but sometimes it was difficult.

"Why haven't they deleted his codes? Why would they still give him access?" She was staring at the computer as she asked her questions, her brows furrowed. "The only plausible reason would be if Dad was still working with them."

"I thought you said he quit."

"That's what I was told."

"By your father?"

She closed her eyes and shook her head, her face hardening. "No. Mr. Manning at the university."

"Then there's your answer."

"It appears so."

Logan leaned forward so that his forearms rested on his knees. "Can you get into your father's files?"

"I'm certainly going to try," Gwynn stated as she began typing again.

Logan found that he liked to watch her work. Her brow would pucker when she found something she either didn't understand or didn't like.

And when she found what she wanted, her wicked grin made his blood quicken.

That smile was in place now.

"You found it, didn't you?" Logan asked.

She looked up and nodded. "It seems my father somehow got access to a very old book. A book that was said to be lost. The *Book of Craigan*."

"What's so special about this book?"

She turned the laptop so he could see a picture of it. The book was extremely thick and very large. Its binding was that of black leather that was aged, but had been well preserved.

But what got Logan's attention were the large connecting spirals in the center of the book. There was no other decoration, no words.

"You've seen the spirals before?"

He inhaled and nodded. "Oh, aye. They were used by the Celts to symbolize the equinoxes. The equinoxes can be powerful tools for Druids. More recently—well, recently to me, before I was brought to your time, Broc and Sonya were on a mission to find an ancient Celtic burial mound."

"I take it they did?" she asked, her violet eyes bright with interest.

"They did. Sonya found an amulet on the body of the dead king inside. The amulet had this same double spiral. If we hadn't found the amulet, which we believe will help us to release Deirdre's twin, then I wouldn't think much of this book."

"But the book is about Eigg."

Logan nodded. "Where the artifact I was sent to find is believed to be. How do we get the book?"

"It's privately owned," she said with a frown. "Many of the ancient books such as this one are. Private collectors will pay thousands, sometimes millions of dollars to have such a relic. Most times these books and other objects are stolen from museums and sold on the black market."

"I take it these black markets are no' good?"

Gwynn tucked her hair behind both ears and shook her head. "Logan, they steal babies and sell them on the black market. Once someone buys something, you'll never see it again. It's like it disappears."

Logan rubbed the back of his neck. "Was this book sold on the black market?"

"I can try to find out."

This time Logan couldn't remain seated. He had to get up and move. He'd bet his immortality that there was something in the *Book of Craigan* that had led Gary Austin to Eigg.

If Gary Austin was searching for the Tablet of Orn, then the likelihood that it was still on Eigg was slim since there were no more Druids to guard it.

Fury ripped through him as he realized he might very well fail his friends.

Logan braced his hands on the doorway leading into the bathroom and let his head hang. Without the Tablet, they wouldn't be able to awaken Laria. Which meant Deirdre wouldn't be killed.

Before Logan could stop it, his claws shot from his fingers and his fangs filled his mouth. He walked into the bathroom so Gwynn wouldn't see him.

And when he saw his reflection, he stilled.

He'd seen his fellow Warriors with their gods unleashed, but he'd never seen himself. He'd never observed the silver filling his eyes.

It was . . . eerie.

Logan peeled back his lips and glimpsed his fangs, startled to see they were larger than he'd realized. With barely a thought, he loosed his hold on his god, Athleus.

In a blink, his tanned skin turned the same dark silver as his eyes. Logan lifted his hand and looked at the silver-tipped claws on his fingers.

He was a monster, a monster Gwynn could never see. She'd run screaming from him. How could he protect her if she feared him?

Logan heard Gwynn rise from the chair. He tamped down his god and turned as Gwynn entered the bathroom.

"Are you okay?" she asked. "You look a little pale."

"I'm worried."

She snorted. "As am I. I found something. Come see."

Logan followed and sank onto the couch next to her. Their shoulders brushed and heat sparked between them, as did the feel of her sweet magic. It grew the longer he was around her. It expanded, increased.

And God help Logan, but he liked the feel of her magic.

The purity of it helped to brighten him. To erase some of the darkness of his past.

"Logan?"

Her husky voice drew his attention. He turned his head to find her eyes dilated and the pulse at her throat rapid and erratic.

The knowledge that she was as affected as he made his balls tighten. The urge, the need, the hunger to taste her lips was so great Logan had to clench his hands to keep from touching her.

With more restraint than he'd ever shown when it came to women, Logan pulled his gaze from hers and stared at the screen. He saw a picture of a man who obviously had wealth, if his clothes meant anything.

"Is he the one who owns the book?" Logan asked.

Gwynn cleared her throat. She really needed to get her raging hormones under control. This reaction to Logan was so not like her.

"Yes," she answered. "Declan Wallace is the grandson of David Wallace, a well-known procurer of ancient artifacts. He's Scottish, and everything in his vast collection is from Scotland's past. Some even date to the time when Rome occupied Britain."

"Who is this David Wallace?"

"He made his fortune, his extremely enormous fortune, I might add, with computer software. Some say it was luck. Others say he made a deal with the devil," she said with a snort.

"Doona dismiss such talk, Gwynn. Remember what I told you about the *droughs*. Deirdre herself has an even greater connection to Satan."

"So he could have made a deal with the Devil?"

Logan shrugged. "It's possible. You say he's Scottish?"

"Yes," she said and read through the bio on the screen. "It says here the Wallaces like to brag that they can trace their family line to the tenth century."

When Logan didn't respond, she looked at him to find him tapping a finger on his knee. "What are you thinking?"

"I'm thinking there could be the possibility of a Druid in his family."

"You make it sound as if Scotland were made up mostly of Druids."

"Nay. I'm wondering if it was so easy for someone to make their fortune, why more people haven't done it?"

Gwynn chuckled. "I see. You think magic had something to do with it."

"I've only been in your time for a short period, but what I've learned is that people are motivated by coin."

"Money," she corrected.

Logan shrugged. "Money. Am I right?"

"You nailed it."

His brow furrowed. "I did what?"

Gwynn laughed and set the laptop aside as she rose to her feet. "I said you nailed it. It's a saying. It means you hit it on the head. You got it right."

"Where are you going?"

"I'm hungry. And I think we should return to Eigg."

He stood next to her. "Why?"

"Those connecting spirals on the book? The same one you say was on the amulet? I saw one etched into a stone yesterday."

Logan was heading for the door before she could get her coat on. "Those spirals were common, but I'd still like to see it."

Gwynn hurried to zip her coat and grab her purse. "We really should buy you a coat."

"I doona need it," Logan said. He shut the door behind them after they stepped into the hallway.

"Don't need it?" she repeated and rolled her eyes. "You've got to be kidding me."

He grinned down at her. "I wouldna dream of it."

"Ah. But you would tease."

Logan chuckled. "I doona need this coat you speak of. The weather doesna affect me as it does you."

"Of course not," Gwynn said with a sigh.

Maybe if she stayed close enough to him, some of his heat would reach her.

But being that close to him had a way of making her body react strangely. Wonderfully, but strangely.

CHAPTER FOURTEEN

Deirdre walked into her beloved Cairn Toul mountain and smiled. The stones had deafened her with their cries of joy on her return.

"I should never have left," she murmured as she paused at the outcropping that overlooked the cavern she used as a great hall.

But she'd had no choice, thanks to the MacLeods. They had forced her to leave, and because of that another *drough* had dared to take her from her time.

A wyrran cooed next to her, its huge yellow eyes gazing at her with the adoration Deirdre craved.

"We're home," she told the wyrran. "It's time to turn this mountain back into what it once was."

The silence inside the mountain made Deirdre itch to hear the tortured screams of the Druids once more. The dungeons would hold Warriors again, and this time she wouldn't make the same mistakes.

Declan had thought he could hold her, thought he could make her bend to his will. He'd been dead wrong, and he would pay for all that he had done.

Deirdre smiled as she thought of all the ways she could

make Declan bellow in agony. She made her way to her chamber, running her fingers along the stones as she did.

She got strength from the stones. They spoke to her, just as she could speak to them. They and the wyrran were the only ones who had never betrayed her.

Deirdre stepped into her chamber and let her gaze wander over the dirt, dust, and spiderwebs that had taken over everything.

A *tsk*ing sounded around her, bouncing off the stones until it reverberated over and over again.

"Have you learned nothing?" the voice said.

Deirdre took a deep breath and turned to the black smoke that seeped from between the cracks in the stone walls. It filled her chamber until she couldn't see her hand before her face.

"I've learned a great deal," Deirdre answered. She was careful to keep her voice even. It had taken just one instance of allowing Him to know she was angry to learn that if she wanted to live, she could never do it again.

He chuckled. "You should have listened to me and forgotten about the artifacts. You should have kept to the course I set for you and killed Lucan and Fallon MacLeod."

"I was in the process of doing just that. I killed Duncan Kerr. Ian would have been mine to control."

The smoke thickened, choking Deirdre. "Do. Not. Lie. You may have killed Duncan, but you went to Mallaig in order to get the artifact."

"I did."

"Even after I told you to let it go?"

The smoke tightened around her, squeezing her so that she couldn't take a breath. "Aye," she managed to get out.

"Why?" the voice boomed.

"I need them. The artifacts will make me stronger," she said between gasping breaths.

Suddenly, the pressure lifted, but the smoke swirled with fury. "You were to have been my greatest achievement, Deirdre."

"I still will be."

"I don't doubt that. Your will to dominate is strong. But I had to put other precautions in place."

And that's when Deirdre realized her master, Satan, had added to Declan's magic to make him stronger. "Declan."

"I thought you might get along better with him."

Deirdre snorted. "Why? You know I won't fail you."

"I want to ensure that you don't. Declan doesn't care about the artifacts. He wants power. He wants to rule. And he wants you."

"I don't want him."

The deep voice laughed, long and low. "I've given him much power, enough magic that he is a perfect match for you."

"You helped him bring me to this time." It wasn't a question, but she wanted Him to admit it.

"I did. I've also helped your cause by getting rid of the Druids."

Deirdre's breath left her in a rush. She needed those Druids in order to gain their magic. "All of them?"

"Oh, there are a few walking about. The Druids at MacLeod Castle are still there. Most of the others have no idea what they are. You should be able to find them easily enough."

She clasped her hands behind her back. "I will conquer this world without Declan Wallace."

"It will be an interesting show," the voice said, a smile evident in the words. "By the way, I thought you might like to know that Ian Kerr was brought with you to this time."

For the first time since her master had arrived Deirdre

smiled. "How fortuitous for me. He will be the first Warrior I find. And he'll be the perfect instrument to penetrate MacLeod Castle."

"Just what I wanted to hear. No more artifacts."

"But I must have them. They will make me stronger."

"That is what I'm for!"

Deirdre lowered her gaze in submission. "I can get the artifacts *and* kill Lucan and Fallon."

"Do you know why the MacLeods want the artifacts so desperately?"

She shrugged. "To prevent me from having them."

"Because, my faithful servant, those artifacts allow them to enter a tomb. The tomb that holds your sleeping sister."

"Laria?" Deirdre whispered in shock.

"Yes. If Laria rises, she will attempt to kill you."

"She doesn't have any magic."

Another laugh, this one dry and angry. "She always did. You never saw it because she hid it so well. Leave the artifacts alone."

"If I do, the MacLeods will awaken her."

"I won't let that happen." The smoke began to drift back into the stones. "Remember, Deirdre. If you don't do what I want I will have Declan replace you. In everything."

The threat was enough to make Deirdre shiver.

But not enough to make her forget the artifacts. Now, more than ever she had to have them. Laria could never awaken. Never.

Deirdre didn't think her twin could kill her, but she didn't want to take the chance, either. As long as she had the artifacts, she would be stronger. And no one would open her sister's tomb.

"That was interesting," said a male voice from behind her.

Deirdre spun around to find Malcolm standing in her doorway with his arms crossed. There was no anger, no surprise, no happiness . . . nothing on his face.

"You shouldn't have seen that," Deirdre said.

Malcolm shrugged, a lock of his golden hair falling over his forehead into his eyes. "Why no'? I've always known you took orders from the devil. I just never realized he visited you before."

Deirdre waved away his words. "We have other concerns. Ian was brought forward with us. I want him found."

"I'll see it done," Malcolm vowed and dropped his arms as he began to turn away.

"Nay. I need you to stay here for the time being."

Malcolm shrugged and resumed his position. "Whatever you'd like."

Deirdre grinned. Malcolm was the perfect Warrior. He had his rage under control, but he would kill anything with one command from her. Even those at MacLeod Castle. All because she had promised him she would leave his precious cousin, Larena, alone.

"I'm going to send the wyrran out."

"Are you sure that's wise?" Malcolm asked. "There are more people about than we are used to."

"I no longer care. I need to find Druids and the artifact. I'm going to send a small group of wyrran to the Isle of Eigg for the artifact."

Malcolm nodded. "We will finish what we began."

Deirdre smiled as the ends of her white hair lifted from the floor and swirled around her. "In more ways than one."

Logan and Gwynn ate a hasty lunch and were on the ferry in less than an hour. The wind was exceptionally harsh and caused large waves, making the ferry move even faster than before.

Gwynn held her stomach and moaned, her complexion paling.

"What is it?" Logan asked.

"The boat is rocking. It's making me sick to my stomach."

Logan looked at the water and allowed a portion of his god to surface. He made sure to keep turned so that no one saw him, and then he used the power his god gave him and commanded the waters to calm.

Instantly, the sea's rough waves disappeared into the regular gently rolling waters.

"Oh, thank God," Gwynn said and closed her eyes.

Logan didn't mind not receiving the credit. Part of him wished he could tell her—show her—what he was, but it wouldn't be wise.

"Odd, though, isn't it?"

"What?" Logan asked.

Gwynn peered over the railing to the water below them. "How the water calmed so suddenly."

"Scotland's weather is always surprising. You never know what you'll get from one moment to the next."

She laughed, her violet eyes bright. "The same holds true for Texas weather."

When they reached Eigg, Gwynn set out with sure steps across the isle. Logan stayed by her side, his gaze on the crowd around him.

Few people paid them any heed. Apparently, Logan was blending in.

Logan spotted a few men wearing kilts, but they were different from his own. More modern, as Gwynn would say. Logan liked the old ways better.

He glanced above him and frowned at the heavy gray clouds hanging low in the sky. "There's a storm coming."

"I think I may need two jackets," Gwynn grumbled. She sniffed and huddled deeper into her jacket.

"A thicker scarf and gloves, I'd say."

She cut her eyes to him and grinned. "You up for more shopping?"

"Ah . . ."

Her laugh sounded around them, lightening Logan's heart. "Yeah. I didn't think so. Most guys would rather be doing anything other than shopping. Don't worry, though. I've already decided I need something thicker than what I have. I'll pick it up sometime today."

"We will get whatever you need." He knew she suffered in the cold weather, and since it was December, it was only going to get colder.

Gwynn's breath puffed around her as she chuckled. "There doesn't seem to be as many people as there were yesterday."

"It's the weather that's coming in. It'll bring snow for sure. And lots of it by the look of the clouds."

"I used to wish every Christmas it would snow where I lived. Sometimes, if we got lucky, every ten years or so we'd get a few flurries that would melt as soon as they hit the ground."

"Christmas?" he asked. He'd learned a lot from her, and even some from the computer, but apparently there was still more for him to assimilate.

"Yeah. It's when we celebrate the birth of Jesus. We decorate our houses with colored lights. Inside our houses we put up trees, which we adorn with lights and ornaments, and then we put our gifts to each other under the tree. On Christmas morning we exchange gifts."

"I see." Though Logan was sure that what he pictured in his head wasn't at all what she was trying to explain.

She laughed again, and he discovered he loved the sound of it.

"I'll show you pictures on the laptop when we get back

to the hotel. It's really a magical season. The songs, the holiday cheer, the parties, and the sales for shopping."

It was Logan's turn to chuckle. "I take it you like to shop."

"Most women do. Mostly I just look. I have expensive tastes, it seems, so I can rarely afford to buy what I want."

Logan frowned, not understanding how she could be so nonchalant about it. "So you cannot afford to buy what you need?"

"Need and want are two different things, Logan. I have all I need and more. Wanting, say, the Jimmy Choo boots I've been eyeing for a couple of months is all about knowing how great they would look with this cashmere sweater dress I have."

He understood all about wanting. Hadn't Logan wanted to go back in time and change his decision to go to Deirdre? Hadn't he wished he had heeded his brother's cries and returned to the warmth of his family's cottage?

Gwynn's small hand touched his arm, and Logan looked up to find he'd stopped walking.

"Are you all right?"

The concern in Gwynn's violet eyes helped to ease the guilt that had begun to choke him. "Aye."

"It's not good to hold everything inside, you know. I did it, and it nearly ruined me."

Logan couldn't imagine Gwynn suffering any kind of guilt. There was a sense of serenity and purity about her. People such as Gwynn didn't make the kind of mistakes Logan had. "How did you do it?"

"There was a time when my father and I didn't speak," she said as she began walking again, this time at a much slower pace. "I resented the fact that he was always at the university. To me, it seemed like he cared more about his research than he did about his family. Many nights I lay awake listening to my mother cry when he didn't come home once again."

"He stayed at the university?"

Gwynn nodded. "There was a couch in his office he would sleep on. He had a closet full of clothes and everything. That was his home, It was more his home than the one he had with us. My resentment turned to hate when I was a teenager. It was always just my mom and me. Always."

"You two were close." Logan could see it in the way she'd smile when she spoke about her mother.

"Yes. We did everything together. No matter how many nights or weeks would pass without my father returning home, she was always so thrilled when he finally did. I never understood how she could be like that. She told me she loved him. As if that made up for the way he treated us."

"Did he no' do things with you?"

"Not at all. I was always in the way. He would take Mom out or bring her home a small gift, tell her he was sorry and wouldn't stay away so long next time. Then he would leave the next morning."

The more Gwynn spoke, the less he liked Gary Austin.

"Five years ago, Mom began to feel run down. It was so unlike her. She'd always had boundless energy. She was always ready to do something, anything. A year went by, and it only got worse.

"I'd moved into my own place by that time, but I began to stay with her to make sure she ate. She could barely get out of bed by then. It was then that I discovered my dad hadn't been to see her in three months. I was going to call him and give him a piece of my mind . . ."

"But she asked you no' to," Logan said.

Gwynn glanced at him and nodded sadly. "She said she didn't want him to see her like that. I finally convinced her she needed to go to the doctor. Turned out she had leukemia. It went untreated for a year, Logan."

He frowned as he tried to recall if he'd heard of whatever the disease was. "What is leukemia?"

"Cancer of the bone marrow. The disease had progressed to a state that not even a bone marrow transplant from me would help her."

"What would you have had to do?"

She lifted a shoulder. "They would go in and take part of my bone marrow to give to her."

"It sounds painful."

"It is, but I would have done it."

Logan wanted to touch her, to pull her into his arms and take away the hurt and pain he saw on her face. The knowledge that she suffered through this alone without her father there to help made him want to rip out Gary's throat.

"Somehow Mom lived another year. It was a horrible time. She was in so much pain and in and out of hospitals. That's how Dad found us. He'd gone home to find the house empty, and a neighbor had told him where we were. As soon as he came to the hospital, he stayed by her side until the day she passed on."

"I'm sorry, Gwynn."

"That's life," she said through a watery smile. "It's been three years, and still it feels like the hurt will never go away."

"It will. Just think of the good memories you had with her."

"I do," Gwynn said with a nod.

Logan looked around to see that they were all alone on the back side of the isle. It was where they had been the day before when Gwynn had heard the wind.

"Tell me how things changed between you and your father," Logan said.

She rolled her eyes and flattened her lips. "I did it for Mom. She wanted us to get along, so I pretended for her sake. It got to be such a habit that by the time she died, most of my anger at him had faded. He was all the family I had left. I had just lost my mother. I wasn't ready to be alone in the world."

"No one is."

A harsh breath left Gwynn's lips, but there was a hint of a smile as well. "I give him credit, he made an effort with me. We had dinner every Sunday night. We talked throughout the week as well. It was more of a relationship than I'd ever had with him."

Logan pulled a strand of hair from her eyelashes. "That's good though."

"Four years ago, had he gone missing, I wouldn't have lifted a finger to find him. And now, I took a leave of absence from my job and used my savings to fly out here. For what? He's not here."

"Nay, but you've discovered yourself. You've discovered who you are what you are. You have magic as old as time flowing through you."

The smile started small, then grew large. "I do, don't I? How many people can say that?"

"Few, I would imagine."

She pulled her hand from her pocket and halted as she touched his arm. "Thank you, Logan."

He looked down into her violet eyes fringed with thick, black lashes and was captivated. Enthralled.

Spellbound.

Their bodies were nearly touching. Logan's gaze dropped to her lips, and he found himself leaning down to kiss her, to finally have the taste of her he'd been craving.

Desire filled him, making him ache to feel her in his arms. He hungered for her taste, craved her touched. Yearned for . . . her.

Suddenly, the feel of Gwynn's magic grew and surrounded him, making him crazy with the unsullied, innocent feel of it. . . . of her.

He had to have her, had to taste her.

"Logan," she whispered.

He groaned at the sound of his name on her lips. She would say it again, he promised himself. She would scream it as he made her peak.

But first . . . a kiss.

Logan's lips were a breath away from touching hers, from slaking the desire that had ridden him tirelessly from the first moment he had seen her.

The sound of footsteps running toward them had him jerking his head up. He cursed his luck when he saw a group of young lads playing. And when he turned back to Gwynn, she was gone.

Logan clenched his hands in an effort to hold back the lust that filled him. He found her about twenty paces from him.

"Here," Gwynn called as she knelt next to something.

Logan's strides ate up the ground as he walked to her. "What is it?"

"The double spirals."

He looked down to find a rock the size of a man's head with the same double spirals that were on the book and the amulet.

"It matches," Gwynn said and rose to stand beside him. "Now what?"

"Now we find the book."

CHAPTER
FIFTEEN

Gwynn couldn't calm her racing heart. Or the ache that wouldn't go away. Ever since she'd seen the desire darken Logan's hazel eyes, she'd known he was going to kiss her.

And she'd desperately wanted him to.

His heat had surrounded her, his nearness like a drug making her think of him. And only him. The world had simply ceased to exist as his head lowered to hers.

Gwynn's eyes had fallen shut and her lips had parted as she waited, breathlessly, for the kiss. When it hadn't come, she'd opened her eyes to find Logan watching a group of boys.

The sheer force of the need spiraling through Gwynn frightened her. Could she give in to the attraction she felt for Logan? Did she dare? Knowing he had traveled through time and was here to fight a force so evil it had brought the entire race of Druids to a grinding halt?

Somehow, Gwynn had managed to take a step away from Logan. And then another, and another, until she'd found the stone.

But not even the frigid air blowing off the water could cool the rampant desire that still burned within her.

"We can't just drive up to this guy's door and ask to see the book," Gwynn pointed out.

Logan looked at her, his forehead creased. "Why no'?"

"It's just not how it's done. Most likely he'll have us thrown off his property."

"Do you have another suggestion then?"

Gwynn lifted her arms and let them fall down to her side, slapping the sides of her legs. "I don't know. All this is new to me, Logan."

"Aye. But it's no' to me."

Unfortunately, he did have a point. "What do you think the book is going to tell us?"

"Who knows?"

"What if I could find out more by asking the wind?"

He stared at her, as if considering her words. "You might be able to learn quite a bit. Especially about where Deirdre is. The trees were always able to tell Sonya such things."

"Then I'll try." Anticipation and excitement rushed through Gwynn's veins. It had frightened her the first time she'd heard the wind, but since then, she'd wanted to hear it again. Wanted to feel its unique touch upon her skin.

"I want to return to where we were yesterday the first time it spoke with me."

The half smile on Logan's lips made the butterflies in Gwynn's stomach flutter again. "Then let us go."

They walked in silence though she was aware of every breath he took. She was even more aware of how often his gaze shifted around them, and even behind them.

"Are you expecting trouble?"

"You're a Druid, Gwynn. I always expect trouble when I'm around Druids. Especially knowing Deirdre is here. And that your father is somehow connected to the Tablet of Orn."

"Wow. Wish I hadn't asked."

He chuckled. "You need no' be worried. I swore to protect you."

With his words still lingering in her ears, Gwynn
reached the spot that had been calling her since she first
saw Eigg. It was even stronger now that she had accepted
she was a Druid and heard the wind.

She smiled as she realized her mother would have
fainted if she knew Gwynn had begun to use her magic
again. But Gwynn would have liked to tell her mother
about these new developments. Particularly the fact that
she could communicate with the wind.

"I'll stand over here," Logan said.

She nodded and smiled when he winked at her. Logan's
charm was infectious. It helped to ease her worries and
fears. And his being near . . . well, he awakened the woman
inside her, the woman she had hidden from the world for
fear of hurt.

A woman who desperately wanted to give in to the
temptation he offered her.

Gwynn let out a deep breath and stood on the cliff.
The waves were white-capping from the rough winds, and
the storm clouds Logan had seen earlier had moved closer
and hung lower than before.

The wind howled around her, brushing against her gently and roughly at the same time. It pushed her, held her.
Comforted her.

Gwynn silently asked the wind where Deirdre was.
When she didn't get an answer, she said aloud, "Can you
tell me where Deirdre is?"

The wind was silent again.

"Open up your magic," Logan said in her ear.

She hadn't known he'd moved behind her, hadn't heard
him close the distance. But knowing he was there if she
needed him helped to steady her, helped to bolster her
courage to reach for the wind.

Gwynn closed her eyes and felt for her magic. It swirled inside her in a white and gold mass, growing stronger every day. When she called to it, it rose up and coiled around her, within her. Through her.

"I feel it."

"As do I."

Logan's voice was oddly rough, as if it took great effort for him to speak. She leaned back against him, and his arms came around her waist.

She could hear his breathing, harsh and erratic, in her ear. But it was the feel of his hard arousal against her back that made her heart drop to her stomach.

And need, swift and stronger than before, stirred.

"Gwynn," Logan said.

She forced herself to forget about the heart-stopping arousal and focus on her magic. Gwynn tried several more times to talk to the wind, but each time she heard nothing in return.

"Something is wrong," she said and gripped Logan's hands as an unknown emotion spiked through her. It was urgent, pressing. "I feel . . ."

"Danger," he said and released her.

Gwynn stumbled forward and waved her arms to keep her balance. When she turned around she found Logan facing two men with guns.

Logan stood between her and them, protecting her just as he'd said.

"What are you doing?" she whispered as she came up behind him.

"You need to hide."

"They have guns."

There was a pause, and then Logan asked, "What are they?"

"The black things they're holding are handguns. The barrel has a hole in it. A small projectile will shoot from that hole and into whatever it's pointed at. It kills without people having to get close."

"Cowards," Logan spat. "Hide. Now."

Gwynn looked around, but there was nowhere for her to go. There were no trees, just the beautiful rolling landscape. And then she looked over the cliff. There, about six feet down was a small ledge.

She didn't hesitate, just sat down and hung her legs over the side. With one more glance at Logan, who still had his attention on the assailants, Gwynn jumped.

With the scream lodged in her throat, she landed heavily and twisted her ankle. "Damn boots," she muttered.

They were gorgeous, but the high heels weren't practical when jumping off a cliff.

The pain of her ankle was nothing compared to her fear for Logan's life. There was no way he would survive being shot by one of the gunmen. If he went down, what would happen to her?

Gwynn glanced at the water below her. She'd have to jump clear of the rocks, which wouldn't be easy—if she managed it at all. Then there were the currents to deal with.

"What are you waiting for?" she heard Logan yell.

"Give us everything ye got," one of the men said.

Logan chuckled. "You'll have to come and get it."

"Give it to us now, or we'll shoot you," the second man said.

Gwynn's heart was in her throat. She climbed up and peered over the edge of the cliff so she could see what was going on. Logan still stood his ground, and the other two weren't looking as confident as before.

But then again, no one could be as assertive as Logan.

"Give us what we want now," the first man yelled.

Logan shook his head.

Then the gun exploded.

Gwynn screamed and covered her mouth as the bullet

slammed into Logan's shoulder. Logan barely moved, and she could have sworn she heard a growl.

A deep, resonating, angry growl.

Gwynn's foot slipped and she started to fall, but she managed to hang on with her fingers. While she was trying to gain another foothold, she heard the men screaming and more gunfire.

When Gwynn once more had her foot secured, she looked over the ledge to see the two men lying on the ground with Logan standing over them.

It was the long, silver claws that curved from his fingers that made her gasp.

The sound had Logan spinning toward her, and her lungs refused to work. The Logan she knew was gone. In his place was a . . . beast with silver skin and claws. And fangs.

"Gwynn," Logan said and took a step toward her. "These men willna hurt you now."

"Did you kill them?"

He paused, then shook his head. "I'd like to. They wouldna have thought twice about shooting you."

That's when she saw the blood that dripped from his wounds. She didn't know whether to be concerned or frightened.

"I willna hurt you."

And oddly, she believed him. Even though her mind screamed for her to be wary.

Gwynn began to climb over the ledge, and when Logan offered her his hand, she hesitantly took it. She noticed how he went out of his way to protect her hands from his long silver claws, which were a shade darker than his skin. She stood before him and looked him up and down.

Logan removed his sweater so she could see the silver covering every inch of his skin. "This is what I am," he said. "This is who I am."

She swallowed to wet her mouth as she looked into what used to be his hazel eyes. Now they were silver from corner to corner. Even the whites of his eyes were silver. "Your eyes."

"Part of being a Warrior."

"So . . . you are one."

He nodded. "You've nothing to fear from me, Gwynn. I swore to protect Druids, just as all the Warriors at MacLeod Castle have."

"Why didn't you tell me you were a Warrior?"

"I wanted to keep it from you. I was afraid you'd be frightened of me."

"I am a little," she admitted. "I've never seen anything like this, except in movies."

She reached out and ran her fingers down one of his claws.

"Careful," he said and pulled his hand back. "They are sharp."

The wounds where the bullets had entered his body were seeping more blood. "I thought Warriors were immortal."

"We are," he said with a slight wince. "My body is getting rid of the bullets."

A moment later, the first bullet exited his body and fell to the ground. It didn't take much longer for the other three to do the same.

And before her eyes his wounds began to knit together, leaving only the blood coating him as a reminder that he had been hit.

"I doona like these guns."

Gwynn couldn't help but smile. "It is a way of life now for most. There are huge guns called missiles that can be launched thousands of miles away to hit us."

"As I said before. Cowards."

Gwynn took a hasty step back as Logan's claws disappeared into his fingers, and the silver faded from his skin. When she glanced into his eyes, they were once more the hazel she had come to know. And love.

"I will always protect you, Gwynn. Even if you tell me to leave now."

She thought about all she'd learned of herself and the past she was linked to. She'd discovered it all because of Logan. If Deirdre was hunting her, she had a better chance of survival with Logan at her side.

Besides, if he wanted to kill her, he'd had plenty of opportunities. One look into his eyes and she couldn't help but believe him. Those hazel eyes flecked with gold were clear and honest as they watched her. Waiting. Hoping.

"I wish you had told me before, but I know now."

Surprise flickered across his face. "You're no' going to ask me to leave?"

"I need a protector, and you've done a good job so far."

Logan grinned and snorted.

Gwynn looked at the two men. "What do we do with them?"

"Nothing. They stay as they lay. They should be glad I didna kill them for threatening you."

If there had been any doubt as to whether Logan would protect her or not, there wasn't any now. Gwynn took a deep breath and slowly let it out.

"The wind wouldn't speak with me. Maybe I'm doing something wrong."

"Or maybe you are no'."

She shrugged. "Regardless, I think it's time we go find the book."

Logan's smile was huge. "Just what I was thinking."

An eerie shriek split the air, sending chills of foreboding over Gwynn's body.

In a blink, Logan had released his god again. He glanced around. "We need to go. Now."

"What is that sound?"

"Wyrran. It means Deirdre is most likely near. If she doesna know of you and your magic, she will as soon as the wyrran report back to her."

Gwynn looked over her shoulder at the cliff and the twenty-foot drop to the water. "We need to get out of here then."

Logan's silver eyes turned to her. "Do you trust me?"

"Yes," she answered without hesitation.

As soon as the word was out of her mouth, Logan's arms wrapped around her. The scream lodged in her throat as he pulled her over the side of the cliff.

Gwynn squeezed her eyes shut and braced herself for the impact with the cold water and the rocks she knew waited below the surface. Then she realized she could no longer hear the wyrran. Or the crashing waves.

"It's all right," Logan said in her ear. "Open your eyes."

Gwynn was pressed against him, his arms like bands of steel holding her close. His smooth, hot skin beneath her hands did nothing to calm her racing heart.

Slowly, Gwynn opened her eyes. And gasped.

"Logan."

He chuckled. "Every Warrior has a certain power. Mine is controlling liquids. We're under the water. No one can see us."

She lifted her head from his chest to look above her. It was like they were in a huge bubble that glided smoothly under the water.

Gwynn spotted fish and even a few dolphins as she continued to watch. "It's amazing."

"It was the only thing I could think of to get you away from the wyrran. They will stop at nothing to get you to Deirdre."

Gwynn swallowed and shifted her gaze to Logan's. Hazel eyes flecked with gold watched her. It was ridiculous for her to ignore the muscles beneath her hands and against her body. Hopeless for her to disregard the desire that returned with a vengeance from earlier, when he had nearly kissed her.

Impossible for her to ignore the passion that heated her blood and darkened Logan's eyes.

One of his hands moved up her back, slowly, seductively, until he cupped the back of her head.

In the water, away from the dangers on land and creatures that could kill her, Gwynn let it all fade away. Until it was only her and Logan.

It was a dangerous game she played by allowing herself to feel the attraction for Logan. But how could she not? What harm would one kiss do?

She had seen her share of relationships. None had lasted long, but that was because she knew to leave before she could get hurt. Or attached.

The same instinct would apply to Logan.

She hoped.

Logan pulled her even closer until his heat surrounded her, warming her against the coolness of the water around them.

Gwynn was surprised when Logan tore off her beanie cap and stuffed it in one of her pockets. He smiled as he ran his fingers through her hair.

The look on his face, as if he had been dying to touch her hair for days, as if he had never before experienced such joy made her breath catch in her throat.

His gaze lowered until he looked into her face. She knew that this time their kiss wouldn't be interrupted.

Gwynn's breathing ratcheted up a notch when his head began to lower to hers. She rose up on her tiptoes until their lips brushed.

Once. Twice.

A charge whipped through her, and when she would

have pulled away, Logan groaned and kissed her again. His lips were soft, but insistent as he nipped at her mouth.

A moan slipped from Gwynn when his tongue licked at her lips before delving into her mouth.

Gwynn clung to him as their tongues mated and dueled. Each stroke of his tongue awoke something within her, something she had never felt before.

It was more than desire, more than passion.

It was . . . a need, deep and consuming.

A yearning profound and uncontrollable.

A longing intense and overwhelming.

And all for Logan.

Only Logan.

Gwynn wound her arms around his neck as he deepened the kiss. It never entered her mind to pull away or break the contact. All she wanted was more. More of the amazing feelings coursing through her. More of the unique sensations rocking her body.

More of the incredible taste of the Warrior in her arms.

She threaded her fingers through his silky, honey-colored hair. His hands shifted until he cupped her bottom and brought her against his hot arousal.

Gwynn groaned and shifted her hips to rub against him.

Logan's hands were everywhere, stroking, caressing, learning. She was inundated with passion that continued to rise and threatened to drown her.

But for the first time in her life, Gwynn wasn't afraid. Not while she was in Logan's arms.

He bent her back over his arm and kissed down her neck. Somehow he had unzipped her jacket and shoved it open. She gasped in pleasure when his hand cupped her breast beneath her sweater.

Need grew until she felt the moisture between her legs. She couldn't get close enough to Logan, couldn't feel enough of him.

And then his thumb grazed her nipple.

Gwynn cried out from the sheer pleasure of it. Logan's mouth claimed hers for another kiss. This one more demanding, more urgent. And hungry.

He ravaged her mouth while his fingers continued to tease her nipple until it was hard and aching. Her breasts swelled, eager for more of his touch.

It was the sound of a boat motoring overhead that caused Logan to break the kiss and lift his head to look above them.

He lowered his gaze to her, then slowly righted her.

"I guess we can't stay down here forever," Gwynn said.

His jaw clenched as he shrugged. "We could always try."

The bad thing was, Gwynn very much wanted to.

CHAPTER
SIXTEEN

It wasn't that Logan was afraid of the automobiles. It was just that he preferred to travel as he usually did. He did have to admit, however, that the car traveled faster than he could.

He glanced over at Gwynn as she drove with her hands gripping the steering wheel so tight her knuckles were white.

They had made it back to Mallaig and purchased the things she'd need when the snow had begun. At first, it was light flakes that danced in the air endlessly.

Then, the rain had begun.

Gwynn had packed all her belongings in the rather small rolling bag.

"We don't know when we'll return, and I don't like being without my stuff," she'd argued.

Logan knew it didn't matter. They could always return to the hotel after they were through searching for the book.

Because he knew they *would* be back.

Gwynn had even taken his few meager belongings, including his tattered kilt, shirt, and boots. They, along with her bag, were packed in the incredibly small car.

With the snow falling even harder, Gwynn had slowed the car until Logan knew he could get out and walk faster. But Gwynn had told him she'd never driven in the snow, and since he didn't know how to drive, that left only her.

"We can pull over and wait out the storm," he offered.

Gwynn shook her head of inky black hair. "I'd rather keep going. I'm afraid if I wait, the roads will only get worse."

"If that's what you want."

"I want to be sitting in front of a warm fire, not driving north where the storm seems to be even worse. But the lady at the hotel said it shouldn't take long to reach Ullapool."

Logan drummed his fingers on his leg. "What is the man's name again?"

"Declan Wallace. Why?"

"I'm no' sure. It's almost as if I should know something about the name, but I doona."

"Maybe you knew a Wallace from your time." She glanced at him, a grin on her face.

Her nose was red, and she hadn't removed her coat. But she was smiling. After all she'd been through, it was enough to make Logan want to reach over and take her hand.

It wasn't something he did with women. Oh, he liked women well enough. Too much, some would say. He charmed them, and he wooed them. But not once had he ever wanted to offer comfort as he did with Gwynn.

"What is it?" Gwynn asked.

Logan shrugged. "I'm still becoming accustomed to riding in this vehicle."

"I can imagine it's quite a change. Do you miss your time?"

"Oh, aye," he admitted. "It was much quieter and there were no' nearly as many people. Everything seems so rushed in your time."

"It's your time as well now," Gwynn reminded him. "But you're right. It is rushed. Everyone is always hurrying here and hurrying there. No one has any patience anymore. There's this thing called road rage. In the US, in some cities the traffic is so horrendous people sit in it for hours. It makes people mad."

"Road rage?"

She nodded. "People have killed others for driving too slow or refusing to let them in a lane, or any number of other offenses. It's just . . . sad."

"I think you would have liked my time." Logan could imagine Gwynn standing in the bailey of MacLeod Castle with the other women.

"I don't know about that. I'm kinda partial to the toilets and showers."

Logan threw back his head and laughed. "Oh, aye, lass. I've found I've grown fond of them as well."

The talk had eased Gwynn's nerves, allowing her to drive with more confidence. Just as Logan had intended.

"Can you tell me what it's like being a Warrior?" she asked.

Logan inhaled a deep breath and slowly released it. "I had only been a Warrior for a century when we found the MacLeods. I was the youngest of the Warriors, but the one thing we all have in common is a past we'd just as soon forget."

"The MacLeods, it was the slaughter of their clan, yes?"

"Aye," Logan nodded. "Fallon, Lucan, and Quinn had lived in the ruin of the castle for three hundred years. They made everyone believe the castle was haunted. It would still be like that if Lucan hadn't saved Cara."

Gwynn grinned and briefly turned her head to him. "What happened?"

"Cara's parents had been killed when she was just a

child. It was wyrran who had killed them, but she didn't know it. She got away and was taken in by the nuns in the village next to MacLeod Castle. One day, she slipped on the edge of the cliffs. Lucan had been watching her, and he got to her in time to save her.

"The rule of the brothers is that no one was allowed in the castle but them. Quinn, had a problem controlling his rage, and Fallon drowned himself in wine so he wouldn't have to listen to his god."

"Wow," Gwynn said softly. "I take it they allowed Cara to stay."

Logan told Gwynn the story of how Cara came to realize she was a Druid and how Deirdre had attacked the castle to try and take her.

"By that time Lucan and Cara had fallen in love. Fallon, being the leader that he was born to be, had stopped drinking. He helped to slow the Warrior from taking Cara, which gave Lucan and the rest of us time to get there and save her."

"So Cara was the first Druid at the castle?"

"She was. It was the MacLeods' idea to open the castle to all Druids as a sanctuary. Any Warrior wishing to fight Deirdre was also welcome."

"How many Warriors are at the castle?"

Logan rested his head against the seat. "The MacLeods, of course. Galen was the next to arrive. Then me, Hayden, and Ramsey. Oh, and then Larena."

"A woman?"

"And Fallon's wife. She's the only female Warrior we know of."

"How neat!"

Logan smiled at the way Gwynn's violet eyes had lit up at the mention of Larena.

"Who else?" Gwynn asked.

"Camdyn, Arran, Broc, and the twins, Ian and Duncan."

Gwynn's smile disappeared. "Except Duncan is gone."

"That he is."

"So that makes twelve Warriors."

He nodded. "We think Ian was pulled to this time because of his link with Duncan. Deirdre had just killed Duncan when she disappeared. That's when me, Ramsey, Camdyn, and Arran decided to come to this time in search of Ian."

"Why is it so important to find him?"

Logan scrubbed a hand down his face. "Because of his god. The rage will be overwhelming. He's always shared his god with his twin."

"And with Duncan gone, Ian has the full strength of his god."

"Precisely. Ian is strong, and any other time I wouldna doubt his ability to control his god. But he's grieving. There was a verra strong bond between Ian and Duncan. He will need us to help him."

"What happens if Deirdre finds him?"

It was what they all feared. "Then Ian might never gain control of his god. He would be Deirdre's to rule."

"I see." Gwynn flattened her lips. "Then we will find Ian once we find my father."

Logan looked at her, amazed once more at her resiliency.

"Do you want to know of the Druids?"

"I do. You told me a little."

"Cara was still learning her magic, but I'm sure by now she's a verra powerful Druid."

The car swerved, and Gwynn gently turned the wheel in the opposite direction until the car straightened. "Icy patch on the road," she explained. "I can't wait to meet Cara."

"She'll welcome you, as will all the Druids. Sonya was the next to arrive. She came because the trees told her she was needed at the castle. She's the one who began Cara's training."

"Can Sonya only talk to the trees?"

"Nay. She can heal. Marcail was saved by Quinn from Deirdre. Marcail comes from a verra formidable line of Druids. The spell to bind our gods was buried deep in her mind by her grandmother. Deirdre's attempt to kill Marcail erased the spell, however."

"That sucks," Gwynn said. "I'm really beginning to hate this Deirdre chick."

Logan chuckled. "We all do."

"But Marcail is safe at the castle?"

"Aye. And carrying Quinn's child."

Gwynn's eyes were huge as she jerked her head to look at him. "You can father children?"

"Apparently. None of us knew for sure, nor had we tried. It was a surprise to Marcail and Quinn as well. The other women take some kind of concoction that prevents pregnancy."

"Interesting. It never occurred to me that a Warrior could have children."

"Marcail also has the ability to take away another's pain."

"That's what her magic does?"

"Aye."

"What happens?"

"She becomes violently ill."

Gwynn's lip curled in distaste. "I'm glad that isn't what I can do. Who else is there?"

"Isla. She was held as Deirdre's prisoner for centuries. Deirdre was able to control Isla's mind and make her do things."

"I take it those things were bad."

"Extremely," Logan said. "Isla was a *mie*, but Deirdre forced her to become *drough*. Because Isla didna become *drough* willingly, the evil never took her. She's the only one who has the ability to control black magic without it consuming her."

"Making her one powerful Druid."

"Aye. She shields the castle and village. If people get too near, they will feel the need to leave immediately. For others who do venture close, they willna see anything other than the countryside."

"Now that's cool," Gwynn said.

Logan followed the wipers on the window as they futilely tried to remove the rapidly falling snow. The storm he had predicted would keep most indoors. It was also a hazard to be in, which was proven to Logan when the car had skidded on the ice.

They would be driving over mountains, and though he wanted to find the book, he didn't think putting Gwynn's life in danger was worth it.

"Maybe we should find another hotel," he said. "The roads are going to be difficult the farther into the Highlands we go."

Gwynn bit her lip, her fingers once more gripping the wheel. "We'll go as far as we can. Tell me more of the Druids."

"With Isla safely away from Deirdre and protected by Hayden, she told us of the artifacts Deirdre was trying to find. The first was at Loch Awe. Imagine Galen's and my surprise when the artifact turned out to be a Druid. Reaghan's clan of Druids is where Laria, Deirdre's twin, had gone to when Deirdre gained too much power."

"Holy smoke," Gwynn murmured. "Each time you tell me of a Druid, the story is more complex than the last."

He shrugged. "I suppose. A spell was cast on Laria to make her sleep until she could be awakened to kill Deirdre."

"Why not kill Deirdre then?"

"Few realized how dangerous Deirdre really was. Laria, however, knew. Reaghan's father then helped cast a spell on Reaghan that made her immortal. With a price. Every ten years Reaghan would lose her memories and begin her life again. Each time a decade passed, it was like a wall went up in Reaghan's mind."

"Hiding the location of Laria."

Logan blinked and gazed at Gwynn. "How did you know?"

She shrugged. "Makes sense to me."

"That's exactly what happened. But Galen and Reaghan fell in love on their way to the castle. Deirdre attacked the castle again in an effort to steal Reaghan. She was struck with a spear and died, but it was her dying that broke the spell. She was able to remember everything then."

"A one up on Deirdre," Gwynn said with a whoop. "Good for y'all."

"Y'all?" Logan repeated the strange word.

"I'm from Texas, Logan. We have our own language," she said with a grin.

Logan scratched his jaw and chuckled.

"Then Sonya and Broc found the amulet, yes?"

"Aye. We need all the artifacts to be able to make it to Laria and awaken her."

Gwynn tucked her hair behind her ear and glanced at him. "Are Broc and Sonya together?"

"They are. Why?"

"It seems that every Druid is matched to a Warrior."

Logan's heart missed a beat. "It appears so."

CHAPTER
SEVENTEEN

Gwynn was thankful for Logan's conversation. She was more nervous about driving on the slick roads than she wanted to admit. But she knew how important it was to seek out Declan Wallace.

Not just for her father, but for the artifact Logan needed.

Yet, as she glanced over and saw him studying the road, she knew he wasn't thinking of the weather. He was thinking about the Druids finding love with the Warriors at MacLeod Castle.

For a moment, Gwynn allowed herself to think about being Logan's. There was no doubt she was attracted to him. Strongly attracted, but he was immortal.

And she was tired of being left behind.

She steeled her heart and her body against Logan. There would be no happy ending for them because she wouldn't allow it. For her own sanity, she had to stay strong in this.

"Just twenty more miles to Ullapool," Logan said.

The time had flown by as they had talked. Hearing about the Druids and Warriors had made Gwynn realize the war Logan and the others were fighting was one that could change the world as she knew it.

If Deirdre was able to prevent Logan and the others from awakening Laria, she could gain the power she sought. Everything would become hers. Every person would be hers to command.

And there would be no one to stop her.

Gwynn followed the road signs to Ullapool, and then through the city to the outskirts. The car was quiet as she and Logan were lost in their own thoughts.

She couldn't help but think that the time Logan was spending helping her find her father was time wasted in not finding the artifact. Or Ian.

Yet, like Logan, she had a suspicion her father and the artifact were somehow connected.

They just had to figure out how. Maybe then they'd find her father. Then he could fill them in on all he knew.

"There," Logan said and pointed to the left.

Gwynn saw the ten-foot-tall hedges that blocked the gated entry from the road. She slowed the car, careful not to brake too quickly on the icy roads, and turned into the drive.

Gwynn stopped next to the speaker box sticking out of the ground and rolled down her window. Snow poured into the car as she punched the button and rubbed her hands together.

"Aye?" the disembodied male voice said through the speaker.

"We've come to see Mr. Wallace if he's available," Gwynn said, her voice raised so the man could hear her.

"You're American." He said it with such distaste that Gwynn rolled her eyes.

"Yes, I am. We're hoping Mr. Wallace can help me lo-cate my father, Professor Gary Austin."

Silence greeted her announcement.

Gwynn sat back and looked at Logan. She shrugged, thinking they had made the trip for nothing when there was a click and the huge black gates began to open.

She hastily rolled up her window and drove through the gates. For just a heartbeat she thought about turning around. There was something . . . off . . . about the mansion.

It was huge, rising four stories. She counted ten chimneys. The mansion stretched far on each side, and she could only imagine how deep the house was. The grounds were perfectly landscaped, even with the snow. The gravel drive had tracks from previous vehicles, and she glimpsed a Jaguar parked near the front door. The house, with its white paint and gray stone accents, drew her gaze again and again.

"Wallace is certainly wealthy," Logan said as he turned his head to peer out the window. "I've never seen anything like this."

"This is impressive, but there are others like this all over the world. You should go to London and see the palace."

"I'd rather no'," Logan said.

Gwynn chuckled and stopped the car. She put it in park and turned off the ignition, but she didn't open the door.

"What is it?" Logan asked.

She swallowed and looked at the mansion. "What if he doesn't know anything about my father?"

"Then we keep looking."

"Where? How?"

Logan's hand covered hers, warm, reassuring. A sizzle of awareness, of his masculine appeal surged through her.

A small frown passed over his face so quickly she thought she might have imagined it.

"We'll find him," Logan said. "Just as I'll find Ian."

"We'll find Ian," she corrected him. "You helped me. I will help you."

The wicked gleam in Logan's eyes that sent Gwynn's heart fluttering in her chest told her he was pleased with her words.

"We need to be careful in there," Logan warned, his face set in hard lines. "We know nothing about Declan Wallace other than he loaned the book to your father. And this place is . . ."

Gwynn nodded as his voice trailed off. "I'll be careful. I promise." She reached for the door handle, but his hand squeezed hers, halting her.

"If there's trouble, Gwynn, I want your vow that you will let me take care of it. I want you to get away as quickly as you can. I'll find you."

"I'm not leaving you in there."

"I'm immortal, remember."

She rolled her eyes. "Immortal, yes, but you can still be killed. If they know about the *Book of Craigan*, it means they know of the Druids. Don't you think it makes sense they'll know about Warriors?"

"Possibly. But my life is nothing compared to yours. We need the Druids to fight Deirdre. We need you."

Gwynn knew Logan wouldn't relent until she agreed. She reluctantly nodded, but she had no intention of leaving him anywhere. He was just as important as she was.

"Good. Let's go talk to Declan Wallace," Logan said.

As one, they exited the car. Gwynn took a moment to lean her head back and look at the mansion. It was huge, the kind they featured on TV shows, the kind that only wealthy people saw the inside of. The kind that people like her could only look at and wonder.

The kind that looked as if it was more than the outside showed.

"Gwynn."

She lowered her gaze to find Logan standing beside her. The snow hadn't let up, and Gwynn was glad she had purchased a warmer hat. It reminded her of the huge fur hats she'd seen Russians wear, but it was warm, and that was all that mattered to her.

No sooner had they reached the top step of the mansion than the doors opened by what Gwynn assumed was the butler.

"Welcome," he said, but his eyes said something else entirely. He opened the door wider to allow them inside. "May I take your coat?"

Gwynn shook her head as she stepped inside and tried not to gawk at the splendor before her. "I think I'll keep it."

The butler rolled his eyes, actually rolled his eyes! Gwynn was so taken aback her mouth fell open.

Logan's soft chuckle beside her told her he'd seen it as well.

"This is good Scottish weather we're having, aye?" Logan said.

The sound of Logan's brogue made the butler pause and look at him. A smile actually appeared on the man's aging face. "That it is. We're in for a fine storm, sir. Follow me, and I'll show you to Mr. Wallace's office where you can await him."

It was Gwynn's turn to roll her eyes as she jabbed Logan in the ribs. "Not fair," she whispered.

He shrugged, and she noticed the way he suddenly held himself stiffly, his nose wrinkling. "We Scots stick together."

"Obviously. Is something wrong?"

His eyes took in everything. "For a moment I thought I smelled . . ." His voice trailed off and he leaned closer to whisper, "Evil."

A tingle raced down Gwynn's spine that was anything

but pleasant. She had the same brief thought when she'd driven up to the house, but no matter how hard she tried she couldn't lay her finger on why.

No more words were exchanged as they entered Wallace's office, and even Gwynn had to admit she liked what she saw. Dark, rich wood covered the walls and the floors. Rugs, probably more expensive than her car, were spread around the room.

A large fire roared in the massive fireplace, which had a couch and two chairs set around it. Across the way was a huge, ornate black desk with small traces of gold on it. It was immaculate. Not a paper out of place.

On the walls were paintings and weapons from every era of Scottish history. And behind the desk was a bookshelf that reached the ceiling, with leather-bound books filling every shelf.

"I'll bring tea," the butler said and closed the door behind him.

"Oh, my," Gwynn said as she turned to look around the office. "This place is amazing."

"He likes to show his wealth," Logan said, his voice flat. "I take it you aren't impressed."

He shook his head. "A man is no' judged on how much coin he has. He's judged on the man he is, his actions and decisions."

She licked her lips and smiled. "Then you are far wealthier than Mr. Wallace."

Instead of pleasing Logan, her words seemed to irritate him.

"Doona say such things," Logan ground out. "I'm no' a good man. I've much to atone for."

"Which you are doing with me. Which you are doing by helping me find my father. Which you are going to do by finding Ian. And let's not forget stopping Deirdre."

Logan blew out a harsh breath and faced the fire so that his back was to her. "When Deirdre is no more, then I'll be able to look my fellow Warriors in the eye."

There was more to Logan's pain than his words said. She took a step toward him to ask when the office doors opened and a maid carried in a tray.

She smiled at Gwynn and Logan as she set the tray down on the table before the fire. "Please let me know if you need anything else."

"Thank you," Logan said, and the maid left.

Gwynn walked to the table and looked at the tray. "I bet it's real silver. The teapot, too."

"Drink some. It will help warm you."

She lowered herself onto the couch and stared at the tray. She was tired of being cold, and though she wasn't much of a tea drinker, with the sugar and cream, she was able to make it drinkable.

Gwynn sighed as the warm liquid slid down her throat. She took several more drinks before she reached for a small cookie and took a bite. "These are delicious. You should try one," she urged Logan. When he didn't reply, she said, "You mentioned you smelled evil. Evil how?"

"Do people normally enter houses so easily?"

She finished off her cookie and took another sip of the tea before she set the cup down. "In my house, yes. In places like this, not really. What are you thinking?"

"I'm thinking we got in almost too easily."

She shrugged and picked up the cup again. "I mentioned my father. I'm sure that's what got us in."

"Maybe. Hopefully."

"And if not?" she asked, unsure if she wanted to hear his answer.

"Then we were allowed in for another reason, one I'm sure I'm no' going to like. Where are your keys to the car?"

Gwynn patted the pocket of her coat. "Here."

"Good." His eyes constantly moved around the office.

But Gwynn knew he wasn't looking at the expensive weapons or fine art. He was looking for danger.

"You're scaring me, Logan," she murmured and scooted to the edge of the couch.

He gave a quick shake of his head. "I wish I didna have to, but there is something wrong here."

"What?"

"It was masked before. But I suddenly feel . . . *drough* magic."

CHAPTER
EIGHTEEN

Gwynn set down her cup carefully and firmly before she stood. "Deirdre?"

"Nay. But nearly as strong." Logan inhaled and let the bitter feel of the magic fill him.

"Then we need to leave."

Logan shook his head slowly. "No' yet."

"What?" Gwynn asked, her eyes wide. "Are you insane?"

"I need to see who this *drough* is. I need to know what the connection is to your father."

"I'd rather not," Gwynn said and came around the couch to stand in front of him. "I'd rather leave."

"And no' learn about your father?" Logan hated to use that argument, but he knew if there was a *drough* with the kind of power he sensed, he had to learn all he could to tell the others.

It was difficult, because he hated to put Gwynn's life in danger. But he had to know.

"You know I have to know about my father," Gwynn said. She crossed her arms over her chest and let out a loud breath. "I've never encountered a *drough* before. I don't know what to expect."

"Expect the unexpected," Logan warned."They think only of themselves and doona hesitate to kill innocents. It could be this *drough* and Declan Wallace are all working with Deirdre."

"That's not reassuring, Logan."

He sighed and wished, not for the first time, that he had another Warrior with him.

Declan tilted his head first one way then the other as he looked in the oval mirror hanging on the wall. He lightly brushed his fingers over the blond hair at his ears. After a few more touches to the hair atop his head, he smiled at himself.

"I am handsome, aren't I," Declan said.

There wasn't a response, but then again, he didn't need one. He'd been born with dashing good looks, but even if he hadn't, his magic could have given him whatever he wanted.

Just as it was doing now.

Declan leaned his shoulder against the wall and inspected his fingernails. "How much longer, Austin?"

"I can't give you that answer."

Declan frowned as he looked at the disheveled professor. Gary Austin took pride in his appearance, or at least he used to. Now his greasy black hair hung lank about his face, and his glasses perched crookedly on his nose.

His button-down striped shirt was half untucked, and his black pants were stained with dirt and food where he had wiped his hands.

"I came to you with the *Book of Craigan* because I was told you were the best at translation."

Gary pushed his glasses up his nose and tossed aside

his pencil. "I am the best at translating ancient Gaelic, but the words change every time I read them."

"It's the magic."

"I know!" Gary yelled. Then he hastily ducked his head. "Each time it changes, it requires a different translation. I cannot find what I need when the words alter."

Declan pushed away from the wall and slowly circled the table where Gary had spread open numerous books as well as a notepad where he had jotted notes.

"You told me you had enough magic to make the book give you its secrets."

"I do, but it's not responding."

Declan stopped behind Gary and laid his hands on the professor's shoulders. "I cannot even touch the book because of my black magic. There are so few Druids in the world now. I need someone who has welcomed their magic as well as used it. I thought that person was you."

Gary turned his head and looked at Declan. "It is me. I'll get you the answers you need."

"Good," Declan said with a smile as he started for the door. "I'd hate to have to look for another Druid and translator."

Before Declan reached the door, there was a knock and his captain, Robbie, walked in.

"We have a problem," Robbie said.

Declan stopped short of snorting. To Robbie, everything was a problem. "What is it now?"

"We have visitors. A Scotsman and a woman who says she's looking for her father, Gary Austin."

Declan looked at Austin to gage his reaction. "Gary, your daughter is here."

"I heard Robbie," Gary answered.

"You doona care?"

Gary impatiently looked up from the book, his lips

curled in a snarl. "Gwynn has always managed to get in my way."

Declan chuckled at the irritation in Gary's eyes. "Does Miss Austin know her father is here?"

"No. She does know he spoke with you. I think she's here only to see if you have talked to the professor recently."

"Let's go see Miss Austin, then," Declan said and walked from the room.

Before Robbie shut the door behind them, Declan looked inside to see Gary working. The threat of death had a way of making people do things they normally wouldn't.

"Do you really think he can find where the Tablet of Orn is?" Robbie asked.

Declan shrugged. "He'd better. I will make his death as painful as possible if he doesna. I need that tablet, Robbie. I must get it before Deirdre does."

"I've no doubt you will."

"Your confidence is staggering," Declan said with a snort.

Robbie grinned. "You didna hire me for my confidence in you."

"Nay. I hired you because you're the best at killing people." Declan paused at the stairs and regarded Robbie. "Who is the man with Gwynn Austin?"

"I have no idea. It was the butler who told me he was a Scot."

Declan tapped his chin with his forefinger. "Why would Miss Austin need to have a man with her?"

"Maybe he's a guide. Maybe he's the one who drove her here."

"Could be," Declan said. "In any event, have your men ready. I may want to detain Miss Austin. For all of Gary's claims, her presence might help to motivate him."

An evil smile split Robbie's lips. "Just what I wanted to hear. Give me two minutes, and my men and I will be in position."

Declan nodded and started down the stairs. Gwynn Austin's arrival hadn't been expected, but it could work to his advantage. If she couldn't make her father work faster, Declan might keep her for himself.

He'd seen a picture of her when he'd had Gary tailed for a month before Declan had approached him. Declan didn't do anything without knowing everything first.

There wasn't a facet of Gary's life that Declan didn't know about. He had even been informed about the special clause in Gena Austin's will that prevented Gary from getting any money unless he maintained a steady relationship with his daughter.

Declan had gotten a good laugh about that. Surveillance on Gary and Gwynn had proven quite comical as Declan watched Gary force smiles and conversation. Gary could never get out of Gwynn's apartment fast enough.

When Declan had asked Gary why he hated his daughter so, Gary's response had been, "she's a waste of oxygen."

Harsh.

But then again, it didn't bother Declan.

He halted in front of the mirror next to his office door and checked his appearance again. He smoothed his hand over his Armani sport coat, and then tugged at the sleeve of his Ermenegildo Zegna French-cuff shirt.

Declan turned his ruby cuff link until it was aligned perfectly. Then he walked to his office door and opened it.

He strode in to find Gwynn seated on his leather couch before the fire. "Welcome, Miss Austin. How can I help you today?"

CHAPTER
NINETEEN

Logan knew the instant he saw Declan Wallace that the *drough* magic he'd felt was Wallace's.

With Gwynn across the room from him, all Logan could do was watch as Declan leaned his blond head over Gwynn's hand and kissed it.

Logan wanted to kill him. To rip him limb from limb for touching Gwynn. To flay the skin from the pompous arse again and again.

"Hello," Gwynn said.

Logan saw a small frown crease her brow, but it was there for only an instant.

"And who is this?" Declan asked as his gaze landed on Logan.

"A friend who has graciously accompanied me," Gwynn said. She rose and walked around the couch until she stood next to Logan.

Declan's smile didn't reach his blue eyes as he stared at them. "Does your friend have a name, Miss Austin?"

"Logan," Logan replied.

The fake smile slipped from Declan's mouth. "Logan?"

"Aye."

Declan fiddled with a ruby at his wrist that seemed to hold the cuff of his shirt together. "What is your surname?"

There was no doubt in Logan's mind that Declan was working with Deirdre. Only someone who knew of the Warriors who had fought against Deirdre would be aware of their names.

"Smith," Gwynn suddenly said.

Logan didn't take his eyes off Declan, but he moved so that his hand brushed Gwynn's.

"Well, Logan Smith," Declan said, the smile plastered back on his face. "Welcome to my home. You've both risked much by venturing out in this storm."

"Gwynn is concerned about her father."

"Aye, as any daughter would be." Declan scratched his cheek as he walked behind his desk and sank into his chair. "Why would you think I've had any contact with your father, Miss Austin? And please, sit, both of you."

Logan would have preferred to take Gwynn's hand and drag her out of the mansion, but with his enhanced hearing, he knew men were taking up position outside the office.

He should have listened to Gwynn. They should have left. But he'd wanted to know whose magic he had felt. Now that he did, he knew their trouble had only just begun.

The click of metal told him the men in the hall had guns as well. Bigger than those held by the attackers on Eigg, if Logan had to guess.

"Well," Gwynn said, glancing at Logan.

He gave her a small nod.

"I heard from my father three weeks ago. He usually checks in pretty often. When I did a GPS search on his phone, I discovered he was in Scotland."

"So you came here," Declan said.

"Yes. I was able to get into his computer system at the university and I learned about you and the *Book of Craigan*."

Declan leaned back in his chair, seemingly enthralled with Gwynn's tale. He braced his elbows on the arms of the chair and steepled his fingers.

Logan clenched his hands into fists when Gwynn took one of the chairs in front of Declan's desk. Logan stayed behind Gwynn, his gaze never leaving Declan.

"How resourceful of you, Miss Austin," Declan said. "The book, as I'm sure you know, is written in an ancient form of Gaelic."

"One that I'm guessing my father could translate," Gwynn said.

Declan nodded. "Indeed. The book didna turn out to be what I had hoped it would be."

"Which was?" Logan probed.

Declan's blue eyes lifted to Logan. "I had hoped it would hold information about some Roman coins that had been stolen from the Ninth Legion."

He could lie, Logan would give him that.

But then again, any *drough* could lie well enough to fool almost anyone.

"I'm sorry you weren't able to find the Roman coins," Gwynn said. "Can you tell me what might have brought my father to Scotland?"

"I'm afraid I can no' tell you what I doona know."

Gwynn licked her lips and scooted to the edge of the chair. "I don't suppose you could tell me when was the last time you spoke to my father? Did he perhaps contact you when he reached Scotland?"

Declan smiled and dropped his hands to his lap. "I spoke to him last at the university when I took back my book."

"I see."

Logan hated to see the defeat in Gwynn's eyes. He couldn't exactly tell her right then that Declan was lying, but Logan would tell her as soon as they were out of this mansion.

If they got out.

"Thank you for seeing me, Mr. Wallace." Gwynn rose and hung the straps of her purse over her shoulder. "I apologize for taking up your time. We'll be going now."

Logan took that opportunity to wrap his fingers around Gwynn's arm and guide her to the door.

They'd gotten three steps away when Declan's voice stopped them.

"I'm afraid you'll be staying, Miss Austin."

Gwynn jerked out of Logan's hold and spun to face Declan. "Excuse me?"

"You heard me," Declan said as he stood. All traces of the welcoming host were gone. "There's no need for me to repeat myself."

"You can't hold me against my will."

Declan laughed, and a moment later the office doors flew open as men rushed in.

Logan counted eight men armed with guns, just as he'd thought. They were dressed all in black. Even though Logan was four centuries away from his own time, there was no mistaking the look of a mercenary.

These men were here to kill.

And Logan knew their target.

Declan came around to the front of his desk and leaned back against it casually. "As for Mr. Smith, he will be killed."

"No."

Logan didn't know who was more shocked at Gwynn's outburst—him, or Declan.

"No one tells me nay," Declan said in a menacing voice.

"I just did," Gwynn said tightly. "I don't have a problem repeating myself."

Logan smiled despite himself.

There was a surge of power from Gwynn that wrapped around Logan. It was like a cocoon, a shield that prevented Declan's black magic from touching him.

Declan threw back his head and laughed. "A Druid? I should have guessed, but your father said you had no magical tendencies."

Gwynn couldn't believe the words coming out of Declan's mouth. "There is much my father doesn't know. I take it he's here then?"

"Of course. He's working for me. He hates you, you know. When I told him you were here, he didna even look up from the book."

Gwynn didn't want the words to hurt her, but they did. She had thought she and her father had come a long way in mending their failed relationship. She didn't know what was truth and what was a lie anymore.

"Ignore him," Logan said from behind her.

Declan straightened from the desk and smiled. "What were the two of you thinking in coming here? Did you think you could just walk in and then waltz out?"

"I've never waltzed," Gwynn said.

She wasn't sure where the sarcasm was coming from, but it felt damned good.

"Americans," Declan spat. "Always so bloody sure of yourselves, aren't you? Well, no' with me. I'm the monster who will keep you awake at night."

"That was my father. I know what you are, Wallace. And your black magic doesn't frighten me."

"It should," Declan said softly.

A tremor went through Gwynn. She hadn't ever used

her magic against another Druid. She wasn't even sure that she could. Her apprehension caused her magic to falter.

"Doona allow his words to get to you," Logan whispered. "You can do this, Gwynn."

"How?" she said barely moving her lips.

"Trust your magic."

With nothing else she could do, Gwynn did as Logan urged. And to her joy, her magic once more filled her. She could battle Declan.

She *would* battle Declan.

"Take him," Declan ordered his men.

Gwynn spun to find Logan dodging and ducking the men aiming to hit him. Logan landed several punches that sent the men falling backward. And they didn't get up.

"Kill him," Declan shouted.

"No!" Gwynn yelled as the semiautomatic rifles discharged.

She winced as four bullets slammed into Logan before he dove and rolled. He came up behind one of the men and with a jerk of his hands, broke the mercenary's neck.

Logan was on his way to the next one when Declan's magic slammed into Gwynn. She tried to push back, but he was too strong.

Her boots slipped on the floor as he pushed her until she hit the wall.

"Get the X90s," ordered one of the mercenaries. "We've got a Warrior."

Gwynn glanced over to see that Logan had released his god and was using his claws to slash through the men.

"He willna be standing for long," Declan said.

And then the first X90 bullet pierced Logan.

Gwynn's stomach fell to her feet when she saw him falter, pain etched across his handsome face.

But it was Declan's laughter that sent her over the edge.

Gwynn called up every last shred of magic within her. She felt it fill her hands, waiting for her.

With a yell she released it, and watched as Declan was lifted off the floor and sailed over his desk to crash into his bookshelves.

CHAPTER TWENTY

Logan's body spasmed painfully, forcing him to drop to one knee. He didn't know how, but Declan's men had managed to put *drough* blood in the bullets.

The amount of *drough* blood in each bullet wasn't significant, but it took only one drop to bring a Warrior to the brink of death.

Logan didn't know how many bullets he had in him. As soon as the first drop of *drough* blood made contact with his body, he'd been unable to heal from the wounds made by the regular bullets.

Through the haze of pain clouding his vision, Logan saw Gwynn hurl Declan across his office. Logan wanted to smile, wanted to give a shout of joy for Gwynn.

But all of that would take away from his concentration on staying on his feet.

Declan's mercenaries who still stood were stealthily moving to surround Gwynn. Logan closed his eyes and called to water, any water that was near. To his surprise, Declan had a pool, and the water answered Logan's call instantly.

"Gwynn," Logan shouted.

She glanced at him, and he waved her to the ground. Gwynn didn't hesitate in dropping flat on her stomach. A heartbeat later the roar of water sounded as it aimed at the mercenaries and Declan, who had gained his feet once more.

"Come on," Gwynn said and put her arm around Logan.

He hadn't seen her move toward him, but none of that mattered. They had to get out of the mansion. Fast. The water wouldn't hold Declan for long.

Logan rose, and with Gwynn's help he made it to the office doors. He couldn't get his legs to move or his muscles to cooperate.

"Wait," Gwynn said as she turned.

The water Logan had called was now slowing down, but it dripped from the walls and ceiling and pooled on the floor, making it difficult for anyone to walk. He kept it contained inside the office, away from them.

Logan smiled when wind busted through the doors and windows, shattering them as it howled. It swept through the office, knocking men off their feet and into the water.

Gwynn had Declan pressed against his bookshelves as he bellowed words that couldn't penetrate the wind. The wind swirled the water, lifting it and using it as a weapon as well.

Logan wanted to use his power over the water again, but his strength was waning.

"Let's go," Gwynn said, draping his arm over her shoulders while wrapping her arm around his waist.

He didn't want to put too much weight on her, but it was either that or fall on his face. Gwynn hurried them along. Every moment counted, and Logan knew it would be a miracle if they were able to leave the mansion at all.

"Almost there," Gwynn said when they reached the front doors.

The wind had blown them open so they didn't have to

stop. The snow was coming down so heavy and thick that it had already coated the car in a deep layer.

"The steps," Logan said thinking of the ice, but he couldn't get any more words out.

He bit back a moan as his muscles continued to spasm. The more the *drough* blood leaked into his system, the faster it would kill him.

Gwynn stepped down as she asked, "What?" And her foot slipped out from underneath her.

Logan felt her push him forward as she fell back. He groaned as he landed heavily in the snow, his feet touching the last of the dozen steps leading up to the mansion.

"Go," Gwynn yelled from behind him.

Logan forced his arms to bend. He tried to rise, but his legs were no longer his to command. Inside him, his god, Athleus, was bellowing with rage—and fear.

Logan knew exactly how Athleus felt. He was supposed to be protecting Gwynn. A fine job he was doing, on his face in the snow.

But he wasn't going to give up easily. He knew Gwynn wouldn't leave without him, so he used his arms to pull himself to the car.

Inch by agonizing, brutal inch he dragged himself.

Behind him, he could hear shouts from the men in the mansion. Logan glanced over his shoulder and saw Gwynn at the bottom of the steps as she faced Declan at the top.

"You willna be leaving," Declan declared.

Logan pulled himself faster. He had to get to the car so that when Gwynn came, they could leave. His blood was on fire, scorching his bones and muscles as it moved through his body.

He didn't have much longer before the *drough* blood took him completely. Already he could feel his strength and everything inside him failing. But he wouldn't stay here and trap Gwynn. He would do whatever he could to get them away.

Logan reached the car and strained to lift his hand to open the door.

"You can go to Hell," he heard Gwynn yell as a blast of air whooshed over him.

Logan used the car door to lift himself up and into the car. He rested his head against the seat and saw the huge fountain with the top layer of frozen water.

He pushed aside his pain and called to the water. It took three attempts, but he finally urged the water to break through the ice.

Taking chunks of the ice with it.

Declan had stood against Gwynn's wind, but when it combined with the water and ice, he barely had time to lift an arm to protect his face before it barreled into him.

In a blink, Gwynn was in the car and the key in the ignition. She started the car and jerked it into reverse. Logan tried to grab the door to close it, but when they sped off down the driveway, it slammed shut on its own.

"Why aren't you healing?" Gwynn asked as she looked at him.

"*Drough* blood," he said, forcing the words past his lips. His body was convulsing, blood soaking everything.

"What?"

He tried to explain, but it was too late. The *drough* blood was draining him of his life. He couldn't even hear the bellows of his god anymore.

Logan's eyes slid closed. And then the world went black.

CHAPTER
TWENTY-ONE

Ian climbed higher and higher into the mountains. The snow had begun two days before, and it hadn't let up since. Snow filled his boots and iced his eyelashes and hair.

His lips were cracked and bleeding.

But none of this stopped the fury of his god.

All Ian knew was that he had to get away from any town. He wasn't sure when in time he was, but he knew he was in Scotland. He'd know these mountains anywhere.

And those mountains would be the only thing that kept people safe from him.

He hoped. He prayed.

Ian's stomach growled. He'd been walking for . . . he'd lost track of days, partly because he couldn't remember anything when his god took over, but also because each day had faded into the next.

But it had been weeks since he'd eaten or even slept. The weaker he became, the easier it would be for his god to take over.

If he was going to fight him, he had to do it at full strength. As much as Ian hated to admit it, he was going to have to find shelter.

His hands bled as he pulled himself up the steep mountain, but they healed all too soon. He wanted to bleed, to hurt. Anything to soothe the grief inside him at Duncan's death.

As usual, when he thought of his twin, anguish overtook him so that he couldn't breathe.

Ian fell to his knees and dropped his head into his hands. Inside, he bellowed his fury and his hatred for the god within him, and for Deirdre, who had dared to kill Duncan.

Most of all, he raged against the sack of wine that had taken him from his friends.

Ian squeezed his eyes closed and dropped his chin to his chest as he leaned back on his haunches. When he could feel his god stirring, he climbed to his feet.

His god was the father of battle. He wanted Ian to fight, blood on Ian's hands, death around him. Death. Always death. And more death.

But Ian somehow kept himself from giving in. It was becoming harder and harder, and he knew there would come a day when he didn't fight his god anymore. He hoped when that day came, one of his brethren from MacLeod Castle would be there to take his head before he could kill innocents.

More hope. More prayers.

Ian walked for hours before he looked up and spotted the opening of a cave. He climbed to it and found that once he got past the narrow entrance, it opened to a huge cavern.

There was no time to build a fire because his god had been denied too long. He wanted control. And Ian was too weak to fight him.

Ian roared and slashed his claws against the side of the cave as he fought—and lost—the struggle with his god.

* * *

Gwynn drove recklessly as she sped down icy roads. It had taken her all of two seconds to realize the only ones who could help Logan were at MacLeod Castle.

A castle that, as far as she knew, didn't exist.

But Logan said it did.

So she drove, glancing at Logan every so often as she did. He was pale, the life seeming to drain from him right before her eyes.

His breathing was ragged. And the blood, it continued to seep from his wounds until the smell of it filled the car.

Gwynn cracked the window and blinked through the tears that gathered in her eyes. "How could I have been so stupid?" she asked herself. "I should have known Dad was working with Declan."

It was just like her father to think only of himself. Logan had told her not to believe Declan's words, but she had no choice. Especially since she'd heard her father say the same hateful things before. He hadn't known she was listening when he shouted them at her mother, but Gwynn had never forgotten.

She let out a yelp of surprise when the car skidded across an icy patch of road, making them slide sideways. The car fishtailed into the oncoming lane where a car was heading right for them.

Gwynn held her breath and took her foot off the accelerator until she could move the car back into her lane. "I hate winter," she muttered. "Why couldn't it be summer? I can drive like the wind during a rainstorm, but give me snow and I'm an idiot."

She kept talking, hoping Logan would hear her and maybe wake up.

Towns flew by in a blur. Mountainside scenes she knew she'd love to stop and look at didn't even make her glance out the window. She had one concern—Logan.

Thankfully, the weather cooperated. A little. The snow had subsided to nothing but flurries. With the heater going full blast to help keep feeling in her fingers, Gwynn never let up on the gas pedal.

"How do I find MacLeod Castle?" she asked Logan. "Logan? Please. Tell me. How do I find the castle?"

Her only response was the rocking of his head as she took a corner on the road that would make a drifter proud.

"Damn," she said. "What if I go to the wrong place? What if I miss it?"

She knew Logan didn't have long before he was gone for good. It had never entered her mind that *drough* blood could take out a Warrior more effectively than anything else.

If she'd known, they would have left as soon as Logan had told her he sensed *drough* magic. She would have made him leave.

Gwynn wiped at her face where a tear had fallen. "Don't you dare die on me, Logan Hamilton. You vowed to protect me. You can't do that as a ghost. Logan! Do you hear me?"

She hit the steering wheel with the heel of her hand. Gwynn hated feeling so helpless. It was made worse because Logan was counting on her to get him help. And she was useless.

Then she had an idea.

Gwynn rolled down the window until the icy wind filled the car. "I need your help," she said, praying her magic worked while she drove. She couldn't take the time to pull over and ask the wind for assistance.

"Please. Where is MacLeod Castle?"

She waited, and waited, but the wind didn't answer.

"Of course not," she muttered.

Gwynn looked at Logan. His lips had begun to turn

blue. Terror wrapped its cold fingers around her and squeezed. The tears she'd held at bay blurred her vision, but she refused to shed them.

When she came to a dead end where she had to turn right or left, she let instinct guide her as Logan had told her to do and turned right. At every turn, every curve, every road she trusted her instinct, hoping beyond hope that it would lead her to MacLeod Castle.

She saw the sea on her left as she drove, the road taking her closer and closer to the cliffs that rose high above the water.

"Please, God, let me be in the right place," she murmured.

She slowed as she turned left off the paved road onto dirt. Gwynn could barely make out a road before her, but she was sure it was one. Every fiber of her being told her to drive down it.

When there was nothing ahead of her but land before the cliffs dropped into the sea, Gwynn stopped the car. She was about to turn around when she felt her magic move within her.

Gwynn turned off the car and got out. She could feel magic around her. Wonderful, beautiful bright magic. Hadn't Logan said there was a shield of some kind around MacLeod Castle?

"Help," she yelled. "I'm with Logan! He's dying! Please, help me . . ." she trailed off as the tears she'd held back finally fell.

There was a flap of wings behind her. Gwynn whirled around to find an indigo Warrior with huge, leathery wings staring at her.

"Logan," she said and pointed into the car. "He was shot with *drough* blood."

"Shite," the Warrior murmured before he yelled, "Fallon!"

In an instant, a black-skinned Warrior stood beside them. "Logan?" he said as he ducked his head inside the car.

"*Drough* blood," the indigo Warrior said.

Fallon nodded as he pulled Logan from the car and draped him over his shoulder. Fallon's black Warrior eyes landed on Gwynn. "Bring her."

"I'll take the car," said another black Warrior with two small braids at either side of his temples.

Gwynn didn't have time to utter a sound as the indigo Warrior scooped her up in his arms and jumped into the air. She clung to him as they rose, his huge wings carrying them through the magic shield she had sensed.

And then she saw the castle. It rose from the cliffs majestically, magically. Its gray stones had been weathered by time until the color was only slightly lighter than those of the cliffs that flanked it on either side.

Gwynn barely had time to look at the castle with its four massive round towers before she was set on her feet in the bailey.

The indigo Warrior took her hand and led her up the stairs and into the castle.

Gwynn saw several women and men rushing up the stairs, most likely to tend to Logan. Thankfully, the quiet indigo Warrior finally released her from his ironclad hold.

She wasn't sure if she would be allowed to follow the others to see Logan. And then suddenly, she didn't think she could as her strength began to wane.

Gwynn gripped the edge of the long table that sat in the middle of the great hall. She smiled as she saw the tapestries that had been mended and hung on the walls. Those tapestries were worth a fortune, but she couldn't imagine them looking as grand anywhere else.

She turned her head and spotted the huge fireplace off

to her right. The fire beckoned as all warmth left her. She was so cold her teeth were chattering. Gwynn would have gladly curled up in the fire if she could.

It was most likely the events at Declan's mansion, the use of her power, and her fear that were making her so cold. She'd been running on an adrenaline rush that was wearing off. Yet this feeling was unlike anything she had ever experienced.

Gwynn had taken only a couple of halting steps toward the fire when the room began to spin and pain slammed into her body. She closed her eyes, but it only made the room spin faster.

She pried open her eyes and tried to focus on the chairs before the fire. If she could only reach them, she'd be able to sit and figure out why she was hurting so. That was all she needed, just to sit down.

Gwynn took another step, and then another. Each time, she felt as if her body were freezing where she stood. She listed to the side as the dizziness grew.

And then she was falling.

Gwynn reached out to grab hold of something, anything, but only air met her fingers.

CHAPTER
TWENTY-TWO

Lucan walked into the castle and tossed the keys to the red car he'd just driven into the bailey in the air. As the keys landed in his palm, he hurried to the stairs.

He had just stepped on the first stair when he turned his head and found the woman who had brought Logan to the castle, lying on the floor.

Lucan threw the keys onto the table and rushed to her. He touched her skin to find it cool and clammy. The blood spreading on the floor wasn't a good sign.

"Cara!" he shouted.

In an instant, his wife was running down the stairs. "What happened?"

"I found her like this."

Cara ran to his side and knelt beside the woman. "There's so much blood."

"I thought it was Logan's because he was bleeding so badly, but with all this blood, I'd say she's wounded, too."

"I need her jacket and sweater removed."

Lucan didn't hesitate to lengthen a black claw and cut through the thick coat, the sweater, and the shirt beneath until only the woman's bra remained.

Cara tilted her head to the side. "She's been shot in the arm."

"It looks to have gone straight through."

"And into her side," Cara said as she rose to her feet. "Bring her, Lucan. We need to get her healed immediately."

Lucan gathered the woman in his arms and followed his wife up the stairs. "She's a Druid."

"Then we really need to save her." Cara pushed open a door to one of the chambers. "I'll get Sonya. Keep pressure on the wounds to slow the bleeding."

Cara pushed up the sleeves to her sweater and ran down the hall to Logan's chamber. She threw open the door to find everyone around the bed.

"Do something," Hayden demanded of Sonya. "He's dying."

"There's so much *drough* blood inside him," Sonya said as she held her hands over Logan's still body.

Cara lifted her gaze from the bed where Logan lay on his side and met the eyes of her brothers-in-law, Fallon and Quinn. "The woman who came with Logan—"

"The Druid?" Fallon asked.

"Aye. She's injured. Badly. The bullet went through her arm and into her side."

Sonya shook her head from the side of Logan's bed. "I cannot be in two places at once."

Broc, Sonya's husband, touched her arm. "I survived with *drough* blood inside me."

"But Deirdre prevented it from affecting you fully."

"Can none of the Druids here do that?"

Sonya frowned. "It will only respond to black magic."

Isla stepped forward. "Then let me try."

"Someone do something." Fallon ran a hand down his face, his frustration showing in the way his lips flattened.

Cara shifted feet. She had learned much about magic

in the four hundred years she had been a Druid. Yet, no one could heal by magic except Sonya.

"I'm holding the *drough* blood at bay," Isla said as she held her hands over Logan's body. "I don't know how long I can, though."

Logan stirred, his groan of pain echoing around the chamber. He opened his eyes and winced when he tried to turn over.

"Nay," Hayden said and put his big hand on Logan's shoulder. "You need to be still."

"Gwynn?" Logan said.

Cara stepped closer to the bed. "She's been injured."

Logan dragged in a ragged breath and clenched his jaw. "Save her," he demanded to the room at large.

"You have too much *drough* blood in you," Quinn began.

"Save her," Logan said more forcefully, which caused him to groan in pain.

Fallon looked at Isla. "Can you hold back the *drough* blood as Deirdre did for Broc?"

"I'm doing it now, but it's been in his system for so long that it's fighting against me."

Fallon nodded. "Sonya, see to Gwynn. We'll keep Logan alive until you return."

Cara let out a breath as she and Sonya raced to the other chamber.

"How bad is Gwynn's wound?" Sonya asked.

Cara shrugged. "She's lost a lot of blood. The bullet is still inside her."

Sonya walked with sure steps to the bed where Lucan was holding towels over Gwynn's wounds. "Let me see," Sonya urged.

Lucan rose and moved away while Cara took her position on the other side of the bed. When Sonya had to heal multiple people, it helped if someone added their magic to hers.

Sonya passed her hand over Gwynn's body and frowned. "The bullet is lodged in her ribs."

"Can you remove it?" Lucan asked.

"I think so."

Cara licked her lips and rubbed her hands together to warm them before she held them palm down over Gwynn's body. Cara closed her eyes and felt her magic move swift and sure to her hands before she released it to mix with Sonya's.

Lucan never got tired of seeing the magic of the Druids at work. He would rather the woman not be injured, but he was confident Sonya could save her. It was Logan he was worried about.

In a matter of moments, the bullet wounds on Gwynn's arm began to close until there was only pink skin showing. It took Sonya longer to dislodge the bullet from the woman's ribs, but with a clink, it fell from the wound onto the floor.

"Finally," Sonya whispered.

That's when Lucan noted the sweat beading the healer's brow. "Is she mended?"

"Nearly."

Lucan let out a sigh several moments later, when Sonya and Cara dropped their arms.

"Gwynn is healed," Sonya announced. "But it will take some time for her body to restore the blood she lost."

Cara covered Gwynn with a blanket, then set about removing her boots. "I'll see to her. Go to Logan."

Lucan held back until Cara smiled at him. "You, too, husband. I know you're worried about Logan."

Lucan winked at her. "Shout if you need me."

"I always need you."

He smiled before he pivoted and strode to Logan's

chamber. Once inside, he walked to his brothers. "Gwynn is healed."

"That's good," Fallon murmured. "I'd tell Logan, but he lost consciousness a few minutes ago."

Lucan crossed his arms over his chest and studied Logan's pale form. "So he was worried about her?"

"You could say that," Quinn said with a snort. "Demanded we heal her before him."

"I've waited four hundred years for the Warriors to return. I never imagined one might show up near death," Fallon said.

Lucan put his hand on his brother's shoulder. "Logan is a fighter. He'll survive."

"By all that's holy," Reaghan exclaimed as she held something small in her hand.

Galen peered over his wife's shoulder. "What is that?"

"A bullet," Sonya answered. "A bullet that was filled with *drough* blood."

"Holy Hell," Quinn muttered.

There was no more talking as Logan let out a silent breath. And his chest didn't rise again.

Without a word, the Druids gathered around the bed and combined their magic with Sonya's. Tense minutes filled with concern and unease passed until finally Logan took a deep breath.

"It's not over," Sonya said before anyone could celebrate. "He's lost too much blood."

Hayden held his arm over Logan's body. "He can have mine."

"And mine," Broc said.

"He can have everyone's blood," Lucan added. "Whatever it takes."

Sonya nodded. "Hayden, you first. Cut deep so the blood flows thick. Hold it over the wound."

"Which one?" Hayden asked. "His back is full of them."

"Pick one," Cara said.

Sonya held her breath as her magic coursed through her and into Logan. Logan's body had begun to shut down as the *drough* blood killed everything within. She wasn't sure if she could save him. He'd had the *drough* blood in him too long. But she wasn't going to give up. Not yet.

"Hurry," she urged as Hayden cut himself for a second time. "The Warrior blood is helping, but not fast enough."

Sonya wasn't surprised when Broc stepped beside Hayden and cut his arm so his blood flowed into another wound.

Soon, each Warrior had taken responsibility for one of Logan's wounds. Sonya blinked away the threat of tears as she saw how the Warriors banded together.

"Almost," she said when she could feel Logan's body begin to work on its own.

Ten minutes later, Sonya not only felt, but saw, his wounds beginning to heal.

"That's enough," she told the Warriors.

She dropped her hands and the other Druids did the same. Sonya was drained, both physically and magically, but she smiled for the first time since Fallon had arrived with Logan's body over his shoulder.

"Good," Broc said as he wrapped an arm around her. "Now someone tell me how the bloody Hell there are bullets with *drough* blood inside them?"

Galen shrugged. "Deirdre?"

"Nay," Lucan said. "I doona think she's here in this time yet."

"Then who?" Fallon asked.

Larena said, "Maybe the person who pulled Deirdre and Ian to this time."

No one groaned out loud, but it was written on their faces.

Sonya took one of the poisoned bullets and wiped off

the blood. "For Logan's attackers to have *drough* blood, they have to have a *drough*."

Hayden shrugged. "Exactly. What's your point?"

She looked at each person in the chamber. "We've all watched as the Druids disappeared, mostly because of Deirdre, but also because they no longer practiced. Whoever did this is not only a *drough*, but is intelligent enough to create something like this."

"You're assuming this *drough* thought up these bullets," Broc said. "It could be someone else."

"Nay, Sonya's right," Quinn said. "Why would someone else no' a Druid create these bullets? How would they know how the *drough* blood would react to us?"

Marcail sighed and spoke for the first time. "Because, my love, they must know of your existence. Not just from stories. They know you're here."

"We're speculating," Reaghan said. "As soon as Logan and Gwynn wake we will learn the details."

"That's my woman," Galen said as he pulled her tight against him. "She's always thinking ahead."

Reaghan rolled her eyes, but she smiled when he kissed her.

Sonya looked at Logan and noticed he wasn't wearing a kilt. "We need to get these clothes off Logan."

Blood was everywhere, even in his boots. Everything was tossed to the side and would be burned later. Isla covered Logan with a blanket while Hayden pulled one of the chairs to the bed and sank into it.

"Until we know what we're dealing with, we need to set up patrols," Fallon said.

Quinn nodded. "I'll take the cliffs."

"I'll keep to the skies," Broc said.

Galen said, "I'll be in the village."

When Fallon looked at Hayden, he raised a blond brow. "I'll be here."

"We can handle the rest," Lucan said to Fallon. "Leave Hayden."

Larena cleared her throat and jabbed Fallon in the ribs. "Are you forgetting me?"

"Never," he said and took her hand. "You'll be with me. Lucan, keep your lookout atop one of the towers."

Hayden watched them leave. Isla ran her hand through his hair before she kissed his forehead. "I'll be back later to see if you need anything."

He nodded and leaned forward in the chair. A moment later, Isla followed the rest of the group out of the chamber.

Only then did Hayden say to Logan, "Wake up, damn you. Wake up and tell me the name of the bastard who did this to you and Gwynn so we can kill them."

CHAPTER
TWENTY-THREE

Declan glared at the shambles that had once been his office. His haven.

Despite his black magic, despite the mercenaries he had hired, and despite the X90s, both Logan and Gwynn had gotten away. Though Declan didn't expect Logan to live long.

No Warrior could withstand a drop of *drough* blood inside them much less the amount contained in the special bullets that had hit Logan.

Despite that, Logan had managed to stay on his feet. Mostly. Declan wanted to know what made the Warrior so different from the others.

"No' that it matters. Logan is dead," Declan mumbled to himself.

That was the only consolation on a day that had turned into hell. However, he would soon have Gwynn under his roof once more. The Druid was too valuable as a tool against Gary.

Also, Gwynn had magic. It might be the inferior *mie* variety, but it was magic.

A grin pulled one side of his lips. He would use Gwynn

to find the Tablet of Orn and warm his bed. Once she became useless, he would kill her and take her magic.

Declan clasped his hands behind his back and inhaled as he heard Robbie approaching. "How many men did you lose?"

"Half."

Declan turned his head toward Robbie. "You're losing men faster than you're replacing them."

"There are always more men, Declan."

Declan shrugged. "True enough. The X90s worked well."

"No' well enough. The bloke wouldna stay down."

"Forget Logan. He's dead by now. The only people who could help Logan are Deirdre and me. I'm no' about to, and since Deirdre has no idea what's going on, she willna be helping him."

Robbie laughed. "You are a cruel git, Declan."

"You have no idea." He waved at his office. "I want this cleaned up immediately," he said and walked from the room.

There was someone he needed to see, someone who would pay for not warning him that a Warrior would enter his home.

December 21st

Logan took in a deep breath and slowly let it out. His body was sore, but it was no longer on fire as it had been.

"It's about damn time you woke."

Logan smiled as he heard Hayden's deep voice. Logan turned his head to find his closest friend sitting beside the bed. Hayden hadn't changed much, except his hair was a little shorter—though still long by most standards.

"You know how I like to keep you waiting."

"No' funny," Hayden said, his expression serious.

"I know. How long have I been unconscious?"

Hayden shrugged and sat back in his chair. "Five hours."

Logan sighed and used his arms to lift himself and scoot backward so he leaned against the headboard. "I take it my wounds were as bad as they felt."

"Worse. You were all but dead when we brought you into the castle."

"How did you find me?"

Hayden's brow creased. "We didna. Gwynn found us."

"That's impossible. I never told her where the castle was."

"Well, she drove up to the shield and began yelling. Broc flew to her first, and once he saw you, he called for Fallon."

Logan ran a hand through his hair, feeling the pull of healing in the muscles in his back and sides. A niggling worry kept intruding on his thoughts, a worry that told him it was important. "Where is Gwynn?"

"She's resting. Sonya healed her."

"So she was injured? I didna dream that?"

"Nay," Hayden said with a shake of his blond head. "The bullet went through her arm and into her side, then lodged in her ribs. Sonya was able to get the bullet out and heal her."

Logan rested his head back against the bed and stared at the ceiling. "Is she awake?"

"No' that I know of. I've been waiting for you."

That was all Logan needed to hear. He threw back the covers, then swore when he saw his nakedness. "I need clothes."

"You need a bath."

"I want to see Gwynn."

"After your bath," Hayden insisted as he stood to block Logan's path. "There's blood all over you still."

"Fine."

Hayden grinned. "You'll find the shower through there."

Logan looked to where Hayden was pointing. "Shower?"

"Doona tell me you doona know what that is."

"I do. I just didna expect to find one in the castle."

"What do you think we did for four centuries? We kept up with the changes of the world."

There was so much catching up Logan needed to do with the others, but first he wanted to see Gwynn for himself. Hayden was right, however. A bath was in order.

"Your clothes are in the chest. We found them in Gwynn's car, though you'll have to borrow a pair of my boots since yours were ruined."

Logan shrugged and opened the door to the bathroom. There was a shower, larger than the one at the hotel, a sink, and a toilet. There was little room to spare. But it was better than having to bath in the sea.

He turned on the shower and found towels on a shelf above the toilet. Logan bathed in record time. Even though he knew Sonya had healed Gwynn, he couldn't stop himself from worrying.

Using the towel to rub the water from his head, Logan walked into his chamber and opened the chest. He pulled a pair of black jeans and a cream long-sleeved shirt from the pile.

He was buttoning his pants when Hayden knocked and opened the door. "I called the others, since we all have questions."

"They can wait until after I see Gwynn," Logan said. He jerked his arms through the sleeves of the shirt, then pulled it over his head.

Logan didn't need to ask Hayden where Gwynn was. He simply followed the feel of her magic to a chamber six doors down and across the hall.

The door was open and when he looked in, Gwynn was still asleep.

"She may sleep for awhile," Sonya said as she rose from her vigil by the bed.

Logan nodded at her, amazed to find her long, curly red hair cut to just below her ears in a riot of curls. Yet it seemed to fit her. "Thank you for saving her. And me."

Sonya rested her hand on his arm. "How do you feel?"

"Slow," he said noting it wasn't only her hair that had changed. Sonya now wore the same type of clothes Gwynn did, and it was odd to see Sonya in anything but the gowns he remembered. "No' as strong as I usually am."

"That's the effects of the *drough* blood. You should recover fully by tomorrow."

Logan looked at Gwynn again, her black hair spread against the white of the pillow. "I'm no' worried about me. Hayden said the bullet went into her ribs."

"Aye. It cracked one rib. Everything is mended now, but as I said, she lost a lot of blood. It sometimes takes the body a while to replenish itself."

The steady rise and fall of Gwynn's chest helped to ease the concern that had banded around Logan's chest.

He wanted to dismiss his worry to forget it. But he couldn't. When it came to Gwynn, everything was different. He couldn't forget her as he had the other women in his past.

And he found he didn't want to.

Which scared the hell out of him.

The underwater kiss they had shared at Eigg had affirmed what he'd suspected since first seeing her. Gwynn's taste, her touch, burned him. Made him hunger . . . made him yearn for more.

"Logan?" Hayden said. "What is it?"

"Nothing. Everything. To me, it feels like I saw you just a few days ago."

"Ah. But for me, it's been almost four hundred years."

Logan glanced at his friend and smiled. "You've changed."

"Aye. As have you."

"Me?" Logan repeated with a shake of his head. "I doona think so."

The fact that Hayden merely smiled only rankled Logan. He hadn't changed. How could he? It had only been a few days for him.

Logan forgot about Hayden and their conversation as Gwynn stirred. She stretched her arms over her head and opened her eyes.

She stared at the gray stone for a few moments before her eyes shifted and she met Logan's gaze. The slow smile that formed made him smile in return.

"Hey," she said.

Logan walked to her side and used her term. "Hey."

Her smiled died as she began to frown. "I thought you had died."

"Nay. You saved me by bringing me here. You should have told me you were injured."

She shrugged. "I didn't know. I never felt anything."

Hayden cleared his throat, reminding Logan that he and Gwynn weren't alone. Logan turned to introduce Hayden to Gwynn, then realized everyone stood in the chamber.

"Oh," Gwynn said and burrowed under the sheets.

Sonya shooed everyone out with her hands. "Interrogations can wait. Let's give Gwynn time to change clothes and get settled."

With a smile and a wink, Sonya closed the door behind her, leaving Logan alone with Gwynn.

He turned to her and fought the desire to take her in his arms. He'd put her in danger. He'd sworn to protect her, yet it had been she who had protected him, even with a bullet in her.

"You're amazing."

She chuckled softly and sat up, keeping the sheet tucked under her arms. "Hardly. I was scared out of my mind, Logan. I had no idea what I was doing."

"Obviously you did. You found your way here."

"Which I can't begin to explain," she said and tucked a strand of hair behind her ears.

Logan sat on the bed at her feet. Though she was covered, the sight of her pink bra straps made his balls tighten. He wanted another taste of her. A long, leisurely taste.

"With magic, I've learned one cannot explain it," he said.

Gwynn glanced at her hands as they played with the blanket. "I thought we'd get all the answers from Declan. I thought he would be able to lead me to my father."

"Declan did lead you to your father."

She laughed dryly. "That's right. He did. My father is working with him."

"Or so Declan says. I wouldna believe everything you heard him say."

"But I do believe my father is working with him. The things Declan said my father said about me? My father has called me those things before. I know they were the truth."

Logan ached for her, for the hurt he saw in her lovely violet eyes. "I'm sorry, Gwynn."

"I should have known," she said. "I should have realized everything my father has said to me since my mother died was a lie. But I had hoped . . ."

"Hope is a powerful thing. Doona underestimate it."

She had the look of a woman who'd had her world crushed. A second time. "I no longer have any hope, Logan."

"There's always hope."

"How can you say that?"

He debated whether to tell her about his past and the guilt he carried, but decided against it. "Look around you. Look at this castle. Feel the magic within it? That is from Druids who escaped Deirdre. Do you feel the power? That is from Warriors who will sacrifice their lives in order to kill Deirdre. Everything you see around you is based on hope. It lives here, breathes here."

"I do see it," she whispered. "I see it in you."

Logan looked down to find her hand near his. He covered it with his own. "Doona give up hope, Gwynn, because if you do, then Deirdre and Declan have won."

"I refuse to allow that."

He smiled and squeezed her hand, glad to see the vulnerability fading from her eyes. "Are you ready to face the others?"

"After a shower. And with some clothes."

"I'm thinking you look fine without your clothes."

She smiled as her gaze lowered to the blanket. "Your charms won't work on me."

"Are you sure?"

CHAPTER
TWENTY-FOUR

There were a few things Gwynn was sure of. That her life had radically changed.

That she was a Druid.

And that Logan's smile made her want to kiss him.

"No, I'm not sure," she answered.

Her heart was pounding slow and hard in her chest. She wanted to be in Logan's arms again. She wanted to feel his lips on hers.

It was foolish, she knew. Logan was a heartache waiting to happen. Yet she couldn't seem to help herself. She wanted him.

Desperately.

Madly.

Intensely.

Despite the threat to her heart, or maybe because of it, Gwynn tucked her legs beneath her and rose up on her knees. Logan's hazel eyes darkened until the gold flecks seemed to glow with his intensity.

He ran the backs of his fingers down her cheek and moved closer to her.

Gwynn edged forward until their bodies were just

inches apart. She didn't understand the pull Logan seemed to have over her. Nor did she understand the depth of the attraction she felt for him.

It was deeper, stronger than anything she'd felt before. And it was glorious. As well as more than a little scary.

For several minutes they simply stared at each other. Then Logan dragged her into his arms and slanted his mouth over hers. It was a kiss meant to claim, a kiss meant to brand her.

And she welcomed it.

Gloried in it.

Eagerly answered it with her own.

Gwynn's fingers plunged into Logan's still wet hair and clung to him, accepting the temptation offered in his hot, demanding kiss. She didn't hold back as he deepened the kiss.

She felt his hunger, felt his focus on her. Gwynn had no choice but to succumb. To yield. To surrender to the onslaught of Logan's devastating kisses.

The desire, the unrelenting thud of passion, pounded through her veins until she shook with it.

She returned his kiss with as much hunger and abandon as he had given her. She left behind the restraint that usually bound her. His kisses were too hot, too wondrous, for her to be anything other than eager and as wanton as he.

As if Logan sensed her unleashed passion, he urged her onward, enticed her to see where this unrelenting desire would take them.

"They are waiting for us," Logan said between kisses.

Gwynn didn't care if the queen herself were downstairs. Nothing mattered but Logan and the unbending passion that gripped her.

She dragged his mouth back to hers. His groan of pleasure made her blood turn to liquid heat.

A gasp of surprise tore from her as Logan's arms tightened around her a moment before he rose from the bed with her in his arms.

Logan moaned at the feel of Gwynn's lean legs around his waist. Even through his jeans and her thin, bright pink panties he could feel the heat of her.

They had no time for kisses, no time for the mounting desire that had built before their first kiss, and most especially afterward.

She had tried to deny it. He had tried to forget it.

But it wouldn't loosen its hold on either of them.

Logan cupped Gwynn's bottom in his hands and rubbed her against his aching cock. He wanted to plunge inside her and hear her scream in pleasure as he filled her again and again. He couldn't remember ever wanting someone as desperately, as urgently as he did Gwynn.

He carried Gwynn to what he suspected was the bathroom door as he continued to glory in the exquisite taste of her kisses.

There was a fire within Gwynn, an inferno whose flames he had fanned and brought to life. It was a blaze he never wanted to go out.

Logan stopped beside the shower and let Gwynn's legs slide to the floor. He longed to look his fill at her entire body, to commit every inch of it to memory. But there wasn't time. Not now. If he didn't get Gwynn downstairs soon, someone would come for them.

He turned on the water and eased back from their frantic kisses. Their harsh breathing was drowned out by the sound of the water.

"You aren't going to finish this, are you?" Gwynn asked.

"I'd like nothing better."

Gwynn reached behind her and unclasped her bra. It fell off her shoulders to the ground. Then she reached down and slowly, seductively stepped out of her panties.

She moved into the shower and turned to look at him. "Then what are you waiting for?"

Logan's mouth went dry as he watched the steam rise above her while the water sliced over her body, from her narrow shoulders to the decadent swell of her pink-tipped breasts and into the valley between them. Rivulets ran down the indent of her waist to her flared hips, into the black curls between her legs, and down those shapely legs to the shower floor.

Logan forgot to breathe as he lifted his gaze and saw Gwynn lean her head back into the water to wet her hair. He followed her hands as she smoothed her hair back from her forehead.

Then she opened her eyes and smiled at him.

Logan had never gotten out of his clothes so fast. In the next breath he was in the shower with Gwynn, the hot water falling over both of them.

There were no words as their mouths found each other again and again, the desire scorching them, consuming them with its potency. Logan hauled her into his arms and sighed as he found her. Skin to skin.

Body to body.

He angled his head and kissed her deeply, fully. Ruthlessly. And she met him stroke for stroke, caress for caress. Eager, needy. Hungry.

Desperation for more of her pushed Logan until he was merciless in his desire to have her as starved for him as he was for her. For everything that was her.

Their kiss was ravenous, their breaths harsh as their hearts pounded. And Logan had to have more. Of her. Of the unquenchable, voracious passion that had taken them.

He reached between them and claimed her breast. His thumb stroked over her nipple with a knowing caress. Gwynn's sudden intake of breath made him smile inwardly. By the time he was done with her, she would be screaming. For him.

Her fingers tightened on his shoulders when he squeezed the turgid peak. Logan turned so that the water sprayed down his back while her breast filled his hand perfectly.

Gwynn's head tilted back, soft moans filling the bathroom as he continued his assault, learning what pleased her, what made her rub her hips against his. What made her dig her nails into his skin.

Logan bent his head, took her nipple in his mouth, and suckled.

Gwynn cried out and arched against him. She didn't think her body could get any hotter. And then Logan's mouth fastened onto her breast. Blind need, fiery and irresistible, took her, pulled her. Drew her into the inferno of desire.

It never entered her mind to pull back. Never had she felt so desperately needy, never so full of yearning as she was now. Her breasts swelled and ached as Logan's skilled hands and tongue learned her. Seduced her.

Devoured her.

She ran her hands over his shoulders and back to feel the steely sinew move beneath her hands. Gwynn couldn't stop touching him. She was greedy as her hands moved over the muscled expanse of his chest that tapered to his trim waist and hips.

Everywhere she touched was hot and hard. Power and strength.

His mouth found hers once more for a kiss urgent and commanding. They were skin to naked skin, limb to limb. And nothing had ever felt so right.

A sigh escaped her as their hands caressed, sculpted each other as they discovered the other. He seized, she yielded. She captured, he surrendered.

Gwynn moaned when his fingers stroked between her thighs. She burned, scalded by the sheer force of Logan's desire. And her own need.

She rocked her hips against his hand as his fingers continued their assault while his mouth trailed kisses down her throat and between her breasts. He nipped at her navel and licked her stomach.

And then suddenly he was kneeling, the water pounding onto his back and spraying her. She looked down at him and watched as he parted her thighs and set his mouth to her curls, to the source of her need.

A breathless gasp escaped as he tongued her softness. She tangled her fingers into his thick, wet hair as he continued to lick her sex.

He was ruthless in his thoroughness, merciless in his attention to her. It was as if he knew exactly where to touch, exactly how to touch in order to give her the most pleasure.

Gwynn's knees threatened to buckle as the passion built until she didn't know if she could stay in her own skin. Logan's large hands held her thighs spread wide while his tongue flicked back and forth rapidly, then slowly and leisurely, over her clitoris.

Her climax was building with each lave of his tongue. Gwynn reached for it, eager to find the exquisite bliss she knew Logan would bring her.

As if sensing she was about to peak, Logan rose in one fluid motion. He lifted her in his arms, his hazel eyes burning bright. He backed her against the wall of the shower, his hard arousal pressed into her stomach.

He nudged her thighs apart with his knee. Once more, she wrapped her legs around his waist and sucked in a breath at the feel of him against her core.

"Gwynn," he said on a moan. "This is what I've wanted."

It was what she had wanted, too. She should have known

that a passion burning this hot couldn't be denied. It might burn out fast, but it would be a wild, astonishing ride.

Flames of desire licked her skin until she was sensitive to every touch, every caress.

Logan suckled her nipple and she cried out, clutching him. The pleasure was so intense it hurt.

He lifted her hips until the broad head of his cock rubbed against her sex. Gwynn dug her fingernails in his shoulders as a shudder of bliss ran through her as he grazed her swollen sex.

And then with one powerful thrust he joined them.

Gwynn's breath caught, locking in her throat as her body wept with joy to finally be joined with Logan's. She tilted her hips as he pushed deeper.

He held her hips as he filled her, stretched her.

Logan had never known such exquisite pleasure before. Had never felt a body as tight as Gwynn's. He dug his fingers into her bottom as he lifted her even closer, drawing himself out of the liquid heat of her sex.

Only to push into her again.

He smiled as she moaned, her lips parted and her eyes closed. He'd never seen anyone so beautiful, never felt such a driving need to claim a woman as his.

But it was exactly what he wanted to do.

He wanted Gwynn. Wanted everyone to know she was his. To lay claim to her so no one, least of all Deirdre or Declan, would dare try and take her away.

Logan angled his hips as he continued to fill Gwynn. He was relentless, heartless in his need to hear her scream with desire.

Her moans turned to soft cries as he pounded into her again and again, harder, deeper. She clung to him, the water from the shower flowing between them and adding to the friction between their bodies.

He could feel his climax nearing. Logan looked down

at their joined bodies to see his cock sunk in her sheath. When he glanced up he saw Gwynn's violet eyes open and watching him.

Logan pulled out of her heat until he was nearly free before thrusting deep again, harder and more powerful than before.

She cried out. And that was just what he needed to hear.

Logan repeated the movement until her breaths came in panting gasps. He felt her body tighten, knew she was close to peaking.

He set up a driving rhythm. Watched as her back bowed, felt her nails break his skin.

And then she screamed his name as she came apart.

Logan barely heard her. The first clamp of her body around his cock sent him over the edge as release swept him. He held her tight against him, as sensations too wonderful and intense to name exploded through him.

Pleasure held them, bound them.

Gwynn opened her eyes to find Logan gazing at her. His heart thundered in time with hers, the heat of their bodies still throbbing where they were joined. Small tremors from the amazing climax still wracked her body.

She'd never known such pleasure and contentment could exist. It wasn't just her body Logan had taken. It was her will to hold him at bay.

CHAPTER
TWENTY-FIVE

Gwynn pushed Logan's wet hair from his eyes as he pulled out of her and lowered her to the ground.

He wrapped an arm around her and held her against his chest. He kissed her slowly, thoroughly, before pulling back. "We need to hurry."

"Give me five minutes."

He nodded and stepped out of the shower. She hurried to wash and rinse her hair as she watched him dry his tall, muscled body.

Gwynn sighed as she recalled the feel of his thick erection inside her.

"What are you smiling about?" Logan asked.

She giggled as she washed herself, mindful of her still sensitive body. "I'm recalling the few moments we just spent."

"It went too quickly. I want an entire night with you."

Gwynn shivered despite the hot water. An entire night? Her knees went weak just thinking about it.

She turned off the water and reached for the towel Logan held out to her. His smile was gone, replaced with a frown. "How much do you think the others know about Declan?" she asked.

"Probably nothing. Deirdre is a formidable opponent. The fact that we now have a second *drough* to fight will make things even more difficult for us. They brought your bag up."

She didn't comment on his change of topic. He was worried, and he had every right to be. By all accounts, both of them should be dead.

Gwynn pulled on a pair of white panties with thin lavender stripes and a matching bra. She got out a pair of light blue jeans, her favorite black V-neck sweater, and her black boots. She quickly combed through her hair and smoothed her hand down her front.

"Okay. I think I'm ready."

Logan smiled and held out his hand for her. Gwynn took it, comforted by his warm, secure hold. The clicking of her boots against the stone floor echoed down the hallways.

With each step, her nerves grew more frazzled. And when they reached the top of the stairs and she looked into the great hall to see everyone sitting at the table, her mouth went dry.

"They are good people," Logan whispered. "You need no' be afraid."

"I'm not the kind of woman who has a lot of friends. I keep to myself."

He squeezed her hand. "I've no' lied to you before. They willna hurt you."

She realized he was right. Yet it wasn't so much meeting new people that made her nervous. These were Logan's friends, his family. What if they didn't want her here? What if they thought her magic wasn't good enough?

Gwynn didn't state any of her fears. She allowed Logan

to think everything was all right as they walked down the steps, his hand at the small of her back.

He had released her hand, a fact that didn't go unnoticed by her. Maybe he didn't want the others to know what had transpired between them.

"We were about to come get you two," said a woman with long, curly chestnut hair and kind mahogany eyes.

Logan chuckled and guided Gwynn to a spot at the table. He waited for her to sit, then took the spot next to her. "Lest you forget, Cara, Gwynn was injured," Logan said with a wink. "Before we begin, I need to introduce all of you to her."

Gwynn licked her lips and let her eyes wander around the room. Beneath the table, Logan's hand took hers again.

"First, our leader," Logan said. "Fallon MacLeod."

Fallon dipped his head of dark brown hair. He wore it long, and his dark green eyes saw much. He smiled and said, "Welcome to MacLeod Castle."

"Thank you," Gwynn replied.

Logan nodded down the table. "And sitting next to Fallon on his left is his lovely wife, Larena."

"The female Warrior," Gwynn said.

Larena's smile was wide and her smoky blue eyes were as vibrant as her golden blonde hair. "Aye. The lone female Warrior, but not the lone female."

Everyone laughed, which put Gwynn at ease.

"Lucan MacLeod and his wife, Cara, are sitting to the right of Fallon."

Lucan bowed his head, and Gwynn realized he was the one who had driven her car to the castle.

She was introduced to Quinn and Marcail, Hayden and Isla, Galen and Reaghan, and Broc and Isla. By the time Logan was done, Gwynn's head was spinning.

"And this," Logan said. "Is Gwynn Austin. She's from Texas."

"Logan has told me about each of you," she said. "I'm glad to finally meet you."

"And we're glad you brought Logan back to us," Hayden said.

Isla leaned her arms on the table and said, "Logan said he never told you where the castle was. How did you know?"

"I have no idea," Gwynn answered. "I just learned a few days ago that I am a Druid and that I can hear the wind."

There was a collective gasp from the women.

"I asked it for help, but it never answered," Gwynn finished.

Reaghan chuckled. "Oh, I think it did. It might not have told you, but it led you to us."

Gwynn hadn't considered that. "I suppose."

"Let's back up," Fallon said. "Start from the beginning, please."

Gwynn sat back as Logan began his tale about arriving in the year 2012 on the same day she met him. He told them how he realized she was a Druid and set out to help her find her father, and how she had helped Logan learn the modern culture.

"Have you found your father, Gwynn?" Cara asked.

Logan frowned. "We're getting to that."

"I was able to get on to the university's network, where I discovered my father had gotten the *Book of Craigan* from a Declan Wallace, who happened to be a Scot."

"That book led Gary to Mallaig," Logan said.

Hayden's brow puckered in a frown. "That's where you were when Deirdre attacked and killed Duncan."

"Aye," Logan said. "I found it more than coincidental that Gary would be there."

Marcail played with one of the tiny braids atop her head. "What is this book?"

Gwynn exchanged a look with Logan before she said, "I was approached by a woman on Eigg who told me I was the Keeper of the Tablet of Orn. The *Book of Craigan*, we think, tells how to get to the Tablet."

Galen ran a hand through his head of dark blond hair. "Damn."

"We saw a picture of the book," Logan said. "Gwynn then told me she had seen on Eigg the same double spiral symbol that was on the book. I knew I had seen it before as well."

Sonya nodded. "The amulet I found."

"That's why the wyrran came," Gwynn said. Every eye in the room focused on her.

Fallon leaned forward and asked softly, "What did you say?"

"Wyrran," Logan answered for her. "I heard them. I got her to safety before they found her. That's when we decided to pay Declan Wallace a visit. To see if he knew where Gary was, but also to see if we could find the book."

"What did you discover?" Broc asked.

"Hell," Gwynn answered before she thought better of it. She forced a laugh and shifted in her seat. "I'm sorry. It was just so . . . awful."

"Logan," Hayden urged.

Logan wrapped his fingers more securely around Gwynn's cold hand. He knew what had happened at Wallace's would likely haunt her for a long time.

"His home was a mansion," Logan began. "They were no' going to allow us entry until Gwynn stated her name. Once inside I felt *drough* magic."

"Deirdre," Lucan said.

Gwynn quirked her lips. "That's what I thought, but Logan said it was different."

"Different how?" Isla asked.

Logan shrugged. "It was still powerful black magic, but it wasna the same. I had felt Deirdre's just a few days earlier, if you recall. I knew it was no' her."

Broc snorted. "It was Wallace."

"Aye," Logan said and sighed. "I realized it too late. By that time he was in the room with us, and I couldna get Gwynn out without danger."

"He confirmed that my father was working for him," Gwynn said, her eyes on the opposite wall. "My fa . . . Gary is translating the text so Declan can find the Tablet."

Logan smiled when Reaghan patted Gwynn's shoulder. "We don't blame you for what your father did."

"Reaghan's right," Quinn said. "You are no' responsible for his actions, Gwynn."

Logan winked at Gwynn when she gripped his hand tighter. "Wallace knew Gwynn was a Druid. He wanted to keep her there, but I wasna about to let that happen. He brought in men, and when their bullets didna put me down he realized what I was."

"One of his men called for X90s," Gwynn said. "I didn't know what they were. All I knew was that suddenly Logan was in pain."

Larena asked, "So how did you escape?"

"Logan used his power over water," Gwynn said with a smile. "The expression on those men's faces when all that water came at them was priceless."

Logan chuckled and shook his head slightly. "Aye, but it didna keep them down for long. Gwynn called the wind. The next thing I knew, it came bursting through the windows. Glass flew everywhere. I doona remember much, but I do recall using what little strength I had to mix the water with her wind."

"We made it to the door," Gwynn said and glanced at Logan. "There was so much blood all over him. And I slipped on the steps. I hoped Logan would make it to my car, because I heard Declan coming up behind me."

Logan ran a hand down his face. "His black magic is powerful. I knew Gwynn would need help, but I couldna even get to my knees. I crawled to the car, praying I didna pass out."

"He made it," Gwynn said, "because the next thing I knew there were water and chunks of ice flying toward Declan. I used that time to run to the car and get the heck outta Dodge."

"What?" Logan asked.

Hayden laughed. "It's an American saying. I'll explain later."

Logan rubbed his jaw. "I managed to tell Gwynn what was wrong with me, but I passed out when I was trying to tell her how to get here."

"You're here," Cara said. "Both of you. And that's all that matters."

Fallon rose and began to pace behind his chair. "Deirdre wasna at Wallace's?"

"I would have felt her magic," Logan said. "But I can almost guarantee that he was the one who brought her to this time."

Sonya let out a large sigh. "But why? If Declan is so powerful, why does he need Deirdre?"

"A good question," Broc said. "One I suspect we will find an answer to soon enough."

Logan released Gwynn's hand and stood. "We need the book, Fallon."

Fallon paused and looked at Logan. "Why?"

"Because if we don't get the Tablet, then Declan or Deirdre will," Gwynn said. "The Druids of Eigg are gone. There is no magic to keep Deirdre away as Logan said there used to be. All they have to do is find its hiding place to take it."

Logan waited impatiently as Fallon considered their words.

It was Larena who stood and said, "Fallon, if you get me there, I can get inside and steal the book."

Galen nodded. "You know she's right, Fallon. And so are Logan and Gwynn. We need the book to find the Tablet."

"How do I know you'll be able to get the Tablet?" Fallon asked Gwynn.

But it was Logan who answered. "Because I'm going to be there to help her."

CHAPTER
TWENTY-SIX

Gwynn looked at Logan and saw in his face the determination and confidence she had come to associate with him. The darkness she'd seen in his eyes had lessened, but it was still there.

"Suppose we do this," Hayden said. "Suppose Larena gets inside Wallace's house and takes the book. What next?"

Broc cracked his knuckles. "We'll need to be sure he doesna have additional magical security after what Logan and Gwynn did."

"He thinks I'm dead," Logan said.

Quinn shook his head of wavy light brown hair. "I disagree. If he knows who you are, he knows the rest of us are here."

"We're speculating," Gwynn said. "These are things Declan never spoke of. Let's go back to what we do know."

Cara chuckled and grinned at Gwynn. "I like her. A lot."

The other women nodded, and Gwynn found herself more pleased than she could have expected.

"I told you," Logan whispered in her ear. "It's impossible no' to like you."

She met his hazel eyes. "Really?"

"Really."

The sound of someone clearing their throat made Gwynn pull away from Logan's hypnotic gaze. Her heart was pounding, her blood heating as she recalled the feel of his large, rough hands on her body.

Gwynn turned her head back to the group and found Marcail's knowing smile directed at her. Gwynn shifted in her seat.

"So what do we know?" Fallon asked.

Gwynn looked around the table before she said, "We know Deirdre is here. She's been here for at least three months."

"We knew that, but how did you know that?" Reaghan asked.

"When Logan described to me what the wyrran were I remembered seeing a video on YouTube about three months ago featuring some new yellow creature. I showed it to Logan and he confirmed it was a wyrran. If they've been spotted, then that means Deirdre is here."

Lucan drummed his fingers on the table and twisted his lips. "We saw the same video."

"Then why did you no' go after Deirdre?" Logan asked. "Broc can find anyone, anywhere. He even found Deirdre four centuries into the future."

Broc laid both of his hands flat on the table as he glared at Logan. "Do you think we have no' tried to get to Deirdre? As soon as we realized she was here in this time, I went looking for her. I couldna find her. There was *drough* magic blocking me."

"Impossible." Logan shook his head, as if he didn't believe Broc's words. "Deirdre never used her magic to hide herself from us before."

Fallon leaned his arms on the back of his chair. "And I doona believe she's doing it now. I think it was Wallace who kept her hidden."

"He did block his magic in his home," Logan said. "At least Broc was able to find Ian. Right?"

Gwynn felt her heart constrict as silence met Logan's question.

"Nay," Quinn finally answered. "The same black magic stopped Broc from locating Ian."

Logan slammed his hands on the table, making Gwynn jump. He rose and began to pace in long, fast steps. Gwynn licked her lips, wanting to reach out to him as his hands raked through his hair.

"So all we know is that Deirdre is here, that we cannot find her or Ian, and that Wallace is another threat we need to deal with," Logan said.

Hayden let out a harsh breath and said, "It appears so. Gaining the book will definitely put a crimp in Wallace's plans."

"But we don't know what they are," Larena reminded them.

"Look for Deirdre again," Logan told Broc.

Broc furrowed his brows. "Why?"

"When was the last time you searched for her?"

"A couple of weeks ago."

"We heard her wyrran on Eigg. I'd bet all the coin I have that Deirdre is at Cairn Toul."

Broc shrugged and closed his eyes. A heartbeat later, his dark eyes snapped open. "Logan is right."

Gwynn smiled at Logan's triumphant look. Her gaze moved to the head of the table where Fallon was watching Logan with narrowed eyes.

"How did you know?" Fallon asked Logan.

Logan threw up his hands. "It was a guess. I knew the first thing Deirdre would do was get to Cairn Toul as fast as she could. It's her haven. Now, she'll go after the Tablet of Orn."

Larena stood and put her hand atop Fallon's. "You know we have to get the book from Declan."

"Aye, but I doona have to like it," Fallon ground out.

Gwynn rose, her gaze locked with Fallon's. "Good. When do we leave?"

"You willna be going back there," Logan declared from behind her.

Gwynn whirled to face him. "Excuse me?"

"I willna have it, Gwynn. You barely got out alive the first time. Wallace made it clear he wants you to work with him . . . And that he wants you in his bed."

Gwynn opened her mouth to reply as Reaghan moved to one side of her and Isla to the other.

"Yelling at him won't get you what you want," Reaghan whispered.

Isla nodded in agreement with Reaghan as she looked at Gwynn. "We deal with this daily. Pick your battles, Gwynn. I hate to admit it, but you going back to Declan's mansion isn't a good idea. Let the others handle this mission."

As her anger at Logan telling her what to do diminished, Gwynn reluctantly agreed. She glared at Logan, though, and took a step toward him. "Fine. But if you come back injured again I'm going to . . ." she paused looking for the right thing to say, ". . . be very angry."

"We'll all return in perfect health," Fallon announced. "Is that no' right, Larena?"

Larena laughed and nodded in agreement. "Contrary to what you may think, my love, I don't like danger."

Fallon's snort, followed by the other Warriors as they looked at their wives, made Gwynn duck her head to hide her smile.

There was something magical about MacLeod Castle,

and it didn't have anything to do with the Druids. It was from the deep, loving bonds that had formed among the people who had made the castle their home.

"I say we go to Declan's tonight," Larena announced.

Logan smiled widely. "Aye. An excellent plan. He willna be expecting it."

"Tonight it is," Fallon said.

Logan found his gaze returning to Gwynn again and again. He'd never felt such fear as he had when Gwynn stated that she would return to Declan's. Logan would do anything—*anything*—to keep her away from Declan.

Thankfully, the others had intervened for him. He knew he'd been an arse to forbid her, but when it came to Gwynn, he couldn't think clearly. He just knew he couldn't allow Declan to get his evil hands on her.

Logan took a deep breath as he looked around the castle. By the saints, he had missed this place, and especially the people within its stone walls.

All that was missing were the four other Warriors.

And Deirdre's, as well as Declan's, death.

Logan's eyes landed on Marcail. The last time he had seen her, her stomach had just begun to swell with Quinn's child. Had she lost the babe? As he stared at her, he could see nothing of her stomach under jeans and a sweater that hung to her hips.

"You had better have a good reason for eyeing my wife as you are, Logan," Quinn said.

Logan looked at Quinn, then back at Marcail. "Did you have the babe?"

Marcail laughed and nudged Quinn with her shoulder. "Tell him."

"If I must," Quinn said, but there was a smile on his lips. "Aye, Logan. We had the babe."

"I was able to craft a shielding spell so that it allowed Marcail to carry her babe to term. Once the babe was born, I shifted part of the spell from Marcail to the child so he could grow," Isla said.

Logan glanced around the castle. "Him? Where is he?"

"Aiden had an errand to run," Marcail said.

Quinn beamed like the proud father he was. "He'll return shortly. He's been anxious to meet you and the others for some time now."

Logan lowered himself back into his seat as he took in all he'd learned. "What of wee Braden and his mother, Fiona? And Odara?"

"Isla used the same spell on Braden," Cara said. "He and Fiona are here as well. They decided to stay at the castle since there was nowhere else for them to go, even after Deirdre was gone. We were their family by then."

Lucan said, "They're with Aiden."

"Odara was another matter," Reaghan said softly. "We begged her to stay."

Galen wrapped Reaghan's hand in both of his. "But she would have none of it. She told us she'd seen too many years, and though she loved it here, she couldna imagine living through four centuries."

"So you just let her go?" Logan asked.

Broc put his hands behind his head as he leaned back in his chair. "Hardly. She also didna have anywhere to go so we built her a small cottage just outside the shield. We visited her daily, making sure she had food, wood to stay warm, and anything else she needed."

"Six months later, Galen went to see her and found her body," Reaghan said. "She'd died in her sleep."

Logan held Reaghan's gaze and said, "I'm sorry. She was a good woman."

"It's what she wanted."

For several long moments, everyone was quiet, lost in their memories. Logan smiled inwardly as he recalled

Odara. She had been old, but she had been mentally strong. She might not have had much magic, but she was a Druid. And she had been part of their family.

"We're going to need to know where Wallace would keep the book," Fallon said. "I doona want Larena spending any more time in his mansion than she has to."

Logan clenched his jaw and tossed up his hands. "The mansion is massive. We only saw the front entrance and his office."

"I might be able to find the blueprints to the house," Gwynn said. "I'm fairly handy with a computer."

Logan should have known Gwynn would be involved somehow. But she had every right to be. Wallace had nearly killed her. He also had Gary Austin, and though Gwynn was angry at the man, he was still her father.

"Is there any way we could extract Gary as well?" Logan asked.

Broc rose and leaned back against the wall, his arms crossed. "That will be tricky. Why do you ask?"

"Because if Wallace loses the book, he'll have no more use for Gary."

"He knew what he was getting into," Gwynn said, her eyes on the floor.

Logan stood and walked to stand next to her, forcing her violet eyes to meet his. "He might no' have, Gwynn."

"Regardless, he wants the Tablet of Orn more than he wants me."

"But he's your father."

Gwynn wrinkled her nose. "A fact I cannot change."

"This argument might be moot," Galen said.

Larena slowly nodded her head. "I agree with Galen. If the book is under security, guarded by both men and magic, I may only have time to get either the book or Gwynn's father."

"The book comes first and foremost," Gwynn stated.

Logan sighed and raked a hand through his hair. "Gwynn's right. We have to get the book so we can find the Tablet before Deirdre or Wallace do."

"Then let's get to work," Quinn said as he banged his hands on the table and rose.

CHAPTER
TWENTY-SEVEN

Deirdre looked with an appreciative eye on her newly clean mountain. Well, as clean as the inside of a mountain could get.

Her wyrran had worked tirelessly, but that was just what they were supposed to do. Her Warriors, most especially Malcolm, had been sent out into the cities to collect a few items she needed. And wanted.

As much as she hated to admit it, she enjoyed the clothes Declan had given her. The pants allowed for much freedom of movement, and she liked how men looked at her when she wore them.

After putting away her new clothes as well as the food and other personal items she'd requested, Deirdre had spent several hours making new wyrran.

"The wyrran were spotted a few months ago," Malcolm said as he entered her chamber. "It was about the same time we arrived here."

"And that concerns me why?" Deirdre asked.

"It concerns you because there was a picture of a wyrran in the newspaper."

Deirdre frowned. "The what?"

"The newspaper. It's like a book only thinner. It comes out once a day and lists the news."

"So?"

"The newspaper also mentioned what they call a website. I asked someone in the town I was just in what that was. It seems there is this place called the internet where information is kept. She showed it to me. There is a video of the wyrran running across a field."

Deirdre held up her hand. "Stop. I have no idea what you're talking about. What's a . . . what did you call it?"

"The internet? Or the video?"

"The video. What is it?"

Malcolm leaned a shoulder against the doorway. "It is a moving picture."

"Oh," she huffed in frustration. "I have so much to catch up on. Maybe we should bring a few people here so they can teach me what I need to know."

"If that's your wish."

"What I wish is to understand this time! The people speak in a way that hurts my ears."

He shrugged indifferently. "It's no' bad once you get used to it."

Deirdre fisted her hands and lowered herself into a chair as she cocked her head to study Malcolm. "Tell me why there's this fuss about my wyrran and the video?"

"Because the video is out there for anyone to see. Your wyrran made the newspapers, Deirdre. It means the MacLeods will see it. They will know we are here."

"Shite," Deirdre murmured. "I had hoped to surprise them."

"No' now."

She rubbed her hands on the soft, smooth black leather pants. "Aye. No use now. The wyrran I sent to the Isle of

Eigg returned without the artifact, but I didn't expect them to find it. They did tell me the Druids are all but gone from the isle."

"Verra odd, since that was their haven."

"My thoughts exactly. I guess when I disappeared, they thought they were safe. But why did they stop using magic? Why would any Druid, *mie* or *drough*, not answer the call of their magic?"

Malcolm's blond brow rose in response. "You'll have to ask one of the Druids."

"The wyrran felt the magic of a few Druids, but they said it was weak. All but one. Hers, they said, was strong. It's her I want."

"And the artifact."

Deirdre smiled. "I already have one artifact. The sword you retrieved from the Celtic burial mound. That artifact will keep the MacLeods from awakening my sister. But having two artifacts, well, that can only help me."

"Are you sure the sword is still here?"

"Of course it is. Where else would it be?" she asked as she stood and walked to a wall at the back of her chamber. She waved her hand over the stone and whispered the words that opened the secret compartment only she could unseal.

Yet when the stones moved to reveal the hideaway, the sword she had placed there was gone.

"Nay," Deirdre choked. "This cannot be."

Behind her, Malcolm snorted. "You were gone from this place for four hundred years. That was plenty of time for the MacLeods to find the sword."

"Nay!" Deirdre screamed as magic charged through her body like lightning.

Her hair lifted around her, destroying everything in its path.

Malcolm closed the door as he exited Deirdre's chamber. He wasn't foolish enough to stay near her when she was in this kind of rage.

Malcolm's lips twisted in a rueful smile as he thought about his cousin, Larena, and the MacLeods finding the sword. It was just what he had expected them to do. Why Deirdre hadn't expected it concerned him.

A lot.

It hadn't taken Gwynn long to find the blueprints for Declan's mansion. It had been built at the end of the nineteenth century by some earl or another. Declan's grandfather had bought it with his first million pounds and set about remodeling it.

Declan had inherited the mansion when he was just ten years old. He'd lived there with nannies and his mother until she died five years later. By the time Declan reached the age of twenty, he'd had new plans drawn up for some improvements.

Gwynn had been ready to give up when she happened to stumble across the blueprints. They showed several hidden access points and underground rooms that hadn't been there previously.

"There's more than this," Gwynn told Fallon, Larena, and Logan. "I just know it. There's no way Declan wouldn't include a few hidden things on the blueprints."

Logan's lips flattened. "Aye. You probably have the right of it."

"How are you going to get the book out?" Gwynn asked Larena. She'd been shocked to discover Larena could turn herself, but only herself, invisible. The power didn't extend to her clothes or anything on her body or in her hands.

Larena ran her finger over the milky stone of the ring on her right hand. "I'll wait until I can get the book out without being seen."

"Naked, you mean," Fallon said with a frown.

Larena lifted a perfectly arched blonde brow. "Do you have another idea?"

"Aye. I go in and get it."

"And be shot full of *drough* blood bullets."

"Better me than you."

Logan and Gwynn chuckled at the couple's bickering. It was obvious to anyone who watched the pair that the love between them was deep.

Larena glanced at Gwynn and began to laugh as well. "I can imagine how we sound to you."

"You sound like two people who care about each other and who have spent several centuries together," Gwynn said.

Fallon threw back his head and laughed. "Verra true."

Logan's smile disappeared as he picked up one of the bullets Sonya's magic had removed. "I think we're going to need more than just me and you watching Larena's back," he said to Fallon.

"Aye. I've already asked Broc to join us. He can fly overhead and watch from above," Fallon said.

"I'm also thinking Hayden would be good to bring along."

There was a snort behind them as Hayden walked into the hall. "As if you even have to ask."

Gwynn's job was done. All she could do was stand back and watch as Logan and the others prepared for their attack. Gwynn felt sick to her stomach thinking about anyone going inside Declan's mansion.

When she had stood on the steps as Logan crawled to her car, Declan had let her feel the full force of his evil. And it was powerful.

She shuddered and rubbed her hands up and down her arms to ward off the chill that had taken hold of her.

"Are you all right?" Logan asked.

Gwynn jumped at the sound of his voice so close to her. She hadn't heard him stir, and she didn't think she'd ever get used to how fast he could move. "Yes."

"You doona look all right."

She managed a wan smile. "I don't want any of y'all to go into that house."

"Have I told you I love your accent?"

She blinked and raised her brows at him. "What?"

"Your accent. What did you call it? Oh, aye. A twang. I like it."

"You're changing the subject."

"Is it working?"

Gwynn smiled despite herself. "Yes."

"Good. Now, I plan on hearing more of your charming accent and odd sayings when I return."

She licked her lips and turned until she faced him. "Wallace's magic is strong. I felt the force of his evil, and it gave me the creeps."

"Deirdre is just as strong or stronger than he is, and we've faced her many times and won."

"No. Declan is different. I've listened to your stories of the battles with Deirdre. Declan will come at you in ways none of you can prepare for. Please. This is a bad idea. Let's return to Eigg. I'll find the Tablet without the book."

Logan ran a hand down his face, his hazel eyes troubled. "Do you have so little faith in us?"

"I'm worried about you. All of you. Maybe attacking so soon isn't a good idea. Waiting a day or two while we head back to Eigg is the right decision."

"Gwynn," Logan said as he grasped her arms. He slid his hands down until their fingers touched. "I may be new to this time, but the others are no'. I remember all too well the feel of that *drough* blood inside me. I doona want to repeat the process anytime soon."

She knew there was nothing she could say to sway him

from the mission. Yes, they needed the book, but it wasn't worth sacrificing anyone's life for it.

Gwynn took a step closer to him, putting them toe to toe. "Tell Larena to concentrate on the book and the book only. We can go back for my father later, once we have the Tablet."

"I will."

"You promised you'd help me find my father, and you did."

His hand lifted and lightly cupped her face. "I always carry through with my vows."

A lock of honey-colored hair fell against his cheek. He caught her hand and turned his head to kiss her palm. Gwynn's heart missed a beat at the intimate gesture.

When he pulled her into his arms she never thought to resist, never worried about who was in the hall and might see them. All that she cared about, all that she wanted was for Logan to hold her and chase away her fears for a few minutes.

As his hands spread over her back, his head dipped and he claimed her mouth. He took. He seized. He captured.

Gwynn surrendered to his demanding, hungry kiss. To the wonder and splendor of his masterful lips as they rekindled the inferno that had been banked but never died.

She plunged her fingers into his hair and pressed her body against his. His arms tightened, holding her close as he angled his mouth to deepen the kiss.

Gwynn squeezed her eyes closed when Logan drew back from the kiss. He pressed her head against his chest and simply held her, his heartbeat sounding in her ear.

"I'll be back," he whispered into her hair.

"Don't make promises you can't keep."

He kissed the top of her head. "I never do."

Gwynn bit her tongue to keep from calling Logan

back as he stepped out of her hold and walked to Fallon and the others. Logan winked, and she forced herself to smile.

The Warriors all had their hands on each other's shoulders except for Fallon, who stood at the end of the line.

"Think of Declan's mansion," Galen told Logan. Then he looked at Gwynn. "And only Declan's mansion."

At Galen's nod, Fallon laid his hand on Galen's shoulders. They were gone in a blink.

CHAPTER
TWENTY-EIGHT

By the time Logan exhaled, Fallon had jumped them to the grounds outside Wallace's mansion. Just seeing the huge white and stone building rising out of the snow made Logan's rage begin to boil.

Declan had meant to kill him. And he had almost taken Gwynn's life.

The broken windows had already been replaced. But Logan saw that part of the huge double front doors was still splintered. Declan hadn't been able to cover up everything. Yet.

Galen whistled long and low. "You were no' kidding, Logan. This place is like a palace."

"Doona let the outside fool you," Logan said. "It's pure evil."

Larena shivered. "Aye. I can feel it."

"It will get worse once you are inside."

Hayden growled. "You're right. It's *drough* magic, but it's different from Deirdre's."

Fallon turned Larena so she faced him. "You doona have to do this."

"Aye, I do," she said softly. "This is for all of us, my

love. For our future, for Logan and Gwynn, and everyone else in the castle."

Logan felt Fallon's frustration as he let out a breath.

"I'd go in your stead if I could," Fallon said.

Larena smiled and rose up on her tiptoes to kiss him. "You know that even if I were able to give you my power, I wouldn't. I'm a Warrior, Fallon. You know this."

"But you're also my wife."

Larena placed her hand on Fallon's cheek and stared deep into his eyes. "Nothing will ever change that."

"Aye," Fallon agreed. "Nothing."

In a blink, Larena's skin turned iridescent as she released her goddess. With one more smile to Fallon, she became invisible until all that remained were her clothes. All but Fallon turned their backs to her so she could remove her clothes.

"I'll give you fifteen minutes. If you are no' out here, we're coming to get you," Fallon said.

Larena chuckled. "I'm going to have a look around. Everywhere. The more we know about Declan and what's inside his home, the better. It will take me more than fifteen minutes."

"Larena," Fallon growled in warning.

Hayden and Logan exchanged grins, because they knew who the winner of this argument would be.

"She has a point," Broc said. "She can no' be seen, Fallon."

"We doona know that!"

Logan turned around at the same time as Hayden and Galen. "Wallace does no' have any Warriors. Just mercenaries."

"I'll be careful." Larena's disembodied voice sounded around them. "I've always returned to you, Fallon."

"You better," Fallon ground out.

Several long moments ticked by until Fallon let out a curse. "God help Wallace if anything happens to her."

There was nothing that could save Wallace from Logan's wrath, but there was no need to tell Fallon that. Logan would take out his vengeance on Wallace with precision and pain. He would suffer terribly for what he had done to Gwynn.

"Care to talk about the kiss we witnessed between you and Gwynn?" Hayden asked.

"Nay," Logan stated.

Broc let out a long-suffering sigh. "As much as I'd like to be involved in this conversation, I must take to the skies."

Logan glanced at Broc, his blond hair now cut to his nape. Broc hadn't bothered to wear a shirt like the rest of them, because he'd just have to remove it or ruin it when his wings sprouted.

Broc's massive wings unfurled, matching the dark blue skin of his Warrior form. "But I'll be listening," he said with a grin just before he leaped into the air.

Logan, Hayden, Galen, and Fallon all waited, hidden near the front gate by a group of shrubs laden with snow. Logan glanced down at his black pants, boots, and shirt. He still couldn't get over how much had changed.

None of his brethren wore their kilts. Instead, they sported the same type of clothes Gwynn had picked out for him. When they had dressed for this mission, Hayden had brought him the gear he had on now. Fatigues, he had called them.

Logan had to admit the pants were easier to move in than the jeans, and wearing all black worked well to help them blend into the night.

That is until they would release their gods and become Warriors.

"Gwynn is pretty," Galen whispered into the silence.

Logan rolled his eyes because he knew there was no way he could convince them not to talk about her. "Aye."

Hayden nodded. "And courageous."

"Intelligent, too," Fallon added.

"She's all those things and more," Logan admitted.

Hayden swiveled his head to him. "How much does she mean to you?"

Logan hadn't allowed himself to think along those lines. He certainly didn't want to give Hayden an answer.

"By that kiss, I'd say a lot," Galen said.

Fallon shifted his feet, his gaze locked on the mansion. "Whatever you might think, Logan, everyone deserves to find happiness. Including you."

Logan frowned. What was that supposed to mean? Did they know he'd gone to Deirdre to become a Warrior?

Impossible.

"Before you left for this time, we all saw a darkness growing inside you," Hayden said.

Logan squeezed his eyes shut. He'd thought he had kept it from them. He'd been so careful.

"It's still there," Hayden continued. "But it does no' seem as great."

Logan met the dark gaze of his closest friend. "There are things I did in my past."

"We've all done things we're ashamed of," Fallon said. "We're your family, Logan. Regardless of what it is, we willna turn you away."

But Logan wasn't so sure of that.

Hayden must have seen his doubt, because he laid a big hand on Logan's shoulder. "Fallon speaks for everyone. I've always thought of you as my brother. You've kept your secrets, but then we all have."

Logan felt as low as a snake's belly. These men were the best men he knew. He didn't belong in their company, didn't deserve to call them friends or family.

Even knowing that, he couldn't walk away like he knew he should. He needed them more than they would ever know.

As soon as Larena stepped inside Declan's mansion she choked on the vile stench of evil that surrounded her. She was cautious with every step she took.

Declan might not have Warriors, but he wasn't a fool. He would have magic in place that could alert him to her presence. Luckily for her, however, all Warriors could sense Druid magic.

Larena quickly stepped to the side as one of Declan's mercenaries walked out of the room she was passing. He carried an Uzi and had two sets of ammo straps crossing over his chest like an X. One carried regular bullets while the other held red-tipped bullets that glowed.

She glanced into the room and grinned when she saw the destruction inside. That must be the office Gwynn and Logan had destroyed.

Larena continued forward. Her search of the ground floor didn't take as long as she thought it would. She was about to start up the stairs when a door was thrown open and two men walked out.

One had the same look as the other mercenaries, but the other was dressed in an expensive Gucci suit. He was clearly used to wearing custom-made clothes.

Declan Wallace.

Larena curled her lip as she watched him walk past. Not even his devastating good looks, golden hair, and bright blue eyes could conceal the malice within him.

"Did you learn what you needed to?" asked the dark-headed man beside him.

Declan smiled. "Enough. She doesna like to give me the information I seek. But I make it worth her while, Robbie."

Fury ripped through Larena. Did Declan have a woman here? A woman held against her will?

And that's when Larena felt it—the *mie* magic.

It was faint, barely discernible through the *drough* magic that permeated the mansion, but there was no denying the presence of a *mie*.

Larena watched Declan and Robbie walk away from her. She was torn between following them and finding the Druid. Larena squeezed her eyes closed as she tried to decide what to do.

If there was a Druid in trouble, she needed to save her. Yet she had found Declan. She should follow him and see if she could learn anything.

It was the muffled scream she heard through the door with her enhanced hearing that made her decision.

Larena waited until Declan was out of sight and no one was around before she reached for the handle on the door and opened it wide enough that she could slip through.

She found herself at the top of a narrow set of stairs that led down into what could only be a dungeon. She set her jaw as anger flared anew.

Larena made not a sound as she descended the stairs to reach the bottom. Cell after cell lined the hallway.

Were they all occupied? Or was Declan merely preparing to fill them? Either way, Larena wasn't going to allow him to succeed.

There was another scream to Larena's left. She ran down the corridor until she reached the very last door. Larena skidded to a halt before the bars and grimaced when she saw the woman, her arms held away from her body by chains hanging from the walls.

The Druid was flinging her head from side to side and using her hands as well as she could to brush against her skin.

"Declan, you bastard. Get them off me!"

Larena looked, but there was nothing but chains on the Druid. It must have been Declan's magic that made the Druid believe that something else was there.

The Druid screeched, huge tears falling from her eyes. "Please! Declan, I swear I won't hold back again. Just get the spiders off me!"

Larena had seen enough. She didn't know how she was going to get the Druid out, but she had to try. Yet when Larena reached for the bars to wrench them open, she felt magic, which made her pause.

She braced herself and reached for the metal bars, only to be pushed backward by the force of the magic.

It was going to take more than just Larena to release this Druid.

As much as she didn't want to leave the *mie*, Larena had no choice. But she would return, she silently promised the Druid.

Larena turned on her heel, the screams of the *mie* following her as she left the dungeon. Larena set her jaw and started up the stairs to the second floor.

There were many rooms to investigate. She thought she might find the book in the library, but that would have been too easy. The next six rooms were empty as well.

It wasn't until she came to the seventh door that she paused outside. She could hear a man moving within, muttering to himself. Her head tilted to the side as she heard the sound of pages flipping.

Larena stepped closer to the door until she was all but pressed against it. She smiled as she raised her hand and knocked.

"What?" grated a harsh voice.

Larena waited until she heard the chair scoot back on the carpet and hard steps start for the door. As soon as the man yanked open the door, she slid past him into the room.

The man looked first one way then the other before he

cursed and slammed the door shut. "Just what I need," he said to himself. "More distractions. As if I didn't have enough already."

His American accent, so much like Gwynn's, caught Larena's attention.

So this was Gary Austin.

CHAPTER
TWENTY-NINE

Gwynn sat at the table and twiddled her thumbs. Literally. Her mind was creating all sorts of scenarios where Logan and the others were hurt. Or worse, killed by Declan.

"They'll be back," Reaghan said as she tossed another log on the fire.

Gwynn forced a smile but didn't comment.

Cara slapped her hands on the arms of her chair and rose. "Well, I have the perfect thing to take our minds off waiting."

"What's that?" Marcail asked.

Isla laughed and started up the steps. "I'll get the boxes down."

"Oh," Marcail said with a huge grin. "Wait for me. I'm coming to help."

Reaghan quickly followed. "Me, too!"

Sonya merely gave Gwynn a wink and began to move furniture around the great hall with Cara.

By this time she found herself more than curious. She stood and hurried to help them lift a heavy chair. "What are y'all doing?"

Cara smiled, her mahogany eyes alight with mischief. "It's December twenty-first. We need to set up the Christmas tree."

Gwynn had completely forgotten about it being December. She'd been so worried about finding her father, then keeping Logan alive, that the time of year had meant nothing to her.

Yet when the others came down with boxes and boxes of decorations and a fourteen-foot artificial tree, she couldn't help but get involved.

Gwynn laughed as Cara and Reaghan climbed the two ladders and began to set up the top of the tree while the rest of them worked on the lower half.

"I'm just glad we finally got a tree that was pre-lit," Isla said as she plugged in the tree and clear lights came on.

"Me, too," Sonya said.

Reaghan asked, "What colors are we using this year?"

"I vote for red and silver," Marcail said.

Gwynn smiled. "That sounds pretty."

"Then red and silver it is," Cara declared.

With the tree fluffed and ready, the boxes of ornaments were next. Gwynn was helpless to stay out of the fun. She loved Christmas, loved decorating her apartment, so she wasn't about to let this opportunity go.

While she, Cara, Sonya, and Marcail decorated the tree, Isla and Reaghan put up the numerous lengths of garland all over the great hall, and the biggest wreath Gwynn had ever seen over the fireplace.

Everything was adorned with clear lights and red and silver ornaments of all shapes and sizes.

It wasn't until they were hanging the last of the ornaments on the garland that Gwynn realized with all the laughter and conversations she had forgotten about her worry over Logan.

She stood back and looked around the hall. "I've never seen anything so beautiful."

Marcail wrapped an arm around Gwynn and squeezed. "We're very glad you were here to help us."

"Definitely," Sonya said.

The others nodded and smiled.

Gwynn took a deep breath and realized she hadn't had so much fun decorating for Christmas since before her mother got sick.

The only thing that would make the night complete was Logan.

Logan's nerves were strung as tight as a bow. Larena had been inside the mansion for almost two hours.

"We'd know if something happened," Galen told Fallon.

Fallon nodded, his jaw clenched.

Logan flexed his fingers. He'd released his god as soon as they had arrived at Wallace's mansion. His god was eager to see the blood of the enemy and to smell their death.

A whoosh of air pushed by them, and for a moment Logan thought it might be Gwynn, since she could communicate with the wind. Then Broc landed behind them and tucked his wings behind his back.

"We need to leave. Now," Broc said as he produced the book.

Fallon growled. "No' without Larena."

"I'm here," she said. "Get us home, my love."

Logan glanced at the mansion as he heard Declan's bellow of fury. He barely had time to smile before he was standing in the middle of the castle's great hall.

He blinked at all the small white lights everywhere, but what really took his breath away was the massive tree in the back corner.

"You're back," Reaghan cried and flew into Galen's arms.

Fallon had immediately taken Larena to their chamber so she could put her clothes back on. Logan heard the others talking to their wives about the mission, but all he wanted to do was find Gwynn.

When his gaze landed on her and he saw her smile, he couldn't stop himself from going to her. He ignored a question someone asked him as he strode to Gwynn.

He stopped in front of her and drank in the sight of her black hair pulled away from her face and her violet eyes watching him.

"We got the book," he said.

Relief poured over her face. "Thank God."

"But we were no' able to get your father."

She shrugged. "The book is more important."

"Is it?"

"You know it is."

"Maybe." He glanced at the tree to the right of them. "What is that?"

"A Christmas tree. Remember when I showed you how people decorated their houses and trees?"

He nodded slowly. "Aye. And where people put presents to others under the tree."

"Right," she said with a bright smile. "You were paying attention."

"I always pay attention when you talk."

Her violet eyes sparkled. "Did you fight Declan?"

"Nay. Larena was in and out of the mansion before Wallace knew what had happened."

"Good."

Logan snorted. "I'd have liked to have another go at him."

"Not when he can stop you with his magic and those bullets."

Suddenly, she turned as Larena and Fallon came down the stairs. Gwynn started toward them, her gaze on the book Larena held in her hands.

Logan fell in step beside Gwynn. He frowned at the faraway look in her eyes, as if she weren't with them at all anymore.

"The *Book of Craigan*," Gwynn said.

Logan blinked at the odd sound of Gwynn's voice. It was deeper, lower, as if it belonged to someone else entirely.

The entire hall had gone deathly quiet. The contentment and cheerfulness of before vanished, replaced with concern as all eyes were on Gwynn.

Logan tugged on a lock of Gwynn's black hair. "Gwynn."

"The book wasn't meant to be read by anyone other than the Keeper." Gwynn's gaze snapped to Larena. "It belongs to me."

Logan shifted his eyes to Fallon to find Fallon watching him. Logan gave a small nod of his head. Fallon, in turn, touched Larena's arm.

"I was bringing it to you," Larena said and held out the book.

The *Book of Craigan* was at least a hand's width thick, if not more, but Gwynn didn't flinch at the weight as she accepted it. As soon as it was in her grasp, she blinked and sucked in a deep breath.

"What just happened?" she asked. Gwynn looked down at the book before turning her eyes to Logan.

Logan shrugged. "It appears you are the Keeper of the Tablet of Orn."

"But what does that mean?"

Isla took a step forward. "I think you'll find the answers in the book."

"What would have happened had Larena not given Gwynn the book?" Quinn asked.

Larena sank into her chair at the table and shuddered. "I don't think I want to find out."

"Me neither," Gwynn said.

Logan guided her to the table. "Are you all right?" he whispered.

She leaned against him, which thrilled him more than it should have. She trusted him, sought his comfort. And he had done nothing but put her in danger since the moment he met her.

Logan clenched his jaw until it felt as if his teeth might crack open. As soon as he had learned about Wallace, Logan should have brought Gwynn to the castle to keep her out of harm's way.

Instead, he had taken her into the viper's nest. He had tainted her wonderful, pure magic with Declan's. And if Logan wasn't careful, if he didn't put some distance between himself and Gwynn, Deirdre was likely to get a hold of her as well.

It took Logan a moment to realize everyone had taken their seats but him. He ignored the question in Hayden's black eyes and made his body lower beside Gwynn.

Galen let out a low whistle. "I felt the book's magic from the moment Larena appeared with it, but once it rested in Gwynn's hands—"

"The magic increased," Lucan finished.

Reaghan's head tilted to the side, her hair moving with her. "The magic within the book is combining with Gwynn's."

"I have little magic," Gwynn said.

Sonya chuckled and shook her head. "On the contrary, Gwynn, despite not using your magic, it's stronger than you realize."

"Open the book," Logan urged her. He could feel her curiosity, but he saw her hesitation, the apprehension in the way she held her lips flat.

Gwynn glanced at him before she tucked a loose strand of hair behind one ear and ran a hand over the cover of the book. A wave of magic surrounded him, encircled him. It sizzled as hot as the rays of the sun, and was as intoxicating as the Druid beside him.

Logan's body hummed with the feel of Gwynn's magic. It filled his lungs and clung to his skin. He was sinking with it. Drowning. Plummeting.

And all he wanted to do was pull Gwynn into his arms. He ached to hold her again and feel her curvy body against his. He yearned to feel her scorching heat surround him. He longed to hear her scream his name again as she peaked.

As if she sensed his need, Gwynn turned her head and met his gaze. Her violet eyes had darkened, her plump lips parted as if she waited for his kiss.

Logan took hold of the last thread of his control and turned his head away. He dragged a deep breath into his body, but it did nothing to calm the need that had arisen, sharp and true.

Out of the corner of his eye, he saw Gwynn open the cover of the book. The leather creaked, and the smell of paper and ink reached him.

"It's in Gaelic," Gwynn said. "I cannot read Gaelic."

"We can," Hayden offered.

Logan put his hand on the book and felt a tingle of magic race up his arm. The magic wound its way through him, becoming a part of him until Logan could barely draw breath.

He clenched his other hand into a fist under the table and locked gazes with Hayden. "Let her try first."

Hayden shrugged. "If she can no' read it, Logan, she can no' read it."

"Give her a moment."

When Gwynn didn't respond, Logan turned his head

and looked at her. Her violet eyes were locked on the book. And they began to glow.

Logan jumped up, ready to yank Gwynn away, when Marcail's hand touched his arm.

"As you said, give her a moment."

"She could be in pain," Logan argued.

Isla shook her head, a smile forming. "She's not. That's her magic, Logan. Watch her. See it grow within her."

Logan swallowed hard as a gust of wind blew open the castle doors and howled through the great hall. It wound around Gwynn once, twice, and then was gone.

But not before it brushed against Logan.

CHAPTER
THIRTY

Gwynn gasped as the force of her magic welled inside her. As soon as she had touched the book, her magic had answered. Almost as if it had been waiting for her to touch the relic.

She could feel everyone in the great hall, especially Logan. He was concerned for her, but he shouldn't be. She could hear the drums and the chanting of the ancient Druids.

They were calling to her, urging her to let her magic through. As soon as she did, the wind answered. It enveloped her, soothed her. And she heard its chorus of joyous cheers.

This is what she was meant to do. There was no fear inside her now about the book or the idea of being the Keeper. The responsibility settled around her shoulders like a comfortable coat. As if she had always worn it and had just needed to be reminded what it felt like.

The wind left the great hall, but it would never be far from her again.

Gwynn blinked and looked down at the book. The letters in the title kept changing, constantly shifting. She waved a hand over them and whispered in Gaelic, "*Cuirstad air.*"

The letters stopped moving instantly.

"Cease," Logan repeated in English.

Gwynn turned the page and began to read. To her surprise, Logan had been right. She could not only read the words but understood them as well.

"What does it say?" Fallon asked.

Gwynn shrugged, but didn't look up from the book. "I've just begun to read. It's telling me how the Druids on Eigg were given the Tablet of Orn to safeguard. Not only did it strengthen their magic, but it helped to protect them as long as it stayed on the isle."

"I thought the Druids of Eigg crafted the artifact," Cara said.

Gwynn shook her head. "Not according to this. It doesn't say who gave it to the Druids, but it already held a great amount of magic before it ever came to Eigg."

"Interesting," Broc said.

"Not sure how that matters," Quinn added.

Gwynn sighed. "It does. It means that as powerful as the Druids of Eigg were, they didn't make the Tablet of Orn."

"She's right. Who would give that kind of artifact to someone else though?" Isla asked.

Gwynn didn't care. All that mattered was that the Tablet of Orn was hers to guard. To protect. It wasn't just Deirdre after it now; Declan sought it as well.

How much information had her father gotten from the book? Was it enough for Declan to attempt to retrieve the tablet from Eigg?

"It will take you weeks to get through that book, Gwynn," Fallon said.

She didn't bother to respond. She'd already read the

first twenty pages. Most of it was the history of the isle and the Druids—her ancestors.

Someone tried to touch the book and jumped back with a shout. Gwynn didn't look up. She was too absorbed in the pages to care what had happened.

"Gwynn," Logan said and put his hand atop the page she was reading.

After a second, she lifted her eyes to him and frowned. "What is it?"

"We've been calling your name for the past five minutes. You didna respond."

"I heard Fallon tell me it would take weeks to get through the book."

"That was several minutes ago."

She shook her head. "Impossible. It was just a few seconds."

Logan's gaze was steady, his hazel eyes holding hers.

Gwynn leaned back and let out a breath. "The book took me, didn't it?"

"It did."

"It's just so interesting. The information it holds on my ancestors is fascinating."

Broc growled. "And bloody irritating."

Gwynn looked from Logan to Broc, then around the table. "What is Broc talking about?"

"He tried to pull the book away from you," Sonya said. "I tried to warn him, but he didn't listen."

"And it zapped me," Broc grumbled.

Gwynn looked at the book and Logan's hand, which was still on it. She turned to him. "Did it hurt you?"

Slowly he shook his head.

"That I find fascinating," Reaghan said.

Isla nodded her head. "As do I."

"What do you think it means?" Galen asked.

Broc rolled his eyes. "It means the sodding book likes Logan."

"It means the book knows something," Marcail said.

Gwynn scooted her chair back from the table and stood. She had to put some distance between herself and the book. And herself and Logan.

Could Marcail be right? Did the book know that Gwynn cared for Logan?

But Gwynn didn't dislike Broc or any of the others. So why had it allowed Logan to touch it without being zapped?

Gwynn walked to the far wall. She leaned back and rested her head against the cool stones. She closed her eyes and recalled how boring her life had been. Now, everything was turned upside down and she was constantly questioning herself and her decisions.

"It's a lot to take in."

Gwynn's eyes flew open to find Reaghan beside her. "You could say that."

"Does the book and its power frighten you?"

"It didn't." Gwynn shrugged. "But it does now that I'm away from it."

Reaghan smiled, and it reached her deep gray eyes. "You've forgotten your magic for years. It will take some getting used to, but you need to learn to trust it. It saved your life as well as Logan's, if you'll recall."

"Yes. It did." So why did she still fear it?

"Logan appears to be settling in well."

Gwynn blinked at the change of topic, but she welcomed it. Anything to keep her from delving too deep into herself. "He's kept an open mind."

"Appearances can be deceiving though, can't they?"

Reaghan was trying to tell her something, but Gwynn wasn't sure what it was. "They can. But that's not Logan."

"It has been four centuries since we've seen him, and you've spent a great deal of time with him recently."

"What are you getting at?"

She picked at the auburn hair that curled around her cheeks. "Get him to talk. He keeps much inside himself. The others have been worried for some time about the darkness he carries."

"What is the darkness?"

"That we don't know. We were hoping you might be able to find out. You see, Gwynn, Logan has always been known as the jokester, the one who is always laughing, always charming."

"I've definitely seen that side of him."

"But you've seen the darkness as well."

It wasn't a question. Gwynn nodded. "I have. It comes and goes. Logan keeps it well hidden."

"He kept it hidden very well for a long time. It's not good for someone to carry that within themselves. For whatever reason, you are Logan's to guard, just as he is yours to lean on in the upcoming days."

Gwynn grew uncomfortable with where the conversation was headed. "Look, Logan is a big boy. He can take care of himself. If he's carried this . . . darkness . . . within himself for so long, it won't interfere with anything now. I know he won't let it."

"It's something to think on." Reaghan smiled and started to walk away. "We could use your help in the kitchen."

Gwynn glanced at the table where the men still sat. Logan was listening to something Lucan was saying. It was as if Logan could feel her gaze, because he turned his head and looked at her.

She smiled and followed Reaghan into the kitchen.

Gwynn didn't know what she expected to find in the castle kitchen, but it wasn't an industrial-sized refrigerator and freezer. She peered through the glass doors and chuckled to find the shelves completely stocked.

"Wow."

Cara laughed. "Yes, it is something. With Galen's appetite, we have to replenish twice a week."

Reaghan let out a dramatic sigh. "I'd love to know how he can eat all that food. It's disturbing how much he eats."

In the middle of the kitchen was a large island complete with a small sink. The top was thick wood that looked as old as the castle itself.

"It's the original worktable," Marcail said when Gwynn touched it. "When we updated the kitchen, we all decided it should remain."

"As well as one of the original ovens," Isla said.

Gwynn turned her head and saw a newer double oven, but not far down the wall from it was an original stone oven. "Amazing. Truly."

"We still use it," Cara said.

Sonya nodded. "The bread tastes the best baked there instead of in the other ovens."

"Bread?" Gwynn repeated. "You bake your own bread?"

Larena laughed and popped a cherry tomato in her mouth. "Not as often as we used to."

"We used to have everything we needed right here at the castle," Cara said. "I still grow many of the herbs we use to cook in my garden."

"And the men still hunt for our meat," Marcail said.

Sonya pulled a cutting knife from a drawer and began to dice some green onions. "Now, we get most of our food from the stores."

Gwynn smiled when she was handed another knife and some potatoes. She quickly set about cleaning and peeling them before she cut them into chunks.

She settled onto a stool as the women began to talk

about everything from clothes to makeup to cutting their hair. Gwynn found herself laughing so hard she was crying.

"We need to make a list of what we want to get the men for presents," Sonya said.

Gwynn licked her lips as she thought of spending Christmas with Logan. "When were y'all planning to head into town to shop?"

"We don't," Marcail said with a roll of her eyes.

Larena elbowed Marcail in the arm and shook her head. "I can go, but because of the spell halting their aging, they need to stay here."

"Going out every once in awhile won't do anything," Isla said. "I've tried to tell the men that."

"They don't want anything to happen to us," Cara said.

Reaghan wiped her hands on a towel. "They could come with us to ensure nothing does."

"Instead, Larena does the shopping for us," Marcail said.

Larena smiled at Gwynn. "We could go together if you'd like."

"Since Logan has returned, I don't see why we can't leave the castle," Sonya said.

Isla shrugged. "We have no idea how long it will take the others to find us."

Almost immediately there was a shout from the great hall. All of the women ran out of the kitchen. Gwynn peered around Cara to find a young man who had the same dark green eyes as Quinn.

"Look who we found on the road home!" the young man shouted.

"Aiden," Marcail said. "It's about time you got home. Oh!"

Two men in medieval breeches and tunics and one in a

kilt stepped into the castle and the Warriors erupted in shouts as they greeted them.

"That's Ramsey, Arran, and Camdyn," Isla said from beside Gwynn. She smiled, blinking away tears. "They've made it home."

CHAPTER
THIRTY-ONE

December 22nd

Deirdre stood at the top of her mountain and closed her eyes against the harsh winter wind that roared by her. The clouds above her were dark gray and hung heavy in the sky.

The snow had begun to fall hours earlier, but not even that had kept her inside.

The empire she had built over centuries had been destroyed in one single blow by the MacLeods. Then, just as she was getting everything back the way it was supposed to be, Declan had interfered.

Deirdre wasn't sure whom she wanted to kill first. Though she was leaning toward Declan. Wouldn't it serve her master right if she killed Declan and took his magic?

She smiled and snuggled into her jacket. Deirdre didn't know much about Declan's plans, but she knew he wanted to rule just as she did.

And she would only rule alone.

With her mind set, she made her way back into the

mountain. She wasn't surprised to find Malcolm leaning casually against the wall opposite her chamber.

"Did you already find what I sent you to town for?" she asked.

He pushed his tall, muscular frame from the wall and raised a brow. "Of course. It's as Declan told you. Clans are no' what they used to be. We'll be hard-pressed to find men for Warriors."

"I don't think so. There has to be some event, some kind of sport where men can prove themselves."

"There are a few."

"Then find me the best of the best. If they cannot be made into a Warrior, then I will find other uses for them."

When Malcolm didn't move, she rolled her eyes and sighed. "What is it?"

"I've found you three who might interest you. They were fighting. It's called extreme fighting. I watched these men. They're verra good."

Deirdre walked to him and ran a long fingernail gently down his cheek. "Perfect. Shall we go and see them?"

She followed Malcolm as he led her to where the men waited in the cavern. With one look, Deirdre was beyond pleased. The men were tall and well honed. Their muscles bulged from use, and the scars on their bodies attested to their skill and wit at winning.

"I'm told you three are good at what you do," she said.

One whistled, his gaze appreciative as he looked her over, and slowly got to his feet. "We do all right."

"An English accent?" she asked, looking at Malcolm.

He shrugged. "Other things," he reminded her.

Deirdre smiled and looked at the other two. "Are either of you Scottish?"

"We both are," the middle one with ginger hair answered.

"Perfect. Malcolm, please escort our English friend to the guest chamber while I have a little chat with these other two."

She waited until Malcolm and the other man were gone before she smiled. Deirdre lifted her hands and felt the rush of her black magic rise to her fingertips. The spell she had memorized centuries earlier to release the gods inside the men tumbled from her lips.

At first nothing happened, and Deirdre feared neither man would become a Warrior. Then the ginger-haired giant clutched his stomach and fell to his knees while the other man looked on.

Deirdre watched in glee as the god inside her new Warrior awoke. The man threw back his head and bellowed in pain as his bones popped and broke, only to heal instantly as his god stretched within him.

"What the bloody Hell is going on?" the second man shouted.

When her new Warrior leaned forward on his hands, his body taking in huge gulps of air, Deirdre turned to the second man. "What is your name?"

"Toby."

"Well, Toby. You may not be a Warrior, but you can be of use to me."

Toby took a step back. "I'm no' sure I want any part of this."

"Too late." Deirdre held up her hand, her magic shooting from her fingers and halting Toby where he stood. "Look in my eyes, Toby. Go on. Look."

When she had the dim-witted fool locked in her gaze, Deirdre used her magic to turn his mind to hers, a vessel for her to command. "Who do you work for, Toby?"

"You," he murmured.

"Good. Now, return to your home. I need men. Special men. They must be unbeatable. The kind of men you don't see every day. When you find these men, I want you to bring them here."

"How?"

She shrugged. "Use whatever means you must. Just bring them here unharmed. Malcolm will give you plenty of coin for you to sell in exchange for whatever they're using for money."

"Yes, mistress."

"Go, Toby. And hurry." Deirdre looked at her new Warrior and found he had gained his feet. "I had hoped one of you would become a Warrior."

"What have you done to me?" he said between gasping breaths.

She smiled, her gaze taking in the deep orange color of his skin, claws, and eyes. "I'll explain everything. First, what's your name?"

"Charlie."

"Well, Charlie. Welcome to your new home. You are a Warrior, and the voice you hear inside you is a god so ancient his name has been lost to the ages. He will give you immortality. He will give you power. But always, you will be mine to control."

Charlie looked over her shoulder and bared his fangs. Deirdre laughed and waited as Malcolm walked to her side.

"So you've found another Warrior," Malcolm said.

"Nay, you have," she said. "Take Charlie to the others and show him what it means to be one of my Warriors. I will send our English friend out to collect more men for me."

Malcolm motioned to Charlie with his chin. "I gave Toby enough coin to last him awhile. He said he knows some men who might be what you're looking for."

Deirdre rubbed her hands together. "Good. By the way, we'll be capturing Declan first. I want him dead."

* * *

It was almost one in the morning before talk turned to the *Book of Craigan* and the artifact. Gwynn tried to stifle her yawns, but the day was catching up with her fast.

There had been much celebrating with the arrival of the other three Warriors. It seems each had arrived in the present year at different times.

Camdyn had been there for almost a month, while Ramsey had arrived two weeks ago, and Arran had just gotten there the day before. They had met up on their way to MacLeod Castle.

Gwynn was happy for Logan and the rest of the castle. The only one missing now was Ian. No one mentioned it, but she saw it in everyone's faces. There was no doubt the people of MacLeod Castle would find Ian and bring him home.

Logan had related their tale to the three new arrivals. There had been countless questions directed at her, which she answered as best she could. Many involved her magic, which she didn't know how to answer.

That's when Ramsey had asked about the book. Gwynn hadn't wanted to get it out again. It was a force she couldn't resist, and even though she knew she had to look through it, she also knew she could never do it alone. Because she might never come out.

"Wait," Cara said. "I want to know what happened at Declan's mansion. Everyone arrived here, then Gwynn saw the book and chaos reigned."

Gwynn gave an apologetic smile to Cara. "I'm sorry."

Marcail shook her head. "No need to apologize."

"I agree," Larena said. "I briefly told Fallon about the mansion, but there are things everyone needs to know. First, Declan is holding a Druid."

"What?" Isla said, her ice blue eyes turning deadly.

"A *mie*," Larena continued. "He has her chained below

the house in what can only be described as a dungeon. It's cold and dark down there, and he had done some kind of magic because she believed there were spiders crawling on her when there were none."

"That bastard," Sonya ground out.

Broc wrapped an arm about her shoulders. "Did you try to release her, Larena?"

Larena nodded. "There was magic barring the cell door. Whoever she is, she tried to resist whatever it was he wanted. In the end he got what he wanted, but he punished her as well."

Gwynn saw Isla's hands clenched on the table. One look around the table told Gwynn that everyone wanted to free this Druid.

"How do we get her out?" Gwynn asked.

Isla's chest heaved with anger. "We do whatever it takes. Even if it means we Druids attack him."

"Nay," Logan said.

Gwynn cringed when Isla turned her ice-blue eyes to Logan.

Logan sighed. "Isla, we will get her out. But we cannot allow any of you near Wallace. You have no idea what he's capable of."

"Logan's correct," Larena said. "From the outside of the mansion, you can feel his black magic. But inside . . . inside is like you stepped into Hell itself."

Gwynn shifted in her seat. "I didn't feel that at his mansion. Did you?" she asked Logan.

"Nay." Logan raked a hand through his honey-colored hair. "Tonight was different though. If I had felt that kind of evil when we drove up to his mansion, we would never have gotten out of the car."

"What do we do now?" Arran asked.

All eyes turned to Fallon at the head of the table. He

leaned back in his chair, his elbows on the arms of his chair and his fingers linked over his stomach.

"There are several things that need be done," he said. "Gwynn and Logan need to find the Tablet of Orn. We need to free the *mie* from Wallace's house. We also need to find and kill both Deirdre and Wallace."

As soon as Fallon finished speaking, the hall erupted with talk as everyone gave their opinions on what should be done first.

Gwynn found her eyes pulled to Logan. He reached beneath the table and took her hand.

"How soon can you read through the book?" he asked.

"A few days."

"I doona know if we have that long."

"Then I will read faster."

He nodded as Fallon slammed his hand on the table for quiet.

"Logan," Fallon said. "What do you think?"

Logan's hazel eyes glanced Gwynn's way before he said, "I think Gwynn and I should head to Eigg to retrieve the artifact. The same time a group storms Wallace's house to free the Druid and Gwynn's father."

"Declan willna be able to be at two places at once," Lucan said with a nod. "I like it."

"You're forgetting Deirdre," Ramsey added.

Hayden frowned. "I'll go with Logan and Gwynn to the isle. They'll need someone to watch their backs."

"Include me in that as well," Ramsey said.

Fallon looked around the table and nodded. "It's decided then. As soon as Gwynn can decipher the book, we'll put the plan into motion."

Gwynn rose and walked to the book where she gathered it in her arms and started up the stairs.

"Where are you going?" Logan asked from behind her.

"We don't have a lot of time. I need to read."

He took the book from her and put his hand on her lower back as he guided her up the stairs. "What you need is rest."

Gwynn's blood began to pound as Logan's hand drifted lower to idly play with her bottom as she walked. By the time they reached her room, her body was on fire.

Logan shut and locked the door behind him. He set aside the book on the table next to the fireplace, then after a long look at her, knelt and stoked the fire until the blaze crackled in the silence.

Gwynn started forward to claim the book when Logan's hands snagged her around her waist and pulled her down next to him on the thick rug.

"I said you need to rest," he murmured as he nuzzled her ear.

Gwynn drank in the desire she saw in Logan's eyes. He said "rest," but he obviously had plans for anything but.

CHAPTER
THIRTY-TWO

Logan groaned at the sweet, exotic taste of Gwynn's lips. She was an addiction, an obsession, and one he would gladly enjoy every day for the rest of his immortal life.

Except, did he have the right?

He knew he wasn't a good man. A good man would never have gone to Deirdre.

Yet, for all his deeds, both decent and foul, Logan couldn't find it in himself to let Gwynn go. He wanted her with a passion that bordered on insanity.

His balls tightened when she raked her nails gently along his scalp before threading her fingers in his hair. The fire that roared next to them was nothing compared to the inferno their desire ignited.

It scorched, it burned.

It consumed.

And Logan willingly—and readily—went into the flames.

He tucked Gwynn's mouth-watering curves against him and rolled so that he was on top. Logan deepened the kiss and let his hand caress down her side until it rested on her flared hip.

Logan slipped his fingers beneath her sweater so he could touch her silky smooth skin. She moaned into his mouth and clutched her arms about his neck tighter.

Her skin was warm beneath his hands, her body pliant and soft. He showed her in his kiss how much he wanted her, how much she meant to him. He might not ever be able to claim her as his own, but he would claim her body this night. This night, he would pretend the future was theirs.

He would pretend that he was the right man for Gwynn.

Logan skimmed his hand up her flat belly until he found her breast. His cupped the orb and gently massaged it. He circled his finger around her nipple through the delicate lace of her bra. She ground her hips against him, her moan music to his ears.

He rolled her turgid nipple between his fingers and lightly pinched. Gwynn's back bowed as she tore her mouth from his and gave a soft cry.

They reached for each other's clothes, tugging, tearing, and laughing as they stripped each other rolling around on the rug. Logan gathered her in his arms and slowly, seductively ran his finger down the curve of her spine.

Gwynn smiled as her eyes drifted shut. He leaned in and took her mouth in a scorching kiss, one meant to conquer and dominate. To capture.

She met him kiss for kiss, giving as much as he demanded. He'd never met anyone who matched his passions, never imagined there would be a woman for him. Yet here she was. In his arms.

Logan held her hips as he ground into her. Her soft gasp filled the chamber. He wanted to be inside her, to feel her damp heat as he filled her.

He used his knees to part her legs and settled between them. It was his turn to moan when her legs loosely wrapped around him. His arousal pulsed with need, eager to plunge inside her.

But not yet. This time he would take it slow and savor every moment.

Gwynn sucked in a breath when Logan's fingers skimmed her softness. His masterful fingers found her and thrust into her aching sex.

She raised her hips to meet his fingers and sighed. He withdrew only to tease her clitoris with slow, teasing circles. Her need gathered and tightened with each flick of his fingers over her.

He was merciless as his slow teasing turned to moving his thumb back and forth over her swollen clitoris faster and faster. Gwynn could feel her climax building. Her body thrummed with it, sought it. And just when she was about to give in, Logan rose up over her.

She opened her eyes to see him kneeling between her legs, his cock jutting upward with a drop glistening on the swollen head.

Gwynn reached for him, wanting to feel his arousal in her hands. Her fingers wrapped around his hot erection. She softly squeezed and smiled when she heard his groan.

She pumped her hands up and down his length. Before she could set up a rhythm, Logan pried her hands away and kissed each palm.

"I wasn't done," she said.

He smiled, and it sent the butterflies churning in her stomach. "Tonight, Gwynn Austin, you are mine."

His words, whispered in a deep, husky voice both erotic and demanding, made whatever argument she might have had fade into nothing.

No man, ever, had spoken to her like that. Like he had dreamed of having her in his arms. Like he wanted the night to last an eternity, just so he could spend it with her.

Men like that didn't exist except in movies and books. But somehow, one was with her. And making love to her.

Gwynn looked into Logan's hazel eyes and knew that

tonight would be special. It would be a night she would
never forget, a night that would be branded into her soul.

An unsteady breath passed through her lips as Logan's
heated gaze swept down her body, lingering on her breasts.
He leaned forward and wrapped his lips around one nipple and laved, licked the sensitive peak until Gwynn's head
was thrashing from side to side.

He repeated the process on her other breast, leaving
Gwynn a quivering mass of need. Her body was on fire,
each nerve ending bunched tight. She lifted her hips, seeking to grind against him, but his hands held her hips down.
She whimpered and dug her nails into the rug.

Logan kissed between the valley of her breasts, then
down her body. He licked her navel and nipped at each
hip bone before he lifted her hips up to meet his mouth.

She cried out at the first swipe of his tongue over her
sex. Gwynn was powerless to move as he held her steady
and used his tongue to raise her need even higher.

Logan watched the pleasure on Gwynn's face while
he feasted on her sex. He felt her muscles tighten as she
neared her orgasm once again. With her eyes closed and
soft cries falling from her beautiful lips, Logan had never
seen a more stunning picture.

He continued to lick her until the last possible moment
before she peaked. When he drew his mouth away, she
opened her eyes.

Her glorious violet eyes were glowing, just as they had
when she had looked at the book. Logan lowered her hips
and guided his throbbing cock to her entrance. She gasped
as the engorged head of his erection pressed into her.

Logan slowly filled her, inch by inch, until she had
taken all of him. He closed his eyes at the exquisite feel of
Gwynn's sheath surrounding him.

He began to move within her, leisurely at first, then

steadily increasing his tempo until he was driving into her. Her nails dug into his back and her legs wrapped around his waist, allowing him to sink even deeper.

She met him thrust for thrust, prolonging their wild ride. She moaned, her head tilted back in pleasure. Something shifted inside Logan, digging deep into his soul, telling Logan he needed Gwynn. Not just to satisfy his body, but to erase his guilt and heal him of his demons.

He thrust harder, faster, deeper as he felt her rise, heard her gasp as she shattered.

Her strangled cry as she came apart beneath him made him smile in satisfaction. But it was just one of many he planned to wring from her that night.

Gwynn had never felt anything so marvelous. Her limbs were liquid, her body not her own. She cracked open her eyes when she felt Logan pull out of her.

He smiled as his large hands caught her hips and turned her onto her stomach. In the next instant, he had her on her hands and knees. Gwynn looked over her shoulder to find him kneeling behind her.

Barely able to hold herself up, Logan filled her from behind with a single thrust. Her already frayed nerves sizzled with this new pleasure.

He withdrew only to thrust into her again. Gwynn closed her eyes and gave herself over to him. She gloried in the feel of his groin meeting her sensitive bottom, of hearing the sound of flesh meeting flesh.

Gwynn leaned back against him, but once more Logan held her hips in his firm hands, refusing to allow her to move. She was helpless against the onslaught of hot, hard cock thrusting repeatedly into her.

Desire swept through her anew, the blaze that had never died out flaring once more. It swept toward her, engulfing her in the mind-blowing pleasure.

Logan kept her still, immobile as he pounded desperately into her. He bent around her, his mouth at her neck as he roared and thrust once more.

Gwynn screamed Logan's name as she felt another climax take her, consume her as waves of pleasure engulfed her. She was falling into an abyss of contentment she never wanted to rise from.

Her body well used, Gwynn found herself smiling as Logan slid out of her. He pulled her with him as he fell to his side. She readily snuggled against his warmth as he spread a blanket over them.

With the fire crackling, the sea wind howling outside, and Logan's chest beneath her cheek, Gwynn had never been happier.

"Tell me of your life before coming to Scotland," Logan asked.

Gwynn chuckled. "I'm not sure I can form a coherent thought after what you just did to me."

"Aye. And the night is just beginning."

She heard the smile in his voice and laughed. "What do you want to know?"

"Everything."

"I already told you about my parents. I didn't have any siblings, nor was there any other family around. I finished high school, went to college, and got a degree in general business because I had no idea what I wanted to do with my life or what career I wanted."

"Career?"

She nodded. "Yep. In order to have money, one has to work. It'd be nice to make money at something you enjoy, but that rarely happens. So, I went to work for a small property management company as their manager. It's decent money, but not exactly what I wanted to do with my life."

"What did you want to do?"

She sighed and glanced up at him. He had one arm around her and the other was bent beneath his head. "I don't know," she admitted.

"Nothing?"

"Well, I always wanted to travel. There's so much of the world I'd like to see and learn. I had always envisioned my first stop to be Scotland," she said with a laugh.

His fingers caressed up and down her back. "Because of your family."

"No, just because I always found it fascinating. I wanted to see every castle."

"Tell me more about your life," he said when she paused.

"There's nothing to tell. I had a cat I adored. I got her when she was just six weeks old and kept her until she died at age seventeen. She was so loving, always purring when I petted her. And she'd drool when she purred."

Logan chuckled. "What was her name?"

"Sheba. You've never seen such bright blue eyes as this cat had. The sweetest thing, too."

"When did she die?"

"Last year."

"You didna get another animal?"

Gwynn shrugged. "I wasn't ready. Enough about me. I want to know more about your life before and after you turned immortal. I imagine you have some great stories."

He was quiet so long Gwynn didn't think he would answer. She shifted so that she rested her chin on his chest and looked at him.

"Logan? What is it?"

His hazel eyes looked from the fire to her. "Do you really want to know?"

"Yes."

"You will regret it, Gwynn."

She reached over and ran her fingers through the hair

at his temple. "I know you keep some secret or deed or something deep inside you. It shows sometimes, despite your smiles. It's a darkness that cannot be hidden."

"A darkness. That's an appropriate name for it."

Gwynn bit her lip and waited. Logan's gaze slid back to the fire.

"My family was poor, but then most were at the time. My father worked hard, as did my mother. I caught the laird's eye with my archery skills, and soon I was training with his soldiers. My younger brother, Ronald, wanted to follow in my footsteps. He idolized me, followed me everywhere."

"You two were close, then?"

"Aye. Verra close. He was six years younger, so it was my duty to keep him out of trouble. Ronald was always more cautious than I. Yet he never backed away from any challenge."

Gwynn smiled at the joy she heard in Logan's words.

"I became the best warrior of my clan," Logan continued. "No one could best me, no' even my laird. Just because I was someone important to my laird, I foolishly thought everyone else would think the same thing."

He paused for a moment. "I remember the first time I heard Deirdre's name. Fear and uncertainty were connected to her name. And each time it was spoken, the fear grew and the uncertainty continued."

Gwynn's heart began to thud painfully slow in her chest. Logan's jaw clenched, and his hand on her back fisted.

"I had heard the tales of the MacLeods and what she had supposedly done. But instead of fearing her as others did, I only saw the power she held. I had made a name for myself in my clan as a warrior, so I decided to find this woman."

Gwynn's heart ached at the distress she heard in his

words. She could well imagine him as a laird's favorite warrior.

"I thought I was meant for more than what I had been given in life. I wasna nobility, but I hungered for the riches, the land, and the titles. I knew I had the sword arm to prove myself, but I had nothing else. My laird assured me I would never want for anything as the commander of his men, but it wasn't enough for me. I had won enough battles and one-on-one attacks to think I was invincible."

Her arms squeezed him. How could he berate himself for things most people thought? No matter how much she wanted to tell him that, she wouldn't interrupt his tale.

"I recall the horrified looks on my parents' faces when I told them I was going to Deirdre. They desperately tried to talk me out of it, but I refused to listen. In my mind, Deirdre had the wherewithal to give me what I wanted most."

His fingers laced with hers, but he wouldn't meet her eyes. Gwynn let her magic surround him, showing him that she was with him.

"Leaving behind my parents, my laird, and my clan was difficult," he continued. "But it was nothing like leaving behind my brother. Ronald didna understand why I was leaving. He followed me into the night, calling my name over and over and begging me to come back or take him with me."

Gwynn blinked away the tears that gathered in her eyes at the agony in Logan's voice.

"He wouldna stop calling my name. I could hear him crying, his young mind no' able to understand where I was going or why. My parents finally intervened. The worst part is, I never looked back. I never went to him and told him farewell. He worshipped me, Gwynn, and I left him standing in the dark crying."

She didn't brush away the tears that fell down her face.

If Logan wouldn't shed the tears himself, she would do it for him.

After a moment, Logan said, "I never stopped, never considered my decision to go to Deirdre foolish. Until I reached Cairn Toul. It was majestic. But as I stood on that mountain, I could hear Ronald's voice in my head begging me to come back. Just as I was turning around to do so, there was suddenly an entrance into the mountain that hadna been there before.

"I forgot my brother as I thought of the life I could have. I hesitated but a moment before I walked inside. It was so dark, so cold, but all I could think about was the magic I'd heard whispered over the land about Deirdre. I was prepared to do anything to have her give me what I wanted."

Gwynn's heart clenched in dread at the words which would come next.

"Of course I'd heard about the Warriors. Who in Scotland hadna? So when I was granted an audience with her I suggested she see if I had a god inside me. I thought it the best way to get what I wanted. It was said the Warriors were the best fighters, so I assumed I had a chance.

"As I gazed at her unnaturally long, white hair and eerie white eyes, I didna sense the evil within her. I was blinded by my greed."

Her tears came faster because she knew what she was hearing, Logan had never told another soul. And now she knew why.

He took a steadying breath and forged ahead. "She didna want to even try to see if I had a god. She looked me over and said I wasna worth anything. I, of course, laughed. I had no idea what I was getting myself into, nor did I care.

"In response, she raised her hand and four men stepped out of the shadows. They were no' Warriors, but by the vacant look in their eyes, I knew they'd been prisoners. Still, it didna stop me from my intent."

Once more Gwynn let her magic surround and comfort him. To her joy, he didn't question it, just accepted it.

"I fought them," he continued. "They were rabid, crazed. But I was skilled and in my right mind. It didna take me long to end them. I proudly displayed the kills to Deirdre, telling her it wouldna hurt to see if I had a god. It never occurred to me that if I didna she wouldna let me go.

"To my amazement, I did have a god inside me. When she said those words in a language I didna understand, I had never felt such pain in my life. Every bone in my body snapped in two. My muscles were pulled apart and my arms wrenched from their sockets. But that was nothing compared to the feel of Athleus rising inside me."

Gwynn rubbed her cheek against his chest while she waited for Logan to finish.

"I tried to hold back my bellows of pain, but in the end it was too much. Even through the haze of agony I heard Deirdre's laughter. I hear it still."

His head turned and he locked his gaze with hers. "Athleus is the god of betrayal. Ironic, is it no'? Now you know the secret I have kept from everyone, the deed I will do anything to atone for."

CHAPTER
THIRTY-THREE

Logan waited for Gwynn to condemn him, waited for her to jump away from him with contempt on her beautiful face.

Instead, she laid her hand over his heart and smiled softly. "You made a mistake, Logan."

"It was more than a mistake."

"If you want to feel guilty because you went to Deirdre, then I cannot stop you. In the end, it was just a matter of time before she found you herself."

He scoffed at her words.

"Fine," she said with a firm set of her lips. "What happened after she unbound your god?"

"When a god is unbound, his rage is vast. Many men can no' withstand the onslaught of the anger and the ferocious need to kill. They fall to their god. Sometimes, I wonder if that would have been easier than seeing firsthand what I had given myself to.

"Between the screams of the dying Druids and the tortured men, Cairn Toul became my Hell. Deirdre thought that because I had come to her I would do what she said. Though I had been naïve and stupid, I realized as soon as I felt Athleus that I had to make a decision. So, I fought him."

"And Deirdre?" Gwynn whispered.

He closed his eyes and tried to keep her from seeing his anguish. "Aye, I fought her. She locked me in the dungeon and tortured me for months. She threatened my family, but I knew to save them I had to act as though I didna care."

"Did she harm them?"

He shrugged. "I doona know. By the time I escaped and returned to them, there was nothing left. No one knew of them or what had happened. Ever since escaping Deirdre, I've done everything in my power to fight her."

He waited for Gwynn to say something, anything, but only silence filled the air. He wasn't surprised. She had wanted to know the awful, sordid details of his past. Now that she knew the truth, it was only a matter of time before everything sunk in and she shut him out of her life.

And he couldn't blame her. Not after what he had done. He didn't deserve to know the heavenly taste of her kisses. Nor did he deserve to have men call him brother, men who would risk their lives for him.

Logan had seen the shock and fury in Duncan's eyes when Deirdre had told him. It was why Logan had never told anyone, not even Hayden. He couldn't bear to lose the only family he had.

"Logan, look at me," Gwynn demanded.

Unable to help himself, he looked down into her beautiful face, her lovely violet eyes. "You doona need to say anything. I know how you feel."

"Actually, you don't. You honor me by telling a story you have kept to yourself all these years."

Honor? He had burdened her with a tale of greed and foolishness that should never be repeated.

"Everyone makes mistakes. You are making up for

yours now. You have been, ever since you decided to fight Deirdre. You found the MacLeods. You've been fighting against her and her evil for decades, Logan. That more than makes up for going to her."

"Doona try to make me look like a hero, Gwynn. The other Warriors at MacLeod Castle were all taken against their will. Their families were killed by Deirdre. How do you think they will look at me when they discover I willingly went to Deirdre? Only her death will atone me of my sin."

Gwynn released a long sigh. "You think the others will be angry about this, don't you?"

"I think they'll hate me," he answered. It was the first time he had admitted it aloud, and he didn't like how badly it hurt to say it. "I betrayed them."

"If you betrayed anyone, Logan, it was yourself. But I wouldn't even say that. You left your family and your little brother. I understand the guilt over that. Did you go to war with other clans?"

"Aye."

"How is that any different from leaving to seek Deirdre? You could have been killed in one of those battles."

Logan squeezed his eyes closed and shook his head. "You are looking for ways to absolve me."

"No. I'm pointing out facts you've refused to see. That darkness inside you is eating you alive. It's destroying the man you really are. You've kept it buried deep, and its driven you in your decisions."

Logan looked at the ceiling. "You didna see Duncan's face when Deirdre told him what I did, Gwynn. There was anger, aye, but also disdain."

"What you did, and do, have control over is your decision to fight against Deirdre. That tells me all I need to know of the man you are, Logan Hamilton."

Logan's chest tightened. Could it really be as simple as Gwynn made it sound? Had he really carried the guilt for nothing?

Her small fingers touched his chin and gently turned his head until his eyes met her violet ones. She smiled and kissed him.

"You will kill Deirdre," she said. "We all will."

Logan kissed her forehead as she snuggled under the covers. "You're an amazing woman, Gwynn."

"Nope. Just one who can see things much clearer than you."

Logan found himself smiling, the guilt he'd shouldered for so long lighter than it had been in ages. It wasn't gone, nor would it disappear until Deirdre was dead.

But Gwynn had helped him. Logan's eyes closed, the smile still in place.

Gwynn woke several hours later to find the fire dying. She crawled out from under the blanket, careful not to wake Logan, and added more wood to the fire.

She rubbed her hands over her icy skin and dug out some sweats and two pairs of socks from her bag. The castle had been modernized, but there were still drafts.

Once her teeth stopped chattering, Gwynn sat before the fire with the *Book of Craigan* in her lap. She had a perfect view of Logan just by lifting her eyes, and though she'd like nothing more than to stay curled up by his side, she had to learn the secrets of the book.

Gwynn felt the pull of the book's magic calling to hers. She opened the thick cover and flipped to the page she had been reading.

The surge of pleasure she felt from the book brought a smile to her face. It seemed to recognize her, to sense she was the Keeper.

Gwynn began to read, becoming absorbed in the words and history of the book. The more she read, the quicker the words came until she was reading faster than she could turn the pages.

Everything about the Druids of Eigg from the time the Tablet of Orn came to the isle until two hundred years ago was in the book.

When Gwynn reached the end, tears welled in her eyes as she read how it became harder and harder for the Druids to hide their magic when they were all together.

Gwynn turned the last page and closed the cover. When she looked up the fire was roaring and Logan was sitting across from her with a pair of jeans on, unbuttoned, and nothing else.

"I woke to find you reading," he said.

She wiped at her eyes. "Did you try and stop me?"

He shook his head. "I was no' going to leave you though."

"I know." She set aside the book and put her hand on the cover. "I read it all. Every page. I know why the Druids aren't on Eigg anymore."

"Why?"

"Their magic was too powerful when they were together. People started to get suspicious and ask too many questions. So the Druids began to leave the isle. I don't think they all meant to leave, but over the years it happened."

Logan poked at the fire. "Aye, I can see that. The Druids are private people. They doona like others interfering. To protect themselves and their magic, they had to take precautions."

"And with Deirdre no longer around, they thought they were safe."

"Precisely."

Gwynn moved her feet closer to the fire to help thaw her toes. "You've not asked me about the Tablet."

Logan shrugged and smiled at her. "I knew you would tell me when you wanted to."

"So much faith in me," she said with a grin.

"It's well deserved."

She'd been joking, but Logan wasn't. She saw it in the way his eyes held hers. His hand came down on hers and his thumb caressed her skin.

She was in way over her head. This was the time she knew she should pull back from Logan to protect herself and her heart, but she couldn't find the will.

And it might already be too late for her heart.

There were feelings growing for Logan, and she was afraid those feelings could very well be love. Instead of making her run, it made her . . . stronger.

"Do you remember how I was pulled to that place on Eigg?" she asked.

Logan nodded. "Of course. Is that where it's at?"

"Kinda. It's under the isle."

"Under?" he repeated with a frown, his honey-colored hair falling forward as he leaned toward her.

Gwynn turned her hand over and linked her fingers with his. "Yes. There are caves all over the isle. This one leads deep beneath the isle."

"It'll be dangerous then. I'll go and get the Tablet."

She laughed because she'd known he'd insist on something like that. "Unfortunately, tough guy, that's not possible. The only one who can take the Tablet from its resting place is the Keeper. I have to go."

"Shite."

"We do this together. Remember?"

He nodded, but his jaw was set. "But I doona have to like it."

"I know." She glanced at the window through the crack in the curtains to see it beginning to lighten outside. "It's early, but we should tell the others."

Logan rose to his feet with the grace of a leopard. "I'll make sure the others are up. You go ahead and take a shower. I think for this trip into Eigg we need to wait for nightfall anyway."

"Probably," Gwynn said and took his hand as he pulled her to her feet. "I'm going to need a week under hot water just to thaw out."

"You should no' have left my side last night. I'd have kept you warm."

She smiled and lifted a brow. "Oh, you kept me warm. And exhausted. I couldn't move for hours."

"I'm losing my touch, then. I should have been able to keep you in bed for days. Maybe we should have another go."

Gwynn laughed and ducked as he reached for her. She raced into the bathroom and tried to close the door before he got in, but he was too quick

Before she knew it, he had her pinned against the door, each of her wrists locked in his grip.

Her smile died as she saw his eyes smoldering with hunger. His jaw was covered with whiskers, and his long light brown hair was disheveled. And he looked incredible.

"I can no' get enough of you," he said.

Gwynn swallowed to wet her mouth. "I know the feeling."

Logan's gaze searched hers. "It frightens you?"

"Yes," she said with a small nod. "I don't allow myself to get close to anyone. I always get hurt when I do."

She waited for him to promise not to hurt her, to tell her that he was different from the rest. But he didn't.

He smiled, but she saw it didn't reach his eyes. Then he

released his grip on her wrists and took a step back. "We've a long day ahead of us. You should get ready."

"Yeah. Okay."

Gwynn moved so he could leave the bathroom, and she couldn't help but feel as if she'd allowed something important, something vital, to slip through her hands.

She hadn't lied to Logan. She was terrified of the feelings he stirred within her. But she wasn't running as she usually did. It wasn't because of the mission or Deirdre or her father.

Gwynn wasn't leaving because of Logan.

She stepped out of the bathroom to tell him that, but he'd already left her room.

"Damn," Gwynn muttered.

She almost ran after Logan, but she held back. It wasn't the time to get into her feelings. As Logan said, they had much planning to do to carry out this mission. Once she had the Tablet of Orn and was back at the castle she could talk to Logan.

Maybe by then she'd know if what she felt was just a full-on case of lust, or something much deeper.

Like love.

CHAPTER
THIRTY-FOUR

Logan strode into his chamber and halted. He stared at the room without really seeing it. His mind, as it had been most of the morning, was on the night he and Gwynn had shared.

He'd told her things he had never thought to tell anyone. It wasn't just the talking they had done, it had been the lovemaking.

There had been many times he'd had shared the night with a woman. But it had only been for the sex. Never for anything else. And never had he felt so different afterward.

With Gwynn, it was another matter entirely. He couldn't think straight, couldn't remember why he should stay away from her.

He was adrift. Aimless. Lost.

Logan had been content on his own. He hadn't wanted or needed anyone. Until Gwynn.

She had changed everything.

"Logan?"

He turned his head slightly at the sound of Galen's voice. "Are the others awake?"

"They're waking now. Is everything all right? You look—"

"I'm fine," Logan interrupted him. "Please have everyone meet in the great hall. Gwynn read the book last night. She knows where the artifact is."

Logan had hoped Galen would leave then. Instead, his friend leaned against the doorway.

"I expected you to sound happier at the news," Galen said.

Logan shrugged and turned his head forward. "I'm beyond ecstatic. I'll be able to finish my original mission."

There was a long pause, and then Galen said, "I'll have the others waiting for you."

As soon as Logan heard Galen's footsteps walking away, he kicked the door shut with his foot. Logan raked a hand through his hair. He could still taste Gwynn on his tongue, still feel her silky skin beneath his hands.

It was everything he could do not to return to her chamber and make love to her again and again until she forgot her fear. And until he could get her out of his system once and for all.

Somehow, Logan knew he would never get her out of his mind. She had penetrated too deeply. She was in his soul, in his mind. In his very being. His every thought centered around her.

He should have been consoled by the fact that he wasn't the only one befuddled by his emotions. Gwynn was feeling them as well. Or at least she was feeling something.

The way the panic had streaked through her violet eyes when she had admitted her fear had made his chest hurt. He didn't want her trepidation. He wanted her body, her lips, and her hands.

He wanted her smile and her laughter.

He wanted to be the one she turned to and the one she trusted.

He wanted to share her past. And her future.

He wanted . . . her.

Logan dropped his chin to his chest and let out a long breath. He couldn't allow himself to be softened, not now. Not when there was a chance he would be in battle soon.

Because there was no way Deirdre and Wallace would allow them to take the Tablet of Orn without some sort of fight. Logan had to be focused. He had to clear his mind of anything and everything but retrieving the artifact.

When he lifted his head, he had shoved Gwynn out of his mind. He changed clothes and ran his fingers through his hair before he made his way downstairs.

Logan wasn't surprised to see everyone except Gwynn in the great hall. He gave a nod of greeting and found a seat at the far end of the table between Ramsey and Arran.

He was filling his plate with food when Gwynn came downstairs, her cheeks flushed and her glorious black hair falling about her shoulders.

Logan pulled his eyes from her and found Hayden watching him. Logan raised a brow at his friend, and a slow smile spread over Hayden's face.

"Good morning," Gwynn said as came around the table.

Logan saw the way her feet missed a step when she noticed where he sat. He wasn't trying to hurt her. He was protecting her by distancing himself.

At least that's what he told himself. He knew it for the lie that it was. He was protecting himself.

"What's the news?" Lucan asked.

Gwynn took a seat beside Hayden, all too aware of where Logan sat. It shouldn't matter. He wasn't hers. They weren't a couple. Yet, he had been by her side since they had arrived at the castle.

She refused to allow it to bother her, however. She'd known that getting close to Logan would likely cause her hurt, and she had accepted that. She needed to prepare herself for it though, or she would find herself in a place she had sworn never to be in again.

Gwynn accepted a plate piled high with eggs, toast, sausage, and bacon. "I read the *Book of Craigan* last night," she announced.

As she expected, she had every eye in the hall. Except Logan's. He stared at his plate.

Gwynn swallowed and looked around the table. "The book is a history of the Druids from the time the Tablet of Orn was given to them. It tells everything."

"Does it tell you where the Tablet is?" Cara asked.

Gwynn nodded. "It does. It also explains that only the Keeper will be able to take it from its resting place."

Fallon sighed. "I knew you would play a part in its recovery. I had hoped to keep you out of danger, but it looks as though you will be in it, Gwynn."

"I'm a big girl," Gwynn said. "I can take care of myself."

Larena set down her fork and wiped her mouth with her napkin. "She did battle Declan."

"Does it say what happened to the Druids?" Reaghan asked.

"It does," Gwynn answered. "A little over two hundred years ago they began to leave the isle because people became suspicious of them and asked too many questions."

Isla frowned. "With that many Druids together, I can imagine their magic was felt even by those who didn't have any."

"So they just . . . left?" Marcail asked.

Gwynn nodded. "I don't think they ever thought that one day there wouldn't be any Druids on Eigg, but over time, their history was lost just as their magic and knowledge of the Tablet's presence were."

"There was no threat of Deirdre, no threat of anyone," Ramsey said. "They had no reason to believe the Tablet would be in danger."

Camdyn grunted. "That was foolish. If the artifact was

so important, someone should have been there to watch over it always."

"I agree," Gwynn said. "But regardless, it wasn't. There are a handful of Druids still on Eigg, but they have little to no magic. They knew I was a Druid, but they had no idea Logan was a Warrior."

Quinn rubbed his chin. "If their history was lost, then it's no' a great leap to think the story of the Warriors was lost as well."

"Which could be good," Hayden said.

Gwynn nibbled on her bacon and fought not to look at Logan. She should have known her admission earlier had hurt him somehow.

"We should leave tonight," Logan said. "It will be better to make our attack in the dark to alert fewer people."

Broc braced his elbows on the table and frowned. "Gwynn, can you find the artifact at night?"

"Yes," she replied, daring Logan to comment.

"Wait," Sonya said. "Where is the Tablet on the isle?"

Gwynn expected Logan to answer, but when he didn't she said, "It's in a cave."

Broc shook his head then. "Nay, Fallon. I wouldna allow them to wait. Gwynn has no' been in the cave before. It will be treacherous to go at night."

"I can do it," Gwynn argued.

Fallon held up his hand when she would have continued. "It's no' that we doona think you capable. You are a Druid, and therefore you should be protected. Since you are the only one able to retrieve the Tablet, we have no choice but to let you go. It's when you go that's in question."

As much as Gwynn would rather go during the day, she knew Logan's thinking was correct. "I think we should go at night as Logan suggested. Declan will be waiting for us."

"I'll bring her in under the water," Logan said. "No one will see us."

Gwynn's stomach flipped when she remembered the last time Logan had used his power and taken her under the sea. It had been their first kiss, the first time she realized no matter how much she knew she shouldn't get close, she couldn't stay away.

"It's a good plan," Arran said.

Hayden gave a quick nod. "Ramsey and I will be there to watch them."

Fallon's gaze swung to Gwynn. "This is your life we're putting at stake."

"No. I'm putting my own life on the line. None of you are making me do something I don't want to do."

"All right," Fallon relented. "Be that as it may, your life will be in danger. If you agree with Logan's plan, then we'll begin to prepare."

Gwynn turned her head and looked at Logan. His hazel eyes met hers, silent and watchful. "I agree with his plan."

She wasn't surprised when Logan looked away quickly, but she wasn't given time to think on it when Isla said, "I want to go with Gwynn."

"Absolutely no'," Hayden said.

Isla turned her ice-blue eyes to him and raised a black brow. "Tread carefully, husband."

"We doona know if you are still immortal or no'."

"And it doesn't matter. Another Druid will be helpful to Gwynn, especially if Declan shows up."

Gwynn smiled when Isla glanced at her. "Isla's right. Declan's black magic is strong. Having another Druid there could definitely be to our advantage."

Hayden blew out a breath. "Isla, you're going to be the death of me."

"You'll keep me safe," Isla said confidently.

Gwynn watched them and the other couples around the table. They had been together hundreds of years and still laughed and loved each other. What did they know that others didn't? What did they do that couples of her time didn't? More people were getting divorced than married, yet, around the table at MacLeod Castle sat six couples all deeply in love.

She wanted that kind of love. To know that no matter what, there would be someone standing beside her, helping her shoulder the weight of her worries or helping her solve some dilemma.

Gwynn had always wanted that kind of relationship. She just hadn't ever been brave enough to give it a try. Her terror of being left behind, of giving her heart to someone only to have them die, kept her alone.

Her worry over losing another person she loved, of feeling helpless as she watched them die had made her create walls around herself. Her own special prison.

How much had she missed out on? How much of life had passed her by as she sat in her small apartment and pretended she'd rather be watching movies than with someone?

Gwynn pushed away her uneaten plate and looked up to find Hayden watching her. His black eyes were too observant, entirely too perceptive.

"We have little time then," Fallon said. "Logan, Gwynn, Hayden, Isla, and Ramsey will go to Eigg for the Tablet. While the rest of us will make sure Wallace has no choice but to fight us."

"And if he's already on Eigg?" Gwynn asked.

When everyone just looked at her, she shrugged. "My father has been studying the book for weeks. He might not have been able to translate it because the words moved around on him, but he—and Declan—know the artifact is somewhere on Eigg. Since we have the book, they will go to Eigg. If Declan doesn't think of it, my father will. He cannot stand to lose."

"Shite," Logan muttered.

Galen smiled and rubbed his hands together. "Then we give Wallace a reason to return to his precious home immediately."

Gwynn smiled as she thought of them destroying Declan's home. She would like to have been a part of that. But she had more important things to do.

But once the artifact was in her hands and safely at MacLeod Castle, she had every intention of going after Declan.

And her father.

CHAPTER
THIRTY-FIVE

Not even the heavy coat Gwynn had borrowed from Isla could stop the cold sea wind from slicing through her. But the view had been too breathtaking to pass up. With all the planning and talking, it had taken nearly the entire day for her to get outside of the castle, but she had managed to slip away unnoticed.

She stomped through the thick snow with a scarf wrapped tight around her neck and heavy wool gloves. The land was coated with a fresh layer of blinding white snow, and the huge boulders jutting up from the ground only added to the majesty of Scotland.

Gwynn inhaled the salty air and continued to the edge of the cliffs. The sea far below her churned, its dark blue waters shifting endlessly. The sound of the waves crashing into the cliffs was calming and exhilarating.

If it had been warmer—lots warmer—Gwynn wouldn't have hesitated to make her way to the water and splash in the waves. She smiled as she glanced down and imagined lying atop one of the massive boulders as the sun warmed her.

"You should see it in the summer," Cara said as she walked toward her.

"I imagine it's just as beautiful."

"It is. There isn't a season I don't love."

Gwynn returned her smile. "Has it been hard living here for four hundred years?"

Cara shrugged and tugged on the end of her ponytail. "I won't lie and say we don't fight. We do. We all do. But then again everyone does. We all knew what we were getting into. The men get to leave because they're immortal, and at least twice a year they take us out as well."

"Is it difficult to return here?"

"Not for me," Cara said with a smile. "We lack for nothing. Would I love to shop more? Sure. But as the years went by, we upgraded the castle to have modern conveniences."

Gwynn bit her lip. It was none of her business, and she would be incredibly rude to ask, but she had to know. "How? None of you work. How do you pay for it?"

Cara laughed and moved her arm as she turned. "We use what the land has given us. And we're imaginative."

"Meaning?"

"Lucan used to build furniture. He made everything inside the castle. We sold many pieces for a time and built up quite a large sum of money. Broc had places around Scotland he had stashed money that we then brought to the castle. Isla makes the best sweets you can imagine. She sold the recipe a hundred years ago, and still makes money off it."

"So you all do something."

Cara nodded. "We pool our money together, though each of us does keep some separate. If we're in need, we do what we need to do."

"Amazing," Gwynn said as she looked at the castle. "I

used to dream of living in a castle when I was a little girl. I swore one day I'd have a castle of my very own."

"You have a home here if you want it," Cara said.

The sincerity in her voice brought tears to Gwynn's eyes. But she didn't know how to answer.

"What will you do after you get the Tablet?" Cara asked.

Gwynn smiled. It never occurred to Cara that Gwynn wouldn't bring the Tablet to the castle. "I have a life waiting for me. I took a leave of absence from my job. I'm supposed to return after New Year's."

"But will you? After all you've been through and all you've learned of yourself and your magic? Can you return?"

"I don't know."

"Then don't think of it now," Cara urged and wound her arm around Gwynn's as they started back to the castle. "Let's enjoy this. All I wanted for Christmas was for everyone to return here. Though we're still missing Ian, Logan did bring you."

"I'm glad he did."

Cara's mahogany eyes flashed through her long lashes as she glanced at Gwynn. "Am I mistaken in thinking there might be something between the two of you?"

Gwynn looked away nervously. "Logan is a good man."

"That he is, but that isn't what I asked. We all saw the kiss he gave you before heading off to Declan's to steal the book."

She swallowed as she recalled that kiss. "Had you asked me this yesterday I would have said there was something between us. Now, I'm not so sure."

"Men," Cara said with a roll of her eyes. "Especially Warriors. They come with pasts that can eat at them."

"Logan told me of his."

Cara halted, her eyes large as she stared at Gwynn.

"He did? He's never told anyone. Not even Hayden, and they are as close as brothers."

"He told me last night."

"Was it too horrific for you?" Cara asked, her face suddenly hard.

Gwynn shook her head, and hastily answered, "Heavens, no. Of course not."

"Good," Cara said with a sigh. "I like you, but—"

"Logan is family," Gwynn finished for her. "You don't have to explain."

Cara started walking again and pulled Gwynn with her. "Is there anything we can do to fix whatever has come between you and Logan?"

"It wouldn't be right. If Logan and I are meant to be, we will be."

Cara's expression said she'd rather help than not. "If that's your wish."

"It is." Gwynn paused at the entrance to the castle and knocked the snow off her boots.

But as she entered the castle, she wondered if she should have taken Cara up on her offer.

Logan watched Gwynn enter the castle with Cara, Gwynn's words still ringing in his ears.

"Well. That was interesting," Hayden said as he walked onto the battlements.

Logan ignored his friend. "Should you no' be with your wife?"

"So you told Gwynn of your past," Hayden said, doing his own ignoring.

"I did."

"And did she take it as well as she told Cara?"

Logan turned his head to Hayden. "Did you spy on their conversation?"

"Aye. Same as you."

Logan knew there was no getting around answering Hayden. He let out a sigh and said, "She took it much better than she told Cara. In the end she was telling me what a good man I am."

"It's what I've known all along. No matter what secret of your past you want kept from me, it willna change our friendship."

"Shall I test it?" Logan asked. His god smiled within him, as eager for a fight as Logan was.

Hayden raised a blond brow. "You should save your energy for tonight and your mission."

"Nay. You have a right to know of my past."

"Stop it, Logan," Hayden warned. "I willna fight you."

But Logan needed an outlet for his frustration. Besides, he should never have kept his secret from Hayden. "I should have told you long ago."

"I already told you. Keep your secret. It doesna matter."

"I went to Deirdre, Hayden. I went to her and begged her to make me into a Warrior. I was sure I had a god inside me. And I wanted all the glory the immortality of being a Warrior would give me."

Logan hid his wince when he saw Hayden's dark eyes widen then narrow. This was what Logan had always feared. This is why he had kept his secret.

He wasn't worthy of being counted among the Warriors at MacLeod Castle.

"Bloody Hell, Logan," Hayden ground out. "Of all the things I thought had happened to you, I never imagined that."

Logan braced his hands on the battlement wall. "I know. I'm more ashamed than I can ever say. While all of you were taken from your families, I went willingly."

"Shite," Hayden said and ran a hand over his face. "Did you align with Deirdre?"

Logan couldn't believe Hayden had asked that question, but then again, he'd have asked it as well. "Never. As soon as I realized what I had become, I fought against her."

For several tense moments Hayden simply stared at Logan before he clamped his huge hand on Logan's shoulder. "You should no' have carried such a burden yourself all these years."

"You are no' appalled?"

Hayden snorted. "Of course, but we all make mistakes. Had I heard about Deirdre and the Warriors before I was taken, I might well have done the same thing as you."

"I thought . . ."

"That we would banish you?"

Logan nodded.

Hayden sighed deeply and let his gaze move slowly over the castle. "We are family. All of us. I've told you before you are the brother I never had. Family forgives each other, Logan, because the only people you can really count on is family."

Logan's throat tightened, refusing to allow any words past. Instead, he nodded.

Hayden began to turn away when he paused and looked at Logan. "Doona be afraid to tell the others, but if you wish to keep your secret, it will never pass my lips."

"Thank you. Brother."

Hayden smiled and turned on his heel.

Logan remained on the battlements, his mind full of Gwynn and all Hayden had said. Logan ran his hand along the gray stones.

The world had changed, but the castle had endured. It had weathered the elements and time with dignity and defiance, poise and pride. It had begun as their fortress and turned into a home.

A home Logan knew Gwynn would find happiness in. At the castle, she could hone her magic and learn from the others. But she wanted to return to her world, to her job. She would still be able to use her magic, but she'd never become the Druid Logan knew she could be.

Logan looked around the castle and land, remembering the battles with Deirdre, the celebrations of weddings, and events that had shaped each of them.

MacLeod Castle hadn't just been a pile of stones to find shelter in. It had become a symbol of hope to everyone who called it home.

Logan turned and strode into the castle. He paused at the landing and looked down from his perch into the great hall. Gwynn stood next to the tree, her arms folded over her chest as she looked at the ornaments.

Despite the upcoming missions, or maybe because of them, Cara and Marcail had wrapped some gifts and were putting them under the tree.

Just as Gwynn had told him it was done.

Logan might have missed out on four centuries, but he wasn't going to miss any more.

"I was told you'd had a vision."

Saffron hated Declan's smooth, cultured voice. She despised everything about him. He held her prisoner now, but one day she would get free. And she would kill him for what he had done to her.

"Saffron," Declan said, his voice falsely sweet. "Shall I bring in more spiders?"

She shuddered just thinking about all those hairy legs crawling on her again. It was her greatest fear, and one Declan used against her with ease. "No."

"I didna think so. Now. Tell me what you saw."

She turned her head to the side and pressed her cheek against the icy brick of the wall. The cold seeped through the bricks and the short-sleeved shirt she wore until she ached with the chill.

"Saffron."

She heard the warning in Declan's voice, knew she was pushing him. "It was nothing."

"I doona care if you saw what shoes I would pick to wear tomorrow," he bellowed in her ear. "I want to know!"

Saffron flinched and tried to scoot away from him, but her chains held her firmly in place. "I saw an island. And two people, a man and a woman."

"What did this woman look like?"

She shifted her arms, making the chains clank together. "She was pretty. Very pretty. She had black hair and the most amazing eyes. They were violet in color."

"Gwynn," Declan ground out.

Saffron squeezed her eyes closed. She had hoped she'd seen someone Declan didn't know. All Saffron could hope for now was that whoever this Gwynn was got away from him safely. And if Gwynn was lucky, the man with her would be able to protect her from Declan.

"I always knew having a Seer would be to my benefit," Declan said. "Get to Eigg with all haste!"

The sound of the metal door slamming shut echoed through the dungeon.

CHAPTER
THIRTY-SIX

Gwynn looked at all the packages being set under the tree. They had been wrapped with care and tied with beautiful ribbons. It brought to mind memories of Gwynn helping her mother wrap presents.

Bing Crosby's Christmas CD had been their favorite to play while wrapping. Then later, while her mother slept, Gwynn would lovingly wrap the gifts she would make for her mother. Or if she had saved enough of her lunch money, she would buy her mother a pair of earrings.

The gifts hadn't been worth anything, but the love in her mother's eyes when she opened the presents had made Gwynn feel like a queen.

Gwynn didn't know if she would still be at the castle for Christmas. The thought of going home to her small, empty apartment made her stomach sink.

But did she dare spend any extra time at the castle? With Logan?

Gwynn pulled Marcail to the far side of the tree so no one could see them, then she lowered her voice to barely above a whisper. "I have a favor."

"Anything," Marcail said.

Gwynn bit her lip and handed Marcail the last of her cash. "I'd like it if someone would find me a kilt for Logan in the Hamilton plaid."

Marcail's turquoise eyes brightened. "Of course. I know just the place. They've replaced the others' kilts, and made some for Quinn and his brothers."

"Good. Keep it between us, please."

"I will."

"Oh," Gwynn said as she stopped Marcail from walking away. "If that isn't enough money, please let me know."

"It'll be plenty," Marcail assured her with a soft smile.

Gwynn knew that Marcail would see that Logan got the kilt whether Gwynn was there or not. She hoped she was able to see his expression when he opened it. He'd been so desolate when he'd tenderly folded his tartan and put it away.

For several minutes she stared at the tree, thinking what Christmas morning could be like with her sitting between Logan's legs on the floor, his arm wrapped around her as they watched everyone open their presents.

Gwynn mentally shook herself and stepped around the tree to find Logan in front of her. "Oh," she gasped, startled by his appearance.

"We leave in half an hour."

"I'll be ready."

He glanced down at her high-heeled boots and frowned. "You will have a verra hard time moving through the caves with those boots."

"They're all I brought with me."

"I've already found who wears your size. Cara has some boots you can borrow."

Gwynn studied Logan. He had detached himself, but not entirely. He still saw to her needs. Just as she knew he would protect her with his life. "Thank you."

"I'd rather you no' be going on this mission."

"I know," she replied and lowered her eyes to the floor as she fiddled with the hem of her white sweater. "But you need me."

"Aye. I do."

Gwynn's gaze snapped to Logan's face. There had been a double meaning in his words, she was sure of it. "You don't want to need me, do you?"

"It doesna matter anymore."

"It does to me."

"Gwynn," Logan said, his voice lowering.

She took a step closer to him. "Yes?" she urged.

He glanced at the tree and shook his head. "I need to prepare for our mission."

Gwynn blew out a frustrated breath. "Men," she mumbled and went to find Cara.

Thirty minutes later, Gwynn had Cara's insulated hiking boots on, and several layers of clothes. She wasn't used to being so confined. But if she wanted to stay warm, she didn't have a choice.

"I feel like the Michelin Man," she grumbled as she retied her scarf for the third time.

"Hayden," Lucan called, just before he tossed something across the hall.

Hayden's hand reached up and snagged the keys from the air. "We'll attempt to bring it back in one piece."

Isla shook her head and looked at Gwynn. "The Land Rover. It's Fallon's favorite."

"Everyone knows what to do," Fallon's voice boomed through the great hall. "If it gets to be too much, return to the castle. I doona want to lose any more lives. Anyone," he said and looked straight at Logan.

Gwynn wasn't sure what that look meant, but she didn't like it. She had no time to think on it as they said their good-byes.

As she, Logan, Isla, Hayden, and Ramsey walked to the

black Land Rover parked in the bailey, Gwynn looked at the other SUV, a Humvee, military style, across from them.

Everyone but Aiden, Fiona, Braden, Cara, and Marcail gathered next to the Humvee.

Gwynn found herself in the backseat of the Land Rover between Logan and Ramsey, while Hayden started the SUV and Isla buckled herself into the front passenger seat.

"How did Sonya and Reaghan convince the others to allow them to go to Declan's?" Gwynn asked.

Isla turned and smiled. "The Warriors might not want to admit it, but they need Druids against Declan."

"Only because he has those bullets," Hayden grumbled as he put the Land Rover into reverse and pressed the gas.

Gwynn kept her eyes on the remaining group as they drove through the castle gates. Just before she lost sight of them, they all placed their hands on each other's shoulders and then were gone.

She turned around and found Hayden's eyes on her through the rearview mirror.

"Why didn't we have Fallon teleport us to Eigg?" Gwynn asked.

"Wallace will be looking for something like that," Ramsey answered. "We thought it best to arrive inconspicuously."

Gwynn didn't think three hunky men climbing out of an expensive SUV was inconspicuous, but who was she to argue?

Deirdre finished zipping her boots and stood to look at Charlie, who lay naked and sprawled across her bed.

"Surely we're no' done," he said with a teasing smile.

"For the moment."

Whatever Charlie said in response was lost to the pounding on Deirdre's door.

"Enter," she called.

The stone door swung open and Malcolm stalked inside.

Deirdre smiled and lifted her chin. "You have news."

"Aye. Fallon and some other Warriors, along with two Druids, have arrived outside of Declan's home."

"They intend to fight him, do they?" Deirdre said as she ambled about her chamber, her mind working through the scenarios. "Interesting."

"It will be difficult for them to engage Declan, since he has gone to Eigg."

She whirled to face Malcolm. "Eigg? He is after the artifact."

"My thoughts as well."

"Then we need to get there. Now." She turned to Charlie. "Get dressed. You're driving us to Eigg."

CHAPTER
THIRTY-SEVEN

The drive to Eigg took longer than Logan would have liked. He was impatient to get to the artifact. And eager for the fight he knew was coming.

Before, when it had only been Deirdre they fought, Logan hadn't worried. The wyrran were easy to kill, and the Warriors Deirdre had were mindless fools.

Their only concern had been Deirdre capturing him.

Now, there were the special bullets that held the *drough* blood to fret over.

And Gwynn. Always he worried about Gwynn's safety, even if she didn't.

Logan glanced over at the Druid sitting in the front. Isla had always been formidable as a Druid. He knew that if she and Wallace clashed it was a battle worth seeing. Wallace was strong, but Isla had the ability to use black magic to make her *mie* magic even more potent.

"We're almost there," Hayden said.

Gwynn had been quiet since they'd left the castle. With her eyes dead ahead, she hadn't so much as looked at Logan the entire trip.

Logan looked at Ramsey to find him staring out the

window into the dark, seemingly calm. Until Logan saw Ramsey's fist clenched on his leg.

Ten minutes later Hayden pulled off the road and put the Land Rover in park. He turned in his seat and looked at Logan and Gwynn. "This is your stop."

Logan nodded and reached to open the door when Isla's hand touched his arm.

"Be careful."

"Always," he replied, but the smile he tried to paste on wouldn't stick.

Gwynn leaned up and hugged Isla. "Don't let Declan capture you."

"He willna get his hands on her," Hayden growled.

Gwynn pulled away from Isla to look at Hayden and Ramsey. "Do whatever you have to do to stay alive. Declan will be merciless."

"So will we," Ramsey vowed.

With a nod to Ramsey, Logan turned his head to Hayden. No words were needed. They had been in battle enough times to know anything could happen.

"We'll be waiting at the meeting point," Hayden said.

"As will we."

Logan climbed out of the SUV and held out his hand to help Gwynn from the vehicle. He closed the door, and a moment later it drove off.

Gwynn released a shaky breath.

"Are you ready?"

She shook her head. "I'm terrified, Logan. I'm scared of what awaits us, I'm petrified that Declan will find us and shoot you with those God-awful bullets again."

Logan gripped her shoulders and turned her to face him. "There's only one thing I want you to worry about, and that's yourself. I will keep anything from getting to you."

"I know," she said and swallowed loudly. "It was just

so much easier talking about doing this while safe at the castle."

"We will be on Eigg before Wallace knows it. It's the others I'm concerned about."

She straightened her shoulders. "You're right. No more pity party for me. They're the ones having to face that psycho."

Logan grinned as he watched her push aside her fears and face the uncertainty that was ahead. There was no other woman who could compare to her. Not her beauty, her bravery, or her loyalty.

She was unique. Special. And he wanted her for his own.

Logan released his god as he took Gwynn's hand and walked her to the shoreline. Her hand shook in his, but she didn't pull back or ask him to wait.

With a wave of his hand he parted the water. "Just like last time," he told her. "We'll walk into the water and it will surround us."

"Okay," she murmured.

It was Gwynn who took the first step forward. Logan moved with her, keeping her steady among the rocks along the shore. Once they were in the water and deep enough, Logan had it surround them, keeping him and Gwynn in a large bubble as they moved.

"I can't see anything in this dark," Gwynn said.

"Doona worry. I can."

"Lucky you. I wish I could."

He bit back his laugh at the irritation in her tone.

Hayden had dropped them off thirty minutes outside of Mallaig, so they had a ways to travel before they reached Eigg.

"You'll tell me when you feel his magic, won't you?" Gwynn asked.

Logan didn't need to ask who "he" was. "Aye."

"You think he'll be on Eigg."

"I know he will. It's what I would do."

She huffed when her toe hit a rock. "And my father. Do you think he'll be here?"

"Possibly," Logan answered after a pause.

They continued on in silence. Logan wished he knew what Gwynn was thinking. She kept it to herself, though.

Not once did she slow or ask to rest as they walked closer and closer to Eigg. He had to steer her to keep her going in the right direction, but her mind was focused, intent. Absorbed.

It wasn't until they reached the edge of Mallaig that Logan felt it, the cloying, suffocating feel of *drough* magic. "Wallace is on Eigg."

Gwynn sighed. "I had hoped he wouldn't be. He knows you can control water."

"Nay. He knows I have a power and that it could be water or wind. Since we battled him together, he has no idea what was your magic and what was my power."

She grinned as she looked at him. "You think of everything."

"I've been doing this for awhile."

"Do you think it will ever stop? This battle for Deirdre, and now Declan, to rule?"

Logan asked himself that question every night. "I have to believe it will."

"There will always be evil in the world, Logan, just as there will always be good."

"Aye. But when that evil is trying to take over, it must be stopped."

"Yes. It must."

Logan took her arm and pulled her to a stop before they reached Eigg. "Gwynn, I . . ." he trailed off, unsure of what he wanted to say.

She merely smiled and walked into his arms as she fit her lips against his. Logan angled his head and slanted his mouth over hers. He kissed her with all the desperation, all the yearning, and all the longing he had within himself.

Her body melted against his, all softness and alluring temptation.

She matched him kiss for kiss, their tongues meeting, mating in a kiss both frantic and demanding. Her sweet, exotic taste would forever be imprinted in his mind, just as she was a part of his very soul.

Logan reluctantly pulled back from the kiss, their breathing harsh and ragged. She turned her head and rested it on his chest.

He closed his eyes and held her tight. He wished she wasn't going into danger, but more than anything he wished she were his.

"I'm glad you're here with me," Gwynn said.

He rubbed his hands up and down her back. "I wouldna allow anyone else."

"Because this was your mission with Duncan."

"Because it is you."

She lifted her face to his, her violet eyes searching. "I didn't come to Scotland to find someone like you. I didn't think a man such as you existed except in my dreams."

"You know my deepest secrets," Logan said as he smoothed back her black hair from her face. "Secrets I thought I would go to my grave with."

"Why did you share them with me?"

"I wanted you to know me. The real me. The one who can no' look himself in the mirror."

"And the one who saved me," she interjected quickly.

"You deserve a better man."

"And what if I found a man who is better than he thinks he is?"

Logan smiled ruefully. "Why would you want me?"

"The question is why wouldn't I want you?"

He opened his mouth to answer her when he felt more *drough* magic. He knew the feel of that magic. Knew it and hated it. "Deirdre," he grumbled.

Gwynn stiffened in his arms. "Where?"

"Verra near. Which way to the cave?"

She closed her eyes, her magic rising like a tidal wave within her. A moment later, her lids opened to show her eyes glowing violet.

"This way," Gwynn said.

Logan jerked, startled to hear the odd sounding voice of Gwynn's once more. She pulled out of his arms and walked with sure steps toward Eigg, dodging rocks and holes as she did.

He kept his gaze on the water above him. The closer they got to Eigg, the shallower the water became. And the easier they would be seen.

Logan flexed his hands, his silver claws clinking together. His god bellowed for blood, but first Logan would see Gwynn get the Tablet.

"The cave is just in front of us," Gwynn said.

Logan wrapped an arm around her waist from behind to halt her. "We need to get inside the cave quickly. I doona want you exposed for longer than necessary."

She turned her head to look at him, her eyes no longer glowing. "I won't let you down."

"I know," he said with a smile. Then he kissed the tip of her nose. "Ready?"

Her fingers locked with his. "I am now."

They took off running, the water parting as they did. The night sky with the moon hanging low shone above them. Logan looked ahead to see the cliffs of Eigg rising out of the water.

They traded the mud of the sea floor for slick rocks and

boulders. The dark, menacing opening of the cave loomed before them. Water dripped down the cliffs from the waves that crashed repeatedly against them.

Logan called to the water to block itself from reaching the cave and sweeping them into the sea as a wave came at Gwynn.

He halted as they entered the cave and looked above him to the ceiling. "How far back is the Tablet?"

"Quite a ways from what the book said."

"God's teeth," Logan cursed and clenched his jaw. "Stay behind me."

Logan might have been in front of her, but he knew every move she made. He was as conscious of her as he was of his god. His every sense was aware of Gwynn. Every breath, each shift of her eyes, every move of her body.

He was cognizant of all of it.

It tore at him the same time it appeased him. Everything about Gwynn turned him about, twisting his usual calm emotions into a whirlpool of chaos.

And he found he liked it.

Logan moved from rock to rock, working his way slowly to the side of the cave where there was a ledge that would make their trek easier.

Behind him, he heard the slightest gasp. He spun around to see Gwynn's foot slip on the damp rock. He yanked her against his chest before she could fall between the jagged rocks.

Her fingers dug into his arms as she clung to him. Logan glanced down between the rocks and inwardly grimaced. He might have used his powers to remove the water that normally filled the cave, but the centuries of waves pounding the rocks had left many with vicious edges that would easily rip the skin from the bone. And the way the rocks and boulders were piled upon each other, one slip between them would ensure a broken bone.

"That was close," Gwynn whispered.

"Too damned close." He held her for a moment longer before he allowed her to pull out of his arms.

Logan ground his teeth together and prayed Gwynn got out of the cave unharmed. He'd never forgive himself if she were injured. Or worse.

He reached the edge of the cave and leaped to the ledge. It supported his weight easily, but it proved as slippery as the rocks.

Logan held out his hand for Gwynn. Once she grasped it, he pulled her beside him. "Now where?" he asked.

She leaned around him and pointed. "Keep going."

He moved forward one slow step at a time. In the darkness he could see the crabs quickly moving out of their way. Water dripped relentlessly from the ceiling, and behind them, the roar of the sea grew stronger as the tide continued to surge against the wall he had put in place.

Gwynn's heart still pounded in her chest from her near fall. Logan might have kept the water out of the cave, but there were dangers aplenty.

She looked at him, his gaze intense as he stared ahead. Although she knew what awaited them, he did not. Still, he forged ahead. Powerful. Compelling. Dominating.

Logan never questioned her as she told him where to go. He simply made certain the water in the cave never touched her.

Gwynn's toe hit a loose rock and it tumbled into a puddle below. Logan stiffened and his head jerked to the side. Gwynn put her hand on his back to let him know she was all right.

"I really doona like you down here," he grumbled.

She looked around and scrunched her face. "Well, neither do I. I'm more of a sit-in-front-of-the-TV kinda gal."

"I thought you liked adventure.

Gwynn heard the teasing lilt of his voice. "Oh, you're

MIDNIGHT'S MASTER

301

funny. The most adventurous thing I ever did before flying over an ocean was attempt the Galleria during Christmas."

"What's the Galleria?"

"A mall. A huge place where there are hundreds of stores. The Galleria is three stories high and just massive. There's even an ice rink inside."

"And you went there?"

She shrugged. "I like to shop. Not that I can afford much, but I still like to look. I usually stay away at Christmas though, because the crowds will mow you down in a heartbeat."

He laughed, which brought a smile to her face. They were in the middle of a cave trying to find an ancient relic while avoiding two *droughs* bent on killing them.

How they could laugh at a time like this was something she couldn't fathom. Yet she knew, she'd rather no one by her side other than Logan.

It was almost too easy for Camdyn and the others to take out the men guarding Wallace's mansion. Camdyn wrinkled his nose as the stench of evil grew stronger the closer to Wallace's house he moved.

Fallon motioned them forward. They moved as silent as a spirit, and as deadly as the sharpest blade. Reaghan and Sonya were ringed by Warriors at all times.

As they entered the house, an older man in a suit stepped into the foyer. Camdyn moved in a blink and had the man in a choke hold.

"Don't kill him," Reaghan said. "He's just a butler."

Camdyn raised a brow, but did as Reaghan asked and used the hold to make the butler fall unconscious instead of breaking his neck.

"This way," Larena whispered as she rose from her crouching position by the door and ran past the stairs.

One by one they followed her. Camdyn and Arran brought up the rear and saw three guards coming down the stairs.

They used their enhanced speed to race up the stairs. Camdyn sliced the neck of one guard as he ran past and broke the second's neck. He looked to find Arran had taken out his guard just as silently.

With a nod, they jumped over the railing and landed next to the door Larena and the others had disappeared through. They entered and followed the narrow steps down into the earth.

It reminded Camdyn too much of Deirdre's dungeons. A place he never wanted to return to.

And then he saw the others standing in front of a cell door.

Camdyn took one look at the chained woman and felt his god's roar for vengeance.

CHAPTER
THIRTY-EIGHT

Logan paused when he reached a series of caves that branched off from the main one. "Which way do we go? There are three other caves besides the one we're in."

"To the right," she said after a long pause.

Logan peered inside and saw nothing but more rock and dripping water. The farther into the caves they went, the darker it became.

"Hold onto me," he said to Gwynn.

Her hands grasped his waist. "I envy you being able to see. It is so dark I can barely see your outline."

"I willna lead you wrong."

"I know."

Her faith in him staggered him, and he was determined she would leave the caves with nary a scratch upon her milky skin.

Step by slow step he led them farther into the cave. The ledge he had been on grew wider in the new cave. Every once in awhile there would be a missing section where he would leap over, then pull Gwynn to him.

It didn't take long to come upon another section of caves. He stopped and looked into each of the yawning entrances. Anyone who didn't know the way could easily become lost.

"Have we reached the next section?" Gwynn asked.

"Aye."

"Good." She moved until her body was pressed against his back. "There should be five caves."

"There are."

"We need the second from the left."

Logan glanced at the rocks they would need to cross to get to the other side. "Of course we do."

Gwynn chuckled and rubbed her face against his back. "I gather it won't be easy."

"Remember the rocks outside the cave?"

"That bad, huh?"

"Worse," he grumbled. "I can no' take the chance of you slipping. Do you trust me?"

"I do."

Her response had been immediate, making Logan smile. He turned so that he faced her. For a brief moment he allowed himself time to look at her as her gaze searched the darkness.

"You're staring at me," she said with a grin.

"Maybe."

She cocked an eyebrow, but her smile never wavered. "Are you laughing at me?"

"Laughing?" he asked in confusion. "Never. Gwynn, I'm amazed at you. I doona know many women who would have done the things you've done and no' be hysterical."

"We Texans are a strong lot," she said with a smile.

Logan wanted to kiss her. He wanted inside her. He wanted . . . her. But it would have to wait until they were out of the caves.

He leaned down and whispered in her ear, "Hold on tight."

Her arms wrapped around his neck as she kissed his cheek. Logan straightened and gauged the distance across the cave. A mortal man might be able to make it if he had a running start, but thankfully Logan wasn't mortal.

He held Gwynn with one arm and leaped across the cave. As soon as he landed, his hand reached out and his claws sunk into the rock to hold them.

"Wait," he said when Gwynn began to move. "The ledge is . . . well, it's no' really a ledge. There's barely room for my feet."

"You cannot carry me the entire way."

He chuckled. "Aye, I could, but I doona think there will be a need. At least no' yet."

"So now what?"

"Now, we get to the next cave."

"How?"

Instead of answering her, Logan bent his legs and jumped again. The second leap was shorter but just as difficult. He lowered Gwynn to the ground, her delightful curves pressed against him, and then reluctantly released her.

"Well," she said after a moment. "That was something I thought never to experience. How far can you jump?"

He shrugged, then remembering she couldn't see in the dark said, "I've no' measured. I can easily jump over a castle wall. We routinely jump from the shore to the top of the cliffs at MacLeod Castle."

She whistled. "Impressive."

"I usually jump midway up the cliffs, then do a second jump to the top."

"But you can jump all the way down?"

"Aye," he said with a smile and took her hand.

The cave's floor was smooth enough that they could walk in the middle. Occasionally Logan would steer them around a large boulder that seemed to grow out of the floor, but all in all, it was easy. If not slippery.

"Do all the caves fill with water?" he asked.

"Yes. At least the ones we will be in do."

He looked above him as he noticed the ceiling began to slant downward so that he hunched over. "And low tide? Does it last long?"

"Not long enough. Did you command all the water out of the caves?"

His lips tightened. "Aye. From anyone looking at the cave, it will appear normal, but the water stops just inside the cave."

"Then why do I hear water?"

He'd hoped she would have gone longer without noticing it, but with no other sound penetrating the caves, it was hard to miss. Logan had heard the water long before now, but hadn't mentioned it because he had hoped they would go in the opposite direction. He should have known better.

"It looks like we're heading toward it, so we should know soon. Doona worry. I'll make sure it doesna harm us."

She nodded, but clutched his shirt tighter. "I know."

Logan had barely taken a dozen steps when he stopped again. This time there were two options. Continue forward, or go right. Right would lead them away from the sound of the water, but would they get that lucky?

"Straight or right?" he asked.

She sighed. "Straight."

As he thought. All the water should have responded to his power. Why there was still water in the caves he didn't understand. He had a nagging suspicion that magic was involved. How involved, was the question.

With Gwynn tight against his back, Logan walked with slow, measured steps. As soon as he saw the drop in the ceiling, he reached behind him and took Gwynn's hand.

"It looks like the floor dips downward. As well as the ceiling."

"How far of a dip?" she asked.

Logan looked past his feet and shook his head. "With the ceiling the way it is, I can no' jump both of us down at once."

"How low is the ceiling?"

He brought her hand up in front of him so she could see how low it hung.

"Oh," she murmured. "That low."

"Aye. I'm going to sit you on the edge while I jump."

"And then?"

He grinned and kissed her hand. "You're going to jump into my arms."

A harsh laugh burst past her lips. "Because I can see so well in the dark."

"I'll be there to catch you."

She let out a deep breath. "I don't have much of a choice. But you better catch me."

The fact that she could make light of their situation proved how unique she was. Gwynn had the uncanny ability to look at life from a different perspective than most people. She found the funny or good or laughable parts and used them to her benefit.

"Here," Logan said as he guided her to the edge. "Now sit. Carefully," he ground out when her foot slipped.

She rolled her eyes. "With the firm grip you have on my arm, I won't be going anywhere. Besides, you need to tell me how close I am to the edge. I can't see, remember?"

"Just doona move," he said and tried to calm his racing heart. He released her arm and braced his hands on his

thighs. He'd had a hold of her, but that didn't mean something couldn't have happened.

She was mortal. Their lives could end so quickly, so
effortlessly, that it amazed him at times that anyone lived
at all.

"Logan?"

"I'm fine," he said.

Her hand reached out, seeking him. He took pity on
her and stepped closer so she could touch him. "I didn't
mean to scare you."

"I know."

"Is it difficult?"

He frowned and turned his head to her. "Is what difficult?"

"Watching mortals die?"

Logan looked ahead and took a deep breath. "More
than you can imagine."

Declan had men at every point of the small isle, yet no
one had seen Gwynn or Logan. But Declan knew they
were there.

"Robbie," Declan ground out.

"We've no' sighted them yet."

"Why no'? They're here."

Robbie's gaze narrowed. "They can no' walk on water.
They had to come by boat. We've stopped every boat.
They have no' been on one."

Declan clasped his hands behind his back, his fury
growing by the moment. "If Logan's power is water, he
could have gotten them to the isle that way. Check the
shoreline."

Robbie repeated his orders over the comlink attached
to him as Declan waited to hear word that Logan and
Gwynn had been found.

Gary walked up beside him, his nostrils flaring in anger. "Gwynn has always been a thorn in my side. She would never have been able to do this on her own. She's not that smart."

"She's a Druid," Declan said. "Or have you forgotten?"

Gary's lips curled in distaste. "How can I? You won't stop reminding me."

"Maybe I should send you out looking for her, Austin. Call to her as a father does a daughter. Despite the hurt I saw in her lovely eyes, she's still a little girl who wants the attention of her daddy."

"I'd rather eat my own arm."

Declan stepped in front of Gary until they were nose to nose. "I'll see that you do. Until then, find your daughter!"

Gary stormed off, his tall, lanky form only made taller by his wool trench coat.

"I really hate that man," Declan said.

Robbie grunted. "We all do. I've seen him watching you. He will try to double-cross you."

"He'll try. They all try."

"But they never win," Robbie finished.

Declan laughed, but it cut off halfway through as he sensed more magic. But it was one he knew, one he had savored for too short a time.

One he had hoped to sense again.

"Deirdre is here," he said.

Robbie turned in a slow circle, his hand on his rifle. "Where?"

"It doesna matter. She'll come to me soon enough."

"Are you sure you want that? She was verra angry at you."

Declan smiled. "I will have Deirdre, Gwynn, *and* the Tablet of Orn before the night is through, Robbie. Just you wait and see."

Robbie touched the com in his ear. "Repeat. I say again. Repeat."

"What is it?" Declan asked as he turned the ruby of his cufflink.

"It's the mansion. We're under attack."

CHAPTER
THIRTY-NINE

Deirdre's eyes narrowed as she stepped off the boat and onto Eigg. "The bastard is already here."

"I know," Malcolm said. "He's standing there."

Deirdre followed where his finger pointed. "So he is. By the way his hands are flapping around, I'd say he wasn't very happy. I wonder if I am the cause of it."

Malcolm tilted his head. "Nay. His . . . it's his mansion. They're under attack."

"Oh, that's perfect. Who?"

Malcolm's maroon Warrior eyes turned to her. "Who else would be so bold?"

"The MacLeods."

"Declan is trying to decide whether to leave or stay. It appears as if . . ." Malcolm paused, concentrating.

Deirdre tapped her toes, impatient to learn more. "What is it?"

"Declan thinks Logan and some woman named Gwynn are already on the isle to get the artifact."

"Nay," Deirdre shouted. "I will not allow them to best me again. Or Declan, for that matter. We leave here with the artifact, Malcolm. Do you understand me?"

For several tense moments he stared at her. "I ken perfectly."

"Good. Find where Logan is."

Gwynn hated not being able to see anything. It was so dark in the caves she couldn't even glimpse her hand in front of her face. If it hadn't been for Logan, she wouldn't have made it past the entrance through the main cave.

Since she was unable to use her eyes, her ears became more sensitive to sound. She grimaced when she heard Logan step and pebbles go bouncing away. Even knowing he was immortal and would heal didn't stop her from worrying.

"Shite," he murmured.

"What is it?" she asked, her face turned in the direction she heard his voice.

There was another curse, this one too low to distinguish. Then there was a soft whooshing sound before she heard him land far below.

"Logan?" she called. He grunted, and she could picture him looking around.

"At least I can stand up straight now."

She smiled, her feet dangling over the edge of the floor. The dampness was soaking through her jeans and thermals, making her shiver against the cool air.

"Are you ready?" Logan asked.

After everything she had been through, how could she say no? Yet, to jump off the ledge without knowing how far down Logan stood was daunting.

"Ah. I think so."

"You're no' afraid, are you?"

She heard the smile in his voice and rolled her eyes. "Me? Nope. I do this sort of thing all the time. I'm an adrenaline junkie," she replied, layering the sarcasm on thick.

"You who brazenly got to know a Warrior."

"Brazenly?" she repeated. "Do people still use that term?"

"You who flew over the ocean. You who braved this cave without knowing what awaited us."

Gwynn put her hands on the rocks where she sat and leaned forward. "Well, if you put it that way."

He chuckled, the sound echoing through the caves. "I willna let you fall, Gwynn."

The smile disappeared, because she knew he wouldn't allow harm to come to her. He had proven it time and again.

"Take your time," Logan said. "I will wait until you're ready."

Gwynn took a deep breath and pushed herself off the ledge before she chickened out all together. The air rushed around her as she squeezed her eyes closed. The next thing she knew, strong arms caught her and hauled her against a muscular chest.

"I've got you," Logan whispered.

She laid her head upon his shoulder and released the breath she had held. "I knew you would."

"Is that why you closed your eyes?"

Gwynn leaned her head back to tell him to stop teasing when his lips descended upon hers. The kiss was soft but commanding, gentle but hungry.

While he cradled her in his arms, Gwynn felt his heart pounding steady and sure. There was nothing about Logan that wasn't brawny or commanding. It was as if he had been born with the knowledge that he could do anything, and had proceeded through life that way.

"We have to continue," he said between kisses.

Gwynn would rather have kept kissing, but the sooner Logan got the Tablet, the sooner Deirdre could be brought to an end. "Yes," she murmured, and wiggled so that she brushed against his arousal.

"God's teeth, what you do to me," Logan hissed.

Gwynn stroked her hand down his cheek. She couldn't begin to tell him what he did to her—or for her. He had changed her life, changed her entire way of thinking.

Logan set her feet upon the ground and took her hand. Then he took a not-so-steady breath. "Ready?"

"I am. We are to proceed until the cave turns to the right. There will be an entrance continuing forward. That's the one we need to take."

"I'll find it."

Gwynn's right hand was laced with Logan's, and she put out her left hand, startled to feel the wall. "Has the cave gotten smaller?"

"A wee bit narrower, aye."

They'd gone about twenty paces when Logan stopped. "I see the turn, but there's nothing in front of us but rock."

"The book said it was hidden. Use your hand to feel along the rocks. You should be able to find it."

"Ah," he said after a moment. "Here it is."

Gwynn tried to ignore the fact that the sound of water was becoming louder, more pronounced. Almost as if it were all around them. She hoped it was just running on top of the caves. And not in them. Because if it was in the caves, that meant Logan's power couldn't move it. Not a good sign.

"Careful," Logan cautioned as he guided her around the rock.

She used her hand to help her, glad she couldn't see the bugs that were surely crawling everywhere. Once she was inside the new tunnel, the water sounded as if it were rushing toward them.

"Forward," she yelled to be heard over the water.

Logan's fingers tightened around her hand, whether to calm her or reassure her she didn't know. Either way, she knew he was worried about the water.

They started walking again. Gwynn couldn't shake the feeling that the walls of the cave were coming closer and closer to her. When she tripped on a loose rock and took a step to the right only to slam against the wall, her suspicion was confirmed.

"I'm all right," she said when she felt Logan turn to her.

She imagined he was frowning. He did that when he knew she was lying, but what point was there in telling him her knee hurt from hitting the rock, or that she would definitely have a bruise between her shoulder blades from the other rock protruding from the wall?

"So the fact you're squeezing my hand means you're fine?" he asked, his voice laced with sarcasm.

"Logan, you cannot protect me from every hurt, no matter how small."

"Aye. I can."

She smiled into the dark. Leave it to a Warrior to think he could shield her from everything. And knowing Logan, he would try.

"We can argue about this later."

"There's no argument," he stated.

Gwynn rolled her eyes. "Just keep going."

No sooner had the words left her mouth than Logan bellowed and released her hand.

"Logan?" Gwynn called as she held out her arms, searching for him.

She could hear him, knew he was close, but something was wrong. "Logan!"

With a tentative step forward, then another, she found him. He was bent over, his hands clutching his head. His body was tense, every muscle bulging as if he were in great pain.

"Logan, talk to me," she begged, worry forming a knot in her stomach.

She didn't care that she'd be stranded in the cave without

Logan. All that mattered was discovering what was wrong, and praying she could fix it somehow.

When he didn't answer, she did the only thing she could do. She wrapped her arms around him and held him. Without being able to see, she couldn't continue on, nor would she leave Logan.

Every moment he didn't move was like a blade in her heart. She didn't know how long they stood like that before his body began to relax.

"Logan?"

"Gwynn," he rasped and reached for her hand.

She shifted to stand in front of him and touched his sweat-soaked face. "What happened?"

"Deirdre."

The hate in his voice caused her to shiver. "What did she want?"

"When I went to her to unbind my god, there was a bond formed. She's tried to use it before, but I was able to ignore her and the wee bit of pain she caused."

"That wasn't a *wee bit*," she mimicked. "Logan, you scared the Hell out of me."

He nodded, his breaths still coming in great gasps. "Deirdre knows we're here. She wants the artifact."

"Well, she can kiss my butt and get in line with everyone else," Gwynn said with more conviction than she felt.

Logan chuckled. "I tend to agree. Shall we continue?"

"Can she do that to you again?"

His shoulders lifted in a shrug while he straightened. "Let's hope no'."

But Gwynn wasn't going to wait around for it to happen. She didn't know much about her magic, but she'd do what she could to stop Deirdre from harming Logan again.

Logan heard the thread of fear in Gwynn's voice and hated it. He made himself lower his hands from the sides of his head and straighten. The pain was fading, but not quick enough for his taste.

"We need to get moving," Logan said as he took hold of Gwynn's arm.

His thoughts of ending Deirdre were quickly pushed aside as he and Gwynn continued toward the sound of the water. It sounded as if the entire ocean was locked in a small space.

The tunnel curved away from the water, and then back toward it. Closer and closer they came to it. Until Logan caught his first glimpse of the water.

"The water grows louder," Gwynn said over the roar.

He gave a light squeeze of her hand. "Aye."

"Is it a waterfall in the caves?"

"I'm afraid no'."

Her steps faltered, then halted altogether. "We have to go through it, don't we?"

Logan pulled his gaze from the churning water and tugged Gwynn around the boulder. Light filtered through the water somehow, giving off a faint glow.

"By the saints," Gwynn said as she caught sight of what was before them. "How deep is it?"

He looked at the massive pool of water and the huge boulders protruding from the depths. "Verra deep."

"Can you use your power?"

"I've been trying. There is magic here, Gwynn. It's preventing the water from listening to my command."

She took a deep breath and shrugged. "Then we'll have to swim it."

Logan had never heard anything so preposterous. "Have you taken a look at the water? Do you no' see the currents? See how the water slams against the boulders and the sides? You'll be crushed."

Her violet eyes flashed with her own anger. "There's

no other choice. We have to go through this to reach the Tablet."

"Nay. I willna put you in that kind of danger."

"It isn't your choice."

"Gwynn, please," Logan begged. He could do many things to protect her, but not in this instance. The water wouldn't hear his call, and it was too powerful. She'd never survive.

Logan couldn't bear the thought.

She faced him and looked into his eyes. "You'll be there with me."

"Doona ask this of me."

"You wanted the Tablet of Orn. You need the Tablet to end Deirdre. I'm trying to give it to you."

He shook his head and took a step back. "There has to be another way. I willna endanger your life."

"My life has been in danger since the moment I arrived in Scotland. And it isn't just Declan. There's Deirdre. And life, in general."

"Exactly. Doona be so careless with your life. It's precious and can end all too suddenly."

Gwynn's gaze was steady, her body rigid. "If it costs me my life in order for you to end Deirdre, it will be worth it."

"No' for me."

It wasn't until the words were out of his mouth that Logan realized how true they were. He'd worked tirelessly since becoming a Warrior to fight Deirdre.

And now, with Gwynn by his side, it didn't matter. Nothing mattered but her.

He still wanted Deirdre dead, but not at any cost as he used to think. There were some things too valuable, too amazing to eagerly toss aside. Gwynn was one.

"We will find another way," he said.

Gwynn sighed and looked to the ground. "If there was

another way, I would have been told by the book. The Druids made sure there was only one way in and one way out to the Tablet."

"Aye, a way that will kill the one seeking it!" Logan raked a hand through his hair as he paced before her.

Gwynn hated the turmoil she saw in him. He wanted the Tablet, but he didn't want to risk her. It was the mere fact that he wanted to put her life ahead of his mission which made her decision.

There was no use trying to talk to him. He wouldn't listen to her. While he worked on coming up with an argument to convince her to turn back, Gwynn began calculating what she would need to do.

The water was deep. The glow that came from the bottom was bright enough for her to make out some images. She hadn't known about the currents until Logan told her, but that was the difference between his eyesight and hers.

She let her gaze roam over Logan's form. She couldn't see every detail, but she didn't need to. It was entrenched in her memory. Every lean muscle, every facial expression. He would be with her forever, even if she couldn't have him for her own.

As she watched his powerful body move with such ease as he paced, she wondered how she had lived before him. He was everything to her. It was no wonder the feelings had grown, and the attraction kindled when she met him.

Meeting him, she had come to like him. Working with him, she had come to trust him.

Knowing him, she had come to love him.

She had known it from his first kiss, but she hadn't wanted to admit it to herself because she feared where they might end up, or more importantly where she might end up. But no one could evade love. It happened when a person least expected it.

And it had happened to her.

It was because of that love she was willing to risk her life for Logan.

Gwynn didn't waste another moment. With as few movements as she could, she removed her scarf and her jacket. Then she jumped off the outcrop of rock and into the water. It sucked her under immediately as the cold slammed into her.

She fought against the water to reach the surface, and when she did, she took a huge breath and wiped her hair from her face. A look over her shoulder told her Logan was no longer there.

Suddenly, he surfaced beside her. "Have you gone completely daft?"

Before she could answer him, the current caught her and dragged her under. She reached up, seeking, searching for Logan. She could see him diving down to her, his face set in determined lines.

Panic began to set in as Gwynn was pulled this way and that, each time bringing her closer and closer to the boulders and cave wall.

Her lungs burned for air, and no matter how hard she tried to get to the surface, the water wouldn't let her go. She screamed, air bubbles swarming around her as she searched for Logan.

She was so preoccupied with looking for Logan and clawing the hair from her face that she didn't see the boulder until it was too late.

The force of the water knocked her into the large rock so viciously that for a moment it pinned her there. Then she was tossed away and around like a leaf in the wind.

CHAPTER
FORTY

"I cannot touch the door," Larena said when she reached for the bars blocking their entrance into the cell.

"Who's there?" asked the woman.

"We're here to save you," Reaghan said as she moved to stand beside Larena. She tested the bars, her lips set in a firm line. "He's used black magic. Only he can unlock the door."

Camdyn watched how the woman's head turned this way and that, her walnut-colored hair matted and hanging limp.

"Camdyn," Fallon said. "Can you do something?"

Camdyn looked at the ground to find dirt beneath him. "Aye, I can try."

He urged the earth to open, to form a tunnel beneath the door barring them from the Druid. The ground shook as a crack formed at his feet and shot under the door into the cell.

Dirt began to fill the crack as it widened, opening until it was wide enough for Camdyn to jump into the hole and duck beneath the door. He bent his legs and jumped beside the Druid.

"Who are you?" she asked as she tilted her head to him.

But her eyes didn't focus on him. "You're blind?" he asked.

Slowly she nodded her head.

Camdyn looked at the others through the bars. He already hated Wallace for harming Logan and Gwynn. Now, he wanted to rip the bastard apart.

With ease, Camdyn gripped the manacles around the Druid's wrists and broke them open. He squatted beside her as she shifted away from him.

He saw the fear on her face, but there was also determination and the will to survive. "Can you stand?"

"I'm . . . I'm not sure."

Her voice was similar to Gwynn's, but not quite the same. "Then I'll carry you, if you'll allow me."

"Who are you?" she asked again.

"I'm Camdyn. I've come with a group to free you."

She cocked her head to the side. "You came for me?"

"We did," Fallon said. "Let's get you out of here, then we'll answer all your questions."

As Camdyn lifted her in his arms, her body went taut. Her eyes widened, turning milky white, then rolled back in her head.

"What did I do?" he asked the others.

"Be still," Reaghan said. "She's having a vision."

Camdyn looked at the dirt-smudged face of the Druid. She was skin and bones, her body light as a feather. But there was no denying something was happening to her, and by the way her magic wrapped around him, consumed him, teased him, Camdyn didn't care.

He kept his expression neutral, but he was on fire. His balls tightened and all the blood in his body rushed to his cock. The more her magic filled her, the more his hunger grew until he thought he might spend where he stood.

All of a sudden, her body went slack in his arms.

"Is she all right?" Broc asked.

Camdyn shook his head. "I doona know. She still breathes."

"I'm fine," the Druid answered. "My name is Saffron, and if all of you want to live, we need to leave now. Declan is on his way."

"You are as Reaghan said? You are a Seer?" Camdyn asked.

"To my deepest regret."

Camdyn locked eyes with Galen before he jumped into the hole and then out on the other side. He commanded the earth to fill the hole until no trace of it remained. And then they were leaving the dungeon.

"If Declan is coming, then we succeeded," Sonya said.

Broc grunted as moved beside her. "Maybe. We shall see."

"What does that mean?"

"It means," Fallon said, "that I'm taking Camdyn, Saffron, you, and Reaghan back to the castle."

Reaghan put her hands on her hips and glared at first Fallon then Galen. "If you're going to find Declan, you will need us."

"I have a thought," Saffron said. "How about we all leave?"

Camdyn grinned at her cheekiness. "Take us back to the castle, then we can check on Logan."

Fallon gave a nod and laid his hands on Camdyn's shoulder.

Gwynn didn't know how much longer she could hold her breath. The surface looked leagues away, and with the hold the current had on her, she knew she wasn't a strong enough swimmer to get away.

She didn't want to die without at least first getting the Tablet for Logan. He needed it.

Strong, sure arms suddenly surrounded her. Gwynn opened her eyes to find Logan in front of her, and then his mouth was on hers. He blew much-needed air past her lips filling her lungs.

Once her lungs were no longer burning quite so badly, she pulled back and looked at him. With a smile and a wink, he wrapped his arms around her and used his feet to guide them around the boulders and toward the surface.

The current spun them about, making Gwynn dizzy and disoriented. She blinked, and when she opened her eyes she saw the cave wall coming at them quickly. There was no time for Logan to turn and take the brunt of the impact.

Gwynn raised her hand and used it to prevent Logan's head from knocking into the rocks. She bit back a scream as the rocks tore through her hand.

All she could do was hold on as Logan swam them to the surface. When their heads broke, she gulped in air. They might have come up from the depths, but the current wasn't done with them yet.

Malcolm watched Deirdre as she knelt before the fire chanting words he didn't understand. They were ancient words. Words of magic.

While the wyrran stood around Deirdre staring at her in awe and the other Warriors watching her with a mixture of fear and wonder, Malcolm felt nothing.

The man he'd been, the man who had risked everything to help Larena and Fallon, was dead. He had died when Deirdre sent her Warriors to kill him, but Sonya had used her magic to keep his body alive.

But Malcolm's soul hadn't survived.

It was part of the reason he was able to control the terrible and horrifying rage that consumed him. He felt the rage, but he didn't care. About anything.

He couldn't care anymore. If he did, if he looked at

what he had become, he'd have to face what he was. And he couldn't do that. He'd explode.

It was easier to bury all his feelings, all his emotions until he was numb. Not even Daal, his god, could fuel the bloodlust that took most Warriors.

Malcolm's gaze drifted back to Deirdre. Her incredibly long white hair billowed around her with the unseen fingers of the wind. The flames from the fire snapped and popped as they grew even higher.

It was the black mist which rose from the fire that caught Malcolm's attention as nothing else could. It hovered over Deirdre, unmoving until it began to swirl around her. Her chanting grew louder, the words coming in a singsong voice.

And the cloud of black smoke grew larger, denser.

Malcolm sensed the great evil of the black smoke. He knew it was the Devil. Whether Deirdre had called it or not was the question.

Deirdre's chanting slowed, then quieted. Whatever she'd done to Logan was finished. But whatever was about to happen to her was just beginning.

The smile on her perfectly sculpted face froze as the mist began to descend around her.

Their small camp grew deathly quiet as they all waited to see what the smoke would do. The wyrran were rocking back and forth and reaching for Deirdre, but their pale yellow hands couldn't touch her.

The other Warriors, however, were showing their fangs and growling.

Malcolm chuckled at their display of rage. It was because of his god that he knew the smoke was the Devil. At one time his god had ruled this land, but the Devil and other demons had tricked them one by one until they'd been locked away.

The gods wanted their world returned to them. And

they wanted to lock *diabhul* away as they'd been imprisoned.

Despite Daal's rage, Malcolm remained as he was and waited. It wasn't long before the mist rose above Deirdre, then vanished. As if it had never been.

Deirdre rose on shaky legs and turned to Malcolm. "We need to be in place and ready for Logan. He will try to trick us, but I won't be fooled."

"What did *diabhul* want?"

Her eerie white eyes bore into him. "*That* is none of your concern."

Malcolm leaned a shoulder against a tree and regarded Deirdre. Whatever the Devil had wanted, it hadn't been good.

It was everything Logan could do to keep Gwynn's head above water. There was a cut on her forehead from where her head had hit a boulder, and there were scrapes on her hand from where she had pushed off the cave wall.

He still couldn't believe she had jumped into the water. He should've known she would do something like that after the way she had argued with him. Logan could still feel the fear that had taken hold of him when he'd seen her dragged under the water.

All he'd been able to think about was getting to Gwynn. And the more he'd tried, the more the currents pulled them apart.

Logan couldn't discern how large the pool of water was, nor where the currents were taking them, but the roof of the cave had begun to lower at an alarming rate.

"Gwynn," he called as a wave of water washed over him. He spit out the water and waited until she looked at him. "Where do we go next?"

"It should be here," she said.

Her body shook from the frigid temperatures of the water and her ordeal. Logan wanted nothing more than to get her out of the water and into dry clothes before she froze to death.

He shook his head. "It's no'."

"It is," she insisted through chattering teeth.

Logan looked through the rough waves ahead and saw where the roof met the water. Splitting the water were many—and various—jagged rocks waiting to rip them to shreds.

There was nowhere for them to go. No landing on the sides to pull up on. No caves to escape to. Just the water.

He gave her a slight shake to gain her attention. "Take a deep breath. We've got to go under so I can swim up back to the cave."

"It's here, Logan," she cried. "I know it."

"We'll find it, but we've got to get out of the water. Now."

She gave a jerky nod. Together they took several deep breaths, and then Logan dove them under. He held onto Gwynn as he kicked them deeper and deeper.

The currents pulled and pushed them, but Logan wasn't about to give up.

And then he saw the light. The same glow he'd seen from above was brighter as it cut through the water. It was almost as if the light beckoned to him.

Gwynn pointed to the light and urged him to go to it with her eyes. Logan gave a kick and took them down toward it. Gwynn squeezed her eyes closed, her hands on her ears as the pressure increased.

The closer they drew to the light, the more it seemed to move away. As they swam, a stream from the light illuminated the wall and Logan saw an opening. His instincts screamed for him to take it.

It was so narrow that only one of them would fit at a time. Logan tapped Gwynn on the shoulder and jerked his chin to the opening.

She glanced at it, then gave him a nod. Logan waited until she turned to face the opening before he gave her a push. Once her feet disappeared he followed.

The tunnel was longer than he expected, but the water helped to push them through. Logan cleared the small tunnel and looked up to see Gwynn's legs moving as she treaded water. He used his arms and kicked to propel him upward.

He surfaced and shook the water from his face. "Are you all right?" he asked as Gwynn turned to him.

His voice echoed in the small chamber. The only sounds were dripping water and their breath.

"Aye," Gwynn said, her teeth clenched tight as her entire body shivered. "Did you see it?"

"See what?"

She smiled and kissed him. "You've found it, Logan. Look down."

Through the water he could see the same light he had seen before entering the tunnel, but he could have sworn the light was in the other pool of water.

"It's the Tablet of Orn," Gwynn whispered, her smile huge.

Logan laughed and wrapped his arms around her. Her violet eyes shone with some vivid emotion that caused his heart to skip a beat. She had nearly died in her effort to help him. Just as he'd promised though, he'd kept her safe.

The feel of her soft body sliding against his brought desire flaring to life. At the moment he didn't care about Deirdre. He didn't care about the Tablet.

All he cared about was Gwynn.

She was alive and in his arms. And he was happy.

Logan looked at her sweet mouth. He knew the feel of

her soft, plump lips against his. He knew the sweet essence of her taste as their tongues danced.

"Logan," she whispered softly. Seductively. Hungrily.

He lowered his head and claimed her lips. A moan tore from his throat at the first contact. He couldn't get enough of her. The more he tasted and touched, the more he had to have.

His tongue slipped through her lips and met hers. Her arms tightened around his neck while he kicked to keep them above the water.

Logan deepened the kiss. He took. He claimed. He savored. It was then he realized he would do whatever it took to persuade Gwynn to return with him to MacLeod Castle. He didn't want to live without her.

He couldn't live without her.

The knowledge shocked him. He broke the kiss and looked at the woman who had turned his world upside down. Without even trying. She had done nothing but be herself. Yet, she had changed his thinking, changed the way he looked at the world.

"You're shivering," he said.

Her forehead puckered. "The water is a wee bit chilly."

"We need to get the Tablet before you catch a chill."

"Underwater again," she said with a sigh.

He ran a thumb over her cheek. "I'd do it myself if I could."

"I know."

After what had happened in the water, Logan was loath to let her go. No matter how many times he tried to command the water, his power wouldn't work. The Druid magic within prevented it.

Gwynn disengaged her arms from his neck and gave him one last smile before she dove beneath the water. Logan knew he couldn't take the Tablet, but he could be there if she needed him.

He followed her down, amazed to find this pool of water calm except for the push of water from the tunnel. With a steady stream of water coming in, the level didn't look as though it had risen. So where was the water going?

Logan forgot about the water as he watched Gwynn's sleek body glide through it. He wanted to make love to her in the water. He wanted her anywhere, everywhere. As long as he could have her.

Was this how Hayden had felt with Isla? The hunger and longing that never ended? The need that clawed to have Gwynn near?

It should terrify Logan, but he found, despite the deep emotions, Gwynn was just what he needed.

Her hair flowed behind her like a black wave. He knew the feel of those heavy tresses, knew they were as silky as they looked and smelled even better.

Logan swam faster until he was even with her as she approached the light. It was blinding in its intensity, but somehow it didn't bother Gwynn.

She reached her hand into the light and turned something. There was a moment of silence, and then a loud bang that shook the cave. Logan grabbed hold of Gwynn as the water suddenly began to drain out of the cavern in a whoosh.

He took the brunt of the fall as they landed on the smooth rock floor. Logan leaned up on his elbow and smoothed the hair out of Gwynn's face. He breathed a sigh of relief when she opened her eyes and smiled.

A deep rumbling began around them, and then on the wall opposite them the rocks crumbled away until moonlight streamed into the cavern.

Logan rose to his feet and helped Gwynn stand. They both faced the door in silence. He could hear the crash of waves nearby, so Logan knew they were on the coast and not deep under the isle as he had feared.

He glanced to his left and saw the waist-high pillar of rock that stood in the center of the cavern.

"We did it," Gwynn said and held out her hand with the Tablet.

Logan looked at the rectangular leather-wrapped shape and smiled. "Nay, Gwynn. *You* did it."

CHAPTER
FORTY-ONE

Gary Austin stared at the wall of water in front of the hidden caves and seethed. Hatred boiled inside him. It festered. It raged.

It devoured.

"So, daughter," he murmured. "You have betrayed me."

But she wouldn't win this night. She wouldn't best him. She'd made him look the fool by stealing the book and learning where the cave was, but in the end, he would be the one holding the prize.

Declan had promised him immortality, and Gary wasn't going to allow that to pass him by.

As he walked among the rocks he looked for another hidden cave. If it hadn't been for the water, Gary would never have known where Gwynn had entered. He doubted she would be exiting the same way. There had to be another way out.

Gary slipped on a rock after a wave knocked into him and felt his ankle roll, as his foot slid between two small boulders. His cry of pain was drowned out by the crumbling of rock ahead of him.

He forgot about the throbbing of his broken ankle as

he pulled himself out from between the rocks and crawled on his belly, soaked by the waves.

There was no way the rocks crumbling in such a fashion was natural. Gary grinned as he reached for the gun Declan had given him.

Gwynn stared at the oblong box in her hand. She had seen magic do many things, but she knew it had taken great magic in order to seal the Tablet beneath so much water, yet not a drop of said water had touched the Tablet until she had taken it from its resting place.

"It's no' quite what I was expecting," Logan said.

Gwynn chuckled, trying hard to forget how cold she was. And wet. "What were you expecting?"

"Well," Logan said with a shrug, "a tablet. A large tablet of stone. No' this," he said as he pointed to it.

Gwynn measured the weight with her hand. "It isn't all that heavy. There is some weight to it, but nothing like a stone tablet should be."

"Is it the Tablet of Orn we found?"

"Yes," Gwynn said with a nod.

Logan's mouth twisted. "There is certainly a large amount of magic coming from it. Do you want to look at it now?"

"I don't know. Maybe."

Logan moved behind her and rested his hands over hers. "We'll do it together."

Gwynn took a deep breath and nodded. "Together."

As one they folded back the soft leather, revealing a wooden box.

"No' what I was expecting," Logan said again.

Gwynn ran her hands over the intricately carved box. Every inch of it was covered in beautiful interconnecting knotwork. "It's stunning. I've never seen anything so beautiful."

"That it is."

She found a latch and flipped it. With a glance at Logan over her shoulder they lifted the lid of the box together. Inside, nestled between deep blue velvet, was a gold cylinder.

The caps on either end of the cylinder were gently rounded. Strips of leather two fingers wide encircled the cylinder at the base of each cap. And in the middle was more gold.

"Oh . . . my."

"Aye," Logan whispered. "Look at the etchings in the gold."

Gwynn could look at nothing else. More Celtic knotwork lavishly covered the gold and even the leather. She couldn't imagine how long it had taken someone to craft such brilliance and do it so wonderfully.

"Is that a lock?" Logan asked. He turned the cylinder in the box, showing a hole that was definitely a lock.

"We're going to need a key," Gwynn said.

Logan searched the cavern. "Where would it be?"

"I never heard anything about a key, Logan. I didn't even know the Tablet was a cylinder. The book didn't mention that."

He moved around her and rubbed the back of his neck. "I recognize some writing mixed in with the knotwork. Maybe that is the Tablet."

"Or maybe there's something inside it. Why else would there be a need for a key?"

"I doona know. Right now, I'm more concerned with getting you warm and safe."

She smiled and put her arm around him. "I am safe. With you."

Just as she had wanted, warmth filled his eyes as he leaned down to place a kiss on her lips. "Have you no' been through enough today?"

"Ah, that would be a definite yes," she said and closed the box. She then covered it with the leather and turned to Logan. She wanted to run her fingers through his wet hair and smooth it back from his face.

"I said before that I feared my feelings for you. I do, I mean, I did. Well, I still do, but that's because I've always run away when things got . . ." She shrugged.

"Too complicated? When people got too close," he offered.

She looked into his eyes and nodded. "Yes. What my father did to me and my mother, and then losing my mother. I was so tired of feeling pain that I shut myself off from everything. Until you."

Gwynn waited for him to say something, and when he didn't, she licked her lips and continued before she lost her nerve. "I did a lot of thinking today, and I don't know what the future holds for me. Or us. But I do know that I want to be with you. For however long you will want me. I may get hurt in the end, but I'd rather have the memories with you than not to have you."

"Gwynn," he said her name softly. "I'm still learning my way in this time, and I'm fighting Deirdre. I doona know what kind of relationship I can offer."

"I understand," she said and rose to her feet to hide the tears that filled her eyes. She knew what Logan said was true, but it didn't stop the hurt.

"Gwynn—"

"Come on," she said. "We need to get to the meeting point before Declan or Deirdre finds us."

"Or me."

Gwynn stilled as she heard her father's voice. She slowly turned to find him standing at the mouth of the cave.

"What do you want?" she demanded.

He laughed and jerked his chin to the box. "You know exactly what I want."

"And you think I'll just hand it to you? The child who was always in the way? The child you didn't want?"

Logan grimaced as he heard the hurt and anger in Gwynn's voice. He wanted to toss Gary into the water so Gwynn would never be troubled by him again, but Gwynn might not forgive Logan if he did.

"If you want the box, you'll have to go through me," Logan said.

Gary laughed derisively. "See this?" he said and lifted the gun. "I give you one guess as to what kind of bullets are loaded in it."

Logan narrowed his eyes and Gary laughed.

"That's right, bucko. X90s. They'll bring you down with one shot. Now, if Gwynn doesn't want to see you dead, she'll hand over the box."

Gwynn stepped in front of Logan, and he promptly moved around her. There was no way he would allow Gwynn to put herself between a bullet and him.

"By the way," Gary continued. "I don't blame you for turning Gwynn down. Who would want someone so plain? Her mother, now there was a beauty."

Logan could feel Gwynn shaking from rage or hurt, he wasn't sure which. And it didn't matter. No parent should speak of their child in such a manner.

"I'll give you one more chance," Logan said. "Drop the gun and leave."

"Or what?" Gary asked.

"Or I'll kill you."

Gary threw back his head and laughed. "The bullets, remember."

Logan pushed Gwynn behind and to the side of him so she could shield herself against the boulders. "I have one question. Do you think those bullets you're so proud of can keep up with me?"

Gary blinked, at a loss for words.

Logan used his incredible speed to race around and behind Gary. With one slash to Gary's hand, the gun dropped. Logan held his claws to Gary's throat.

"I asked you nicely to leave," Logan said. "You didna. You threatened me, and you were hateful to your daughter. For that I should kill you."

"Gwynn won't let you," Gary said with a sneer.

Logan shifted his eyes and met Gwynn's gaze. Her expression gave away nothing. She was angry now, but if Logan killed Gary, Gwynn would regret it later.

So Logan tossed him aside. "Run."

Gary looked up at him from the ground. "I can't. My ankle is broken."

Logan shrugged and grabbed Gwynn's hand as he led her from the cave. "Then stay. I doona care."

They exited the cave, Gwynn as silent as the stones around them. They had gone but ten steps when a shot rang out, blowing shards of rock around Gwynn's face.

Logan whirled around, his god loosened and ready for battle. But before he could go back and finish off Gary, the rocks began to shift to block the opening as water once more filled the cavern.

"The water willna listen to me," Logan said.

Gwynn put her hand on his arm. Logan turned his head to find her eyes glowing violet again.

"Evil is not allowed inside. Only the Keeper and those with good in them are allowed in the sacred cave. And out."

She blinked and the glow was gone. Her gaze turned to Logan. "My father wasn't a good man."

"But he was your father."

"Yes. He was."

After a moment, Gwynn turned away and Logan followed. He waved his arm over the water and watched the sea part. Just as they were about to step into the water, Gwynn gave a scream as she was yanked backward.

Logan turned and found a strand of white hair around his throat. He clawed at the hair, hatred burning in his gut as he stared at Deirdre.

"I told you I would get the artifact," Deirdre said. "Now I will have a Druid to kill and steal her magic. How sweet of you to find her for me, Logan."

Logan struggled to breathe as Deirdre tightened her hair around his neck. "Bitch," he ground out.

"If you had any idea what I've been through I'm not sure you'd say that. I hear you've met Declan." She rolled her eyes. "Fool actually thought I would share power with him."

Logan could care less. He glanced to his left to find Gwynn on the ground unconscious as Malcolm stood over her. Malcolm's maroon eyes met his, and Logan knew, regardless of their friendship, he would kill him if Malcolm harmed her.

"Now," Deirdre said. "Where were we? You were giving me the artifact."

She motioned to the wyrran surrounding her to retrieve the box that had fallen from Gwynn's arms. Logan silently urged Gwynn to wake, to use whatever magic she could to get away.

Deirdre peeled back the flaps of thin leather and looked at the box. She glanced up at Logan. "I imagine you're hating this. Picture how angry I was to learn the sword I had taken was stolen."

"My heart . . . bleeds," Logan said as his air was cut off.

There was a loud bellow Logan would recognize anywhere, and a heartbeat later a ball of fire was lobbed at the wyrran.

Logan looked for Hayden and found him and Ramsey coming at Deirdre from opposite sides. There was a large *whoosh* as Broc dove from the sky, taking a wyrran with him before ripping him in half.

Suddenly, Larena in all her iridescent glory was standing in front of Malcolm. Logan's attention was diverted when the MacLeod brothers surrounded Deirdre.

Quinn sliced off her hair, giving Logan the time he needed to dive to the ground while he clawed away the strands that remained. When he gained his feet, he found all the Warriors fighting.

Logan rushed to Gwynn. Just before he reached her, an orange Warrior came at him. Logan sliced open his chest and knocked him aside.

He saw Gwynn's chest rising and falling as she breathed, saw her eyes flutter open. He took a step toward her and was rushed by the orange Warrior again.

Gwynn opened her eyes to a battle around her. She looked at the ground, but the Tablet of Orn was gone. Then her eyes locked on a tall, beautiful woman with white hair that flowed to the ground. She used it as a weapon, slashing and impaling, grasping and choking.

Gwynn didn't need an introduction. She knew it was Deirdre who had attacked. And who had the Tablet.

Despite the ache in her body and the chill that had settled in her bones, Gwynn got to her feet. She took a deep breath and called to her magic.

It answered with a surge so powerful it nearly buckled her knees. Gwynn's body swayed as her magic swirled through her, growing stronger and stronger until she couldn't contain it.

At the same time she lobbed a blast of magic from her hand, she called to the wind. The blast of the wind sent several wyrran tumbling into the water.

Gwynn turned and glimpsed a flash of silver to her left. She watched, mesmerized as Logan fought. He was . . . magnificent. His fury was a thing of majesty. He fought with dazzling artistry and elegance mixed with deadly purpose and danger too palpable to disregard.

When the wind blasted around him, he sank his silver

claws into the Warrior he'd been fighting and looked to the water. A huge watery arm rose out of the sea, the hand unfurling. Logan directed the hand at Deirdre, and Gwynn watched as the fist closed around her.

Logan smiled, satisfaction filling him as Deirdre's frantic screams filled the air while Gwynn's wind slammed the wyrran into the cliffs, breaking every bone in their small bodies. With a toss, Logan threw Deirdre far out into the sea. The remaining wyrran and Warriors were quick to follow her. All but Malcolm.

Malcolm faced them, his kilt torn and blood coating him from the battle. His eyes were on Larena, though it was apparent he would take on anyone.

"Malcolm," Larena said and took a step toward him.

Fallon took hold of Larena's arm and pulled her back.

Malcolm bared his fangs at Fallon.

"What has happened to you?" Broc demanded.

Malcolm laughed, the sound as hollow as his eyes. "Deirdre found me. It seems I had a god inside me, but none of you bothered to tell me."

Fallon glanced at Ramsey. "You were no' dealing with your injuries well, Malcolm. Larena thought it would be better if you didna know yet."

"When were you going to tell me?" Malcolm demanded.

Larena shrugged. "I had hoped I never would. I thought you were safe at the castle."

"You were wrong!" Malcolm bellowed.

"It doesna matter now," Logan said. "You are a Warrior. It's up to you to decide what side you will fight for."

Malcolm laughed again and took a step back. "My choice has already been made."

"That's no' a choice," Quinn said. "You know what she did to us. You heard the stories."

Malcolm shrugged, his face indifferent. "What's done is done."

"Did you kill Duncan?" Arran demanded.

Malcolm looked at the Warrior and nodded. "I did. It is what Deirdre commanded."

"Nay, Malcolm," Logan said. "Sometimes people make the wrong decisions. You can change your mind."

Malcolm knew what he had done, knew Logan had gone to Deirdre. Logan waited for Malcolm to tell the others, but the Warrior simply raised a blond brow.

Logan blew out a deep breath and looked at the maroon Warrior before him. "I went to Deirdre, Malcolm. I wanted to be a Warrior. Her Warrior. It was a mistake, and one that cost me everything."

For long moments Malcolm held his gaze. Logan thought he had gotten through to him, but then Malcolm looked to Larena.

"I'm no' the man I once was. I'm the verra thing you're fighting against."

Lightning struck behind them, causing all of them to turn around. When they turned back, Malcolm was gone.

They stood in silence as the events of the day settled into their souls.

"I want revenge on Malcolm for what he did to Duncan," Arran said.

Ramsey put a hand on Arran's shoulder. "Do you recall how it was when your god was first unbound? We have no idea what Deirdre has done to Malcolm."

"You doona blame him for Duncan's death?" Arran asked in disbelief.

Hayden said, "Nay. I blame Deirdre."

Logan felt every eye turn to him then. The secret he had carried for so long was now out in the open. He felt lighter for having shared it, but the load had already been lifted after telling Gwynn.

"I should have told you," Logan said to Fallon. "All of you."

Fallon shrugged. "As you told Malcolm, we all make mistakes."

"I see the man who came to us and fought with us," Lucan said. "That's enough for me."

"For all of us," Ramsey said.

One by one they nodded. Logan looked down at Gwynn to hide the emotion that clogged his throat. She smiled, and he pulled her against his side.

"Let's go home," he said.

Hayden lifted the box Deirdre had dropped and smiled. "Home."

CHAPTER
FORTY-TWO

Declan stared at the empty cell where Saffron had been held for over two years. She had been his crowning glory. A Seer. They were the rarest of all Druids.

And now she was gone.

"Gary is dead. We found his body floating in the sea," Robbie said. "All the men left on Eigg are dead."

"And Deirdre?"

Robbie shrugged. "There was no trace of her. I did find several dead wyrran."

"Gwynn and Logan?"

"Gone."

Declan turned the ruby cuff link over and over. "I've lost Saffron. Gary is gone. There's no trace of Deirdre. And Gwynn and Logan have gotten away with the artifact. Have I got it all?"

"We doona know if they retrieved the Tablet."

"Oh, they have it. But no' for long," Declan vowed.

He turned on his heel and left the dungeon. He had plans to make.

* * *

December 23rd

Gwynn came awake to find herself at the castle. After the battle with Deirdre, Gwynn had been so cold and her head pounding so badly she had passed out. At least she was warm, and judging by the way her body no longer ached Sonya had healed her.

She blinked at the ceiling a couple of times before she turned her head and found Logan sitting beside the fire. His gaze was on the flames, his fist propped against his chin as he leaned on the arm of the chair. Gwynn wondered what he was thinking. He looked so pensive, so unlike the Logan she had come to know.

She stirred and his head swiveled toward her.

"You're awake," he said as he rose to his feet and came toward her.

"I am. And warm now."

"Thankfully," he said. "I told them my secret, Gwynn."

She smiled. "I told you they wouldn't care."

"So you did."

"How long did I sleep?"

He shrugged. "A few hours. I figured you deserved it after all you've been through."

Gwynn wrinkled her nose. "I'd rather not repeat anything like that again. I didn't think I was going to come out of that alive."

"I'd rather no' have you scare me like that again either."

She looked into his hazel eyes. "You seem . . . lighter. The darkness is gone."

"It is. With my secret out, I'm no' weighted down as was. You helped with that."

"Good."

Logan glanced at the window. "It's snowing again."

Gwynn knew she shouldn't take the chance and get hurt by him again, but she lifted the covers. "I'm cold."

A slow, seductive smile split Logan's face. "I was hoping you'd say that."

A giggle escaped her as he shed his shirt and jeans and climbed into bed. His arms wrapped around her as their limbs tangled together.

The smiles melted away as their gazes locked and his head lowered to hers. The kiss was unhurried and leisurely and full of such hunger and longing that it made Gwynn's stomach plummet to her feet.

The kiss was filled with need and desire, but unlike the kisses from before it was slow. Sensual. Powerfully arousing.

She could feel the longing within him, sense the hunger rising each time their tongues met.

She reveled in the kiss, met him stroke for stroke as the intensity increased. He rolled her onto her back, his hands touching her everywhere.

The second time his mouth fit against hers, she was in a maelstrom of hunger and urgency. Her hands slid over the hard sinew of his shoulders and around his neck.

"God's teeth! I can think of naught but you," Logan said.

Gwynn leaned back her head as he began to kiss down her throat, leaving a trail of hot, wet kisses that made chills race over her body.

Her hands roamed the breadth and width of his back, his muscles moving and bunching beneath her palms. He kissed her again, a fiery, frenzied, soul-stirring kiss.

He took. He claimed. He seduced.

With one kiss she was aroused. Needy. Hungry. For Logan and the passion his touch wrought. She clenched her legs together and moaned at the spike of desire that filled her.

Without warning, Logan rose on his elbows and looked down at her. His fingertips brushed the undersides of her breasts, which instantly swelled and ached for his touch.

"I want to feel your skin," he said between kisses.

She sighed as Logan's weight settled over her. The feel of him, the way he felt against her, over her, in her was the only thing she needed.

The one thing she would beg for.

His hot, hard arousal rested against her stomach while he kissed her again and again, making her throb and tremble for more. When his fingers skimmed over her already hard and aching nipple, Gwynn cried out and arched her back, seeking more of his touch.

He cupped her breast and teased the tiny bud until Gwynn was rotating her hips against him, seeking the release she knew he could give her. When she could stand the torment no more, he shifted to her other breast.

Gwynn's skin felt as if it were on fire. She burned for Logan, for his caress. And when his hot, wet mouth fastened on her breast, she plunged her hands into his hair and held on as he took her higher.

He shifted and began to kiss down her stomach, his hands holding her thighs apart. Gwynn forced her eyes to open and watched as he fit first one shoulder then the other beneath her legs.

Logan rose up on his knees and moved her calves until they rested on his shoulders. His large hands gripped her hips as he rubbed the swollen head of his cock against her sensitive flesh before he pushed inside her. Once. Twice.

Gwynn gripped the sheets and cried out at the pleasure that pulsed through her. His erection slid into her slowly, his body straining above her.

"So damned tight," he said.

With one last thrust he was seated to the hilt. His hazel gaze seared hers as he began to move. Short, quick strokes, and long, hard thrusts. The alternating feel of him knotted her desire tighter and tighter.

She reveled in the sensation of his hard, steely length plunging inside her again and again. Harder. Faster. An instinct, primal and fierce, took her, plunged her in a wild and intense ride.

She moaned, her head thrashing side to side as she heard their bodies meeting, felt the slide of his body as sweat glistened along their skin.

He filled her deeper than before. Yet it wasn't enough. She couldn't get enough of him, of this raw, untamed desire that had overtaken them.

She grasped the need that held her and let it take her where it would. It compelled her, urged her to let Logan pull her ever higher.

Her breaths came in panting gasps. Each time he pounded into her, penetrating deeper, her body tightened and tightened.

With her muscles locked, the release came suddenly and with such intensity that she screamed. Wave after wave of glorious release wracked her, her senses shattered and her body forever Logan's, eternally linked.

But even then he wasn't done with her.

Logan wanted her to remember this night, he wanted it emblazoned on her memory—and his.

She had the most magnificent body he had ever seen. Skin had never felt so soft, hair had never been so silky, and no touch had ever burned him as hers did.

Logan filled his hands with her breasts as he continued to move within her. He teased and pinched her nipples before he ran his hands down her body.

He shrugged her legs from his shoulders and leaned over her. He cupped her buttocks and felt the hot, dewy essence of her against his cock. Then he pulled out of her until only the head of his rod remained. With one hard thrust he filled her.

She moaned his name. Her mane of black hair was tangled about her, her fingers clawing at the blankets while he withdrew and thrust.

Holding firmly onto her hips, he set a driving rhythm. Her sheath clutched him, holding him firmly as he filled her. He held her pinned beneath him. Her legs locked around his waist, her hands touching him everywhere. And she moaned for more, called out his name as he filled her.

He drove into her relentlessly, carrying them both to an apex of unthinkable pleasure, of carnal delights of which he had never experienced.

And never would with another woman.

"Logan," she cried.

He felt her body stiffen. Knew she was close to peaking again. Desire erupted swift and true. It swept through him, consuming him with the need to brand Gwynn as his own.

She tightened around him a heartbeat before she screamed his name, her back bowed and her skin flushing with her climax as her amazing violet eyes glowed as she met his gaze.

While her sheath spasmed around him, Logan kept pounding into her. The feel of her scorching wet body clamping around him, caressing his cock pushed him over the edge.

He released her hips and fell over her, his breathing harsh, ragged. His hips pumped desperately, urgently, as she clamped around him one last time.

She pulled him into a chasm of never-ending pleasure, of bliss so blinding, so pure it made his chest ache with emotions he didn't dare try to name.

Logan's forehead lowered to Gwynn's as they held each other. Safe. Secure.

CHAPTER
FORTY-THREE

December 24th

Gwynn tied the bow on Logan's present and looked at the silver paper and red bow. She hoped he liked his gift. Marcail had also gotten another shirt, a new sporran, and even boots. But those would come from the others.

Gwynn ran her hand over the package and rose from the floor of her chamber. She walked out of her room and into the hall to the tree.

It had been two days since their return from Eigg. Many times she'd tried to talk to Logan about their relationship, but each time he would change the subject.

Gwynn knew when a decision had been made. As much as she wanted to be with Logan, she needed more than their nights together. For too long she had refused to get close to someone, but now that's what she wanted.

She wanted more than the sex. She wanted a relationship. She wanted a future.

She wanted love.

Gwynn put his gift under the tree behind other gifts

and stood. Everyone was supposed to draw names, but by the sheer number of presents, many more had been bought.

"Are you sure?" Fallon asked her as he walked up next to her.

Gwynn inhaled and slowly let out the breath as she faced him. "I can't stay and ignore what's between me and Logan. If I remain, things will continue on as they are."

"Maybe that's a good thing. Maybe that will develop into more."

"The thing is, I need to know it will develop into more."

"I think you're making a mistake, Gwynn. You belong here. No' just because of Logan, but because you're a Druid."

She swallowed past the lump in her throat. She wanted nothing more than to remain, but if she stayed without Logan talking about whatever was between them, she knew she was going to get hurt.

"I can't."

He nodded and looked at the tree. "I wish you would wait until tomorrow."

"Another night of him evading my questions about us will destroy me," she confessed. "I love him, Fallon. I love him as I thought I would never love a person."

"He's going to be furious when he returns and you are no' here."

Gwynn shrugged and pulled on her coat. "I've left him a note that explains everything."

Larena walked out of the kitchen and hugged her tightly. "We will miss you. I hope you return soon."

"Me, too," she said and wiped her eyes. "I've said my good-byes to everyone. I cannot linger anymore. It's time to go."

Fallon sighed and shared a look with his wife before he turned to Gwynn. "Are you sure you want me to jump you to the airport? I can jump you home with Galen's help."

"I already bought my ticket, and after everything I've been through, I'm not afraid of flying anymore."

Gwynn looked once more at the castle that in a short time had become her home. Her gaze landed on the huge Christmas tree, and she smiled. When she blinked she stood in the middle of Edinburgh Airport.

She looked around, astounded that no one noticed them.

Fallon chuckled. "They doona pay attention. Godspeed, Gwynn Austin."

"Godspeed, Fallon."

As she waved, he disappeared. Gwynn pulled up the handle to her bag and started toward the ticket counter.

The small box in Logan's pocket was burning a hole through his jeans. He had been trying to get out of the castle to shop for Gwynn for two days without being obvious.

He'd had his chance this morning and taken it. Yet, a sense of foreboding almost had him staying behind. He couldn't shake the feeling that something had happened.

"Hurry," he urged Hayden.

"If you tell me that again I'm going to make you walk home," Hayden said through clenched teeth, his hands gripping the steering wheel tightly.

Logan drummed his fingers on his leg, thinking of the gift he had purchased. He didn't know what a Badgley Mischka was, but Gwynn had wanted it. "Do you think she'll like it?"

Hayden rolled his eyes. "For the thousandth time, aye, I think Gwynn will love the purse. She told Isla it was the one she wanted."

"Did I spend enough, though? There was a bigger one."

"Logan," Hayden warned.

Logan threw up his hands. "I'm in knots, Hayden.

She's been trying to talk to me about what's between us for days. I have no' known what to say, so I've put her off."

"No' a good move."

"I know. I kept telling myself I should let her go, but with every hour we're together, I find it more difficult, until I realized I can no'. I may no' be good enough for her, but I want her. If she still wants me."

Hayden chuckled. "There's no' a question of that, my brother. I've seen the way she looks at you. When are you going to give her the ring?"

"I guess it depends on how things go tonight and tomorrow morning."

Hayden slowed as he turned off the paved road to the dirt road that led to the castle. "She's a good woman, and you are a good man. Everything will be all right, Logan."

But as soon as Logan walked into the castle, he knew nothing was all right. It was the way Larena looked at him.

"Where is she?" he asked. "Where is Gwynn?"

Fallon rose from the table, his face grave. "She left a note in your chamber."

"Where. Is. She?" Logan demanded again.

Isla shifted in her chair before the hearth. "At the airport. She's going home."

Logan felt as if the floor had been snatched from beneath him. He shook his head, unable to believe what he was hearing.

"Nay. She wouldna go. No' on Christmas Eve."

"Read the note," Broc said. "I'm sure it will explain her reasoning."

Logan turned to glare at Fallon. "Take me to her. I want her to tell me why she's leaving. I'll no' read it from a letter."

Fallon raised a brow, a hint of a smile appearing as he lifted his hand. "If that's what you want."

"It's what I want."

In an instant he and Fallon were in a crowded building, people milling about everywhere.

"I'll wait here," Fallon said. "Good luck finding her."

Logan rolled his eyes and looked around. He tried to recall everything Gwynn had told him about airports. A gate. She had to leave through a gate.

"But which gate?" he mumbled.

After several questions, and with his speed, he was able to get around security to the terminals where the gates were. He paused beside a huge screen that listed all the flights to determine which gate was hers.

"Gate six," he repeated as he read.

Logan's strides ate up the floor as he stalked to gate six. When he found Gwynn sitting alone staring at her hands in her lap he didn't know whether to laugh or shake her.

He walked over and stopped in front of her. It took a moment, but her head lifted. When she saw him, her beautiful violet eyes widened in surprise.

"Logan," she whispered as she slowly stood.

"What are you doing here?" he asked.

She looked around. "What does it look like? I'm going home."

"Why?"

"Why?" Her voice took on a hard edge. "You dare to ask me why after not talking to me about us, about what's between us."

He clenched his fists at his sides. "I didna know what to say."

"How about say what you're feeling? Something like, 'I like you, Gwynn. I'd like to see where this goes,' or 'Sorry, Gwynn. I'd rather not see you anymore.' See how that works?"

"It's no' that easy."

She snorted. "Don't talk to me about easy. Do you have any idea what it cost me bringing it up every day and night to try and get you to tell me something, some hint about how you felt?"

"I thought you knew. I would no' have been with you if I didna care."

"I have to be told, Logan. I have to hear it. Showing it is great, but I need the words. I put my love out there for you time and again."

Logan itched to take her in his arms and wipe away the tears he saw gathering in her eyes. "Did you tell me you loved me?"

She blinked. "No. Why would I?"

"Then why would I? You asked about us, Gwynn, but you didn't tell me how you felt either."

"Oh, but I did, mister. Don't you dare turn this on me. On Eigg, after we found the Tablet, I told you I wanted to see where this would lead, that I wanted to be with you."

Logan glanced at the floor. "Aye, you did, and I was taken off guard by it. I didna answer then because I was trying to convince myself I wasna the man for you."

She slapped her hands on her legs. "You're right. I don't need a man thinking for me. Let me make those decisions."

"I love you."

Gwynn opened her mouth, ready for another retort, when his words penetrated her haze of anger. She closed her mouth as the tears she'd been holding back fell.

"I love you with all my heart, Gwynn Austin."

She swallowed past the lump in her throat and looked into Logan's hazel eyes. "You've had my heart from the moment I met you."

Logan smiled and held out his arms. Gwynn stepped into them and wrapped her arms around him. "I love you. I love you. I love you."

He tilted her head so he could kiss her, a kiss that drew applause from those around them.

Gwynn, laughing, broke the kiss. Logan winked at two old ladies watching them. He looked down at Gwynn and asked, "Are you ready to go to the castle?"

"I'm ready to go home. Our home."

EPILOGUE

December 25th

Logan couldn't stop smiling as everyone at the castle sat around the tree. He'd heard from Gwynn what Christmas was, but being back with his family and having Gwynn by his side made Christmas even more special than it would have been.

He'd hid his nervousness as Gwynn opened her present. When she held the black handbag, she had let out a whoop and thrown her arms around him.

"It's Logan's turn to open his presents," Hayden said.

Logan shifted uneasily.

Gwynn, who sat between his legs on the floor, smiled at him over her shoulder. "I agree. And he opens mine first."

She moved out of his arms and reached for a large present under the tree before turning and handing it to him. Logan looked down at the red sparkly paper with the silver ribbon and merely held it.

No one had ever given him a gift, and he wasn't sure if he knew how to react.

"Open, baby," Gwynn urged.

Logan swallowed and undid the bow before tearing into the paper as he'd watched the others do. When he opened the box and saw the Hamilton tartan, new and perfect, his throat closed.

Gwynn's hand cupped his cheek, and when he looked up he saw her crying. His own vision swam as he tried desperately to find his voice.

"This is perfect," he finally managed. He pulled Gwynn into his arms and kissed her.

"There's more," Isla said as she began to stack boxes in front of him.

With Gwynn by his side he opened boxes to find new boots, a sporran, and several shirts. He was overwhelmed, but immensely grateful.

"Oh," Cara said sadly. "That's all the gifts."

Logan looked at Gwynn and said, "No' exactly."

Gwynn frowned and glanced around her. "Logan, all the presents are gone."

"I kept one aside." He pulled the ring from his pocket and held out his palm so she could see the three-carat garnet. "I doona know how I lived before you, but I can no' live without you. There will be danger, battles, and evil we must destroy. Yet, there's no one I'd rather have by my side. Gwynn Austin, will you be my wife?"

Gwynn's entire body shook. She looked down at his hand, tears filling her eyes. Carefully, she picked up the garnet and slid it onto her left ring finger before raising her gaze to him. "Yes, Logan. My answer is yes."

Shouts and clapping erupted in the hall as Logan pulled her into his arms. Which was the only place she ever wanted to be.

Who would have guessed that traveling to Scotland would give her everything she'd ever dreamed of? She had her own Highlander, the family she'd always wanted, and even her castle.

Regardless of the days ahead of them, Gwynn would treasure each moment with Logan.

Camdyn smiled and clapped, as joyous as the others at Logan and Gwynn's happiness. He heard Cara happily announce that it had been four hundred years since the last wedding at the castle, and it was time for more.

Camdyn looked at Ramsey and Arran. Those two he could see finding their mates. As for him . . . there wasn't a woman for him. Not anymore, at least.

His gaze was then drawn to Saffron, who sat between Isla and Larena. He'd heard her screams in the middle of the night as the nightmares assaulted her. The other Druids were doing what they could, but whatever Declan had done to her so far evaded their magic.

As for her blindness, he'd been staggered to learn Declan had been the cause of it. He'd spelled her somehow that took away her sight, yet for that handicap, she managed well.

Her being a Seer, and now living at the castle, was a boon none of them had expected. How it would play out in the coming weeks and months was what interested Camdyn.

Deirdre drummed her long nails on the stones in her chamber. She'd been busy creating new wyrran and finding another Warrior since her defeat at Eigg. She'd also been punished.

Her master had been furious. Even now she could feel the flames along her skin from his anger, but it didn't stop her planning her next move to acquire the artifacts.

Regardless of what her master told her, she had to stop Laria from waking. No matter the costs. When she had gathered the artifacts and proved herself to *diabhul* once more, he would see she'd been right.

"You wanted to see me," Malcolm said as he strolled into her chamber.

She looked the Warrior up and down. "I have a chore for you. On the winter solstice I cast a spell that finally revealed there was a Druid near Edinburgh. I did not see her face or discover her name, but there is a way we can draw her out."

"How?"

"There is a school of children where she works. I want you to kill every child there."

For an instant Malcolm couldn't breathe. He knew the evil inside him. He knew what Deirdre was. But killing children was another matter entirely.

"Why do you hesitate?" Deidre asked. "I'm sending my newest Warrior to MacLeod Castle in order to kill them and get the artifacts. If you want your precious cousin, Larena, to stay alive, you will obey me on this."

Malcolm gave a slow, single nod of his head. "I will see it done. But if Larena is harmed—"

"Do not think to threaten me, Warrior," Deirdre said as she rose, her hair lashing out and wrapping around his throat. "You have been useful, but don't think you cannot be replaced."

Malcolm yanked Deirdre's hair from his throat, but only because she allowed him to. "I need the address to the school."

Deirdre's smile was cold and calculating as she handed him a piece of paper.

Malcolm turned on his heel and walked from her chamber and out of her mountain. If there had been the smallest thread of feeling left in him, by the time he was done with the children, it would be dead.

Just as his soul was.

* * *

Ian opened his eyes in his dark cave and groaned when he saw the claw marks that scored the stone. Had he gotten loose from the cave? Had he done the unthinkable and killed an innocent?

There were no answers, only a hole in his memories that frustrated him.

His stomach rumbled in hunger. Did he have time to hunt before his god threatened again? Did he dare take the chance?

Since he had no idea how long it had been since he last ate, or even how long he had been unconscious, Ian knew he had to keep up his strength to fight his god.

He pulled himself up and took a deep breath before he left the cave. The snow that fell was thick and heavy as it blanketed the slopes of the mountains. He hadn't gone far when he found the tracks of a stag.

The thrill of the hunt coursed through Ian as he ran through the thick snow tracking the stag. When he found it standing beside a frozen loch, Ian used his speed to sneak up on the deer and slice its throat with his claw.

The stag was dead before it hit the ground.

Ian peeled back his lips, his fangs filling his mouth as he roared in triumph. He loved hunting, and it had appeased his god—for a short time.

Now, Farmire called for more hunting, more blood. More death.

Ian tried to ignore his god and lifted the stag on his shoulder. But Farmire was persistent. He raged inside Ian, his rage palpable as it burned.

Ian struggled to keep walking, desperate to make it to the cave before Farmire took over. He was just a few steps from the entrance when Farmire's roar inside his mind deafened him.

His knees hit the ground, the snow cutting his skin.

Ian let the stag drop as he clutched his head. Fear spiked within him as he realized Farmire's control was growing. He was able to take over Ian faster each time.

As the darkness began to close in on Ian, he wondered how much longer he would remember who he was before Farmire took over completely.

Read on for an excerpt from

MIDNIGHT'S LOVER

the next exciting installment in
the Dark Warriors series

**Coming next month from
Donna Grant and St. Martin's Paperbacks!**

Danielle stumbled in the snow. She had been fighting to keep on her feet for hours, but this time, she didn't bother. She turned as she fell and lay on her back in the snow.

When the sun had crested the mountains that morning, she had seen just where she was. And it terrified her. She was deep in the mountains.

With no roads or towns in sight. She kept telling herself she'd find something over the next rise, but every time there was nothing.

Just more snow. More mountains.

Warmth was a distant memory.

The dampness penetrated her jacket, making her shiver even more. She was starving and wanted nothing more than to curl up on her couch and turn on the tele while sipping some hot tea.

To her horror, several hours ago the key had spoken to her. It had urged Danielle to continue going deeper into the mountains.

Maybe she had gone east the entire time and hadn't known it. But if there was one thing she knew, after this event she would carry a compass with her at all times.

Exhaustion weighed heavily upon her, and the cold only hampered things. It took more effort than she wanted to admit just putting one foot in front of the other.

Twice already she'd had to backtrack and find another trail because she'd been so intent on staying upright she hadn't realized she'd almost walked off a cliff or into a boulder.

Since she was alone, she needed to be vigilant. She needed to be aware of her surroundings. If she wasn't careful, she'd find herself frozen to death or falling off a mountain. And neither sounded very appealing.

Danielle let out a loud sigh and climbed wearily to her feet. She looked around, wondering, waiting to hear the inhuman shrieks she had heard last night.

Her stomach growled. She lifted a handful of snow and munched on it, as she had the entire day. It might help quench her thirst, but it was doing nothing for her hunger.

"The next rise," she said to herself. "I'll find a road or a village at the next rise."

At least she hoped she would, since the sun was sinking fast. Danielle had walked nonstop since the accident. Her feet would probably hurt, if she could actually feel them. Which was probably a good thing since she had never walked so long or far in stilettos before.

She needed to rest, to eat a hot meal. But that could be a long time coming.

"They're going to find me in the spring. I'll have frozen to death because either my magic isn't working or the stupid key got me lost on purpose."

She lifted one foot in front of the other and started walking.

"I hope the MacLeods are the friendly sort," she said to herself. "If I survive this and discover they aren't, I'll scream. Loud. And long."

This is what she had come to—talking to herself. But

the quiet had begun to weigh on her earlier. With no one else around, Danielle didn't see the harm in speaking to herself.

She snorted, then wiped at her nose. "At least no harm yet. Who knows if I'll be sane by the time I get out of the mountains?"

She scratched her cheek, then stilled. She could have sworn she had seen movement out of the corner of her eye. The trees were thick, and the snow concealed footsteps, but she'd been sure a shape had moved quickly and quietly.

She turned her head and peered through the trees. The snow had lessened, the flakes swirling in their dance upon the air. It was eerily quiet on the mountain, moreso than before. As if the woods knew there was a predator near.

Again, just out of the corner of her eye she saw movement. Danielle whirled around, and this time she caught a spot of pale yellow.

Her heart pounded in her chest. *Yellow*?

She recalled the radio announcer talking about yellow creatures before her wreck. He'd called them dangerous. Teeth and claws, he'd said.

Danielle inhaled deeply, and remembered everything Aunt Josie had told her about being a Druid. Danielle had never used her magic in defense before, but she was about to learn.

She called to her magic. Instantly, she felt it move and expand within her. She was surprised it had answered her so swiftly. Surprised, and gratified.

She moved in a circle, her eyes looking for the creatures. Always they were just on the edge of her vision. It was as if they were toying with her.

"Find other prey," she commanded, and let a small amount of her magic shoot from her hand.

Her magic filled the silence, but there was no hiss of hurt or other sound to let her know she had hit her target. Was she so tired she was seeing things? Was her mind playing tricks on her, as it had when she was a child?

Danielle lowered her hand and adjusted her purse on her shoulder. She was thankful no one else had seen her act so foolishly. With a sigh, she started walking again.

She'd taken two steps when she heard the first shriek.

It was unnatural and caused the hairs on her arms and neck to stand on end. Just as the night before, she didn't hesitate as she began to run. It didn't matter that she had no idea what had made that sound. All she knew was that it was strange and sinister.

The knee-high snow hampered her from moving as fast as she wanted. To make matters worse, the shrieks continued louder and longer. And they grew closer.

What kind of creature made that sound? And how many were there? Two? Three? Or more? Danielle didn't want to find out. All she could think of was the yellow creatures everyone was talking about.

She kept running, kept moving. A chance look over her shoulder showed her the nightmare was coming true. Small yellow creatures were jumping from tree to tree as they chased her.

Danielle's blood pounded in her ears, her heart thumping wildly in her chest. She gripped the trees and rocks to make it to the top of the mountain, sliding on the ice on several occasions. With the cold air stinging her lungs, Danielle started down the other side of the mountain with barely a glance at it. She spotted a valley below, with a frozen loch. Maybe she could find a place to hide there.

Her knee crumpled underneath her as she started down the mountain, causing her to roll a couple of times in the snow. She managed to right herself and get back on her feet. Then her foot hit a patch of ice, and she went tumbling again.

Her arm slammed into a boulder hidden by the snow. Pain exploded throughout her body. She wrapped her arms around her head and tried to use her body to slide down the mountain, feet first.

The snow and the ice weren't slowing the yellow creatures, however. They continued after her, their shrieks causing her ears to ring from the unholy sound.

The snow was packed so hard that it cut her hands and face whenever she had the misfortune of connecting with it. She would have preferred to make the trip down on her feet, but at least she was moving fast. It might give her an advantage over the beasts.

She was moving so quickly that she couldn't stop herself when she saw the edge of the cliff coming at her. A scream lodged in her throat as she slid off the cliff and hung in midair for a moment before plummeting.

Her arms and legs flailed around as she sought some kind of hold. She barely had time to register that she was falling before she landed with a small tumble in a thick patch of snow.

Danielle had no time to make sure she was unhurt as she climbed out of the snow and began to run again. The shrieks continued, and if she lived through this, she knew she would recall the sound until the day she died.

She made for the loch, her lungs seizing and her body protesting the abuse. She was halfway to the loch when one of the yellow beasts landed in front of her.

She screamed and skidded to a halt, one of her heels twisting and causing her to roll her ankle. The creature's huge yellow eyes glared maliciously at her while it snapped its mouthful of teeth. It couldn't close its lips around its teeth, which gave it a menacing, ugly look.

And then more surrounded her.

Danielle directed a blast of magic at them. It sent the creatures tumbling back and shaking their heads as if to clear them, but they rose and came at her again.

If her magic couldn't help her, then she was doomed. But she wasn't about to give up without a fight. She sent another, more powerful, blast at them. This time all but one got up. With each step they took toward her, Danielle retreated.

Their long claws snapped as if they wanted to slice her open. They began running at her one at a time to see how close they could get to her.

For magic she hadn't used in quite a while, Danielle was happy with how quickly it was responding to her. But she couldn't keep the beasts away, no matter what. One got close enough to grab the strap of her purse, sending it flying through the air to land ten paces away from her. Danielle tried to reach for her purse, but the creatures kept coming at her, preventing her from doing anything other than using her magic.

Then the sound of a roar, loud and vicious, echoed through the valley.

The creatures quieted and lifted their heads, their eyes darting about. Danielle could feel their trepidation. Whatever had just made that roar was something that gave the creatures pause. The only question was, would its source help Danielle, or come after her as well?

Danielle seized the moment and tried to slink away. She was almost past one of the beasts when it turned its evil eyes to her and let out a vicious shriek right before it raised its claws at her face.

Ian had awoken to the sound of wyrran. He'd tracked and killed four the day before. Maybe they'd come to him this time. It had felt good to kill evil again, felt right to use his

Warrior abilities to help those at MacLeod Castle in the only way he could.

Then he felt the magic. He'd never felt anything so . . . glorious, so amazing in all his days. It took just a moment to realize the wyrran were chasing a Druid.

Ian had loosened his god before he'd reached the entrance to his cave. He used his speed to follow the Druid's magic. As he ran, he saw the trail made in the snow, as well as the wyrran tracks.

When he crested the hill and saw the wyrran surrounding the Druid, Ian had tilted back his head and let loose a roar. He started toward them wanting, needing . . . *craving* to kill the wyrran.

Then one of them cut the Druid. Her scream of pain sent him barreling into the wyrran. He decapitated one as he ran past it. Another he impaled on his claws and tossed it into the air as he put himself between the Druid and the wyrran.

Ian turned and faced the remaining seven wyrran. He bared his fangs as he bent his legs and flexed his claws. Farmire roared with approval inside him.

This was what Ian needed. Battle. Death. Blood.

He wanted the wyrran's blood to coat the ground until the snow was no longer white. He sought to wipe the creatures from existence, just as he desired to erase any evidence of Deirdre.

Ian was prepared when the wyrran all came at him at once. Even while slashing at the wyrran and evading their claws he noticed two had gone after the Druid, pushing her farther and farther onto the frozen loch.

"Nay!" Ian bellowed, to try and stop her.

She had no way of knowing the ice was very thin in places because he broke through it every day, and she was nearing a spot he had used just the day before.

He snapped the neck of a wyrran, and slammed two of

the others' heads together. He used his claws and sank them through the other two wyrran's hearts.

Then he turned to the Druid. "Doona move!" he shouted.

But she was too intent on the wyrran coming after her. She kept her gaze on the wyrran and one of her hands in the pocket of the cloaklike garment she wore.

Ian stepped onto the ice, but it groaned under his weight. Normally he didn't care because he wanted to be in the water, but the Druid wouldn't survive the temperatures.

"The ice is too thin!" he said again.

The Druid's eyes lifted to his. Ian found himself staring into eyes as bright as emeralds, a heartbeat before there was a loud crack, and the ice split beneath her feet. . . .

Fueled by dragon magic.
Enflamed by human desire . . .

DON'T MISS DONNA GRANT'S EXCLUSIVE DARK KING E-BOOK TRILOGY

DARK CRAVING
Available in August 2012

NIGHT'S AWAKENING
Available in September 2012

DAWN'S DESIRE
Available in October 2012

FROM ST. MARTIN'S PRESS